SHOCKWAVE

SHOCKWAVE

Colin Forbes

GUILD PUBLISHING
LONDON · NEW YORK · SYDNEY · TORONTO

This edition published 1990 by
Guild Publishing
by arrangement with Pan Books Ltd

CN 1137

Printed and bound in West Germany
by Mohndruck, Gütersloh

AUTHOR'S NOTE

All the characters portrayed are creatures of the author's imagination and bear no relationship to any living person. Also, the organization, World Security & Communications, again has no equivalent in real life anywhere in the world.

FOR JANE

CONTENTS

Prologue

At 4 a.m. it was purely by chance that Bob Newman first heard that Tweed had murdered and then raped a girl.

Returning from a London party, he was driving down Radnor Walk when he saw the unmarked vans parked by the kerb in front of Tweed's terrace house. Men in civilian clothes moved up and down the steps leading into the narrow three-storey building.

They walked quickly, as though in a hurry to complete some urgent assignment. A uniformed policeman stood under a lamp, his hands clasped behind his back. Otherwise the street was deserted.

Newman slowed his Mercedes 280E, parked it a dozen yards from the rear van. He cupped his hand to mask the lighting of a cigarette while he watched. One dark-haired man in a business suit he recognized as he hurried back inside the house. Harris, Harvey – some such name. Special Branch . . .

Two men in boiler suits emerged from inside the rear van. They carried a long plastic body-bag into the building. It looked very much as though the Clean-Up Squad was at work.

Newman climbed out of the car, locked it, strolled up to the entrance to the house. The uniformed policeman stopped him.

'You can't go in there, sir. Best get back to your car and go home . . .'

'I know the man who lives here. What's going on?'

The policeman looked uncertain how to reply. He

glanced up the steps and the dark-haired man peered out. Harvey. That was his name, Newman remembered. Chief Inspector Ronald Harvey. A thick-headed bureaucrat. He hustled down the steps to confront the new arrival.

'Newman, what are you doing here at this hour? Did Tweed phone you?'

'Why would he do that at this time of night?' Newman countered.

That was when Howard, Director of the Secret Service, appeared framed in the doorway. But not the immaculate Howard that Newman was accustomed to seeing. Tall, in his fifties, his plump reddish face was disfigured with a stubble of unshaven hair. His tie was badly knotted, his shirt had a crumpled look – everything about him suggested a man hastily summoned out of bed. His expression was grim and Newman could have sworn he was still feeling dazed.

'Better come in, Bob,' he mumbled. 'This is a terrible business. And the Minister is here . . .'

He was talking as he led the way along a narrow hall, mounting the staircase to the first floor. Harvey followed close on Newman's heels, protesting.

'This is no time to let a foreign correspondent into here.'

'I'll take full responsibility.' Howard addressed him over his shoulder, still ascending the steps. 'And you know perfectly well Newman is fully vetted, has often worked with us.'

'Which Minister are you talking about?' Newman asked.

'Minister for External Security. Buckmaster in person, which I could do without. Brace yourself, Bob. It's in here . . .'

*   *   *

Howard stiffened himself, walked very erect into Tweed's bedroom. The place seemed full of people. Curtains closed over the window, Newman noted. But his gaze focused on where 'it' lay. On Tweed's bed.

The girl would have been in her late twenties, early thirties, Newman estimated. A mass of beautiful blonde hair spread like a wave over the pillow. She lay with the sheet pulled down, exposing her naked body, her long legs, knees pressed together. A brutal sight. Her tongue protruded, flopped to her left side from between well-shaped lips. In life she had been glamorous. Her greenish eyes were wide open, staring sightless at the ceiling. Her neck was horribly bruised. She looked bloody awful, Newman was thinking.

A man in a dark suit, also unshaven, straightened up, reached down to lift a black bag off the floor. The doctor. Removing a pair of surgical gloves, he dropped them inside the open bag he'd perched on a chair, closed the bag.

Harvey plunged in. 'Well, Doctor, what are your findings?'

The doctor, short, plump with thinning white hair, raised his eyebrows. 'For heaven's sake, you'll have to wait for the autopsy. I'm not given to making guesses.'

'Perhaps not,' a fresh voice drawled, 'but you can tell me a few preliminary conclusions. Time, my dear chap, is of the essence, considering the murderer's identity.'

Newman swung round. A tall slim man stood in the doorway to the bathroom. His thick brown hair fell down the sides of his face. In his mid forties, he stood six feet and his aura of authority dominated the room. Unlike the others, he was freshly shaven and his swift-moving brown eyes were alert. He wore an expensive check sports jacket, a spotless white shirt, blue tie with a regimental tie clip sporting the symbol of the airborne forces. Lance Buckmaster. The Minister for External Security. Noted for his attention to presenting a faultless appearance. The tone was clipped, public school.

'You know the Minister, Bob,' Howard said to Newman.

'We have met.'

'And I'm still waiting, Doctor, for a reply,' Buckmaster said with a snap.

The doctor sighed, pursed his lips. 'The girl was strangled and then savagely raped. More I can't say before—'

'The autopsy,' Buckmaster interjected impatiently. 'We know the form. But how do you interpret the sequence – strangulation first, then rape. Why not the other way round?'

'Despite the victim's slimness she looks agile and strong. If she'd fought the rape there'd have been skin from her attacker under the fingernails. There may be a trace under her index finger, but nothing more. And that's subject to the autopsy,' the doctor repeated firmly. 'I'd like to go now.' He looked at the group of waiting men. 'The preliminary examination is finished as far as I am concerned . . .'

Nodding to Howard, he walked out without a glance at Buckmaster. Harvey checked with the photographer, the forensic expert, who both said they didn't need the body any more. Two waiting men in boiler suits carefully wrapped the corpse inside a canvas swathe, lifted it on to a stretcher, removed it from the room on their way downstairs. Buckmaster, hands clasped behind his erect back, paced the room restlessly, pushed a shock of hair over his head.

'Why assume it was Tweed?' asked Newman, staring at Howard.

'Because he lived here.' It was Harvey who answered. Wearing plastic gloves, he was picking up a pipe from a glass bowl to slip it inside a transparent bag. 'He even smoked his pipe before he did the job.'

14

'May I look at that pipe?' Newman persisted. 'It's full of tobacco and barely been smoked.'

'So he had a few puffs before he grabbed her round the neck and got on with the job . . .'

Newman walked over to a small wall cupboard. 'Can I look inside here?'

'You cannot,' Harvey informed him. He sealed the bag holding the pipe. 'What's inside it that interests you?'

'Maybe a tin of tobacco.'

'Then we'll have a look at it, shall we?' Harvey stretched out a gloved hand, opened the door. A tin of tobacco rested on the shelf. He prised off the lid. Newman leant forward, sniffed at the half-empty tin. A stale musty odour.

'Satisfied?' Harvey replaced the lid, put the tin back on the shelf. 'And Tweed has disappeared—'

'Looks like he's run for it,' Buckmaster interjected. 'Our best hope is he'll do away with himself. All this has to be kept under wraps, Newman. You've signed the Official Secrets Act.'

'And the neighbours?' Newman enquired.

'A rumour will be spread Tweed has gone off on another insurance investigation. He had nothing to do with his neighbours. All they know about Tweed is he's supposed to be Chief Claims Investigator for an insurance company with a lot of business abroad. Howard told me that.'

'And you want this kept under wraps,' Newman reminded him. 'So what are you doing here – you're highly recognizable with your picture in the papers at every opportunity . . .'

'Don't quite like how you phrased that.' Buckmaster's tone was aggressive. 'You are talking to a Minister of the Crown, in case you've forgotten. As to my presence, Howard phoned me. And I've left my Daimler and driver round two corners from here. And it's time I left.' He

15

looked at Howard. 'I will be in touch with you by nine this morning. See you're available in your office.'

He pulled out a folded check golfing cap from his pocket and rammed it low over his forehead. He sneered at Newman. 'You think anyone will recognize me now on my way back to my car?'

He walked out of the room. Howard shrugged his shoulders as they were left alone. 'He's got a point. He normally never wears anything on his head—' He broke off as Buckmaster reappeared in the doorway.

'Funny business this. I'd never have associated a man like Tweed with such an atrocity.'

Then he was gone again. Howard waved his hands with the air of a man lost. 'And I'd never have thought Buckmaster capable of such a human remark. People are a funny mixture . . .'

'How did you first hear about this business?' Newman asked in a low voice.

'Anonymous phone call. Woke me up. "Tweed is in desperate trouble at his apartment in Radnor Walk. Better get over there before the police do." I think those were his exact words . . .'

'So it was a man who made the call? Recognize the voice? I want you to think – think hard.'

'No, I don't think I've heard that voice before. I dressed quickly. I was on my own. Cynthia is away, fortunately. I arrived about 1.30 a.m. The door wasn't locked. I found that out when I'd pressed the bell and no one came. I walked inside, came upstairs . . . and found her lying on the bed. No sign of anyone else. I phoned Buckmaster. Only thing I could do. When he arrived he alerted the Clean-Up Squad. We can't have a scandal like this made public. It would destroy the Service . . .'

'Who is – was – the girl?' Newman asked crisply.

Howard, still in a state of shock, stared at Newman. The foreign correspondent was in his early forties, well-built, of medium height and with light brown hair verging on sandy-coloured. Even at that hour he had an alert look, as aura of controlled energy. The normally droll smile was absent.

'We've no idea of her identity,' Howard replied. 'They've torn the place to pieces and couldn't even find a handbag. Of course now they're recalling the fact that Tweed's wife left him several years ago for a Greek shipping magnate, that he hasn't had a lot to do with women since . . .'

'He likes girls,' Newman interjected sharply. 'He's been on the edge of having an affair more than once. But he blotted out his wife by dedicating himself to his job. You know that.'

'I thought I did . . .'

'Not you, too? That's great. That's really great.' Newman slapped a hand against his thigh, heard a noise, turned to find Harvey had come back.

'One thing strikes me as odd, Mr Newman,' he began, his manner officious. 'How you happened to turn up here at this hour?'

'I'd been to a party at Cipriani's in The Strand which went on all hours. To sober up I walked back to my flat in Beresforde Road. I wasn't sleepy, so I decided to drive round London a bit to tire myself.'

'That's a jolly long walk, if you don't mind my saying so,' Harvey remarked and smiled in a twisted way. Newman could have hit him.

'So what the hell are you getting at?' he asked quietly.

'Nothing. At the moment. But we can check your story later – find witnesses who saw you leave Cipriani's. Get someone to do the same walk at the same time, see how long it takes . . .'

'Why not do the walk yourself?' Newman rapped back. 'Might help to take an inch or two off your waistline.'

17

'No need to get personal. The main thing is, where is Tweed at this moment?'

Kneeling in front of the safe in his first-floor office at Park Crescent, headquarters of the Secret Service, Tweed turned the dial to the last numbers of the combination lock, hauled open the door.

The curtains were drawn over the windows looking towards Regent's Park and he hadn't turned on the light. He used a flash to see what he was doing. Pulling open a drawer, he took out several stacks of banknotes in German marks and Swiss francs. He arranged them neatly in the executive case open by his side, then concealed the bank-notes with several layers of insurance magazines and four paperbacks. He locked the case, closed the safe door, spun the combination dial, stood up.

In his mid forties, Tweed had a compact build, dark hair and wore horn-rim glasses. In repose his face was that of a kindly man with exceptional intelligence. The eyes behind the lenses were watchful and wary. He wore a business suit which lacked the elegance of his chief, Howard. The Deputy Director of the SIS was a man you could pass in the street without noticing, an effect he'd been careful to cultivate.

Still using the flashlight, he perched the case on his desk, took out his key ring, used the two keys which unlocked the specially reinforced bottom right-hand drawer. Reaching down, he delved beneath three code books, hauled out the six passports with his photograph – minus glasses – and all in different names. He chose the passport with the name William Sanders, thrust it in his breast pocket. The other five he spread out flat at the bottom of the executive case. He re-locked the drawer, stood up, and that was when someone switched on the main light.

*   *   *

Paula Grey, his attractive assistant, closed the door, leaned against it. In her early thirties, her raven black hair gleamed in the overhead light. She had excellent bone structure, a well-shaped determined chin, a good figure and long legs. She was wearing a dark blue gaberdine suit, a white blouse with a pussy bow, her check coat folded over one arm. The February early morning was chilly, with a hint of snow to come in the air.

Tweed, enduring high tension, concealed his shock well. His mind went cold as ice. His voice was completely normal when he asked the question.

'What on earth are you doing here at this hour?'

'I might ask you the same thing.' She nodded towards his suitcase standing next to the desk. 'Going somewhere? You never told me. And something's wrong. I can tell.'

His right hand went automatically towards his pocket for his pipe. Then he remembered he'd given up smoking the damned thing. His mind was moving at extraordinary speed.

'Something cropped up unexpectedly. I'm going abroad for a short time . . .'

She walked towards him, her movements swift and graceful. She put both her hands on his shoulders.

'This is Paula. Remember me? I came in to do some work – I couldn't sleep. Now, what's wrong?'

'Brace yourself. I'm going to be accused of murder and rape. A beautiful young girl I've never seen before. She's lying in my bed at Radnor Walk. Now you'd better ask the question – did I do it?'

It was the only hint of emotion he showed. She clenched her teeth, shook him. Tried to. He stood immovable. 'What the devil are you talking about? How dare you ask me that.' Her voice quavered with emotion, then she regained control. 'Are you mad? Fleeing like a common criminal. You're the Deputy

19

Director – in case you've forgotten. You must stay and fight it. Find out what really happened.'

'Can't. I have a secret project I was controlling. Only one other person over here knows about it. I have to remain free to carry that project through. A lot is at stake – maybe even the security of the whole western world. Which sounds melodramatic. I'm leaving, Paula. Catching the earliest plane to Brussels.'

'Why Brussels? And I still don't see why you're so certain you'll be accused of this dreadful thing,' she protested.

'Because someone very clever and ruthless has planned this frame-up. So they may have planted some more damning "evidence" somewhere in my flat. I had no time to search thoroughly. And why Brussels? That's only the first stage. I have to find a bolt-hole – somewhere I can operate from. They'll lock me up when they find that poor girl. Everything points to me as the murderer, the rapist. Who do you think I could trust with that hanging over me? No one for certain—'

'You bloody fool,' she snapped. 'You can trust me. I'm coming with you. My case packed for an emergency is in that cupboard over there. And a couple is less conspicuous than a man on his own . . .'

'Out of the question.'

Tweed forcibly removed her hands, walked across to the stand near the door, donned his old Burberry. He picked up the executive case, his suitcase. He paused by the door, looked back at her.

'Your job could be at stake. You live for your job. Stay here and keep the home fires burning.'

He left the room, closing the door behind him. That was when Tweed began running and running and running. The nightmare had started.

PART ONE

The Fugitive – Tweed

1

At 7 a.m. the same morning Lance Buckmaster arrived at the headquarters of the company he had founded in Threadneedle Street, World Security & Communications Ltd. To avoid any risk of being noticed he drove his wife's Volvo station wagon.

The twenty-storey building was empty at that hour. Buckmaster parked the Volvo in the underground garage, used the special key to open the executive elevator door, ascended to the eighteenth floor. Gareth Morgan, his deputy and confidante, waited for him in the large office with windows overlooking the City. A white mist obscured the view, gave the high-rise buildings a ghostly look. It was going to be a bleak February.

'It worked.' Buckmaster threw his check cap on a couch, strode across the room and lolled in his executive chair. 'Special Branch bought it, swallowed it – hook, line and sinker.'

'And Tweed?' his deputy enquired.

Gareth Morgan was forty-two years old and looked more like fifty-two. Five feet six, he was overweight for his height and his body resembled a large turnip in shape. He had small neat feet and moved with agility. Dark-haired, he had shrewd beady eyes, was clean-shaven and showed the beginnings of a jowl. A slow deliberate talker, he fixed his small eyes on the subject he was conversing with, as though exerting a hypnotic effect. He was a man of great energy, ability and ruthlessness. Buckmaster's wife, Leonora, had once told a woman friend,

'Lance and Morgan go well together. Two of the world's greatest con men . . .'

'Tweed has vanished off the face of the earth,' Buck-master informed his subordinate in his lofty voice. 'Which is just what we hoped for – that he'd run for it.'

'Don't underestimate that man,' Morgan warned as he lit a cigar. 'He'll have headed for Europe . . .'

'So it makes your job easier. We have WS & C offices with trained staffs all over the Continent. I'm putting you in charge of the operation. Locate Tweed and eliminate him. Essential you make it look like an accident . . .'

Morgan pursed his thick lips, his expression grim. 'You mean go over there myself? I have to mind the shop here. When you became a Minister you appointed me Man-aging Director. Remember?'

'You like moving about.' Buckmaster's tone was brus-que. 'The assignment should be right up your street. You fly to Europe, put the boot in to our top people, get them looking, then fly back here. Like a Kissinger shuttle, Gareth.' He checked his watch. 'And I'm not supposed to be here. I'm leaving shortly for the Ministry.'

Morgan ran a thick thumb across his jowl, puffed at his cigar. Buckmaster was right: he shouldn't be in the building. When he'd been appointed a Minister he'd handed over his parcel of shares to his wife, Leonora. And the idea did appeal to Morgan: a Kissinger-like shuttle. Appealed to his ego. He'd use the company executive jet.

'I'll have to return here frequently,' he said eventually. 'I find Leonora is becoming a bit active – curious about things – as chairman. And she's become chummy with that accountant, Ted Doyle . . .'

'Curious about what?' Buckmaster demanded.

'Company figures. The balance sheet. So far I've kept her away from the secret files. When is that fifty-million pound loan coming in? I can't bluff the City for ever.'

'Soon. And you've left off a zero. It will be five hundred million.'

'As much as that?' Morgan concealed his shock. 'That should put us back in business nicely. But where the hell can you raise that money?'

Buckmaster stood up, donned his check cap. 'Leave that to me. You deal with Tweed. And quickly . . .'

'It may take time,' Morgan warned. 'I told you not to underestimate him.'

'Not too much time. The deadline is running out. Fly to the Continent today. I'm off . . .'

Morgan sat in the leather chair facing Buckmaster's desk for some time after his chief had left, his bulk squeezed between the arms. He had come a long way since his early days as a security guard with a small outfit, had climbed with Buckmaster.

He recalled as almost yesterday the advertisement in *The Times* for an experienced administrator to join a new security organization. He'd called the number in the ad. from Cardiff and Buckmaster had answered the phone. Buckmaster had been off-hand in his reaction.

'I don't know you have the experience I need . . .'

'But I do have a first-class ticket from Cardiff to London in my fist. And I'm calling from the station. The express leaves in five minutes – I can see it from where I'm speaking. Give me fifteen minutes of your time and you'll hire me. If you decide not to I'll walk straight out of your office and you'll never see me again. Only four minutes now before that express begins to move . . .'

The audacious ploy had worked. Buckmaster had warned him there would be no question of paying his fare. Morgan had replied he paid his own way. He boarded the express with two minutes to spare.

It was Morgan's handling of the attempted bank raid a few days earlier in Cardiff which turned the trick. It had made the national press. Instead of travelling with the

25

security truck carrying the money, Morgan had checked out the area round the bank the previous day. On the morning of the delivery he hid in an alley armed with a baseball bat concealed under his raincoat. Two armed men had jumped from a car as the money was being carried towards the bank. Morgan had appeared behind them, had first smashed the skull of the man carrying a machine-pistol and then crushed the kneecap of the second robber armed with an automatic.

At the interview Buckmaster had explained he was founding a new security firm specializing in protecting high-risk and valuable cargoes. His first reaction was to reject Morgan until he remembered the abortive Cardiff robbery.

'Routine. That's where established firms make their mistake,' Morgan had told him, speaking rapidly and with an air of total authority. 'And they use one of three alternative routes in recognizable trucks. The vehicles must be varied in appearance, the destination told to the driver in code as he leaves the depot – by you or me. We must have dummy runs to confuse the intelligence systems of the professional robbers. And I hire every member of the staff – I can smell a wrong 'un a hundred yards away . . . We infiltrate informants into the underworld to organize our own counter-espionage apparatus . . . In certain countries on the Continent we use tougher methods . . .'

'On the Continent?'

Buckmaster, who normally dominated a conversation, had found himself taken aback by the scale Morgan foresaw they would operate on.

'Of course.' Morgan had waved the unlit cigar he'd held clenched between his teeth. 'It is an international organization we are thinking of. Europe first, then the States . . .'

'And when could you start?' Buckmaster had eventually asked.

26

'As your right-hand man, now. I brought my packed case. It's waiting in the lobby . . .'

Buckmaster had hired him on the spot. A decision he had never regretted. Morgan had suggested the name, World Security & Communications. And that was twenty years ago. Long before Buckmaster's eyes had turned to politics and he'd become the youngest MP in the Commons, leaving Morgan to run the largest security organization in the world. It had expanded by leaps and bounds.

And that, Morgan thought as he stirred in the chair, was when I advised caution. That we consolidate what we had built up; but Buckmaster had the bit between his teeth. More offices had been opened up in many countries. Too many too quickly.

'And one day I'll own the whole outfit,' he said to himself. 'Providing it doesn't go bust first.' Through nominees he'd bought up a major holding in the company. Morgan thought of only one person in the world. Gareth Morgan.

Stretching, he yawned. He'd been up all night. First things first. The tracking down of Tweed.

2

Tweed moved fast. He caught the first Sabena flight to Brussels, using the William Sanders passport at London Airport. Arriving in the Belgian capital, he took a cab to the Hilton on the Boulevard de Waterloo.

He booked in at the special executive reception on the eighteenth floor, reserving an executive suite on the twentieth floor. Dumping his case inside the suite, he left the hotel.

He hired a BMW from Hertz, showing a driving licence in the name of William Sanders. He parked the car in an underground garage near the hotel. He could have parked it in the Hilton garage, but if he needed to leave suddenly that might be dangerous.

'Do you really think we can disappear into the blue?' Paula asked as they walked back to the hotel.

'If we keep moving . . .'

The presence of Paula Grey was one thing he hadn't counted on. She had followed him in a second taxi to London Airport, taking her case with her. His first realization that he was not alone came when he booked a return Business-Class ticket at the Sabena counter. He turned and Paula was standing behind him.

'A Business-Class return to Brussels,' she informed the airline clerk.

Collecting her ticket, she came up behind him again as he checked in for the flight. Tweed was unable to argue with her – it was too public and the last thing he wanted was to draw attention to himself. They were sitting alongside each other in the half-empty aircraft before he could protest.

'What on earth do you think you're doing?'

'Coming with you. I told you. Back at the office.'

'I can't risk having you with me. There are things you don't know. You could be in terrible danger.'

'I've been there before. Remember Rotterdam? For starters?'

'I want you to catch the first flight back from Brussels. I'm a common fugitive – wanted for murder and rape. It's a queer feeling I can tell you . . .'

'So you need every bit of support you can get. Back at the office you said something about a secret project. Is that why you have to go underground?'

28

'Yes. And don't ask me about it.'

'I'm not leaving you,' she warned him. 'Tell me later what really happened to you last night. First we must decide what to do, where to go, who we can trust.'

Tweed, reacting automatically to the danger, still felt stunned. Paula, he recognized, was thinking with her usual clarity. She had summed up his immediate task in a nutshell. For the first time he wavered in his determination to get rid of her. She sensed his uncertainty.

'Well, for starters, who can we trust?'

'No one,' he'd said bleakly. 'Absolutely no one – they'll react as soon as they guess I've left the country. The first move will be to alert all my known contacts, to request that I be held incommunicado if I approach any of them . . .'

'And you really think someone like Chief Inspector Kuhlmann of the German Federal Police is going to swallow this absurd idea that you're a murderer and a rapist?'

'He won't have any option . . .'

They had argued like this until the plane touched down in Belgium: Tweed uncharacteristically negative; Paula positive and working out escape routes. Tweed's mood changed as soon as they reached Brussels, reserving the suite at the Hilton, hiring the car.

Returning to the Hilton, they went straight up to the suite. It was Paula who had insisted they share the suite against all Tweed's objections.

'If we book a separate one for me,' she pointed out, 'I may have to show my passport. Being registered as Paula Grey will lead the baying hounds straight to you – once they grasp that I've disappeared too. I can sleep on a couch if they haven't twin beds . . .'

'They had twin beds the last time I was here,' Tweed recalled.

'Stop being so Victorian,' she'd snapped. 'If you register I can pass as your wife . . .'

It was Paula who, on the way back to the hotel, had dived into a shop, emerging with a folder full of Michelin road maps of different areas of Europe. 'Need these to plan our route,' she'd said briskly.

Now Tweed was staring from the suite window at the panoramic view over the city. Close by reared the immense domed bulk of the Palais de Justice, a complex so large it covered a greater area than St Peter's in Rome. He found it ironic.

'If they catch up with me now,' he mused, 'I suppose that's where they'll take me . . .'

'Oh do shut up and look at these maps with me. Where are we heading for when we leave here?'

'Switzerland might be best.' Tweed shook off his mood of resignation, leaned over her shoulder to study the maps. Again her driving force was animating him, pushing back an insidious sensation of inertia. 'I'll have to risk contacting Arthur Beck, Chief of the Federal Police in Berne. Switzerland being neutral, it might be our best bet.'

She carefully concealed her satisfaction at this first use of the word 'our'. Tweed's finger traced a route through Liège to the east and then down through the Ardennes, a remote hilly district.

'Not much traffic if we can make it into the forest,' he said. 'Definitely our best chance of not being spotted.'

'But where do we go from there? How can we safely cross into West Germany – assuming the alert has gone out by then?'

'Our best chance is to drive along the secondary roads in the Ardennes into Luxembourg. There's no check on crossing that border. Then, if we get lucky we drive over the Luxembourg frontier into Germany, head south down the Rhine for the Black Forest. There's a small place where I think we could slip over the German border into Switzerland. It's one hell of a long shot.'

'So we follow that route,' Paula said firmly.

'The big question is – will we ever reach the Swiss border?'

Paula asked the question which had preyed on her mind while they were drinking coffee from room service in Tweed's suite. She took a deep breath, nerved herself, dived in.

'Isn't it about time you told me what really happened back at your flat in Radnor Walk?'

'Like an idiot, I walked straight into a carefully prepared trap. If one of my staff had done the same thing I do believe I'd have fired him. I was so incredibly stupid I still don't know what got into me.'

Paula crossed her legs on the couch, facing Tweed who sat bolt upright in an executive chair. 'Well, what did you do?' she coaxed.

'I was working late at the office as you know. You'd gone home and only Monica was left in the building with me. She took the call and said it was for me. The caller would only tell her his name was Klaus. I guessed it was one of my circle of private informants on the Continent – the people even you don't know about. I've promised them all total confidentiality.' He paused, sipped at his coffee.

'I know you have these people. Go on,' Paula encouraged him.

'I took the call. It sounded like Klaus Richter, although there was a lot of background noise. People chatting, laughing. He said he'd flown over urgently to see me and asked me to come to the Cheshire Cheese, that pub in Fleet Street, at ten o'clock that night. He sounded edgy. I agreed. Where I made my mistake was in not checking back with his number in Freiburg at the edge of the Black Forest. Although they'd probably

31

covered that.' He spoke the last words grimly.

'Who is "they"?' Paula asked.

'I've no idea who's behind the conspiracy – because that's what it has to be. And a very dangerous conspiracy since I suspect it's connected with the secret project I was controlling alone. Don't ask me about that. I arrived at the Cheshire Cheese early deliberately – to spy out the land . . .'

'Your usual ploy in such cases. You did have all your marbles,' she encouraged him again.

'It was 9.45 when I entered the pub. Place was crowded. I ordered a glass of wine and sat in the corner where I could survey the whole place. No sign of Richter. I waited and waited. It was just before closing time when a girl dropped an envelope in my lap. Unsealed. The message inside was brief. *Came early. Had to leave. Being followed. Meet you at Radnor Walk. K.* I'd just time to read it when the girl returned. She whispered that Klaus told her she must take the message from me after I'd read it. A clever touch that. Klaus was a very careful man. I let her take it . . .'

'Seen that girl before?'

'Never. Head wrapped in a scarf and tied over her chin. It *was* a cold night. About thirty at a guess. About five foot ten, well dressed, pale white complexion, blue eyes. Then she was gone . . .'

Tweed stared into the distance, recalling the incident. Paula prodded again.

'So what was your next move?'

'As I said, it was late, near closing time. I walked back all the way from Fleet Street to Radnor Walk, which took a while . . .'

'To check that *you* weren't being followed?'

'Exactly, I wasn't. At least not on foot. There was an Audi which passed me soon after I'd left the pub. I believe now the driver – I didn't see who it was – was

32

checking that I had left the pub. Eventually, after midnight, I arrived at Radnor Walk. The front door was slightly ajar. No trace of any forcing of the two security locks. I crept inside, picked up that heavy walking stick with the weighted tip I keep in the umbrella stand, explored the ground floor. Nothing. I had the strong feeling the place was empty. Then I went upstairs . . .'

He drank more black coffee slowly, the faraway look in his eyes again. This time Paula waited in silence. He put down the cup, stared straight at her.

'I entered the bedroom and the bedside light was on. I saw her at once, lying face up in my bed. The sheet rumpled. Brutally strangled. Big bruises round the neck.' Tweed was now speaking in a normal detached tone. 'The sheets had been pulled down over her long legs. She was naked, had a good figure. I soon realized she'd been raped – no need to go into the details. I also realized it was the perfect frame – that I'd be accused.'

Why?' Paula was leaning forward, watching Tweed carefully. 'You knew the girl?'

'Never seen her in my life. The murderer had added some subtle touches. My pipe, filled with tobacco, partially smoked, lay in a glass bowl.'

'You gave up that pipe several weeks ago. You said you were a wet smoker and didn't enjoy it.'

'Which is one thing about me the murderer doesn't know. But it doesn't mean a damned thing. I could have tried the pipe again before I set about her. A glass I'd left in the kitchen in the morning was on the bedside table – with a drop of wine in it. Chablis. From a bottle on another table which was almost empty. The glass would still have my fingerprints on it, I'm sure.'

'Could they still feel so sure you were guilty? People like Howard, for God's sake.'

'No option.' Tweed was cleaning his glasses with his handkerchief, a mannerism which Paula welcomed

33

seeing. Relating what had happened was calming him. 'And no alibi,' he went on. 'I was walking back for over an hour through deserted streets. I doubt if anyone at the Cheshire Cheese would remember me – I was deliberately making myself inconspicuous . . .

'The girl who gave you the message from Richter. She knows you were there.'

'And is obviously part of the plot, hired to hand me the note, and take it off me afterwards. No evidence . . .'

'This Klaus Richter in Freiburg,' she suggested. 'Could he help?' She frowned. 'You used the past tense when referring to him. Why?'

'Because I think he's probably dead,' Tweed replied. 'The people who organized this are professionals – and ruthless as hell. What they did to that girl proves that. They've left no loose ends, I'm sure.'

'What on earth did you do after you'd found this unknown girl in your house?'

'Thought fast. I could see a noose had been thrown round my neck I'd maybe never get free from. The only answer was to run – in the hope that I can escape being apprehended while I find out what's happening to the project I was working on. As I said earlier, I'm a fugutive. We can't trust anyone . . .'

'There's Newman – and Marler.'

'A horrific crime like the one at Radnor Walk makes a man an outcast, a pariah without friends. We're on our own. Someone is counting on that.'

'But we're not just going to sit here until they come for us?'

'No. Instead we'll do the unexpected.'

3

'I've found out Tweed caught an early flight to Brussels. I'm having the staff of our office there check every hotel. I flew over copies of that photograph of Tweed you gave me,' Morgan reported as he drove the Daimler beyond Exeter towards Dartmoor.

His bulk was squeezed inside the chauffeur's uniform, which did not fit his turnip-like shape too well. A chauffeur's peaked cap was pulled down over his high forehead. Buckmaster sat beside him, staring at the bleak snowbound slopes of the moor.

Morgan had adopted his disguise because, as a Minister, Buckmaster was not supposed to have any further connection with the world-wide security organization they had built up. Buckmaster ran a hand over his lean face.

'It's essential at least to keep Tweed harassed and fearful – on the move until you can locate him and do the job.'

'There is one complication.' Morgan leered. 'Paula Grey has also disappeared you said earlier. Looks as though he's taken his bedmate with him to keep himself warm.'

'There's no record that their relationship is anything but professional,' Buckmaster snapped in a puritanical tone. 'That means they may be more alert. Bear that in mind. And if this Grey woman is with him when you pinpoint their whereabouts – she'll have to go too.'

'That can be attended to. I've contacted Armand Horowitz and he's meeting me in Brussels.'

35

'So, you've gone to the top,' Buckmaster commented as they turned on to the Okehampton road. It was getting dark.

'You need a real professional on a job like this,' Morgan responded. 'Horowitz has never failed to take out a target.'

'Don't want to hear about it. No details, no pack drill.'

Morgan subsided into silence. Buckmaster's habit of distancing himself from the seamier side of the company worried him. He had little doubt that if anything went wrong Buckmaster would let him drop over the cliff. Which, he reflected, is why he pays me one hundred thousand pounds a year. But, he also reflected, it means I'll have to watch my back. Treachery was the name of the game in politics. In business too. Because he had grasped this fact was why Morgan had risen so high.

'What are you going to do next about Tweed?' Buckmaster asked as Morgan turned off the Okehampton road and drove through the snow towards Moretonhampstead.

'Tell you in a minute. I'd better get out of these togs – I also suggest you sit in the rear of the car before we arrive at Tavey Grange.'

He stopped the car on the grass verge of the deserted road. Getting out, he tossed the cap on the seat, wrestled off the uniform, exposing the lightweight dark suit he wore under it. While Buckmaster sat impatiently in the rear and drummed his fingers on his knee, Morgan put on an expensive black overcoat, the collar trimmed with astrakhan, buttoned it up, got back behind the wheel and resumed driving.

Passing between the granite houses lining the main street of Moretonhampstead, he drove on, his headlights picking out the bends in the serpentine road. Tavey Grange lay half a mile beyond the Manor House Hotel. He answered Buckmaster's question as he turned off the road between lodge gates and proceeded down the long

36

drive across open parkland. A half-moon was rising and the snow-covered slopes of Dartmoor glowed weirdly.

'I'm taking the chopper from your helipad here back to London. Tomorrow I'll take Stieber with me to Brussels, pick up the trail there.'

'You'd better know – unofficially – that an alert for Tweed has now gone out secretly to our counter-espionage friends and certain police chiefs in Europe. Locate and hold is the order.'

'That might handicap me.' Morgan grunted. 'Wish you hadn't done that.'

'Had to. It was the obvious reaction I had to make as Minister. If I'd held my hand it would have looked suspicious. The PM agreed. It will serve the purpose of isolating Mr Tweed from his old buddies, keep him running like a scared fox.'

'If you say so.'

Morgan felt more comfortable as he approached the Grange, still hidden by a copse of trees. It was only in London they had to keep up the pretence that Buck-master had nothing to do with his company. The servants at the house were mostly foreigners who didn't know their arse from their elbow, as Morgan put it to himself.

They passed the copse and the lights of a large Elizabethan house came into view. Tall stately chimneys, the lights shining from behind mullion-paned windows. Morgan reduced speed and checked his appearance in the rear-view mirror, driving with one hand. Wanted to look his elegant best for the bitch, his nominal company chief, Leonora Buckmaster. He combed his hair. In the rear Buckmaster made a gentle hissing noise between his teeth. The sooner Morgan boarded the chopper and pushed off the better.

Leonora Buckmaster came to the front doorway as the Daimler pulled up. Morgan jumped out, opened the rear door. Buckmaster alighted. His wife called out in her well-modulated voice.

'Drinks are ready in the library. Then straight into dinner. I'm famished. Good evening, Gareth.'

'Good evening, ma'am.' Morgan dipped in a little bow and gave her his best smile.

Leonora Buckmaster was ten years younger than her husband. A slim blonde creature, she wore a Valentino black and white dress. Her husband gave her a hug and hurried inside, saying he was going to take a quick bath, then he'd be down for drinks.

'A drink in the library for you, Gareth?' she enquired.

He pecked her on the cheek. She managed to conceal the physical revulsion she always felt from close contact with this man. She might be chairman of the company with Lance's block of shares in her name, but Gareth Morgan was managing director and ran the organization.

'That would be nice, Leonora,' he agreed after closing and locking the car. The garage man would put the Daimler to bed. He followed her into the library, produced his cigar case, then hesitated.

'Not in here. Out on the terrace,' she informed him. 'I've got a drink. Do pour your own. Leave some in the bottle . . ..'

It was not a friendly joke: Morgan was aware she thought he drank too heavily. To hell with her, he thought and kept his coat on in the warm book-lined room. He poured half a glass of neat Scotch, raised it to Leonora who had seated herself in an arm chair, erect and elegant.

'Chin-chin,' said Morgan and drank a heavy slug.

He opened the door to the terrace spanning the full width of the rear of the mansion, closed it behind him. The ice-cold air hit him. He lit his Havana, took a deep satisfying puff. Leonora was getting to be a pain, probing into the affairs of the company. At least he'd kept the vital figures away from her.

He strolled along the terrace below which the grassy slopes fell away steeply towards an ornamental lake. A cottonwool mist was floating down towards the lake from the ridge in the moonlight.

On the terrace he took his decision. He'd board the chopper when he'd finished his drink, tell the pilot to take him to London Airport. His suitcase was in the boot of the Daimler. He could get a couple of hamburgers and a glass of beer at the airport, then catch the evening flight to Brussels. Get after Tweed.

At SIS headquarters in Park Crescent, London, Howard sat behind Tweed's desk, facing Bob Newman. Monica, Tweed's close associate for many years, sat at her desk, her head bent over some files while the two men talked.

'Do you really think Tweed is guilty?' Newman demanded point-blank.

'It's inconceivable, I agree,' responded Howard, waving a well-manicured hand, his plump face pink with embarrassment at the directness of Newman. 'But he made a great mistake fleeing the country. And taking Paula with him. Doesn't look good for his case . . .'

'His case!' Newman exploded. 'You talk like a bloody prosecuting counsel. He obviously had his reasons. What was he working on? And how do you know he's fled the country?'

'Can't talk about what he was working on,' Howard said stiffly. He paused. 'Didn't even know myself until I talked with the PM this afternoon. And you won't like this, but since you're fully vetted and have worked with Tweed in the past . . .' Another wave of the hand. 'A general alert has been sent out to certain security personnel in other countries to locate and hold him when found. All very hush-hush. The press mustn't get on to it – and you *are* the press. I'm invoking the Official Secrets Act form you signed on that one. Have to. Sorry and all that . . .'

'I said,' Newman repeated slowly, 'how do you know he's fled the country?'

'Well, Buckmaster gave the order. Check with airports, seaports. Show his photograph. Only to top security personnel, of course.'

'Of course!' Newman interjected ironically. 'Do get to the point of what I asked.'

'Jim Corcoran at London Airport made discreet enquiries. Found a girl with a good memory who remembered him checking in early this morning for a flight to Brussels. Appeared to have a girl with him. From the description Corcoran obtained I'm afraid it could be Paula Grey . . .'

'Makes sense,' Newman commented.

'Makes sense!' Howard's pompous manner changed, his voice went up several decibels. 'If it was Paula that means I have two of my staff as fugitives from justice . . .'

'Balls!' Newman lit a cigarette. 'Buckmaster's doing this all on his own?'

'Well . . .' Howard showed more indecision. 'Actually I wasn't privy to the decision to send the alert.'

Wasn't privy to . . . Newman controlled himself with an effort. Howard really was the most bombastic prig. 'Then who was?' he demanded.

'Buckmaster – after due consultation with the PM I was told at Downing Street to issue a discreet alert.' He leaned forward. 'I might tell you I persuaded her to cut down the list Buckmaster had drawn up of people to be informed. Only those I feel we can trust to keep it under wraps have been contacted.'

'Who are they?'

40

Howard hesitated again 'Why do you want to know?'

'For Christ's sake – because I believe Tweed is innocent, that he's been framed up to the hilt. And I'm going to do something about it, not just sit here on my tod wringing my hands.

'I can't do anything else, Bob,' Howard said quietly, 'except sit here on my tod, as you put it. I needed to know that you're also convinced it's a conspiracy. It's not a view I can admit to officially. I'm very relieved you're going into action – and you might like to know I reworded the signal Buckmaster was sending, made it, shall we say less positive.'

'Buckmaster seems to be running this outfit these days,' Newman snapped. 'I don't like that either . . .'

It was a recent experiment on the part of the PM – to create a new ministry to oversee the security services. The Ministry for External Security. The first man to be appointed as Minister, Lance Buckmaster, had seemed logical. He was youngish, energetic and a good orator.

It had seemed even more logical to choose this MP since he'd built up a vast international organization devoted to security. World Security & Communications specialized in the safe movement of high-risk cargoes – gold bullion, old-master paintings, large consignments of banknotes.

But WS & C as it was now known world wide had carried the development of security to the ultimate. It handled secret data for the research departments of major companies. It had gone into the communications field, using its own satellites to provide a watertight method for directors talking about vital topics over the phone from, say, Frankfurt to Washington, supplying the coded systems.

With all this experience behind him, Buckmaster had proved a natural choice to control the new Ministry. The snag was it had deliberately not been made clear how much power he wielded over the Secret Service. Howard was still able to report direct to the PM. She had insisted on retaining ultimate control. Howard waved his hand a third time before speaking his mind.

'Just between you and me it's a running dogfight between myself and Buckmaster. I won't let him come here often. There are certain files I refuse to let him see. It may cost me my job, but so far the PM has backed me.'

'And what about Turnip Top, as the press has labelled Gareth Morgan? I met him at a party. His conversation is a lie a minute. His policy is to ingratiate himself with anyone who might be useful to him, a nauseating spectacle. But I detect something sinister behind the showbiz front, the big cigar.'

'I wouldn't have said sinister. Why use that epithet?'

'Rumours from contacts I have. Hidden inside WS & C is a well-organized industrial espionage section – run by an unpleasant character with a dubious background. Helmut Stieber. Not his real name, by the way. His father came from Czechoslovakia. Married an English girl. Both are dead. Stieber is Morgan's deputy. Spends most of his time on the Continent. Also rumoured they used strongarm tactics during one of Buckmaster's many takeover bids to build up his conglomerate. Even to sabotaging competitors' plants.'

'I didn't know that.' Howard sat up straight. 'I can tell you one thing – Morgan isn't allowed anywhere near this place. But some of Buckmaster's requests for data I suspect emanate from Morgan . . .'

He broke off as Marler strolled in after tapping lightly on the door. In his early thirties, he was supposed to be the coming man at SIS. Among his talents was that he was the most deadly marksman in Western Europe.

Slim in build, wearing an expensively cut sports jacket and slacks, he was clean-shaven, had a strong face and spoke in a high-pitched drawl.

'Evenin', Bob. Haven't seen a story from you for ages. Living off the proceeds of that bestseller you wrote, *Kruger: The Computer That Failed*?'

Marler, five feet seven, perched his backside on Paula's desk and swung his legs. Newman looked at him with no particular liking. He'd noted that Howard had clammed up as the new arrival appeared. Why?

'You know perfectly well, Marler, that these days I only go after a story I think is really worthwhile. That's the advantage of being financially independent.'

'So you won't be doing a piece on the somewhat grisly events at Radnor Walk?'

'There's a "D" notice on that,' Howard snapped. 'We've led the press to believe some foreign diplomat was involved in a wild party. Drugs and all that. Put them off the scent.'

'Jolly good idea.' Marler lit a king-size cigarette. 'Can't have the world thinking Tweed broke loose at long last, had his way with an attractive girl and then throttled the poor dear . . .'

'You have such a nice way of putting things,' Newman commented. 'Life and soul of any party, you'd be.'

'Keep your hair on, old chum. I know it's a bit of a shaker.' He addressed Howard. 'Since Tweed appears to have scooted, are you sending out a general alert, setting the hounds after him?'

'All options are still under consideration,' Howard told him stiffly.

'Fair enough. Just came in to say I've been summoned to the presence. Thought you ought to know . . .'

'You mean the PM?' Howard's sense of outrage was clear in his tone.

'Lordy, no. Lance Buckmaster, our esteemed Minister for External Security has asked me to attend him down at the ancestral home, Tavey Grange on Dartmoor.'

'Why?'

'I'll know when I get there, won't I? I'd better get moving. It's a quite a drive – even at night. Our posh new Minister never sleeps.' He glanced at Newman as he stood up. 'The Radnor Walk episode would give you something to get your teeth into. Assuming you're still on Tweed's side . . .'

'Are you?' Newman rapped out.

'I always keep an open mind . . .'

'Because there's not much going on inside it?' Newman suggested.

Marler gave a mock salute, left the office without replying.

'You don't trust him,' Newman said with a slight sense of shock.

'You asked me earlier who had been informed in Europe. If you ever quote me I'll deny I ever said it.' Howard was now looking uncharacteristically grim. He spoke in a monotone. 'Chief Inspector Benoit of the Brussels Criminal Police. Arthur Beck, chief of Swiss Federal Police in Berne. Pierre Loriot at Interpol in Paris. Gunnar Hornberg of SAPO in Stockholm. René Lasalle of French Counter-Intelligence in Paris. And Chief Inspector Otto Kuhlmann, head of Federal Criminal Police in Wiesbaden. That completes the list.'

'Thank you.' Newman paused as Howard stood up to leave. 'It will be a miracle if the news doesn't leak out. And you really have closed him in.'

'The list was much longer as drawn up by Buckmaster,' Howard replied as he reached the door.

'And the signals included details of the crime committed at Radnor Walk?'

'Those men are his friends of quite a few years . . .'

'But will they still be his friends after receiving the signal you sent?'

'I edited the Ministry version,' Howard told him. 'My signal used the phrase "alleged offence". I must go now.

Good luck, Bob. I can't do another damned thing.'

He left the room and Newman swung round to face Monica who had remained like a piece of the furniture during the whole time since he'd arrived. Now she held one finger to her lips, picked up a portable radio from the kneehole beneath her desk and switched it on. Carrying it over, she placed it on Tweed's desk, switched it on, found a music programme, kept it on low volume and sat down close to Newman.

'Why that?' he asked.

'In case the Ministry has bugged the office. Some odd people with papers bearing Buckmaster's signature have been here.'

'Surely Howard realizes the danger? Yet he let me talk . . .'

'He can't believe a Minister would do that. I can – I've met the Right Honourable Lance Buckmaster. Honourable? You have to be joking. He's one of the biggest con men in politics, and that's saying something. Of course I may be prejudiced – he called me Old Faithful.'

'Patronizing swine . . .'

'Oh, he did it on purpose – to try and needle me. Part of his stock-in-trade when he wants to take over an organization. He sows dissension. Howard thinks Marler is in the running for his job.'

'Marler wouldn't play. I don't like him, but he's a cynical bastard and won't be taken in by the likes of Buckmaster.'

'Are you sure? It's a big carrot he's dangling in front of Marler's nose. That has unsettled Howard – all part of the well-known Buckmaster technique.' She leaned closer. 'Am I right in thinking you really believe Tweed had nothing to do with that beastly murder?'

'Yes.'

'Then you might like to know Tweed took a large sum of money with him. A small fortune in Swiss francs and

45

German marks. It's missing from the safe and only two people had the combination. Tweed and myself.'

'So he's OK for funds. That worried me . . .'

'And, Bob, he's also taken six dummy passports in different names, all carrying his photo . . .'

'Anyone know about that?'

'Only me. He kept them in his bottom right-hand drawer. I'm the only one besides Tweed with keys. I checked while I was on my own. Plus international driving licences in the same names. He's up to something.'

'He needs back-up. I have to find him.'

'He does have Paula with him as far as we know,' Monica reminded him.

'He needs more than that. I'm leaving for Brussels today. I always carry a large sum in one thousand Swiss franc notes.' Newman frowned as he worked it out. 'I won't even go back to my flat just in case someone is watching it. I can buy what I need in Brussels – clothes, shaving kit. Luckily it won't seem odd at the airport, travelling without a suitcase. Businessmen are travelling there and back in a day.'

'If only we knew who was behind all this,' Monica mused.

'I'll have to find out, won't I? Remember, I'm used to doing just that – as a foreign correspondent.'

4

Morgan had missed the last flight to Brussels the previous evening. Fog had delayed the landing of his chopper at London Airport. He stayed overnight at the nearby Penta Hotel.

In the morning he ate a large breakfast – double portion of ham and fried eggs, plenty of cream in his coffee. After he'd booked his Brussels flight he used a public phone to call Stieber, his Chief of Security, in Threadneedle Street. He gave Stieber the number he was calling from, told him to call him back from outside. Stieber was back on the line in five minutes. His cold voice, with a hint of the Czech accent he'd never eliminated, sounded a shade excited.

'The bug in you-know-who's office worked. It came over a treat on the radio transmitter when I played it back . . .'

'Give me the guts, then pick up your case from the office and get your backside out here. London Airport, Terminal One. At Sabena's reservation counter. Buy yourself a Business-Class ticket. From Brussels you'll fly on by yourself to Frankfurt, then maybe Freiburg. I'll instruct you on the plane. You have one and a half hours to get here. Give me your news. Fast . . .'

'Marler was on his way to see the chief on Dartmoor. What is really interesting is Bob Newman is getting into the act in some way.'

'The foreign correspondent?' Morgan's tone was sharp. 'So what is he up to?'

'I don't know. I think after Howard left the room there was maybe a further conversation between Newman and someone else . . .'

'You *think*?'

'Wait for me to finish, please. A radio was turned on and it played music, which I found odd. So there could have been conversation I didn't pick up – scrambled by the radio.'

'You're guessing. Unless Newman is a smart cookie. Forget Newman. He's a has-been. Get your arse over here.'

*   *   *

The evening before Morgan phoned Stieber, Marler had driven his second-hand red Porsche to Dartmoor. After dark he stopped at a Little Chef, had a quick meal of scrambled eggs and coffee, then continued his journey.

It was ten o'clock when he turned in between the lodge gates and guided the Porsche down the winding drive to Tavey Grange. Leonora appeared behind the Spanish butler, Fernandez, who opened the nail-studded front door.

'Mr Marler?' She gave him her best smile, liking what she saw under the porch lantern. 'Please come in. José will take your case up to your room. Have you had dinner? I've kept something for you. Lance is making long-distance calls from his study – he's looking forward to seeing you in the morning. A drink for you?'

Marler extended his hand, smiled back. Leonora had small, well-shaped hands and clasped his warmly. Marler, normally cold and distant, could exert considerable charm with attractive women.

'Very kind of you, Mrs Buckmaster. But I grabbed something to stay the pangs of hunger on the way down. If your husband isn't going to be available until mornin' I think I'd just as soon get some kip. Long drive and all that . . .'

Leonora escorted him up the massive oak staircase to his room at the back, wished him a good night's sleep and walked slowly back along the landing. She had excellent legs. Marler, still holding the executive case he'd refused to hand to José, noted the curtains were drawn the full length of the large room. He began his check.

There was no key to the door. Opening the executive case, he extracted a rubber wedge, jammed it under the door. He next pulled back a section of curtain, opened one of the mullion-paned windows. Icy air flooded into the heated room.

With a flashlight – also taken from the executive case –

48

he examined the exterior, leaning out. The beam illuminated the deserted terrace one floor down. He swivelled it to check the outside wall. No fire-escape, no convenient drainpipe anyone could shin up. But to the right of the window he'd opened he found an old ivy creeper clawed to the brickwork. A ready-made ladder for an intruder who wanted to search his possessions during the night.

He closed the window, drew the curtain back across it, glanced round the room. A small heavy porcelain vase on a side table caught his eye. He placed it carefully on the window ledge behind the curtain. That would make enough noise to waken him.

Satisfied with his precautions, he had a wash in the luxurious bathroom, cleaned his teeth, undressed and got into bed. What would the morning bring? He was still uncertain of Buckmaster's motive for wanting to see him.

The following morning, while Morgan was waiting for Stieber at London Airport, Buckmaster joined Marler in the dining-room.

'Good of you to come,' he announced breezily. 'Hope you don't mind, this will be a working breakfast.'

'You talk, I'll listen,' Marler replied and continued piling marmalade on his buttered toast.

'I'm not too happy with the way things are run at Park Crescent – under the present regime, I mean.' Buckmaster poured coffee for himself, Marler said nothing.

'What I'm getting at is our friend, Howard. Nice chap, right sort of background, but is niceness enough?'

'He's proved satisfactory to the PM so far.'

'So far. That's the operative phrase. But what about Tweed and the new emergency? If the Radnor Walk horror becomes public it would be the greatest scandal in the history of the Service. Can we afford that? Some of my advisers think the simplest solution would be if Tweed never came back.' Buckmaster paused to digest some crinkly bacon. 'I understand you are one of the best marksmen in Europe,' he remarked as though apropos of nothing in particular.

'What exactly are you proposing, Minister?' Marler demanded.

'Oh, no definite proposal, my dear chap. Just thinking aloud. Looking at the problem from all angles. And from what I hear you are the person most likely to smoke Tweed out of his hideaway, wherever that may be.'

'I wouldn't count on that,' Marler parried.

'We know he took a flight to Brussels with that girl, Paula Grey.' Buckmaster pushed a cardboard-backed envelope across the table with his fork. 'Inside are two photos, one of Tweed, the other of the Grey woman. I suggest you start with flying to Brussels today. We've notified Benoit that Tweed is wanted. Also Kuhlmann, Loriot, Lasalle and Arthur Beck.'

'You mean I could use them to help in the search?' Marler probed.

Buckmaster paused in the act of forking a strip of bacon into his mouth. 'Well, it would be entirely up to you to decide whether that really is the best way to go about solving this problem. If you see what I mean.'

'I'm not sure I do.'

'I glanced through your personnel file last night. An abbreviated version, I suspect. Howard is still a little jealous of his authority, hasn't yet quite grasped the new set-up since my Ministry was established. I got the impression you're something of a lone wolf. I like that.'

'And you're authorizing me to leave for Brussels, to handle the problem in any way I see fit? Have I understood you?'

'Broadly speaking, yes. In the interests of the Service. Draw any amount of expenses you need. There's my authority for you to do that inside the envelope. Mission unspecified, of course. For your protection.' Buckmaster gave his public smile now so well-known from his pictures in the press.

'Supposing I did solve the problem for you . . .'

'Not for me,' Buckmaster corrected him quickly. 'For the reputation of the Service. I'm only a cog in the machinery.'

'I was going to say,' Marler persisted, 'where would that leave me?'

'A good question.' Buckmaster dabbed at his thin lips with his napkin. 'We all have to think of ourselves from time to time, don't we?' Again, the public smile, showing two rows of perfect teeth. 'You have to remember that with Tweed gone the post of Deputy Director becomes vacant.' Buckmaster leant back in his chair, brushed a hand through his hair. 'And when it's all over who knows? Howard might decide the time had arrived for him to think of retirement.'

'No sign of that at the moment,' Marler pressed him.

'I wouldn't be too sure. Tweed was Howard's appointment. He might think it the honourable thing to do. With a little gentle persuasion . . .'

Buckmaster jumped up suddenly, left his chair standing away from the table. 'Let me show you something before you leave for Brussels. Upstairs in my study . . .'

He took the treads up the great staircase two at a time, a demonstration of his boyish energy. Marler followed at a slower pace. Inside the panelled room Buckmaster picked up a malacca cane, pointed to the wall over the fireplace.

The badge of the Airborne Division had been enlarged in colour and framed as a centrepiece. Below it was Buckmaster's beret, worn during his Army service. Four photographs of the wearer showed him in the act of jumping from an aircraft.

51

'We were taught to go for the jugular,' Buckmaster remarked.

'That was in the Army.'

'Oh, come, man. This is a war we're fighting now. A war to preserve the SIS against all enemies, against all who put its reputation in peril. Agreed?'

'I'm listening . . .'

Buckmaster folded his arms, leaned against his desk, still gripping the malacca. Almost as though he was posing for a fresh picture to be taken.

'You really are a close-mouthed character. I like that. Makes for good security. Now, you've had time to sleep on the problem. What's your first move against Tweed?'

'Search, locate, destroy. I'd better get moving now. I want to be in Brussels today . . .'

'This conversation never took place.' Buckmaster stood upright, towering over his guest. 'I have some phone calls to make. I'd give you a lift to London in the chopper which arrived back last night, but I'm inspecting a certain defence establishment *en route*.'

'And I have my car . . .'

Buckmaster watched the slim marksman leave. Everything was working out well: security and police chiefs on the Continent had been alerted; the whole apparatus of WS & C was looking for Tweed under Morgan's iron hand; and now he had Marler in the manhunt.

Buckmaster was banking most on Marler. He had one great advantage over all the others. He was working from the *inside*.

Marler collected his suitcase and executive case from his room and ran down the staircase in search of Leonora Buckmaster to pay his respects. To his surprise she was waiting in the large hall, wearing a mink-lined raincoat open at the front. Underneath it she was clad in a close-fitting N. Peal black sweater which showed off her figure to full advantage. A Liberty scarf was wrapped round her head and she picked up a travelling case.

'Could you possibly give me a lift to town if that's where you're going next?'

'My pleasure. Car's outside, rarin' to go.'

Marler concealed his surprise and opened the passenger door of the Porsche. She swung her shapely legs inside and began talking as he switched on the ignition.

'The chauffeur has a touch of the flu. Hence the Daimler isn't available . . .'

As the car moved away from the Elizabethan pile Marler glanced in his wing mirror. Behind him was the stable area, now used as garages. He saw a uniformed chauffeur polishing the bonnet of the Daimler just before he turned under a stone archway on to the drive.

'In any case . . .' Leonora laid a hand on his arm. '. . . I wanted to talk to you about this and that.'

They were well on their way, bypassing Exeter, before she spoke again in her throaty voice. The mist had lifted in the night and Marler was making good time.

'You're with General & Cumbria Assurance, my husband told me. One of the top executives. You're concerned with ensuring – and insuring – VIPs' security against kidnapping?'

'That's right.'

Marler decided Buckmaster was good at security if he didn't let his wife know that General & Cumbria was a cover organization masking the SIS.

'So you must be a real expert on all forms of security,' Leonora continued.

'I would hope so.'

'I'm sure you know that when Lance became a Minister he had to transfer his block of shares in WS to me – in my name. I'm the chairman and I can do what I like.'

53

'Really?' Marlet was concentrating on his driving.

'I don't too much like the man, Gareth Morgan, Lance appointed as managing director. He runs the whole organization as though I didn't exist.'

'You sound a trifle irked.'

'More than a trifle. The fact is I'm looking for someone who one day could take over from Morgan. A horrid man. And I've got another problem.'

'Unfortunately life is full of them . . .'

'Don't be so coy.' She nudged him playfully in the ribs with her elbow. 'I feel you are a man I can talk to – knowing that whatever I say won't go any further.'

'Up to you to decide that, Mrs Buckmaster.'

'Please, Leonora.' She slid out of the sleeves of her coat, lit a cigarette, took a deep drag. 'The fact is my husband is playing around with women. One mistress I could ignore – but he's now on his sixth. I find that a bit much.'

'Are you sure? Rather dangerous – his being a Minister and all that.'

'Of course I'm sure. I could give you names. But he's very discreet. His training in security helps the bastard. Doubt if I could prove anything. Not sure I want to – it would ruin his career. Then he'd want his shares back. It could end up as a public dogfight. Not in my interest.' She spoke coolly. 'And it might lead to an investigation of my own background.'

'So, mum's the word. And why tell me all this?'

'I have to talk to someone. You don't imagine I could confide in my best friends, do you? They're the ones who'd love to dish the dirt. You're neutral. Besides, I wanted to put you in the picture. In case I can lever out that toad, Morgan.'

The rest of the journey she went silent, smoking and staring into the distance until Marler pulled up in front of the HQ of World Security in Threadneedle Street. He refused her invitation to join her for 'a cup of coffee, or something stronger.'

'Frightfully kind of you,' he said to her as they stood by the kerb. 'Trouble is I've an urgent appointment with one of those VIPs you mentioned. A millionaire. Business calls . . .'

He drove back to London Airport and stopped in the long-term garage. He sat there for a few minutes. Something of a record – to be 'head-hunted' by the husband and then the wife on the same day. A bright future spread out before him. Then he grabbed both cases and made for the airline counter to buy a ticket. To Brussels.

5

Tweed muddied the trail leading to him. After spending one night at the Hilton he reserved the suite for a week and paid in advance. He explained to the blonde girl receptionist who controlled the executive suites that he had to go to Bruges on business.

'We may have to stay there overnight but I need to have accommodation available for when we get back . . .'

After an early morning breakfast with Paula, he walked with her to the garage where the BMW was parked. They put their cases in the boot and within ten minutes he was leaving the outskirts of Brussels, heading east for Liège – the opposite direction to Bruges.

'Do you think the trick will work if they trace us to the Hilton?' Paula asked.

'It will confuse them. That is what we have to do from now on. Throw out smokescreens.'

Before midday they were across the border into Luxembourg, surrounded by cliffs looming over the narrow serpentine road. No other traffic in either direction. Paula's head was bent over the map, acting as navigator for the route to the point where they would attempt the crossing into Germany.

'Do we assume German security has been informed?' she wondered.

'Yes. We always assume the worst. If we can only slip inside Germany we can make for the autobahn and then for the Black Forest area.'

'You have a plan?'

'Ultimate objective Switzerland. Arthur Beck may or may not be cooperative. We can't assume he will be. After all, a murderer and a rapist isn't the type of person anyone wants to get mixed up with . . .'

'And you're assuming they'll believe that about you? Friends and allies for years?'

'That goes out of the window when you become an outlaw. I'm working on the premise we have no friends anywhere. We're on our own this time.'

'There's Newman and Marler. They'll never swallow the frame-up.'

'No friends anywhere,' Tweed repeated, twisting the wheel as he followed the lonely road through the limestone gulch. 'We will know something in less than two hours. That's when we'll hit the German border.'

Chief Inspector Kuhlmann of the Federal Police in Wiesbaden was chewing on his cigar as he read the *Most Secret* signal from London. His assistant, Kurt Meyer, watched his chief.

Kuhlmann was a small wide-shouldered man with dark hair and a mouth which was also wide. In his forties, he had thick dark eyebrows and an aggressive thrust to his jaw. His movements suggested great energy and he threw the signal on to his desk.

'You've read it, Kurt. What's your reaction?'

'This Tweed sounds a monster . . .'

'That's because you've never met him. He's totally incapable of committing any type of crime, let alone murder and rape – that signal is oddly worded, coming from Howard.'

He strolled over to the window, lit his cigar, stared down as plain-clothes policemen hurried across the courtyard one storey below. He grunted as Meyer took the two photos from the envelope delivered by secret courier. One of Tweed, the other of a dark-haired girl with an attractive face and intelligent eyes.

'What do we do?' Meyer asked. 'The Minister in Bonn suggested we circulate all frontier posts, after phoning them . . .'

'The Minister is a cretin. Another politician. Always pass the buck. Well,' Kuhlmann removed his cigar to gesture with it. 'He's passed the buck to me so let's get creative.'

'Creative?'

'The Minister said we ought to circulate Tweed's photo as well. It occurs to me we're just about to circulate the picture of that man, Stein, suspected of wholesale fraud – so maybe we get them mixed up, Kurt.'

'Mixed up?'

'That's it. The instructions are to have Stein followed without his realizing it. Not sufficient evidence for an arrest. So we send out Stein's photo as Tweed, and Tweed's as Stein.'

'Why are we protecting this Tweed?' Meyer enquired.

'Partly because I've known him for years. He's incapable of throttling a cat, let alone a woman. And the wording of the signal from Howard is intriguing. *Whereabouts required because of alleged complicity in the murder and*

57

rape of an unknown woman. Please report direct to me. Repeat direct to me. Howard. He's sending me a message.'

'I still don't understand . . .'

'But then you're not supposed to – nor is anyone else except me. Howard doesn't believe a word of this crap. Something very funny is going on back in London. Better get on with it. Don't forget to switch those photos. A whole pile of messages are going out. Be surprising if we didn't slip up on one of them.'

Paula was tense as they approached the German frontier post beyond Echternach in Luxembourg. Tweed, who had refused to let her take over the wheel, appeared outwardly to be perfectly relaxed as he stopped and presented the passport in the name of William Sanders.

'What is the purpose of your journey to the Federal Republic?' asked the Passport Control official in German.

Some instinct made Tweed reply in German. 'We're taking a late holiday now the package-deal tourists have gone home.'

The official stared hard at Tweed and slowly turned the pages of the passport. Tweed put an affectionate hand on Paula's neck and she managed a wan smile. The official seemed to take for ever examining the passport before he handed it back and waved them on.

'Oh, my God,' said Paula as they drove out of sight of the frontier post, 'my palms are wet inside my gloves.'

'So what a good job you were wearing them. They look for little giveaway signs like that. Now we're inside Germany and we can keep moving.'

'What route?' asked Paula. 'And it's beginning to snow.'

'A devious one. I'm doubling back to Trier, still inside Germany, then on to Mainz and Frankfurt.'

58

'That's a funny way to Switzerland. And surely we'll be passing close to Wiesbaden, the HQ of the Kriminal-polizei?'

'Which is the last area Kuhlmann will expect to find us in if the hounds have been loosed. The route from there? South on the autobahn. Later we'll move on to the E35 – the autobahn to Basle in Switzerland. The idea is to move faster than London will ever dream we could. Later, you can take over the wheel.'

'I'd like that. It will take my mind off things – with no limit on the autobahn. I'm really beginning to think we might make it.'

Arriving at the Mayfair, the most expensive hotel in Brussels, on the Avenue Louise, Morgan immediately called the World Security office on Avenue Franklin Roosevelt. Horowitz sat in an armchair in Morgan's room, listening.

'I'm at the Mayfair, George,' Morgan began. 'Have you any info on the subject I told you was top priority?'

'Yes, we have. He's in Brussels. Very close to where you're speaking from. Maybe it would be best if you came over here.'

'Expect me in ten minutes.'

Armand Horowitz had been staring into space, mentally checking the measures he must take to trace Tweed. Six feet tall, he was in his forties, had a long bony face tapering to a pointed jaw. Clean-shaven, he wore steel-rimmed glasses and moved with calculated deliber-ation. He had already killed fifteen men – top indus-trialists and other VIPs.

His secret opinion of Morgan was not high. The Welsh-man was too fond of high living. His manner was too flamboyant for Horowitz's taste. But he paid the huge fee Horowitz demanded for accepting an 'assignment'.

Inside the luxurious villa on Avenue Franklin Roosevelt George Evans, chief of European Operations for World Security, greeted the two men in his office overlooking a trim lawn with a light covering of snow. Also in his forties – Morgan disliked older men in positions of power – Evans was a large heavily built man, simian arms hanging by his sides, with a moon-like face and dark hair. He reminded Horowitz of an ape.

'Get to it,' snapped Morgan as he whipped off his overcoat, refused any refreshments and eased his bulk into an armchair.

'Tweed, I suspect, is both tricky and cunning . . .'

'I didn't come here for a pen portrait. Where is he? Close to the Mayfair you said on the phone.'

'Since then I've had another report from one of my top security agents.' Evans played with a pencil as he leaned over his desk, staring at Morgan, who stared back with a bleak expression. All these people needed a boot up the backside at regular intervals to keep them up to scratch. 'My agent', Evans continued smoothly, 'phoned while you were on your way over here. We doubt whether Tweed and his mistress, Paula Grey, will ever return to the Hilton where he was staying . . .'

'Chapter and verse,' Morgan snapped.

'I was just coming to that. My agent took a dummy package to the Hilton, addressed to Tweed, marked "Personal and Confidential". Reception at the Hilton said no one of that name was staying there. My agent said Tweed was attached to the European Commission and often travelled incognito – under a different name. He had a forged authority signed by one of the Commissioners who is away on holiday. He also showed the photo of Tweed you sent over with the courier who travelled here by night ferry. The girl receptionist was reluctant to give any information. My agent chatted her up and she let slip Tweed and the Grey woman left early this morning after booking their suite – and paying for it – for another week.'

'He's slipped the net,' Morgan muttered half to himself.

'You said Paula Grey was his mistress,' Horowitz intervened in his slow way of speaking. Evans stirred in his chair: there was something sinister about Horowitz which made him feel uneasy. 'What positive proof have you about their relationship?' Horowitz enquired.

'Well.' Evans spread his large hands. 'From her photograph she's attractive and younger, so one makes the natural assumption . . .'

'Which could be quite wrong . . .'

'Does it matter?' Evans, conscious of his position, resented contradiction from the hired help. Then he became aware of the eyes behind the steel-rimmed lenses gazing at him and felt uncomfortable.

'It might matter a lot to me in my job,' Horowitz informed him. 'Knowing the true relationship between two people who are in flight can be most helpful.'

'Well, we haven't actually photographic evidence of copulation,' Evans responded brusquely.

Morgan watched the exchange with secret satisfaction. No harm in taking Evans down a peg. Horowitz nodded thoughtfully.

'Thank you for the data, Mr Evans,' he said politely.

'How did you get on to this Hilton business?' demanded Morgan.

'I've had my whole staff touring the best hotels in town. The extract from the file on Tweed you sent with the courier made the point he often stays at top places because he thinks he's less likely to be noticed.'

'And that's all you have?'

'No. I didn't stop there. Another group of my agents have toured the car hire firms, using the same tactics. Tweed has hired a BMW under the name William

61

Sanders. The doorman at the Hilton saw them driving east early. Here is the registration number.'

He passed a slip of folded paper to Morgan who handed it to Horowitz without looking at it. Standing up, he slipped on his overcoat, his expression still bleak.

'You lost him,' he told Evans. 'What are you going to do next?'

'Tweed was seen driving *east* out of the city. A logical move if I was in his shoes – Belgium is too close to Britain. He has to be heading for Holland, Germany or France . . .'

'Then alert our organizations in those countries. Pick up his trail . . .'

'If I may make a suggestion,' Horowitz, also standing, addressed Evans. 'You said you'd read an extract from Tweed's file, detailing some of his techniques . . .'

'Only an extract. Someone in London must be blocking complete access . . .'

'I was about to say,' Horowitz continued, 'that Tweed must have assumed something like this would happen.' He's a pro. So it's likely he'll change his normal habits. He could still be here, staying at some small hotel. Why not switch your agents to checking those places?'

'Do it,' said Morgan. 'I'll be back in a minute for a private word.' He marched to the door, followed by Horowitz who put his soft trilby back on his head, pulling the brim down. Outside in the corridor Morgan stood near the mahogany door he'd closed.

'What do you think? Holland, Germany, France?'

'Oh, definitely Germany,' Horowitz said promptly. 'Holland is a cul-de-sac, leading him nowhere. And with all the terrorist problems the French face their borders are watched closely. I would make for the Federal Republic.'

'Wait here.' Morgan went back into Evans' office, closed the door, marched back to the desk behind which

Evans was sitting, phone in his hand and about to use it. 'Put that thing down.' Morgan leaned across the desk, his face close to Evans's.

'That was a real cock-up, wasn't it? You had him in the palm of your hand and let him escape. Now, just for once try and earn that over-inflated salary we pay you. Use the satellite phone for top security. Call Frankfurt, tell them I'm coming. And while I'm on my way all our operatives in Germany hit the streets – with copies of Tweed's photo, and Grey's. All the hotels. But they're to concentrate also on car hire firms. Tweed may decide to switch that BMW for something else. I want a fix on that man. And fast.'

'Understood. I'll then fly to Frankfurt myself to oversee the operation. I may see you on the same plane.'

'I hope not.' Morgan straightened up. For the first time he smiled as he took a cigar from his case, laid it on the desk. 'Havana. May give you inspiration. I'm relying on you . . .'

He left the office. Horowitz stood in the corridor, hands in his trench-coat pocket, staring up at a framed portrait of the founder, Lance Buckmaster.

'No inspiration there for you,' Morgan commented as they walked to the elevator. 'We'll catch the first flight to Frankfurt after we've picked up our bags from the Mayfair. That way we should be ahead of Tweed.'

'Don't bank on it. I'm beginning to build up a vague picture of this man. A formidable opponent, I suspect. I shall want a met forecast for the weather over the whole of Western Europe. And while you go straight back to the hotel I want to buy some road maps.'

As Morgan walked back to the Mayfair alone he felt satisfied. He'd shaken up Evans, first bawling him out then ending up with a show of confidence in him with the Havana. The only way you kept the top brass in line, reminded them who was the boss.

6

Chief Inspector Kuhlmann put down the phone and looked at Kurt Meyer as though he'd never seen him before. It was a technique he employed when grilling a suspect he knew well. Meyer felt confused as he sat behind his desk and started examining a file.

'We've pinpointed him,' Kuhlmann said eventually. 'Stein crossed the border near Echternach in Luxembourg a few hours ago. He's on our patch.'

'Stein?'

'Tweed, you dumb bastard. Travelling in a BMW with a girl. Sounds like Paula Grey. The frontier post spotted him from the photos we rushed to the western frontier. I have the registration number too.'

'Shouldn't we record it?' Meyer, young and lean-faced, had his pen poised over a pad.

'It's in my head.' Kuhlmann walked over to a large-scale wall-map of the Federal Republic. 'I wonder where he's making for? Could be anywhere except near Wiesbaden, near me.'

'Shouldn't we inform the Minister?'

'Not yet, we haven't caught Tweed yet. That phone call never happened. Your job hangs by a thread,' he informed his subordinate cheerfully.

Hands thrust inside his jacket pockets, Kuhlmann went over to the window and stared down into the courtyard again. He had omitted to tell Meyer Tweed's BMW was being followed by an unmarked police car, a vehicle which would be replaced by another later to allay suspicion. Kuhlmann was notorious for playing a lone hand. The web was being spun, he thought. The big question was who was the spider?

Newman boarded the aircraft for Brussels at London Airport, fastened his seat belt. Into the empty seat beside him a passenger joined him. Newman turned his head slowly. His fellow passenger was Marler.

'Didn't know I was on your tail, old chum, did you?'

Newman clasped his hands. He said nothing until the machine was ready for take-off, moving forward to the main runway. When he responded it was in a monotone, as though reciting a catechism.

'You phoned Julia, who practically runs the house where I've an apartment in South Ken. Presumably from the airport. She told you I'd left with a bag. You waited at the entrance to Terminal One, saw me arrive in a taxi. You then followed me to the ticket reservation counter, chatted up the girl afterwards, found I'd booked a Business-Class seat to Brussels, did the same yourself and waited outside the final departure lounge until you saw me boarding.'

'Ten out of ten. And I kidded myself up you hadn't seen me.'

The plane lifted off the ground, climbed steeply through a dense cloud-bank, emerged into brilliant sunlight. Below was a sea of unbroken cloud like endless mountain ranges.

'Now you can tell me what you're up to,' Newman demanded.

'We're both on the same side. Trying to find Tweed and Paula, to protect them.'

'Well, that's reassuring, isn't it?' Newman suggested ironically.

'Cryptic remark.'

'Not really. Here comes the $64,000 question. Do you think he did it?' Newman lowered his voice. 'Strangled and then raped that girl?'

'You have to be joking.'

'I have a funny sense of humour. Maybe not on your waveband. You haven't answered the question. And who sent you?'

'I thought you knew.' Marler's tone was flippant. 'When Tweed is out of action, Howard is in control.'

Newman remained silent for the rest of the flight. He was thinking furiously. He had never liked Marler, although he recognized his great ability. Now he didn't trust him. Why? Some sixth sense he'd learned not to ignore.

He had two options, he thought, as the plane began the descent to Brussels. One, he could ditch Marler. It wouldn't be too easy, but he knew he could manage it. Two, he could go along with Marler, pretend to accept him at face value, and this way he could keep an eye on him. He decided on the second option as the wheels touched down.

Remembering where Tweed had stayed once during a desperate operation in the past. Newman told the cab driver to take them to the Brussels Hilton. He went up to his room while Marler went to his, dumped his bag on the bed, ran back to the elevator and walked out of the hotel.

It took him a few minutes to find a public phone booth. He took out his small notebook, found the number for Kriminalpolizei in Wiesbaden, dialled Kuhlmann's personal number.

To his relief the Chief Inspector answered the phone himself. His voice sounded as gravelly as ever, charged with energy. He told Newman to hold on and the Englishman heard him call out in German.

'Kurt, take that file down to the Registry and lock it away yourself. The combination hasn't been changed . . .' A pause. 'OK, Newman, what can I do for you?'

'Have you received a message from London to apprehend Tweed?'

'Where are you speaking from . . .'

'A public call box, of course . . .'

'OK. Keep your hair on. I had to check. The answer to your question is yes. Partially. Newman, what was the weather like when me met in Lübeck?'

'A bloody heatwave. Why . . . Oh, I see. Yes, it is me. You said partially. What does that mean?'

'Sounded like you,' Kuhlmann said calmly. 'I had to be sure. You think he did it?'

'For God's sake!' Newman was unusually vehement. 'Have you lost your marbles. He's innocent. It has to be some kind of conspiracy. Who's behind it I don't know. But Tweed badly needs help, back-up. I'm in Brussels. He came here but I'm sure he didn't linger. Not with the wolves after him. And he has Paula with him. I just don't know where to start looking.'

'Frankfurt might be a good place to start. Don't come here. Call me and I'll meet you somewhere. I've decided where. At the Frankfurt Hof. We'll fix a time over the phone. Speak to me only.' The tone of voice changed. 'I'll see to it – and thanks for calling, Lothar. Bye . . .'

Newman guessed Kurt had returned to the office. Kurt Who? And Kuhlmann was obviously trusting no one except himself. It was getting worse. The stench of treachery in the air.

As he re-entered the vast lobby of the Hilton Newman stopped, then moved to the right into the sitting area. Marler was standing at the reception counter, talking to one of the girls. He had an envelope in his hand. Newman watched him stuffing banknotes into the envelope, sealing it, writing on the front. Then he disappeared and the girl also vanished. Newman guessed they had gone to the security vault behind the counter. He was waiting when Marler reappeared.

'Unpacked your bag?' Marler enquired and lit a king-sized cigarette.

'Not yet. I had some coffee. I saw you at the counter.'

'Let's stroll a bit down the Boulevard de Waterloo,' Marler suggested. He waited until they were outside before speaking again.

'While you were quenching your thirst I was busy making a few enquiries. By devious means, of course. Tweed has been here. He reserved an executive suite for another week – but Tweed has gone. And won't be coming back is my guess.'

'How did you find that out? Hotels don't give information about guests easily.'

'Oh, I simply told the girl I'd agreed to leave a large sum of money I owed to a friend. Showed her Tweed's photo. Asked for a safety deposit box after she'd seen me cramming Belgian banknotes in an envelope. Two large denomination bills on top, the rest a small sum. Gave her the key, got a receipt, told her my friend was travelling incognito. She wrote *William Sanders* on the envelope she'd put the key inside. I *can* read upside down. Now all we have to decide is where to look next for him.'

'Frankfurt,' Newman said, and left it at that.

George Evans just managed to catch the same flight as Morgan and Horowitz, but the last seat available was Economy Class. When the plane landed at Frankfurt he left the airport first, bypassing the wait at the carousel which held up his colleagues.

World Security HQ was in Kaiserstrasse, a new building with armoured plate glass windows and a system of scanners covering the entrance and all corridors. Arriving an hour later, Morgan stepped out of the cab and looked around while Horowitz paid.

Morgan didn't like Frankfurt. He liked Hamburg and Münich, but he called Frankfurt the Machine City. Too much traffic clogging the streets, too many high-rise buildings, too little greenery. A concrete fortress of a place.

His first act on entering was to test the security. He walked straight towards the bank of elevators. Two uniformed guards intercepted him, one reached for his suitcase.

'I'm Morgan. I run this show,' he snapped and waved his pass in their faces. 'And I'm short of time . . .'

'I'm sorry, sir,' one of the guards replied in English, 'but we have to check your case with the X-ray machine.'

Horowitz, more stoical, was already at the counter while his case passed through the type of machine used at airports. Morgan waited while his own case was processed, biting his lips.

'George Evans is expecting me. He may not have got here yet.'

'He's in his office now. Just stand in front of this screen while I call him . . .'

'What the hell for?'

'So he can see you on the screen in his office. All identities of callers have to be confirmed . . .'

The guard was talking to Evans as Morgan glared at the screen, then took out a cigar and clamped his teeth on it.

'If you're seeing me, get these people off my back, George – we're supposed to be running an operation . . .'

'You can go up now, Mr Morgan,' said the guard, replacing the phone. 'Room 401, fourth floor.'

'I run this outfit. I know where the hired help lives . . .'

Inside the elevator Horowitz made his comment. 'They were doing their job. And the security is reasonably good.'

'You have to keep people on their toes.' Morgan chuckled, a wheezing sound. 'Management must manage.'

Evans got his blow in first as he stood at the door, ushered them into a large office overlooking the Kaiserstrasse. Venetian blinds were half-closed over the windows to avoid any risk of observation from the buildings opposite.

'We've traced Tweed. I'm expecting another call from our informant. The connection was broken as you came up . . .' He broke off as his phone rang. 'Hello. That you, Kurt again? Make it snappy – I have important visitors.'

He listened, said yes, he'd grasped it. 'Keep me up-to-date on their progress. What we need to know is where they're heading for – so we can be ready for them. The money will be waiting in the usual safety deposit. Bye, Kurt.'

He offered drinks and Morgan said he'd have a double Scotch. Horowitz shook his head, nursed his small case on his lap and glanced at Morgan. On the plane his employer had downed several drinks: Morgan was a man who drank heavily. Maybe the pressure of the job was getting to him. No excuse.

'Tweed', Evans began as he handed a cut-glass tumbler to Morgan, 'has arrived in Germany. With Paula Grey, so far as we know. With a woman, anyway. He actually came into Frankfurt in his hired BMW, then changed it for a Mercedes. Here is the registration.'

Another folded slip changed hands, was again passed on to Horowitz. Evans looked pleased with himself as he settled behind his large antique desk. In his armchair Morgan drank half the Scotch, smacked his lips, scowled.

'A Mercedes. That doesn't help. This country is lousy with them. Look at the taxis – all Mercedes.'

'Which is maybe why Tweed chose that make,' Horowitz suggested in his quiet voice. 'Have you a toilet here?' he asked his host.

Evans gestured towards a door and Morgan waited until he was alone with Evans before he asked the question.

'How are we getting this info so fast? Who is Kurt?'

'I don't like to advertise my contacts.' Evans glanced at the closed toilet door, leaned forward, lowered his voice. 'Kurt Meyer. Chief Inspector Kuhlmann's assistant – an inside track right into the centre of the Kriminalpolizei at Wiesbaden. I can tell you that isn't easy to arrange.'

'But it's your job to do things like that. You've got something on this Kurt Meyer?'

'Pornographic pictures taken in a high-class bordello. And he's married. We pay him to put icing on the cake, and tie him to us. I have receipts signed by Meyer in the safe – he didn't want to provide them but a little arm-twisting works wonders.

'And that's all we know?' Morgan demanded. 'That Tweed and his girl friend are driving somewhere in a Mercedes?'

'No, that isn't all we know.' Evans made no attempt to conceal his satisfaction. 'Unmarked police cars are following him. They're using the leapfrog technique, one vehicle taking over from another at regular intervals. They radio in reports of their locations to Wiesbaden. When he can, Kurt then passes them on to me – from an outside phone, of course. *We* now have operatives following Tweed.'

Morgan twirled his cigar between his thick stubby fingers as he thought about it. Evans's news was better than he'd ever hoped for.

'Where was the latest sighting?' he asked.

'On the autobahn, heading south towards Karlsruhe. He could turn off east or west, of course . . .'

71

'Not west. He won't risk France. But he might head east.' Morgan put the cigar in his mouth, lit it as Evans pushed a heavy Rosenthal bowl towards him. 'He could just be heading for Russia via the Czech border . . .'

'From the little I've grasped about him I'd say that was unlikely, to say the least.'

'But it would be a good rumour to spread, step up the pressure all round. Feed it into the grapevine, use your press contacts.' He blew smoke into the air. 'But on no account let anyone know we're interested.'

'You know we have a department devoted to doing just that. Feeding rumours on behalf of a client about to make a take-over bid – rumours about the bid victim . . .'

'But no names,' Morgan warned. 'Just rumours about a highly placed British official defecting to the East.' He looked up as Horowitz reappeared. 'We have a tail already locked on to Tweed. Driving south on the autobahn. You'll have to be careful. The German police are tracking him – unmarked cars.'

Horowitz, tall and thin in the trench coat he still wore, and carrying the case he never let out of his sight, stared at both men. There was something remote, detached in his ice-blue eyes. Again Evans felt disturbed: it was almost like a hangman measuring his latest customer for the drop.

'I find that curious,' Horowitz remarked. 'I understood from you, Morgan, some kind of alert had been sent out. If so, why hasn't Tweed been arrested?'

'No idea.' Morgan disliked people who brought up insoluble problems. 'What do you propose to do?'

'I'd like an executive jet placed at my disposal at Frankfurt Airport. The company jet. To fly me to the small airport outside Freiburg near the Black Forest.'

'Consider it done,' Morgan replied before Evans could speak.

'It may be an hour or two before I arrive to board the

jet,' Horowitz continued. 'I have to pick up a helper. I'm on my way now.'

Evans watched him leave, noted how silently he closed the door behind him. He let out his breath. 'I'm not sorry to see him go – it's like having death in the room.'

'Maybe that's his trade.'

Armand Horowitz walked a hundred yards along Kaiser-strasse, disassociating himself from World Security before he hailed a cab. Looking back, he could see the complex of radio masts and satellite dishes on the roof of the building he'd left. WS operated a highly sophisticated communications system. But Horowitz, who had been born in Hungary, was no slouch himself at communications.

He had spent a while in the toilet, most of the time with his ear to the stethoscope-like instrument he'd pressed against the closed door. He'd heard quite clearly Evans's reference to his inside track with the Kriminalpolizei at Wiesbaden, to Kurt Meyer's treachery. Secret knowledge, Horowitz always felt, was power.

As the cab drove out of Frankfurt to the address on the way to the airport, Horowitz, sitting erect, case in his lap, reflected he was the only real professional in this game. He'd developed a contempt for men like Morgan and Evans. They carefully distanced themselves from the dirty work, but didn't hesitate to employ his services. Evans had been distinctly uncomfortable about Horowitz's presence in his office.

The cab stopped at the street intersection he'd been given, his passenger paid him, took time drawing on his gloves until the cab was gone. Horowitz then walked the last hundred yards to the decrepit villa standing back from the airport highway, pushed open the left-hand iron grille gate. He walked up the moss-infested path, mounted the steps and pressed the bell-push two times, paused, then gave one long press. He'd seen no reason to reveal to Morgan and Evans that his helper was a woman.

7

Newman arrived at Frankfurt an hour later than Morgan. With Marler he took a cab to the Hessischer Hof, one of the two best hotels in the city. They registered and avoided using a porter. As the elevator ascended Newman made his flat statement.

'Wait in your room – or in the hotel. I have to go and check with someone.'

'I don't actually recall anyone putting you in charge . . .'

'Then get off my back and I'll work on my own.'

'No need to get shirty,' Marler responded mildly as they walked along a quiet, carpeted corridor. 'If that's the way you want to play it, fair enough. I'll mooch about the hotel . . .'

Newman dumped his bag, took out two spare suits, hung them on a hanger, left the case lid open and left the Hessischer Hof. He walked across the small park on the far side of the street towards the vast exhibition centre, glancing back frequently: he'd chosen this route because it was impossible for Marler to follow him without being seen.

From a public phone booth he called Otto Kuhlmann who answered immediately.

'I'm in Frankfurt. The heatwave man in Lübeck . . .'

'Meeting point changed. Can you be near the ticket

office at the *Hauptbahnhof* one hour from now?'

'I'll be waiting for you there . . .'

It was only a short walk to the main rail station. Newman went straight there. He spent half an hour in the restaurant, drinking coffee. When he emerged on to the vast concourse he saw Kuhlmann standing at the entrance to one of the platforms opposite the ticket office. The German saw him at once, walked over, shook hands, greeted him in his own language.

'Let's just stroll up and down, Bob. That way we can talk without being overheard.'

'You don't believe this incredible accusation against Tweed?' Newman asked him point-blank.

'No. Neither does Howard. But what about you? Any doubts?' Kuhlmann challenged.

'None whatsoever. Why the devil do you think I came haring over here? To try and find Tweed, give him some back-up, find out what the hell is going on.'

The tannoy was calling out a message about an express leaving for Basle in Switzerland. Passengers were hurrying to barriers. A locomotive was gliding in, hauling a trainload of coaches. Kuhlmann, inches shorter than Newman, wearing his normal dark suit, which emphasized the great width of his shoulders, took his time replying.

'There's the stench of treachery and conspiracy high up in London,' he commented eventually. 'Tweed – with Paula Grey, I assume – at this moment is driving south along the autobahn from Frankfurt. He crossed the Luxembourg border in a hired BMW with Belgian number plates. Since then – in Frankfurt – he changed cars. Now he's in a black Mercedes. My men picked him up as he came over the Luxembourg border. They're following him in unmarked cars. I thought only I knew this. I haven't told my Minister.'

'You said Howard doesn't think him guilty. That surprises me. How do you know?'

'Because the signal he sent spoke of *alleged complicity* in murder and rape, and only asked for his whereabouts. It also was emphatic that I reported back to him alone. I haven't even done that yet.'

'Why not?'

'Because my men tracking Tweed have reported a complication. Someone else is playing the same game – following him with a series of cars. I found out who they are just before I left to see you. Gave me cause to think, pause.'

'Who is it then?'

'Prepare yourself for a shock. The registration numbers of two of the cars were radioed back to me. I called Vehicle Registration. The cars belong to World Security & Communications GmbH. Lance Buckmaster's international colossus before he became your Minister for External Security. The damned fools omitted to *hire* cars.'

Newman was stunned. They walked in silence while he absorbed this new twist. He stopped to let a woman with a pram rush past him. Kuhlmann lit a cigar. They began walking again.

'You have to be quite sure about this?' Newman queried.

'I thought you knew me well enough by now to know I'm careful – very careful – about what I say,' Kuhlmann growled. 'Maybe you can also work out why I'm in no hurry to communicate with anyone in London. Who can we trust?'

'Maybe someone high up in WS is playing his own game. Buckmaster no longer has any control over his company.'

'Not like you to be naïve. We've had trouble with that outfit before now. They were suspected of trying to smuggle restricted high-tech equipment into East Germany. Aboard one of their own security trucks. I grilled a man called George Evans, the managing director of their operations here on the Continent. A crook if I ever saw one. I just hadn't enough evidence to bring the case to court.'

'What are you saying?' Newman asked, wanting the German to confirm his own growing suspicion.

'I'm saying that officially the WS organization is now run by Buckmaster's wife, Leonora. She has his block of shares. I did a little research at the time of the East German business. But do you think even a man like Evans, managing director for Europe, would risk his position by going into business on his own? I cross-examined him. He's not the type. He'd only carry out orders – coming from Lance Buckmaster.'

'And you think he's still doing that?'

'Yes!' Kuhlmann was emphatic. 'What it's all about is what I can't fathom. But now you can see why I'm in no hurry to contact London. First, Tweed is a man I like, admire. Someone is trying to put the fix on him – whoever they are they're not getting help from me. Second, I have a score to settle with World Security. They were guilty as hell over the East German business and made me look a fool. I even got a reprimand from my creep of a Minister. So now I watch and wait.'

'You're really relying on me.' Newman faced Kuhlmann, confronted him.

'Yes, I am. You have freedom of movement. I haven't.'

'I don't even know where Tweed is,' Newman pressed.

'So, you call me at regular intervals. Let's give you a code name. Felix. Speak only to me. I've worked out Tweed can't drive for ever – even if Paula Grey gives a hand with the wheel. Somewhere he's got to stop. I'll know when he does – and where. I'll have a police chopper waiting at Frankfurt Airport to fly you to the nearest airfield.' Kuhlmann took an envelope from his breast pocket, gave it to Newman. 'The pilot's name is Egon Wrede. That letter identifies you, authorizes you to be flown anywhere you tell Wrede. Best I can do . . .'

'Wait! There's something odd you haven't told me. Why did you think up this secret system of approaching only you? Code name Felix, etc. Sounds as though you don't trust anyone except yourself.'

'I don't. There's a lot of power behind this thing. Best I can do,' he repeated and walked away.

Tweed checked the small notebook he rested on his knee. Paula was behind the wheel of the Mercedes moving at between 140 and 160 k.p.h. – about ninety miles an hour. Ahead the autobahn E 35 stretched away into the distance. They were well south of Karlsruhe and approaching Offenbach with Freiburg beyond.

Paula had at last persuaded Tweed to hand over the driving to her for awhile. No great burden – she loved speed. Out of the corner of her eye she saw Tweed glance again in the wing mirror.

'They're still with us?' she asked.

'Indeed they are,' he said calmly as though working on a crossword puzzle. 'Seven cars spread out behind us and that silver Merc a quarter of a mile ahead. That makes eight cars – I've double-checked the registration numbers,' he remarked, glancing down at his notebook.

'It's a bloody convoy.'

'It's exactly that. Which is what I don't understand. Eight cars tracking us all this distance. At first I thought they were police cars.'

'Why shouldn't they be? They're probably looking for us now.'

'Because it's too many – even for using the leapfrog system. If Kuhlmann was waiting to pounce – waiting to

78

see where we're making for – he'd use four cars at the most. Eight suggests two different groups.'

'Who could they be?'

'Your guess is as good as mine. It's OK for me to talk?'

'I want you to . . .'

She loved the speed but was only too aware of the danger of slipping into a hypnotic daze. The four-lane highway curved and straightened and curved. The scenery which might have relieved the monotony, kept her alert, was non-existent. It was like driving along an endless concrete canal. But she kept up her high speed. Tweed was desperately anxious to get to Freiburg and it was late afternoon already.

'What do we do when we reach Freiburg?' she enquired.

'*Before* we get to Freiburg,' he corrected her. 'I take over the wheel and we lose them, the whole shooting match.'

'Don't see how . . .'

'You will. Just keep moving.'

Horowitz gazed out of the window of the descending Sikorsky. Freiburg airfield came up to meet him. Alongside sat a girl in her early thirties with titian hair, good bone-structure and an excellent figure concealed beneath the windcheater she wore. Tight denims clung to her legs and she wore knee-length leather boots.

Horowitz had picked up Eva Hendrix from the villa on the way to Frankfurt Airport. It wasn't her real name and – like Horowitz – she'd been born in Hungary. Normally he mistrusted the use of women but he foresaw the opportunity of infiltrating her into Tweed's company in the future.

'Where are we going first?' she asked as the machine touched down with a bump.

'World Security HQ in Freiburg.'

'Funny place to have an office – I thought they had a main HQ in Basle, thirty minutes down the autobahn from Freiburg.'

'They have. Freiburg is more discreet. On the edge of the Black Forest.'

'Good place to bury the bodies,' she joked with black humour.

Horowitz froze for a few seconds. She had come nearer to the truth than she ever dreamed. Too busy lighting a cigarette, she didn't notice his expression. She glanced out of the window into the dark as the pilot entered the cabin.

'Oh my God, it's started to snow.'

'So for once the met forecast people got it right. Which is helpful.'

He didn't explain why it was going to be helpful and the pilot told him the car he'd specified was waiting for them. Horowitz nodded as he followed Hendrix out of the cabin, carrying the case he'd picked up from the Frankfurt villa in one hand, his executive case in the other.

Horowitz, who preferred travelling light, had suitcases with clothes packed deposited at various locations all over Europe. The car was a Ford, as he'd requested. Nothing flashy. He had perfected the technique of not being noticed to a fine art. Eva Hendrix started to chatter in her persuasive voice while the uniformed chauffeur drove them into the ancient town of Freiburg. The snowflakes were larger now, the windscreen wipers flicked back and forth.

'Is it a seduction job again?' she whispered.

'Not exactly. More an infiltration – if the chance arises.'

He feeds out information as though each word costs him money, she thought. Well, he was paying so let him get on with it in his peculiar way. She glanced at his strong profile, staring ahead at the snowbound road. He wasn't queer, she felt sure, so did he have a woman every now and again she wondered? If he did it would be a clinical performance, precise and calculated, like everything he did. Not for me, she decided.

'I'm not interested in you sexually,' he remarked, spacing out the words in his deliberate way. 'Just in the work you can do for me.'

Christ! she thought. A man who can read a woman's mind. It was supposed to work the other way round. When they arrived at the HQ of World Security in Freiburg the closed gates were opened for them immediately. At least someone with the car's description and registration number had been told they were coming.

Inside the lobby Horowitz handed the uniformed guard the letter of introduction Gareth Morgan had supplied.

'We've no photograph of you, Mr Schmidt,' the guard complained.

'Read the note at the bottom. You're not very good at checking documents, are you? Mr Morgan wouldn't like that.'

So far as he knew, no photograph had ever been taken of Horowitz. He'd been very careful about that. The photos in his collection of passports were blurred images of the real man – and without the steel-rimmed glasses he habitually wore.

'Sorry, sir,' the guard apologized. 'The chief's office is available for you. I'll take you up there – unless you'd like some refreshment first?'

'Nothing for me . . .'

'I'm starving,' Hendrix complained. 'I'd like a good steak, cooked rare, and a drink. A double vodka-martini.'

'See to her wants. Feed her. She can stay down here in that sitting area. Now, take me to the office,' Horowitz ordered the guard.

The office was a large room on the first floor equipped

81

with a desk on which perched three phones in different colours. Horowitz told the guard he wanted to call the Frankfurt office. Privately.

'I'll leave you alone, then. The blue phone is the one to use.'

Horowitz waited until the guard had gone, then placed his bags on a couch and studied the room. High up in one corner was a camera aimed at the desk. They do trust each other, Horowitz thought. Dragging a chair over, he stood on it, took off his scarf and wrapped it round the observation lens.

Before using the phone he checked the room minutely. He found the tape recorder attached to a small alcove carved out from underneath the desk. His keen hearing had caught the whirring of the tape. They'd probably switched it on by remote control while he was on his way up. This was one call they wouldn't be recording.

Crouching down, he examined the machine. He used the manual switch to turn it off. Then he extracted the cassette, hauling out the length of tape which had been recording and stuffed both items in his jacket pocket. He was seated at the desk, about to dial Frankfurt, when the door was thrown open and a uniformed guard entered the room. He pointed at the camera.

'That has to be left alone . . .'

Horowitz replaced the phone, stood up slowly without a word, walked slowly up to the guard. His right hand took hold of the guard's tie and collar and he threw him backwards through the doorway. The guard hit the far wall and slid to the floor.

'I have already said I wish to make a call privately. Stay out of this room. If there is another intruder I will break both his arms.'

The guard, still slumped on the floor, gazed at the slate-grey eyes behind the glasses. He had never felt so frightened. Horowitz had spoken quietly, the words spaced out. He closed the door and went back to the desk, sat down, dialled the number from memory. He was still wearing kid gloves.

'I wish to speak immediately to Gareth Morgan. No need for my name. He is expecting the call.'

'Morgan here,' a familiar voice rasped within thirty seconds. 'Is that . . .'

'No names are necessary. I'm speaking from your Freiburg office. Can you tell me where the subject is now?'

'Yes. A car radioed in only a few minutes ago. Coming straight towards you. On autobahn E 35. About midway between Offenbach and Freiburg . . .'

'Then I'd better go. You arranged for that vehicle I requested when I called from Frankfurt Airport? With a *reliable* driver?'

'I dealt with it personally. Driver's name is Oscar. He should be waiting for you in the transport yard at the back.'

'And the subject is still in the same vehicle?'

'He is . . .'

'Goodbye, then.'

Horowitz picked up his cases, retrieved his scarf from the camera, keeping clear of the lens, took the elevator downstairs. Eva Hendrix, an empty glass on the plate glass table, was sitting waiting for her food. Horowitz dumped his suitcase beside her.

'Look after that. I'll be back in a few minutes.'

He went out of the front entrance, made his way round to the back of the building as snow fell on him. He was hardly aware of the chill in the night air, his mind totally concentrated on his job. He found the enormous twelve-wheeler refrigerated truck parked inside a large shed with the doors open. A man sat in the cab attached to the trailer vehicle, smoking a cigarette, reading a newspaper. He folded the paper, opened the door, jumped out and threw his cigarette out into the snow as soon as he saw Horowitz.

'I'm Schmidt,' Horowitz said, examining the driver. 'Who are you?'

'Oscar. I need identification for this job.'

Horowitz handed him the authorization signed by Evans. Oscar read it carefully by the sidelights of his huge vehicle. The engine was purring like a tiger. Oscar reminded Horowitz of the Michelin tyre man – short and tubby, his belly bulging behind his belt, round-headed. But there was nothing amusing about Oscar. His rubbery face, unsmiling, was the prototype of the 'heavy' seen in 'B' films.' He handed the sheet back and Horowitz showed him the piece of paper with the registration number of Tweed's Mercedes. Oscar glanced at the paper and handed that back.

'You can remember the number?' Horowitz asked.

'It's my job to remember things like that. What make of car? What colour? Where?'

'A Mercedes. Colour black. Now driving down the E 35 from Offenburg. One man, one girl inside. What is that contraption mounted over the cab?'

'Show you, then I'm off.'

Oscar climbed nimbly back inside the cab, slammed the door shut and pressed a switch. On top of the cab was a very big circular disc with a grille over it like miniature venetian blinds. When Oscar pressed the switch half way a lamp like a huge searchlight came on, so strong Horowitz had to dip his head. The driver pressed the switch fully down and the beam became of blinding intensity. Peering up, Horowitz saw the narrow 'blinds' had swivelled to become mere rims. He guessed its purpose. It must have a range of three hundred yards.

He stood aside and the great vehicle moved ponderously out of the garage. Oscar sounded his deafening horn three times and the gates to the yard swung open.

Horowitz watched it turn on to the road and vanish. It should, he reflected, be more than large enough to finish the job.

Returning to the front entrance, he found Hendrix still waiting for her food, smoking yet another cigarette. He bent over to speak so only she could hear him.

'We're leaving now. On foot. So put your coat on and then we can get out of here . . .'

'I'm waiting for those sluggards to bring my steak.'

'No, you're not. I booked two rooms at the Hotel Colombi from Frankfurt Airport. You can have an eight-course dinner there, if you can cope with it. And I may not need your services now, so you could be on a train back to Frankfurt tomorrow.'

'The snow is getting worse. I'll get soaked . . .'

'Put this scarf round your head. Then get moving, woman. No more yacking. You know I don't like attention drawn to myself.'

As they plodded through the snow, which was falling even more heavily, Horowitz had a mental picture of Tweed in his Mercedes driving towards Freiburg, while Oscar in his refrigerated truck drove towards Tweed.

8

Night. Tweed had taken over the wheel from Paula. Visibility was bad. The falling snow was approaching blizzard conditions. He had the heaters full on. He was driving at 100 k.p.h. His undimmed headlights showed the curve of the autobahn ahead far enough to keep up that speed.

'It's getting worse,' said Paula. 'I calculate we're within twenty miles of the turn-off to Freiburg. Do we go on?'

'Yes. The vehicles are still behind us. We have to shake all of them off.'

The headlights behind him were blurred, the gap between pursued and pursuers had widened, but they were there. And the silver Mercedes was still somewhere ahead of them. He shifted his position: he was beginning to feel stiff and achy.

The view beyond the windscreen was weird. A belt of heavy snow along the highway south, the neon lights cast a weird light over the snow, reflecting back a ghostly glow. There were few headlights coming in the opposite direction beyond the barrier, and few travelling in his direction. He yawned.

'Isn't it getting too hot?' Paula suggested, looking up from her map. 'I'm happy to turn down the heating.'

He reached a hand out and switched off both heaters. There was a danger he'd lose his concentration if too much warmth built up. The belt of snow rolled on and on and on. Tweed straightened up, pushed his back hard against the seat, anything to keep alert.

'Will the snow make your manoeuvre to lose them more difficult?' Paula asked.

'Could make it easier. We can't be seen so easily. Please keep an eye on the signs. I need to know we're approaching the Freiburg turn-off well in advance.'

'Will do. We're coming up to one soon, but it's not the one for Freiburg.'

Oscar sat inside his parked truck at the top of the slip road leading down on to the E 35 for traffic heading along the autobahn to Freiburg and Basle. His engine was running and his windscreen wipers whipped back and forth to keep the glass clear of snow.

He held a high-powered pair of night-glasses pressed close to his eyes. From his vantage point he could see vehicles approaching from the north a good way off. The snow was falling more lightly, thank God, which increased his range of vision.

The manoeuvre he had planned was highly dangerous and quite illegal. He was banking on the size of the truck to make it easy, not all that dangerous and successful. He wore gloves, as he had since he'd first entered the vehicle – stolen from a food depot a hundred miles to the north. And he had added a subtle touch for afterwards when the police investigated the catastrophe. On the seat beside him was a half-empty bottle of bourbon – also handled with gloves.

An ex-amateur racing driver, Oscar was confident that after the 'accident' he could execute the necessary U-turn to head south again. If some other car became embroiled, bad luck. Only an army tank crashing into his truck could put it out of action. And that was what he had once driven when he had done his military service – driven a Leopard tank.

When the police eventually found the abandoned truck they'd assume the driver who'd stolen it had been drunk. The bottle of bourbon would convince them of that. Oscar felt sure he'd foreseen every contingency. But that was what Schmidt was paying him nine thousand marks for. Attention to detail.

He stiffened. A Mercedes was approaching. The snow had almost stopped falling and he had a clear view. A lone woman driving. In any case, it was the wrong registration number. The car seemed to float towards him. And she must be doing 140 k.p.h. Stupid cow – in these conditions. No wonder there were pile-ups on the autobahn. Probably racing on to meet her lover, he thought. The car seemed to take ages to reach the point where the slip road entered the autobahn. Then she was gone.

The incident reassured Oscar. He'd have plenty of time

to drive down when the target vehicle came into sight. He lit a cigarette, then frowned. The weather was changing. The snow had stopped coming down. The temperature had dropped suddenly. In the distance over the autobahn it was becoming hazy. Creeping in from both sides was a freezing fog. He lifted the pair of binoculars to his eyes again. At the moment he'd still have time to drive down on to the autobahn – providing the freezing fog came no closer.

'We're approaching another turn-off,' Paula warned. 'Still not the one to Freiburg, but we're getting closer.'

'I congratulate you on spotting that sign,' Tweed replied and gripped the wheel more firmly.

A sinister white vapour was floating over the autobahn. Snake-like curls of mist drifted downwards. His windscreen was icing up. The wipers kept knocking slivers of the ice off the windscreen. He turned up the heater. Raw cold was penetrating the interior of the Mercedes. The silver car ahead had disappeared. Could it have driven up the turn-off? He doubted it.

'It's stopped snowing,' Paula remarked, 'but this fog is going to make it difficult for you.'

'So we're lucky there's nothing just ahead of us.'

'The trouble is I can't see any more how close our friends behind us are. Let's hope they keep well back. We don't want one of them slamming up our rear.'

It was a thought which had occurred to Tweed. He wriggled and sat up straighter. For no particular reason he felt more alert and in control. Second wind. The adrenalin was flowing again. Probably the arrival of the fresh hazard had triggered it off. He would have liked to reduce speed but he was worried about what might be coming up behind him.

The ice made a crackling sound now as it froze harder and the wipers shifted it. In his headlights the endless lane ahead gleamed like glass. The surface was becoming very treacherous. Paula yelled an urgent warning.

'Oh, my God! Look what's coming. He must be mad . . .'

In the distance a huge truck was advancing towards them on collision course, its headlights blazing. Then mounted on top of the cab another light came on, a powerful beam like a great eye glaring at them. Paula froze with terror. The searchlight beam became much stronger, blinding her as the monster rumbled on towards them. Even above the sound of their own engine she could hear the drumming beat of Oscar's souped-up motor.

Tweed's mouth tightened. His eyes flickered for a second to the rear view mirror. No sign of any traffic behind his Mercedes. He kept his speed, resisted the temptation to lessen the pressure on the accelerator. The two vehicles rushed towards each other. The gap was closing to collision point in seconds.

'He's crazy as a fox,' Paula gasped.

'Brace yourself!' Tweed ordered.

He could see now it was an immense refrigerated truck weighing God knew how many tons. It would crush his car like an eggshell with its size and the combined speeds. He knew instantly the driver was intent on killing them. Still he kept up his speed, stayed in the same lane as the oncoming juggernaut.

Oscar was crouched over his wheel, his dead cigarette hung from the corner of his thin mouth. This was the target – everything was right. Number and sex of the people inside. Registration number. He pushed his foot down and the truck shook with the power of its movement. Oscar leant back in his seat, away from the wheel, ready for the shock . . .

Paula closed her eyes. She knew she was dead. The thought flashed through her mind that at least she would die with Tweed . . .

Behind the wheel Tweed sat immobile as a waxwork figure. His mind was as cold as the ice forming on the windscreen. The driver of the truck must now have assumed he was petrified with fright, unable to think, maybe even asleep as sometimes happened.

Tweed calculated the combined speeds of the two vehicles as best he could, his mind moving like lightning. When he judged the moment was right – that he could turn the Mercedes faster than the truck driver could alter the onward rush of his mammoth – he swung the wheel to the left, switching to the outer lane. The juggernaut loomed over him. He was skidding. Tweed drove into the skid, the car responded, he was free of the skid. The wall of the truck slid past on his right, inches away.

Oscar swore foully, then blinked. Headlights were racing towards him. Instinctively he swung the wheel and the truck hit the car. There was a grinding crunch of metal as the front of the car telescoped, a second crashing sound as the car behind it rammed into the wreckage – followed by a third. The truck was skidding all over the autobahn, skating over the ice-rink surface. Oscar fought desperately for control, saw the outer metal barrier rear up before him, swivelled his foot – too late – for the brake. The truck smashed into the barrier, broke through it, lurched down an embankment.

The cab separated from the trailer which turned over on its side, sliding down the slope. Freed of its burden, the cab sped on, rammed into a low concrete wall. Oscar was hurled through the windscreen like a fighter pilot jerking forward at G-speed. When the police found him later his head was almost severed from his neck, lolled through the fractured opening in a macabre way, the dead cigarette still tucked in the corner of the dead man's mouth.

*   *   *

'I don't know how you managed it . . .'

Paula used a handkerchief to wipe sweat off her brow, to dry her hands. She was breathing deeply, her breasts heaving, fighting to get a grip on herself. Tweed said the first thing that came into his head.

'Neither do I, but I did. At a cost. You realize there was a major pile-up? Lord knows how many vehicles – all of them following us, I suspect. How close to the Freiburg turn-off?'

He asked to switch her mind to something else, and because it was essential to leave the autobahn after what had just happened. He reduced speed and carefully wiped each of his own damp hands on his coat. Paula was already studying the map, looking up to check a sign.

'It's the next turn-off. We're stopping in Freiburg?'

'Yes, I know the place. Spent six months at the University once to learn German. We'll stay there the night. You'll find it relaxes you. Freiburg has a first-rate hotel.'

'What's it called?'

'The Colombi.'

9

On their way to the Hotel Colombi, their shoulders stooped to ward off the falling snow, Horowitz paused when he saw a car hire firm which was still open. Eva grumbled as she stood in the cold, carrying her case.

'I want something to eat,' she protested, clasping her coat collar round her slim neck.

Horowitz's patience was exhausted. Smiling, he put down his luggage, placed both hands on her shoulders. A good four inches taller than his companion, he bent down to speak to her.

'If I have any more moaning from you they'll find your body in a ditch. How would you like to end up that way?'

She trembled as he stared straight at her, and not with the cold. 'I'm sorry. What are we doing?' Her teeth chattered, and again not with the cold.

'I am going to hire a car. We'll then drive the last few metres to the Colombi. Are we feeling better now?'

'I'm OK. Anything you say, Armand . . .'

Horowitz used a driving licence in the name of Vogel to hire an Audi. The formalities completed, he drove away along the cobbled streets of the old town. It was important to have transport, mobility. He reserved two rooms at the luxurious hotel which had a large reception hall and modern curving staircases leading to the first floor. Hendrix mellowed in the warmth and the palatial surroundings, said she'd go up to her room to get ready for dinner. Horowitz handed his suitcase to a porter with his room key.

'I'll see you in the bar,' he told Hendrix.

It was with a sense of relief that he made his way alone into the bar and ordered a glass of champagne. At that time of year there were few people about and he sat at a table by himself. An infrequent drinker, he sipped his champagne. A radio playing somewhere was interrupted by a news flash. Horowitz froze, his glass half-way to his lips.

'A major pile-up on the E 35 near Freiburg . . . reported eight cars involved . . . heavy casualties . . . also reported a large refrigerated truck driving north along the southbound lane caused the latest holocaust . . . the truck driver believed to have died in the pile-up . . . more details in our next news bulletin . . .'

Horowitz put down his glass still half full. He ordered a second glass, checked his watch. When Eva Hendrix arrived he pointed at his own glass.

'You can finish that up before you start on the one I ordered for you. I have to go out – something I forgot to attend to. Start dinner without me – I may be a while.'

'And I got myself all dressed up for you . . .' She saw his expression and stopped. She was wearing a green off-the-shoulder dress which hugged her figure. 'Don't worry,' she went on quickly, 'I'll start dinner and see you when you get back . . .'

And maybe, she thought, if I'm lucky he'll be away a long time and I'll meet an interesting man. Horowitz was not even looking at her: opening his executive case, he lifted the base, sorted through several documents, found what he was looking for and shut the case. Still holding on to it, he nodded and went out to where the Audi was parked.

It took him half an hour's fast driving up the autobahn to reach the disaster point. Police cars with blue lights flashing, revolving. Uniformed police everywhere. Beyond, a glimpse of carnage – the pile-up on the southbound lane resembled a scrap metal yard. Police were directing the traffic, waving traffic on. He pulled up on the hard shoulder, switched off and got out.

He was careful to approach one of the older policemen: the younger ones gave out no information, delighted in exerting their brief authority by telling you to move on. The policeman he spoke to stood with his hands on his hips, had grey hair showing beneath his peaked cap. Horowitz began the speech he had rehearsed.

'I'm a state official, a commissioner of taxes.' He showed the forged document. 'I heard about this awful accident on the radio and I'm worried sick . . .'

'You think someone you know might be involved?' the policeman asked sympathetically.

'Yes. My wife. She was driving from Frankfurt and phoned me to say she was leaving late. But she could have arrived here about the time of the accident . . .'

'Registration number? We have managed to find all of those at least.' The policeman immediately regretted his choice of the last two words. 'What make of car?'

'A Mercedes.' Horowitz hesitated. 'You have a list of the numbers? You have? Would you mind if I looked down the list? I'd sooner see it listed for myself. I'm in a state of shock.'

The policeman nodded again, took a folded sheet of paper from his tunic pocket, unfolded it, handed it to Horowitz and held a flashlight while the tax commissioner checked the numbers, moving his index finger slowly down the list. Horowitz let out a deep sigh.

'She's not included. Thank God. Do you mind if I do a U-turn through that smashed barrier and get back to Freiburg? I may have missed her coming out here.'

'I'll guide you out, sir. This is your lucky night. No one survived that. Freezing fog and still they drive at high speed. Madness.'

'There's a lot of it about in the world. And thank you for being so helpful, officer . . .'

Horowitz drove back to Freiburg in a philosophical mood – the registration number of Tweed's Mercedes had not been on the list. He was still loose, roaming about somewhere. The question was where? He tried to think himself into Tweed's position: what would he do?

By the time he had arrived back at the Hotel Colombi he had decided. He was going to have a busy day tomorrow.

Tweed got lost driving into Freiburg. They had altered the street route system since last he'd been in the place. He found himself in front of the main station.

'I think the bookstall is still open in the ticket hall,' Paula said. 'I'll nip out and try to get a street guide.'

She returned a few minutes later with an air of triumph, waving a folded map. Sitting beside Tweed, she stopped before opening the map and looked at him.

'If you want to go on further I'm game. Is it safe to stop so close to that accident? That truck driver tried to kill us – and he knew where to locate us exactly. Lord knows how but maybe we should get out of here.'

'You're dog-tired and hungry . . .'

'I told you, I'm game.'

'I'm dog-tired and hungry too,' he told her. 'and that's when I'm likely to make a major mistake. I know Freiburg. Let's see if we can find the Colombi Hotel.'

'It's on the Rotteck Ring. I saw an advertisement for it in the booking hall. Give me a moment.' Tweed waited and looked round. Modern buildings in front of the station he didn't recall – obviously erected since his stay years ago in Freiburg.

'Got it! And it's so easy. See that street over there – Eisenbahnstrasse? We simply go down there and turn left into the Rotteck Ring. The hotel is on the far side of the Ring.'

'Let's get moving, then. I could do with a bath and I expect you could. Then a decent dinner. The food is fabulous.'

It was only a short distance and Paula spotted the Colombi as they turned a corner. Quite suddenly Tweed pulled in at the kerb before they reached the hotel. Leaving the engine running he drummed his fingers on the wheel.

'What's the matter?' asked Paula. 'You're suffering a delayed reaction from that appalling business on the auto-bahn aren't you?'

'No. But a few minutes ago I said I was dog-tired and hungry. I also said that was when I was likely to make a major mistake. I think I was just on the verge of making one.'

'I don't understand. We can talk about it when we're settled inside the Colombi in the warmth . . .'

'Which is the mistake I was about to make.' He leaned back in his seat. 'Think, Paula. I'm wanted for murder and rape. So in London they're bound to have looked at my file – which gives some of my personal techniques while abroad. One is that I often stay at a first-class hotel to merge into the background. The Colombi is among the "Thirty Best Hotels in Germany" list – and we were followed close to Freiburg . . .'

'But,' Paula hesitated, then went on, 'it must have been a massacre when you evaded that truck. I heard it – a terrible sound of vehicles crashing into each other. They may all be dead.'

'More than possible. But someone sent those cars after us and whoever he is, he'll soon know we weren't involved. They'll check the car registration numbers.'

'You think then some high-powered organization is behind that pursuit. Probably the police . . .'

'And maybe someone else. I told you, eight cars following us was too many for one outfit. So we go to the Colombi, someone knows that habit of mine, we're walking into a trap.'

'Yes, you could be right,' she agreed. 'So what do we do?'

'Stay at a much smaller hotel, the one I stayed at when I was here to learn German. The Oberkirch on Schusterstrasse. It has the advantage of being tucked away behind the Munster – and there used to be a large car park there. Don't bother with the map. I know where I am now. I turn into the Kaiser-Josephstrasse, then turn off that down a side street and we're in the Munsterplatz . . .'

Tweed turned down the Kaiser-Josephstrasse, a long cobbled street bisecting the town from east to west. It was almost deserted at that hour, in the wintry weather. A yellow tram ran along the centre and the street was lined on both sides with closed shops.

Turning into the Munsterplatz, Tweed saw cars parked,

covered with a coating of snow. He drove round slowly, the wheels bumping over the icy cobbles, found an empty slot behind two rows of cars under the lee of the Munster, drove into it.

'We're nicely tucked away here in case someone comes looking for us,' he remarked as he switched off the engine. 'It's only a short walk to the hotel. Mind your footing.'

'The main thing is we're within sight of sanctuary for the night,' Paula said cheerfully. 'I don't really care how far it is. I'm stiff as a board and want to stretch my legs.'

Carrying their cases, they moved across the square, lonely and silent at night. The only sound was the crunch of their feet on the crusted snow. The great spire of the Munster loomed above them like an arrow pointing to heaven. Tweed turned into the Schusterstrasse, which was also deserted. Icicles were suspended from the roof gutters like daggers, gleaming in the light from ancient lanterns attached to the walls.

'It's a lovely place,' Paula remarked.

The street was narrow, cobbled, full of old buildings which were joined together and went back to medieval times. Tweed nodded towards a small four-storey building on the left-hand side of the street. It had cream-washed walls, brown shutters and beyond its rooftop he could see the tip of the Munster spire.

'The Hotel Oberkirch,' he said. 'Refuge at last.'

'Even from the outside it looks cosy,' Paula observed, keeping up a cheerful note. 'I think I'll skip the bath, settle for a nice hot dinner.'

'I'll join you,' said Tweed as he held open the door for her.

A wave of pure warmth met them. Outside it was below freezing point. Inside the temperature must be forty degrees higher, at least, Tweed reckoned. He reserved two rooms in the name James Gage and arranged to meet Paula in the dining-room.

They stood in front of a blazing log-fire before they parted. Paula crouched down, held out her frozen hands towards the fire. They began to tingle almost unbearably. She gritted her teeth, held her hands in the same position. The tingle began to fade, she stood up.

'What are we going to do tomorrow?' she whispered. 'Keep on the move?'

'I haven't decided yet. I think better on a full stomach – but I know one thing I'm doing immediately after breakfast.'

'Which is?'

'Find the local car hire outfit. Exchange the Mercedes for a BMW . . .'

'We had one of those when we drove from Brussels to Frankfurt,' she objected.

'So it will confuse the trackers mightily – especially since I think they picked us up at the Luxembourg border crossing, then followed us in our Mercedes down the autobahn.'

It was late in the evening when Newman left the Hessischer Hof in Frankfurt and walked across the little wooded park. He had left Marler in the bar, saying he was going upstairs for a shower.

For the third time that day he called Kuhlmann from the public box. He wasn't sure the police chief would still be in his office but the gravelly voice answered immediately.

'Felix here,' Newman said. 'No more developments, I suppose?'

'You suppose wrong. There was a newsflash I caught of a big pile-up on the E 35 autobahn outside Freiburg . . .'

'God! Not Tweed?' Newman let the name slip in his anxiety.

'No,' Kuhlmann assured him promptly. 'I know definitely – I've phoned Freiburg police HQ – they've a list of the registration numbers of the eight cars involved from a radio car on the spot. Your associate is not on the list. But I think he was somewhere near the disaster. Eight of my men were killed in the pile-up.'

'That's appalling. You must be feeling sick . . .'

'Not sick – grim. Look, Newman, supposing we meet where we met before? Say in three-quarters of an hour from now?'

'I'll be there . . .'

Newman, puzzled, replaced the receiver. He had slipped up in using Tweed's name because it had sounded as though he'd been one of the casualties. But Kuhlmann had also slipped up – using 'Newman' at the end of the conversation. And Kuhlmann *never* slipped up. Unless intentionally.

Kuhlmann looked at his assistant, Kurt Meyer, as he replaced his own phone. Meyer had his head buried in files he was comparing, apparently oblivious to everything going on round him.

'I'm leaving for the night,' he informed Meyer. 'You expect to be here much longer?'

'Maybe another two hours, Chief. I'm still trying to make head or tail of this Gruninger case.'

'Get lucky . . .'

Kuhlmann left his office after slipping on his dark topcoat and scarf. He walked down to the next floor where two men sat working at desks facing each other. He leaned on the door he had closed, pursed his lips before speaking.

'This is just between the three of us. Friedl, I think it is possible Kurt Meyer may leave the building shortly. I want you to follow him without being spotted. See where he goes, who he contacts. Bork, you go with Friedl. Take that camera with you – the miniature job Zeiss developed for us where you get a picture within a minute of taking the shot.

The night version. No flash-bulbs. If Meyer meets someone I want his picture taken in the utmost secrecy. Think you can handle it?'

'No trouble at all,' Friedl replied. 'It so happens with the weather changing I bought a new windcheater and also a beret this morning. Meyer has never seen them. And I'll wear phoney glasses. He won't spot me.'

'If you can,' Kuhlmann ordered, 'meet me in the bar of the Canadian Pacific Hotel to report any findings. I'll wait there till midnight. See you . . .'

Kurt Meyer left the Kriminalpolizei HQ at Wiesbaden ten minutes after Kuhlmann had gone. He drove towards Frankfurt, stopping on the way to make a call from a public booth. George Evans answered the phone himself, working late in his office in the Kaiserstrasse.

'Kurt here. I have urgent information. There have been serious developments. Can we meet? You'd want to know at once.'

'Where are you calling from?' Evans asked.

'A public call-box, of course. On the way to Frankfurt from Wiesbaden . . .'

'So you have transport?'

'Yes. My own Passat.'

'I'll meet you in the lobby of the Frankfurter Hof half an hour from now. It had better be important.'

He slammed down the phone before Meyer could reply, stared across his desk at Gareth Morgan, perched like a large evil gnome on the edge of his chair, cuddling a glass of Scotch.

'That was my Wiesbaden contact, Kurt Meyer. I'm meeting him, as you must have heard, at the Frankfurter Hof.'

Morgan swallowed the rest of his drink, wiped his mouth with the back of his hand. He sat frowning, staring back at Evans, then decided.

'May be to do with that newsflash we heard about the pile-up near Freiburg. You said one of your men was reporting to you when he cut out.'

'He cut out all right. Or was cut out, more likely. He was just saying: *Tweed is somewhere ahead of us but in this fog*— Then he let out the most chilling yell – *Ahhhhhhh* – and the link went blank.'

Imitating the scream of agony he'd lifted his voice. Morgan pursed his lips with distaste. Any dramatics were his department. He stood up, placed the empty glass on Evans's desk where the damp base left a ring on the highly polished surface. Evans affected not to notice the sloppy touch.

'I think I'll come with you, hear what this Meyer has to say for myself. You can introduce me as your bodyguard . . .'

'Is that wise? Putting yourself on view? And Meyer is running scared.'

'I'd like to hear for myself,' Morgan repeated. 'Got it?'

He saw no reason to explain that Buckmaster had emphasized he wanted Morgan to supervise the whole Tweed operation personally. And Evans might not handle this creep so he obtained every scrap of information available.

'By the way,' he continued as Evans fetched the coats from a cupboard, helped Morgan on with his black overcoat, 'your running expenses here are astronomic. I was going through the figures. Do you really need thirty operatives in Frankfurt? We have to watch expenses if we're to make a profit.'

'I was told by London that expense was no object. It was the image which counted – if we're to hold our position as the largest security organization on the Continent.

'But you do have a budget?' Morgan persisted.

He was well aware that the reference to 'London' meant Lance Buckmaster.

'What's a budget?' Evans asked airily.

Morgan grunted. 'Let's get off to see this chap at the Frankfurter Hof.'

'I still think your coming is risky . . .'

'We're in the risk business – in case you hadn't realized it.'

'I'm damned sure it was an attempt to kill Tweed,' Kuhlmann told Newman as they again strolled up and down the concourse of the main station.

It was much quieter at this hour. The whole tempo of the *Hauptbahnhof* had changed. It was almost empty of passengers and the few there sat huddled on seats. The tannoy seemed to have gone to sleep.

'What makes you think that?' asked Newman.

'I had unmarked cars following him. They reported that four other cars were also doing the same thing. We know who they were now – security guards from the World Security apparatus. Why am I sure? A stolen refrigerated truck drives the wrong way up the autobahn – that was seen by a driver coming up the northbound lane – and Tweed's Mercedes was somewhere not far ahead. Two sets of skid marks were found afterwards – one by the wheels of a car, the other by the truck before the driver went through the barrier and was killed. Oh, yes, that was an assassination attempt.'

'And where do you think Tweed is now?'

'Somewhere in Freiburg would be my best bet. They'd driven all the way from Brussels. The last section was through near blizzard conditions. The incident must have shocked them, so logically they'd rest up for the night.'

'Is that police chopper at Frankfurt Airport still standing by? Egon Wrede was the name of the pilot?'

'Yes to both questions. And Wrede will still be fresh. He's an expert at catnapping while he waits. And he'll have collected food from the airport.'

102

'Then I'm using it to fly straight to Freiburg.'

'I hoped you'd say that.' Newman had stopped walking for a few moments, his mind racing. Kuhlmann brushed past his right side, strolled round behind him, came up on his left side and his wide mouth broke into a grin. 'Better check your pockets. Careful. Nothing on view.'

Newman felt inside his right-hand pocket. He froze. He could recognize the feel of a gun. He checked his left-hand pocket and again his fingers touched metal.

'A Walther .38 automatic,' Kuhlmann told him. 'It's OK – the safety's on. Spare mags in the other pocket. Better take this bit of paper . . .'

Newman read the typed sheet quickly. An authorization to carry the weapon. On official headed paper. Signed by Kuhlmann himself.

'How did you manage that trick?' he asked.

'I used to know a pickpocket when I was on the beat a million years ago. A real pro. He taught me all he knew. Then I put him away for two years. Are you wondering why I've kitted you up?'

'Yes.'

They were strolling again to keep warm. 'Three of the World Security guards dragged out of the carnage down near Freiburg were armed. Which was naughty. No authorization. You may need protection. Tweed certainly does. Best I can do . . .'

Kuhlmann walked away. Newman also left the station, found a cab and was back at the Hessischer Hof inside ten minutes. During that time he took his decision about Marler: to continue keeping an eye on him. He brought him out of the bar.

'We're leaving now. Give you the details in the cab. Get your bag. Don't ask questions – you'll get no answers.'

'Supposing I won't leave unless you tell me what's going on?' Marler challenged him as they walked across the lobby.

'Then I'll dump you . . .'

'Meet you down here in five minutes.'

10

'We'll go to the bar,' Morgan said after they'd met Kurt Meyer.

'That's rather public,' Meyer protested.

'Not if we sit in that dark corner,' Morgan snapped, taking charge of the situation. He ordered a large cognac for himself and left Evans to deal with the other drinks. Then he leaned forward, tapped Meyer on the knee.

'You've never seen me after this meeting. Get any funny ideas and certain interesting photographs will be shown to your wife. She'll enjoy them, I'm sure.'

'I swear . . .'

'Don't. I can't abide bad language.' Morgan sat back, satisfied he was dominating the proceedings, waited until the drinks had been served, paid for by Evans. He leaned forward again, his voice a hissing whisper.

'Tell all. Make it quick.'

'Someone called Newman rang Kuhlmann. . .' He paused to watch the effect of his statement. Morgan remained very still, his eyes fixed on Meyer's like inert beads. 'I remembered Kuhlmann making a reference to Robert Newman, the foreign correspondent. Maybe that's who it was . . .'

'I'm waiting for the guts,' Morgan hissed again.

'Well, this Newman was told by my chief that Tweed wasn't involved in the big car pile-up on the autobahn near Freiburg. But he said he thought Tweed was somewhere near the pile-up when it happened. Then Kuhlmann made an arrangement to meet this Newman . . .'

'Where?' prompted Morgan.

'At the place they'd met before. He gave no indication where that was. They were to meet in three-quarters of an hour. And that was about it. You have heard the news-flash . . .'

'We heard. Everybody has heard,' Morgan told him. 'Time you walked. Not yet. Evans has something for you while I get a drink.'

Morgan padded over to the low curved bar, ordered another cognac. While he was at the bar Evans slipped an envelope containing banknotes under the table to Meyer.

'I don't like that man,' Meyer complained. 'In future I only deal with you.'

'You deal with who we say you will. Say thank you for your present, then push off before he returns.'

'Thank you.'

Meyer stuffed the envelope into his breast pocket, took a quick glance round the dimly lit bar and hurried out of the hotel. Morgan downed his cognac, licked his lips, came back, slipped into his overcoat and without a word made for the exit. Evans followed.

They climbed into the rear of the waiting stretched black Mercedes limousine, the chauffeur closed the door and sat behind the wheel, waiting for instructions. Morgan leaned forward, spoke through the opening in the glass screen dividing rear from front.

'Put on the radio. Music.' He waited until the chauffeur found a programme. 'Now take us back to Kaiserstrasse.' He closed the glass panel.

'He won't be able to hear a word we say now,' he commented.

'Hans is completely trustworthy,' Evans protested as the car moved away from the hotel's steps.

'No one is completely trustworthy. If Meyer got it right –

and I think the little creep did – Horowitz has made a balls-up of eliminating Tweed. Like I said, you can't trust anyone. Is the Lear jet which flew him down there back here?'

'Yes. With a fresh crew waiting at the airport in case of need . . .'

'Which is more expense. I wonder what that's costing? It would be cheaper to let them stay at home on a stand-by retainer.'

'I had orders from London.'

'I know. To keep the jet ready on a round-the-clock basis. Well, they'll earn their money – the crew. I'm flying to Freiburg tonight to take personal control.'

'Horowitz won't like that. He likes to operate on his own. And his track record is excellent.'

'His track record just got smeared. When we reach HQ leave me alone in your office. Use another phone to call Horowitz – you can contact him, I suppose?'

'In an emergency. He phoned me from Freiburg. He's staying at the Colombi . . .'

'Some dump of a boarding house?'

'Actually . . .' Evans sounded smug. 'It's the best hotel they have in Freiburg, and listed among the thirty best in the Federal Republic.'

'More expense. No wonder his fees come so high. I've changed my mind. Don't call Horowitz. Under no circumstances let him know I'm flying there tonight. Instead call the airport, make sure that jet crew is ready – and write out an authorization placing the Lear at my complete disposal. No time limit.'

Lance Buckmaster was in his study, the door locked, at Tavey Grange, when the call from Morgan came through. It was being transmitted by satellite via the radio-receiver dish nestling among the Tudor chimneys.

'Hold on a minute,' Buckmaster ordered.

He held his hand over the phone. 'Sonia, go to your room at once. I'll join you later.'

Sonia Dreyfus, twenty-seven, with long dark hair, daughter of a wealthy industrialist, sat naked to the waist on a long leather couch. She had a good figure. Whipping on a sweater she gathered up her clothes and left the study. She'd learned that when Lance said move, you moved. And what luck that his silly bitch of a wife, Leonora, was up in London at the Belgravia apartment.

'Carry on. What is it?' Buckmaster's upper crust voice floated up into the stratosphere and back down to Frankfurt.

Morgan was wily in his wording. 'The first attempt was made on the subject for treatment. We now know his location. The attempt smoked him out . . .'

'But was not successful? Is that what you're telling me in your roundabout manner?'

'Your assumption is correct.'

'I want the problem dealt with quickly. Report to me here – if I am here – when it's out of the way. I have to go now, urgent matters to attend to. Good-night.'

In Frankfurt, Morgan put down the phone, used a silk handkerchief to wipe sweat off his forehead. That had gone easier than he'd expected. *Urgent matters to attend to*? At this hour? Buckmaster was probably screwing his latest mistress, Sonia Dreyfus. By Morgan's count – and he believed in keeping track of such juicy info – this would be number six. One of these days Leonora was going to react.

He pressed the intercom switch, told the Welshman to come and see him. When Evans entered Morgan was leaning back in his chair, trimming the tip from a cigar.

'This Newman business is a complication I don't need,' he began.

'You think it is *the* Robert Newman, the foreign correspondent, as Meyer suggested?'

107

'I don't think, I know.' He made a ritual of lighting the cigar, revolving the match round the tip. 'Newman and Tweed have collaborated in the past. I was told Newman has full vetting. Now we hear he's cooperating with Kuhlmann. It has all the hallmarks of a conspiracy. This tells me.' He tweaked his pointed nose with his index finger.

'Maybe Newman has heard the rumours – that Tweed is fleeing to the East, senses a good story. These reporters will go to any lengths to make money, get a sensational scoop. No morals at all.'

Morgan raised an eyebrow, said nothing while he got his cigar going. That was pretty good, coming from Evans, considering some of the things he'd done without a qualm.

'It's not for money,' Morgan corrected him. 'You've forgotten – not so long ago Newman got lucky, wrote an international bestseller, *Kruger: The Computer that Failed*. Made him financially independent for life.' He puffed at his cigar, blew a perfect smoke circle which drifted towards the overhead fluorescent strip. 'We may have to remove him from this vale of sorrows in due course.'

'The potential body count is rising,' Evans objected. 'Tweed, the Grey woman, now Newman.'

'So you'd better get ready to shell out a large fee to friend Horowitz – after I've put my foot up his backside. I'm leaving now. You may not see me for a while. Look after the shop in my absence. . .'

Five minutes later Morgan was sitting in the rear of the limo on his way to the airport. He'd seen no reason to tell Evans that after Freiburg he'd fly back to London. It was necessary to keep an eye on what Leonora was up to. After all, she might be chairman, but he was managing director.

Newman and Marler arrived at Frankfurt Airport at 1 a.m. The chief of security, a thick-set man called Kuhn, examined the letter from Kuhlmann and then escorted them into the icy air of the airport to where the police Sikorsky was waiting.

Wrede also examined the document, then welcomed them aboard. They climbed the step-ladder and Wrede, an amiable man, showed them to their seats.

'You're taking us to Freiburg, please, near the Black Forest,' Newman told him.

'I know. I was told over the phone. Coffee in this thermos, sandwiches here.' He handed them two large greaseproof packets.

Wrede, a small roly-poly man – Newman almost expected to see jam on the sleeves of his woollen pullover – was about to retract the ladder prior to closing the door, joining his co-pilot, when Kuhn came running across the tarmac.

Wrede listened, came back to Newman. 'Sorry, there's an urgent phone call for you. You can take it in the security chief's office.'

'Come with you,' Marler suggested.

'You'll stay where you are . . .'

He joined Kuhn at the foot of the ladder and they hurried back to the main airport building. On the way Newman noticed a Lear jet parked under lights, close to a hanger. Some millionaire's plaything. For something to say he asked the question.

'Whose jet is that?'

'Belongs to World Security. A crew stands by twenty-four hours a day, seven days a week. Costs them a fortune – many times more than I'll earn in a lifetime.'

Newman stared at the jet again. His memory automatically registered the serial number painted on the fuselage. Inside the office he picked up the receiver lying off its cradle. Kuhn tactfully left the office.

'Who is it?' Newman asked cautiously. 'This is Felix . . .'

'Kuhlmann here. Hoped I'd catch you before you flew off. I have heard rumours our friend who escaped the pile-up is fleeing to the East. Absurd, I know. Trouble is the Minister also heard them. He's ordered all frontier posts to keep on the alert. Especially those leading to East Germany and Czechoslovakia. Switzerland as well,' he added. 'The heat is really on.'

'Thanks for letting me know. I'm taking off in the next few minutes.'

It was a very worried Newman who walked back to the Sikorsky. The sooner he reached Freiburg the better.

11

When the Lear jet carrying Morgan landed at Freiburg airfield he ordered the crew to find accommodation in the town, to call him at the Colombi so he could contact them, to have the jet ready for immediate departure. He omitted to thank them for a smooth flight: no point in coddling the paid help.

The car he'd told Evans to have ready for him transported him through the night to the Colombi. The room he'd ordered Evans to reserve by phone was ready. It was 2.30 a.m. when he knocked on the door of Horowitz's room.

'He may be asleep,' the night porter had pointed out.

'Then he'll just have to wake up.'

There was a light under the door but it was several minutes before the door opened a few inches on the chain. Horowitz, flat against the wall on the opening side, wearing a dressing gown, clasped the Browning .32 automatic inside his right-hand pocket.

'Who is it?' he called out in German.

'Speak bloody English for Christ's sake . . .'

'I said,' Horowitz repeated in English, 'who is it?'

'Me. Morgan. Surely you can recognize my voice. Hurry it up. It's half-past two in the morning.'

'Put both your hands through the gap and then show your face,' Horowitz ordered.

Fuming, Morgan did as he'd been told. Glaring through the gap, he saw Horowitz come into view, the Browning pointed at his ample stomach. Horowitz closed the door, released the chain, opened it. As soon as Morgan was inside he relocked the door quietly, put back the chain, slipped the Browning back into his pocket.

'Where did you get the weapon?' Morgan demanded as he sank into an armchair.

'From a friend near Freiburg who keeps things for me. What are you doing here?' he asked in the same quiet tone. 'Everything is under control.'

Morgan's eyes swept round the room. The bedclothes were rumpled, a lamp on the bedside table was on, a paperback novel lay face down on the bed, splayed open. A bottle of mineral water and a glass stood on a table.

'Sure,' Morgan said sarcastically, 'everything is under control. Tweed is still wandering around God knows where, but still living.'

'God may not know where, but I have an idea,' Horowitz replied as he poured himself a glass of water and drank some slowly, his eyes on Morgan. 'And you haven't answered my question – what are you doing here?'

'Finding out what the devil isn't going on.' Morgan leaned forward and glared at Horowitz who had hauled a chair forward and was sitting close to him.' 'You were paid a small fortune to do this job. *Avec vitesse* . . .'

'Don't ever try to pass for a Frenchman,' Horowitz remarked mildly. 'You'd be spotted as soon as you opened your mouth. I told you, everything is under control.'

'Well tell me how. What do you propose to do next?

And what was that remark about God not knowing but you do – where Tweed is? Where is he?'

'Oh, he has to be holed up somewhere in Freiburg. You want a few details? Incidentally, only half the agreed fee has been paid . . .'

'You get the balance when Tweed's lying on a slab.'

'Which was part of our agreement, and still is. I suppose the Lear jet flew you here from Frankfurt? You know, you're rushing about too much. And you're overweight. You should watch it, my friend. You could easily have flown down in the morning.'

Morgan gritted his teeth. 'I got to my present position by moving faster than the opposition. Also, my boss – who is ultimately your boss – is getting impatient. He wants results and he wants them fast. Lying in bed reading a paperback is not what we paid you for . . .'

'Actually, that is exactly what you paid me for.' There was an edge to Horowitz's tone. 'Instead of dashing all over the place in the middle of the night I prefer to *think* – really you should try it sometime. On the basis of the little I've learned about my target from the extracts from the file you gave me I can do that.'

'I'm listening,' snapped Morgan and took out his cigar case.

'While you are, I'd sooner you didn't smoke in here. I have to sleep in this atmosphere . . .'

'Jesus!' Morgan put away the cigar case, took out a hip flask and swallowed a generous slug of cognac. 'That's better. I'm still listening.'

'Tweed had been driving for at least twelve hours I calculate by the time of the pile-up on the autobahn. Incidentally, no danger of Oscar, the truck driver, talking . . .'

'I was going to ask you about that. The newsflash was vague. At least the one we heard in Frankfurt.'

'Since then we've had a very detailed news bulletin.

112

You'll grasp what I mean when I tell you it was amusingly titled – The Headless Maniac. Severed heads don't talk, so far as I know. He muffed the job – but the weather conditions were exceptional. As I was saying, Tweed had driven for many hours to reach Freiburg from Brussels in a day. Even allowing for his lady companion taking over the wheel, they'd both be very tired. Freiburg was their nearest refuge. Tweed would want a good meal and a good night's rest. He's here somewhere, I assure you.'

'Then how do you find him?'

'First by getting up early in the morning. My alarm is set for six. I can get by on three hours' sleep quite happily. I shall tour the town – which I know well – on foot before it wakes up . . .'

'On foot? Looking for what?'

'His parked Mercedes, of course. I have the registration number . . .'

'You could drive round faster.'

'Yes, and miss his car. It's not too large – Freiburg – and I walk fast. My long legs. Also I have from the photos you showed me the images of Tweed and Paula Grey imprinted on my mind. I might even see one of them. On foot.'

'OK.' Morgan was mellowing under the influence of the large slug of cognac he'd swallowed. 'But there's a complication. It's called Robert Newman. He was in Frankfurt – and secretly meeting Otto Kuhlmann.'

'I see.' Horowitz's long lean face became serious. 'Could he possibly be coming here?'

'Work it out for yourself. Police cars were tracking Tweed as well as our own. One of our drivers recognized a plain-clothes driver from Wiesbaden. All dead now. But Kuhlmann told Newman about the pile-up, so . . .'

'I'm ahead of you. The foreign correspondent could arrive in Freiburg, and the file said they'd worked closely together in the past. As the French say, Newman is *formidable*. I shall have to take extra precautions. Are you staying here?' A wisp of a dry smile crossed Horowitz's features. 'Or flying back to Frankfurt when you leave me?'

'Good God! What do you think I am? Superman? I need a good night's kip after what I've been through today.'

Horowitz stood up. 'Then I suggest you go to your room and get your beauty sleep. Don't join me if you see me in the breakfast room. Just give me your room number.'

'Sixteen.' Morgan stood up, suddenly weary and flaked out. He stifled a yawn. Must keep up an image of command and energy in front of this cool snake. He lowered his voice. 'Try and make it a quick kill.'

'I move at my own pace. One planned "accident" has gone wrong due to the weather. You'll get your money's worth. As you have in the past. Good-night.'

The Sikorsky descended vertically through the darkness to Freiburg airfield. Newman gazed down at the snowbound landscape, felt the wheels bump, the rotors slowing and turned to Marler seated alongside him.

'We've arrived. There's a police car parked close to the tarmac. Leave me to do the talking if we're approached.'

'Since I don't have a clue what this is about I'm hardly likely to have much to say.'

As they descended the ladder after Newman had thanked the pilot, a uniformed policeman, his peaked cap rimmed with snow, greeted them when they stepped on *terra firma*. A tall giant, he extended his identity folder with his left hand and shook Newman's hand with his right.

'Mr Newman, I believe,' he said in English. 'Chief Inspector Kuhlmann asked us to meet you. Sergeant Andris at your service. Where do you wish us to drive you to?'

'Before we leave, Sergeant Andris, I see there's a Lear jet parked over there. Could you tell me when it arrived, who it belongs to, and who, if anyone, flew in here?'

114

Newman already knew the answer to its ownership. The registration number on the fuselage was the same as that painted on the machine he'd observed waiting at Frankfurt. A jet would cover the distance far more quickly than a chopper.

'I watched it land about an hour ago. It nearly ran out of runway. It belongs to World Security. One man alighted, a short heavily-built man wearing a dark overcoat, the lapels trimmed with astrakhan fur. Clean-shaven, in his forties at a guess, he moved quickly and had the small feet you often see with very well-built men. A Mercedes was waiting for him. I have acute hearing and just caught his instruction to the driver. The Hotel Colombi.'

'Thank you. Excellent powers of observation you have. And we also would like to be driven to the Colombi.' Newman paused. 'We'd like to arrive quietly. Could you stop your car nearby, out of sight of the entrance to the Colombi?'

Andris glanced at Marler as he held open the door. Settled in the rear seat next to Newman, Marler spoke in a low voice.

'He'll know me again. He photographs people with his eyes.'

'So behave yourself while you're in the Black Forest area,' Newman responded, glanced back at the Lear, closed his eyes and dozed.

He woke up as the car slowed and stopped by the kerb. Andris had carried out his instructions to the letter. The car was parked a dozen yards away from the light flooding out from the entrance to the Colombi.

At Newman's suggestion, Marler joined him in his room after depositing his bag in his own accommodation. Marler never seemed to tire and looked fresh as paint. He'd run an electric razor over his growth of stubble before arriving.

'And who do you think was the mysterious passenger who flew in before us?' he enquired.

115

'Gareth Morgan,' Newman said promptly. 'Description fitted him perfectly. I've met the louse. Have you?'

'No.' Marler omitted to mention his trip to Tavey Grange, his interview with Buckmaster. 'If this Morgan knows you is it a good idea to stay here? You could run into him.'

'I intend to. And his presence suggests we're very close to Tweed. Morgan likes to supervise operations himself.'

'Operations?'

'Yes.' Newman sagged into a chair, gestured for Marler to sit down. 'There was a horrific pile-up on the south-bound autobahn just outside Freiburg late yesterday evening – and the cars following Tweed were World Security jobs. So it's beginning to add up. Tweed escaped the pile-up . . .'

Newman watched Marler's reaction closely.

'Thank God for that,' Marler replied blandly and lit a king-size cigarette, a sign of inner tension. 'What', he continued, 'is beginning to add up?'

'The identity of the people who want Tweed out of the way. Permanently. World Security. At least they're mixed up in this business somewhere – otherwise why should they be so anxious to follow him?'

'But you haven't asked the main question,' Marler objected. '*Why* should anyone want him eliminated. Just supposing you're right. And there's a hell of a lot of supposition in your thinking. Or is there something you're not telling me?'

'What on earth gave you that idea?'

Newman yawned. He wanted sleep, to be fresh for the many tasks he had to undertake in a few hours. The main point now was to get Marler back in his room, to feel sure he'd stay there for the rest of the night.

'I'll tell you what gave me that idea,' Marler rapped back. 'You keep disappearing, making mysterious phone calls I suspect. For some reason you knew it was a good idea for us to fly to Freiburg, that Tweed is in this area. You're not clairvoyant.'

'Why not push off and get some shut-eye?'

Marler stood up slowly. 'I'm beginning to get the feeling that for some crazy reason you don't trust me . . .'

'And that's crazy reasoning. You'll feel more relaxed in the morning.' He mimicked Marler's voice. 'Be a good chap, get back to your room. Maybe we can talk some more after a good breakfast.'

Marler left the room without a word. Newman waited for a few seconds, then tiptoed to the door, opened it quietly in time to see Marler's back disappearing into his own bedroom further down the corridor. Newman checked his watch and waited fifteen minutes. Satisfied Marler was not reappearing, he closed the door, leant against it, forced himself to think.

He must set his alarm clock early, get out of the hotel, explore the town for some sign of Tweed and Paula. Try the smaller places. Tweed could have switched his habits. Then a confrontation with Gareth Morgan, preferably in the dining-room. If he could throw the top man at World Security off balance, Morgan might just let something slip.

12

Armand Horowitz walked out of the front entrance of the Colombi the following morning shortly after streaks of grey light had appeared over the Black Forest.

He wore rubber overshoes – the snow had become hard as a rock overnight, its surface solid ice in many places.

He walked into the old part of the town – most of Freiburg – in the direction of the Munster.

Despite the sub-zero temperature he was clad only in a lightweight raincoat and a silk scarf, his head bare. Horowitz could stand any amount of cold, found it invigorating. Walking at a steady pace, he checked the registration number of every Mercedes parked by the kerb.

Inside the briefcase he carried in his right hand was a Pentax camera. At least the outer casing appeared to be a camera. Horowitz, an explosives expert, had sat up half the night in his room preparing the bomb which contained Semtex explosive. Attached to its back were four magnetic feet.

When he found Tweed's car it would be a simple matter to bend down, adjust the trembler mechanism by moving the shutter speed dial, then clamp the device to the underside of the car with the magnetic legs. The trembler would trigger the bomb when the car began to climb the slightest incline.

When the Mercedes had exploded Horowitz, on hearing the news over the radio, planned to call the local newspaper anonymously. He'd say he represented a splinter group of Baader–Meinhof, that they had 'executed' the industrialist, Martin Schuler. It would be assumed they'd mistaken the target. Another 'accident'.

Horowitz had collected the bomb from the same contact outside Freiburg who had supplied him with the Browning automatic and certain other equipment. He walked along the Kaiser-Josephstrasse where some shops were already open. Cleaning women with spades were levering ice off the sidewalk, pushing the slabs into the gutter.

He had changed his mind about checking the Munster-platz car-park next. Tweed, he decided, would hide on the perimeter of the town, ready for a swift departure in an emergency. He turned along Schusterstrasse. In the distance was the Hotel Oberkirch.

Horowitz kept moving at his even pace, watching his footing. Just before reaching the Oberkirch he turned right again along a shopping arcade which led him out into Oberlinden, another street of ancient buildings. Every variety of paving had been used: cobbles, pavé and pebble mosaic. He reached one of the medieval gates, Schwabentor, the road passing under a tall decorated tower. He changed direction again, checking more parked Mercedes.

Now he was moving down Konvikstrasse, a narrow curving street. The old houses had dormer windows projecting from the roofs, leafless creepers stretching down the walls from window boxes high up. The water from a fountain surrounded by a circular stone basin was a frozen jet suspended in mid-air. The water in the basin was a solid sheet of blue-grey ice.

Tweed was also up early. He washed, shaved, dressed quickly and made a brief phone call. The car-hire firm he'd found in the directory was open for business. He left the hotel, hurried to the Munsterplatz. He was sitting behind the wheel, about to turn on the ignition, when he got out again.

He had to wrench the hood open and ice cracked. He checked the engine. No sign of tampering. He closed the hood and crouched down to check the underside of the vehicle. Again, all seemed well. He was driving slowly out of the square when he saw the tall man with steel-rimmed glasses in his wing mirror. Carrying a briefcase, he had paused and was examining a parked Mercedes. Tweed drove off, disappeared round a corner.

He exchanged the Mercedes for a BMW, using an international driving-licence with a fresh pseudonym, James

119

Gage. Before breakfast was served at the Oberkirch he had parked the BMW in the same slot beneath the Munster. The moment he arrived back he knew something had happened. Paula was waiting for him in the hall, an odd expression on her face.

Paula unlocked the door of her bedroom, stood aside, ushered Tweed into the room. He took four paces beyond the doorway, paused for a fraction of a second, then turned to speak to Paula who was relocking the door.

'You might have told me,' he chided her.

'I thought it would be a wonderful surprise.'

'It is.' Tweed turned back to grasp the hand of Newman who had stood up from the chair he'd sat in. 'And how did you find me?' was his first question.

Newman grinned. Nothing wrong with Tweed's mind: his first thought had been that if Newman could find him someone else could.

'It's all right,' he assured him. 'I used a long-shot trick in case I was coming to Freiburg. And I know this town. It was here that I picked up the trail of Kruger – remember, I explained how in my book.'

He took a folded telegram from his pocket, handed it to Tweed. It read: *Gerald seriously ill in St Thomas's, London. Please contact his brother urgently*. The telegram was addressed to Robert Newman, care of Hotel Colombi, Freiburg. Tweed handed the telegram back.

'I don't understand.'

'I sent it from the post office at the main station in Frankfurt, knowing the hotel would hang on to it for a week or two. They gave it to me when I arrived at the Colombi last night. This morning I toured all the smaller hotels, showed them the telegram, then your photograph. No one even questioned what your name was. That telegram acted as a kind of *Open Sesame*, as I thought it would.

120

When I arrived here they told me you booked in last night and called Paula's room. It's a gambit I used several times when I was an active foreign correspondent, tracking someone.'

'Clever.' Tweed sank into a chair, relieved. He reflected that the only two people in the world he could fully trust were now with him.

'Want to hear what I've found out?' Newman asked. 'Kuhlmann, by the way, is on your side. Doesn't believe for a moment you were involved in that murder and rape of a girl . . .'

'Have they identified her yet? I'd never seen her before in my life . . .'

'Paula has told me all you explained to her about that night. Now listen to me. I have to get back to the Colombi to have a crack at Gareth Morgan. Going back to that night in Radnor Walk, I was strolling back from a late party . . .'

While Paula perched on the edge of her bed, Tweed listened with great concentration to every word Newman said. Afterwards he could have written down the whole of the foreign correspondent's account. The warmth of the room steamed up his glasses. As he cleaned them on his handkerchief he recalled he had seen someone else perform the same action. A tall thin man with steel-rimmed glasses who had paused by a parked Mercedes at the edge of the Munsterplatz. Why had that incident come back to him?

'. . . and then we were driven from Freiburg airfield in the police car to the Colombi,' Newman concluded.

'We?'

'Marler flew with me from Frankfurt. Sorry, left that bit out. He's back at the Colombi. I've been keeping him in the dark about what I've been doing . . .'

'Why?' Tweed asked, his eyes alert.

'You'll say it's because I don't like him. Frankly I'm not sure we can trust him on this one.'

'Very wise,' interjected Paula.

'Why don't you trust him?' Tweed prodded.

'The way things are, a lot of people might assume your job will be vacant soon. I've a feeling Marler would very much like to be Deputy Director in your place.'

'It's possible.' Tweed considered for a moment. 'He's ambitious. Nothing wrong with that. I don't think that you're right, but you're sensible to take precautions. I'm a fugitive from justice. Best keep it between the three of us for the moment. Bob, could you go over that scene you witnessed at my apartment that night. Buckmaster was there, you said?'

'Yes. Howard phoned him after he came to the apartment himself.'

'And you said he was the only one who was clean-shaven – that is, looked freshly shaved. At that hour.'

'Yes. What are you driving at?'

'Only that if a man has an assignation with a girl he often takes care to shave himself before they meet.'

'My God!' Newman stood up abruptly. 'You don't mean that it could have been Buckmaster who . . .'

'I don't draw any theoretical conclusions.' Tweed blinked, looked at both his companions. 'I think it's about time you both knew what this is all about. The secret project I mentioned to Paula – without telling her all the details. It affects the whole security of the West.'

Tweed began talking after Newman and Paula had pulled chairs close to him, speaking in a low voice, against the sound of music from the bedside radio he'd switched on. The precaution seemed unnecessary to Newman: Tweed and Paula had arrived only the previous night and without any advance booking. As Tweed went on talking, he understood the reason for Tweed's ultra caution.

'With the aid of two British computer scientists, Arthur

122

Wilson and Liam Fennan, the Americans have cracked the Strategic Defence Initiative problem. They've found a fairly cheap way of ensuring a defence system can be hoisted into the atmosphere which will guarantee no Soviet rockets launched against the West will get through the screen . . .'

'You mean this system is watertight, absolutely fool-proof?' Newman sounded incredulous.

'They've done exactly that. And Washington accepts it could never have been achieved without the work put in by Wilson and Fennan. To simplify a complex problem, a giant computer called Able One – or *Shockwave* as we call it – has been built. It's really two huge computers linked together, their systems merged like twins. Since we con-tributed so much Washington is supplying us with the second of the only two *Shockwaves* in existence.'

'How and when?' asked Newman.

'Our *Shockwave* is on the way from the United States. We're going to install it at Fylingdales in Yorkshire. It has one drawback – a limited range. But once the system is functioning we can protect ourselves and the whole of Western Europe. *Shockwave* can detect up to five hundred rockets in flight – and destroy every one within seconds of being launched. The rockets and their payload would detonate over the Soviet Union. It's an amazing – and totally unexpected – breakthrough. The Russians are years behind us.'

'How is it being transported?' Newman pressed.

'That's what worries me. I wanted it brought in by one of the giant transport planes the US have. But someone persuaded the PM that it would be safer with such a huge cargo to bring it across the Atlantic by freighter, the *Lampedusa*.'

'So this is the secret project you referred to,' Paula remarked. 'How many people know about this clandestine voyage?'

'Only three in Britain and three in the US – the President himself, the Chairman of the Joint Chiefs of Staff, Admiral Tremayne, and Cord Dillon, Deputy Director CIA.'

'Where is the *Lampedusa* now?' asked Newman.

'On the high seas. I calculate it's about midway across the Atlantic, and due to berth at Plymouth in the early hours of the morning it arrives. Arrangements have been made to offload *Shockwave* at night, to transfer it to a huge trailer. The police will escort it to Yorkshire. Roads will be closed to give it free passage.'

'You did say that using this freighter worries you. Who are the three people in Britain who know about it? Who persuaded the PM to bring it by sea?'

'Lots of questions.' Tweed gave a wry smile. 'And the three people are the PM, myself and Lance Buckmaster. It was the Minister, Buckmaster, who opted for sea transport.'

No one spoke for a short while. Newman and Paula were absorbing the magnitude of what Tweed had revealed. Tweed checked his watch: they'd be serving early breakfast in the dining-room. But there was more to tell. His tone was calm.

'You had better know everything – in case anything happens to me. Someone else would then have to carry on the task . . .'

'What task?' Paula interjected.

'Patience. We have to communicate with the wireless operator aboard the *Lampedusa* as soon as we can – to check that all is well. The crew has been hand-picked by Cord Dillon, Deputy Director of the CIA. He personally vetted every man. Dillon, as you know, is an old colleague of mine. In London I had a secret system of communication by radio with their wireless op.'

124

He opened his battered briefcase, took out a thick code book.

'We have a system of code signals to be exchanged at specific intervals. I am Monitor. Buckmaster also personally has the code system – he uses the Admiralty's communication network. I used our high-tech communications system in our other building further along Park Crescent. At nine in the evening I called the *Lampedusa* – the evening of the murder at Radnor Walk – and all was well.' He looked at both of them. 'I'm now telling you something no one else in the world must know. Unknown to anyone except Dillon and the wireless op aboard, I invented a simple check system. I insert into the communication the signal "Tr*a*y" – not Troy. The wireless op should then respond with "Helen is OK". The second trick signal is "White". The response from the *Lampedusa*, if all is well, should be a reference to "Cowes" – the yachting port on the Isle of Wight. Buckmaster has no knowledge of this secret check system. Now, you both know something about codes. See if this makes sense.'

He handed the code book first to Newman and sat back while the foreign correspondent studied it. Newman nodded, handed it on to Paula.

'You've kept it simple. One question. The wireless op aboard that vessel presumably has a duplicate of this code book?'

'He has . . .'

'But does *his* code book contain the two trick signals with the required responses?'

'No, it doesn't,' Tweed replied. 'He carries that data only in his memory. Cord Dillon agreed that would be safer.'

'Seems quite clear to me,' Paula said, handing back the code book. 'But it seems useless to me now – you can't contact the *Lampedusa* because you've no equipment to transmit a signal.'

'You're right. At the moment.' Tweed paused. 'But if I can get Arthur Beck's cooperation I can use his high-powered transceivers from either Zürich or Berne . . .'

'That's assuming Beck is as helpful as Kuhlmann,' she pointed out. 'Which is a highly dangerous assumption. Arthur Beck is, after all, head of the Swiss Federal Police.'

'And I've further bad news,' Newman told him. 'Kuhlmann warned in Frankfurt that an alert has been sent to all frontier posts on the East German, Czech and Swiss borders.'

'East German and Czech?' Tweed sounded stunned. 'Why those borders?'

'Because someone has spread the rumour you're fleeing to the East.'

'That someone has been very busy.' Tweed looked unusually grim. 'But there is a roundabout way I might be able to slip across the frontier into Switzerland, then contact Beck. The hounds have been loosed on me, so it won't be easy.' He looked at Paula. 'I think we ought to split up. You stay with Newman and I'll go on alone . . .'

'Forget it!' she snapped. 'I've come with you this far. If you think you can just drop me overboard you've lost your marbles . . .'

'And,' Newman broke in, 'it took me one hell of a job tracing you. Face it, you need help. Think of *Shockwave*, of what is at stake. We worked as a team on other dangerous operations in London – but nothing as vitally important as this.'

'You're right, of course.' Tweed spread his hands in a gesture of surrender. 'We'll work together again. Now I have to decide our next move – and fast. Freiburg could turn into a trap.'

'And it could be a great mistake to leave here now,' Paula persisted. 'From what Bob has told us I'm convinced Buckmaster and World Security is behind this. They may well be watching all the exits from Freiburg.'

126

'She's right,' Newman agreed. 'Some of those cars involved in the big pile-up contained World Security men who were following you. And they have an office in Freiburg. Quite close to the Colombi, I noticed.'

'Breakfast first,' Tweed decided. 'I'll think better after a good meal. And Paula hasn't eaten for hours either. What are you going to do, Bob? Join us?'

'No. Just promise me you'll stay here. Good. I'm going back to the Colombi. I'm looking forward to a cosy little chat with Mr Gareth Morgan . . .'

On the first floor of the World Security building near the Colombi, Morgan sat in the local commander's office with Horowitz. It was a conceit of Buckmaster's originating from his days with the Airborne Division that he conferred pseudo-military titles on top personnel. In Freiburg the top man was 'Commander' Ken Crombie, a stern-faced thirty-year-old who had served in the same airborne division as Buckmaster. Morgan loathed him, was waiting for the first excuse to remove him, but concealed his dislike. Sitting offside to Crombie's desk he gave an oily smile.

'I'm very pleased with the way you're running this apparatus. The fact that you speak German makes you the perfect man for the job. And I gather you have stationed cars at all exits from Freiburg to watch out for Tweed's Mercedes?'

Horowitz grunted. 'Fat lot of good that will do. Tweed is nobody's fool. He's changed the Mercedes for a BMW again.' He reached for a pad in front of Crombie, used his pen to write neatly on it, pushed it back across the desk.

'That's the registration number they should be looking for. You'd better get on the blower, Crombie. Your cars do have radio contact, I presume?'

'You're sure about this information . . .' Crombie's general air of pompous self-confidence faded as his eyes met

127

Horowitz's. He jumped up. 'Excuse me', he said to Morgan, 'while I dash to the communications centre . . .'

'How did you come up with that?' demanded Morgan.

'I spent over two hours early this morning checking every Mercedes parked in Freiburg. No sign of Tweed's vehicle. Then I toured the car-hire people, showed them an insurance certificate in the name Weber. Told them a Mercedes with Tweed's registration number had ground up against my car when he overtook. Naturally the agency he'd handed it back to immediately checked the car for damage. While the receptionist was absent I checked his record book. There it was in black and white. The Merc changed for a BMW. In the name of James Gage. So now we know who we're looking for. I'll be touring all over Freiburg looking for that BMW when I leave here. Which I think should be now . . .'

Morgan sat thinking for several minutes before Crombie returned. Horowitz was like a machine, relentless until he'd completed his assignment. Even Morgan found it frightening.

'You've contacted them all?' he asked when Crombie came back. 'Good. We might have thought of checking the car-hire people ourselves. I'm off for some breakfast.'

And in my report, he thought as he climbed the steps of the Colombi, I'll put that *Crombie* might have thought of that but he didn't.

'Mind if I join you? Shortage of places.'

Morgan was piling fried eggs and bacon into his mouth when he looked up. He chewed the food for longer than was necessary. He immediately recognized the man sitting opposite as Robert Newman, foreign correspondent. His picture had appeared in the newspapers often enough. He concealed his sense of shock by taking his time plastering a piece of toast with butter. Then he

128

smiled and buttered up his companion instead of the toast.

'Don't I know you? Yes, it's coming back to me. You're the famous correspondent who broke the Kruger scandal and wrote that blockbuster of a book afterwards. Made you rich. Good for you. I was a green security guard at the time.'

'But you've come a long way since, Morgan, weaselling your way up to the top. MD of World Security. Buckmaster's trusted servant.'

Newman ordered one fried egg and bacon from the waiter who had appeared, said he'd have coffee. Morgan had stopped eating, was wiping his thick lips with his napkin when Newman looked at him again, smiling affably.

'I don't like your language, Newman. Weaselling and servant were the words you used, I believe.' His expression and tone were ugly. He recovered quickly. He had to find out what Newman was doing, where he was staying. 'First thing in the morning,' he went on, 'I never am at my best until I've had breakfast.' He smiled again. 'Your reputation for getting a story is international. What might you be working on now? Another Kruger to chase?'

'You might say that. A different form of Kruger. But in the field of fraud again, yes.'

It had been a shot in the dark, the first thing which came into Newman's head. The reaction surprised him. Morgan's eyes stared at him as though he could hardly believe he'd heard correctly. For a moment he was at a loss for something to say. Then the crocodile smile appeared again.

'You're staying here – or just in for the excellent breakfast they serve?'

'Oh, yes, I'm staying here, as you are. Department of coincidence. How is the security business? Tell me, do you often cooperate with the police?'

'Depends.' Morgan gave himself time to think. That also

was near the mark – bearing in mind Kuhlmann's troops had also been following Tweed. This was a dangerous opponent – Morgan decided to deal with him aggressively, to frighten him, but Newman struck first.

'I've heard rumours that a British agent is on his way to the East, identity unknown.' Newman leaned across the table his voice low, grim. 'What intrigues me is where those rumours came from, who started them? You mentioned Kruger – well, I hunted him down and I'm going to hunt down whoever initiated these rumours. And more important, why?'

'Sounds like a dangerous mission . . .' Morgan began.

'Very dangerous. For the guilty men. I smell a conspiracy. I hear the police are investigating World Security . . .'

'That's a lie . . .'

'Well, you should certainly recognize one.' Newman switched moods, became amiable. 'And this isn't the first time that the police have been interested in you. There was that case of high-tech equipment being smuggled into East Germany – at least your organization attempted it and then failed.'

'You just listen to me for a moment.' Morgan had regained his self-control. He spoke in measured tones. 'You have a reputation for working on your own. A lone wolf is what you have been called. One day you'll come up against something you can't handle. It will blow up in your face.'

'You mean a car bomb?' Newman enquired casually.

'I never said anything of the sort. I didn't ask you to sit at my table. If you must stay there, shut up.'

'Just thought I'd warn you,' Newman continued in the same affable manner. He drank some coffee. 'After all, your job is on the block. Buckmaster drops people who become an embarrassment to him. Doesn't give them a second thought, however long they've served him. And

130

you've just dropped butter on your suit.'

Morgan glanced down, used his napkin to wipe the butter from his sleeve. He forced himself to eat more toast and marmalade. He felt badly shaken. He never knew the details of how Horowitz carried out his assignments, but there had been a case of a car blowing up a hostile director of a company Buckmaster had taken over. And Newman's use of the word 'conspiracy' had rattled him.

He looked round the restaurant where most of the tables were occupied. A short slim man in his thirties sat by himself. Morgan's eyes passed over him. The presence of Marler meant nothing to him.

Within minutes of returning to his room, Newman heard a gentle tapping on his door. It was Marler, wearing a bulky raincoat. Newman told him to sit down, asked if he was going somewhere.

'Yes. Here. From my room.' He slipped off the raincoat, felt inside one of the pockets. 'This was the best way to conceal this.' He produced the special compact camera developed by the boffins in the Engine Room in the Park Crescent basement.

'Handy little gadget,' Marler went on. 'Easy to hide and when you take photographs it develops and prints them within a minute.' He extracted two prints from his breast pocket, perched them on Newman's lap.

'Where did you get these?'

'You weren't the only one up early this morning. I tapped on your door, no answer, so I guessed you'd gone out. I went out myself. I positioned myself where I couldn't be seen but I'd a perfect view of the entrance to the World Security offices down the street. Those are pictures of three men who left or entered the building separately.'

'I see.' Newman masked his puzzlement by studying the three prints. Was Marler cleverly trying to build up

131

confidence? He felt uncertain, but still not sure enough to reveal to the agent Tweed's whereabouts.

Marler, reading his mind, watched him with amusement. Sooner or later he'd gain Newman's trust. He'd no doubt about his ability to do that.

'This one is Gareth Morgan, the man I set out to shake to the core at breakfast,' Newman eventually remarked. 'The other two I don't know. I don't like the look of the tall man with steel-rimmed glasses.'

'Your sixth sense is getting quite good. Keep working at it. You're looking at Armand Horowitz, a Mittel-European, and one of the world's most successful assassins. A real pro, Armand. No suspicion has ever attached itself to him and yet my contacts tell me he's killed at least fifteen men. All for a big fee. And in every case the murder was passed off as an accident.'

'How do you know all this – if he's kept under cover so well?'

'Never believe a word anyone says, do you?'

'Not without positive corroboration. I was an active foreign correspondent once – and noted for reliability.'

Marler sighed. 'All right. Once Tweed sent me underground. I posed as the finest marksman in Europe, for sale only for a monumentally high price. We even built up a "background" for me – I was supposed to have knocked off several top political and industrial figures. I got lucky – I was hired for a job which put me on the inside of a gang of monsters Tweed was after. The man who hired me told me if I'd refused he'd have hired Armand Horowitz.'

'And you think Morgan has hired him to take out a fresh target?'

'Obvious, I'd have thought. His target is Tweed.'

13

Later that day, just before twilight, a carload of four
armed World Security men saw Tweed's BMW leaving
Freiburg, heading south on the E 35 autobahn towards
Switzerland. As the Mercedes began its pursuit, Savage,
the driver, a man in his thirties, gave the order to his
companion in the front passenger seat.

'Warn HQ immediately . . .'

His companion picked up the microphone. They had a
direct radio link on a high-frequency waveband. He gave
the day's call signal.

'Champagne here. Eiger now proceeding south on
E 35. We are escorting. Over and out.'

Listening to the amplified message in the communications complex in the basement of World Security HQ near
the Colombi, Horowitz pursed his thin lips. He had
caught the note of triumph in the operator's voice. Beside
him sat Eva Hendrix.

The large basement room had a clinical appearance,
the walls painted white, the steel tables supporting every
type of sophisticated apparatus. Including the satellite
system for receiving messages from the dish perched on
the building's roof.

'I wonder,' commented Horowitz and stood up.

'What's the matter?' asked Hendrix. 'We've got him.
And you were right – you said you thought Eiger would
head for Switzerland.'

Eiger was the code name Horowitz had given for
Tweed. Hendrix also stood up and slipped on her fur-

lined jacket. She wore underneath it a thick polo-necked sweater, a loose skirt and knee-length boots with flat heels. She guessed Horowitz was ready to leave. They had an Audi waiting for them outside.

'We're joining Savage?' she asked.

'Yes. It's the only thing to do at this stage. I can catch them up on the autobahn.'

Savage pressed his foot down as the Tweed BMW increased speed suddenly. There was a one-hundred-yard gap between the two vehicles and they had the autobahn to themselves. The speedometer on the dashboard of the Mercedes crept up from 140 k.p.h. to above 150 k.p.h. – approximately one hundred miles per hour.

'What's he up to?' asked the passenger in the front seat as he extracted a Luger .45 from his briefcase.

'Trying to shake us. He won't. Get ready. At this speed he'll go clear off the autobahn.'

Savage calculated they were approaching a long wide curve, the ideal spot for the killing ground. And still there was no other traffic on the autobahn. It was the time of day.

The previous day Savage had been behind the wheel of his silver Mercedes driving *ahead* of Tweed minutes before the catastrophic pile-up. Which is why he'd escaped undamaged, even alive. The bones of his lean face were taut with concentration. A tough Geordie from Newcastle, he had his eye on Evans's job. Too soft for this type of work. If he could eliminate Tweed he'd score a lot of Brownie points with Morgan.

'I'm going to close the gap, so be ready,' he warned his companion.

'He's crossing into the next lane? Why?'

'I'm going to close the gap. Get ready, I said . . .'

The man with the Luger pressed the button which

134

lowered his window. Air hammered inside the car like the slipstream of an aircraft taking off. The forearm of the hand holding the Luger rested firmly on the window edge. He took careful aim as the Mercedes rushed forward, the gap closed.

Behind the wheel of the BMW, Newman kept glancing in his rear view mirror. He nodded to Marler by his side.

'They're falling for it. Up to you.'

Marler used the seat retracting lever, pushed himself back to the fullest extent. They were alone in the car. Marler pressed down the arm-rest, began wriggling and squeezing himself through the gap between the two seats. Only a man as small and slim as Marler could have conducted the manoeuvre.

As Marler slithered into the rear of the car Newman increased his speed further, drawing away from the pursuing Mercedes for several seconds. Which distracted the man with the Luger who was about to press the trigger. The range had altered, become too great. He glanced at Savage, but the driver was already stepping up his own speed.

In the rear of the BMW Marler hauled the sniperscope rifle he'd obtained from his friend outside Freiburg from under the travelling rugs. He released the safety catch, lowered the window on the right side. The two cars remained in their different lanes but the gap was again closing.

It was closing because Newman had seen in his mirror that Marler was in position. He had gently lost speed. Even the small reduction in tempo was closing the gap in seconds. Inside the Mercedes Savage smiled thinly. Jerry would wait with his Luger until suddenly they were within yards of the BMW. The gun held eight rounds. Jerry would empty the weapon. At least two shots were bound

135

to find their target. In his mirror he saw another vehicle coming up behind him in the distance, its headlights like two small eyes. To hell with it. They'd be away, long gone before it arrived . . .

Approaching the Mercedes from the rear Horowitz sat in the passenger seat, a pair of night-glasses pressed against his eyes, his steel-rimmed spectacles pushed up over his forehead. Behind the wheel Hendrix was demonstrating that when a woman driver is good she's very good.

Horowitz lowered his binoculars, sat relaxed with them in his lap. Hendrix glanced at him.

'What's going to happen?'

'Exactly what I am wondering.'

She didn't say any more. Horowitz was not a man you questioned. She always had the impression of iron self-control. And he could spend hours travelling with some-one without saying one word. She could read nothing from his expression. Suddenly he leaned forward. She had a sensation of intense concentration. He spoke tersely.

'Drive a little faster. But keep a good distance behind that Mercedes.'

Inside the BMW Marler had kept the barrel out of sight below the level of the window. He looped the strap round the handle of the door to give maximum stability. The Mercedes was rushing towards them like a torpedo. The Luger was fired twice. There was no chance to fire it a third time.

Marler raised the muzzle, the front right tyre of the Mercedes leapt into his sight, he fired four times. Two of the high explosive bullets he'd fed into the rifle hit their mark. The target wheel unsheathed lengths of rubber, scattered them over the snowbound highway. Savage felt the car going out of control, slithering into a lethal skid, compounded by the speed at which he was travelling. The

Mercedes skated across the autobahn, swivelling in a half-circle. The rear struck the crash barrier with immense force, smashed through it and then the vehicle turned over and over on its sides, rolling across a field. It was slowing down when it burst into flames, became a fireball, lighting up the night like a small bomb detonating.

Black oily smoke rose from the funeral pyre as Newman continued to drive on. Marler reloaded the rifle after closing the window. He lit one of his king-size cigarettes.

'Good shooting,' Newman observed.

'Fair to middling. I suspect only two out of four hit the mark. It should have been at least three . . .'

'Well, you saved us. I'm taking the next turn-off, returning to Freiburg.'

'Jolly good idea. I'm getting a bit peckish.'

'That was horrible,' Eva Hendrix gasped as she slowed down, worried about skid-marks as they passed the fireball.

'It was worse. It was amateurish,' Horowitz commented. 'I find it pathetic. They *will* send boys to do men's work. And keep your speed as it is – I'm watching the northbound lane.'

She glanced at him again and he sat with his back pressed hard against his seat. He was holding the night glasses close to his eyes again, scanning the empty northbound lanes of the autobahn.

'Expecting something?' she asked, then wished she hadn't spoken.

'Yes,' Horowitz replied simply.

Several cars skimmed past on the northbound lanes. Horowitz scanned the registration numbers of each car which was a BMW. About ten minutes later he grunted as a pair of headlights appeared and sped towards them. The

137

registration number came up clearly. Two men in the car. One driving, one smoking in the back. Neither of them Tweed. Of course. The car raced past, was gone.

'Take the next turn-off. Then drive us back to Freiburg. You can press your dainty foot down,' Horowitz suggested.

'What's happening? Where's Tweed?'

'If I were Tweed I'd have gone only one way. East out of Freiburg into the Black Forest. And Evans will have called off the watchdogs at the Freiburg exits. Another amateur . . .'

It gave Horowitz no pleasure to find he was right when they'd arrived back at World Security HQ on Rotteck Ring. Evans explained as he poured drinks in his office for Hendrix and himself.

'Once I had the report the BMW had been spotted I called in the operatives from the other exit points. The cost of running a total lookout like that is considerable. All those involved are on overtime. And we've been ordered to cut costs.'

'By whom, if I may enquire? No, nothing for me,' Horowitz remarked when offered a drink.

'By Morgan. Nothing else you require, I imagine? I gather Savage is continuing to track Eiger? We've had no radio report from him for a while.'

Horowitz gave Hendrix a warning glance. Keep your mouth shut. Let Evans find out another of his teams was *kaput* in due course. Maybe he'd have to talk fast to the police. That was what he was paid for.

'Where is Morgan now?' he enquired.

'Pushed off back to London, didn't he? Flew there in the Lear jet from Freiburg. Went as though the hounds of hell were after him.'

'Maybe he felt they were.'

138

It was a relief to Horowitz to hear Morgan was hundreds of miles away. Now perhaps he could do the job he'd been paid for without interruption. He stared at Evans who was consuming a large Scotch. These people drank too much.

'You asked if there was anything else I required,' he reminded him. 'Yes, there is. I need five of your German shepherd tracker dogs. With German handlers. The fiercer the better. I want them now. Plus an unmarked wired van to transport them.'

'That would leave me without guard dogs,' Evans protested. 'I have only five left in reserve. The rest are hired out . . .'

'I said I needed five. So that's fine.' Horowitz was still gazing at Evans whose eyes dropped. 'I understood that Morgan had told you to supply me with anything I wanted.'

'That's correct, but I didn't expect to be left without any dogs. We've quoted for a contract which includes those animals . . .'

'Then you'd better inform your potential customer he'll have to do without guard dogs.'

'And I have no unmarked van with a wired compartment left,' Evans informed him with scarcely concealed satisfaction.

'Go and buy one. A station wagon. Preferably a Volvo. And get your technical department to build a wire cage in the rear compartment for the dogs. I'll need the vehicle ready five hours from now.' He saw Evans open his mouth to protest. His tone became cold. 'Do I have to tell you how to fulfil a simple request like that quickly? You're supposed to hold down your job because you're effective.'

Evans's ruddy face became redder still. He sat behind his desk, picked up the phone and gave the instructions in German. He told the man he was speaking to he needed

139

the vehicle ready in four hours, slammed down the phone.

'That's better,' Horowitz commented softly. 'Now I want you to take Hendrix and myself to that side office overlooking the operations room. The office with a one-way mirror so we can watch.'

'And what precisely would you like to watch?' Evans snapped.

Horowitz continued as though he hadn't heard the interruption.

'Assemble in the operations room all the men who were watching the other exits from Freiburg – all except those checking the one Eiger left by. You had a large-scale map to control the operation? Good. Put that on a wall where I can see it from the one-way mirror window. What time did Savage report in on his radio that he'd spotted Tweed's BMW leaving, that he was starting to follow the vehicle?'

'At exactly 4.15 p.m.'

'Thank you. When you have assembled all the watchers, find out the times they left their exits. In which sequence. There'd be a few minutes' delay between one radio message being transmitted and the next.'

'I'll have to call some of them back. They'll have gone off duty . . .'

'Then call them back.'

'I don't see what you're getting at,' Hendrix ventured as she sat down inside the office next to the operations room with another glass of vodka.

Horowitz stood, hands in his coat pocket, staring through the 'window' which had a mirror on the other side, making it impossible for the men gathering in the operations room to see him. On the table where Hendrix sat was perched a two-way microphone which would enable Horowitz to communicate with Evans when the conference started.

'The whole thing was a cock-up,' he said, standing with his back to Hendrix. 'Cobbled together without proper research and planning. It was Tweed who did the planning. Neither of the two men in that BMW we saw speeding back up the north lane to Freiburg was Tweed. The key time is 4.15 p.m.'

'I still don't get it . . .'

'And neither does Evans, I'm sure,' Horowitz said sardonically. 'I'm certain now that there was synchronization of watches between Tweed and the two men in the BMW. Timed to the minute – so when the BMW was spotted leaving Freiburg by Savage – and reported to this operations room – Tweed drove out of Freiburg ten minutes later at the outside.'

'But which way?'

'That is what I am attempting to discover. The vital time span is approximately 4.15 p.m. to 4.25 p.m. – say 4.30 p.m. at the latest. We have to hope one of those watchers was observant even after he'd heard the bird had flown. And I must remind Evans of something else . . .'

He walked back to the table with his deliberate tread, picked up the microphone, pressed the switch and spoke to Evans who stood looking at the enlarged wall map of Freiburg while operatives entered and sat in the rows of chairs facing the wall.

'Evans,' Horowitz said into the mike, 'you haven't forgotten the screen for projecting the target's picture?'

'It's being brought in at this moment,' Evans responded in a terse edgy tone.

'Show it first when everyone is seated, please . . .'

The lights in the operations room went out as Horowitz began speaking. The twenty operatives, all men, stirred restlessly. The amplifier added a curiously sinister, eerie tone to Horowitz's voice. The projectionist flashed

Tweed's picture on the screen. A head-and-shoulders three-quarter view, his face in repose. Horowitz spoke again, still standing, holding the mike close to his lips which distorted his speech to a sibilant hiss.

'All of you were waiting at your designated exits from Freiburg. You were on the lookout for this man, Eiger, travelling in a BMW with a specific registration number.' Horowitz paused.

From where he stood he saw rows of the backs of heads tilted upwards, staring fixedly at the screen. The projectionist was holding the image of Tweed steady. Horowitz waited, hoping the image imprinted on their minds would trigger off a memory. He continued speaking.

'I want you to wipe out of your minds any thought of that BMW. The vital time is between 4.15 p.m. and 4.30 p.m. – the period when you were being released from duty, no longer on the lookout. But even as you waited, maybe smoked a cigarette before returning to base, you subconsciously saw another car.'

He paused again, allowing them to soak up each statement before adding further data to their minds. He spoke again. His voice had an almost hypnotic effect on his audience as they sat motionless.

'Another car, but a different make. Not a BMW. Probably not a Mercedes. And inside that car was Eiger, the man who you see now on the screen. Think back, gentlemen. Please concentrate.'

'I just drove straight back to HQ,' a voice reported.

'At what time?' Horowitz demanded.

'At exactly 4.20 p.m. when I received the order over the radio to abandon surveillance.'

'One of you may well have seen this man,' Horowitz persisted. 'He could have been dressed in any garb. Maybe he wore some kind of headgear to change his appearance . . .'

'An astrakhan fur hat,' another voice called out

142

excitedly. 'That's what he wore. I thought the features were familiar.'

'Where did you see him? What vehicle was he driving?'

'A blue Audi. I was stationed at the Schwabentor, at the edge of the Altstadt. He came from the direction of the Konvikstrasse and turned away from the city along the Schwarzwaldstrasse. I'm sorry, but at the time the fur hats fooled me. In any case, we'd been called off duty, so I guessed someone else had picked him up.'

'No need to apologize. Have you any idea of the time when you made that sighting?'

'I can tell you exactly. It was 4.30 p.m. – I monitored it for the record. The radio signal had just come through to return to base.'

'You used the word "hats" – in the plural. Why?' Horowitz prodded gently.

'Because the girl sitting beside him also wore a fur hat.'

'Thank you for your help, gentlemen. That is all for now.'

Horowitz switched off the microphone and turned to Hendrix who had just finished her vodka.

'If you need another drink, make it coffee. We want clear heads for tonight.'

'Tonight?' she asked. 'That sounds like no sleep.'

'I don't need sleep.' Horowitz sat down opposite her and made a clenched fist gesture. 'It all fits. As I suspected, Tweed did the planning. He foresaw all the exits would be watched. He handed over his BMW to two other men and it acted as the decoy vehicle. At 4.15 p.m. It leaves Freiburg and drives south down the E 35 autobahn. Savage reports he has tabbed it. Evans falls for the trick, calls off all other watchers one by one. Fifteen minutes later Tweed is driving the new vehicle he has hired – an Audi – out of the city. Everything was carefully synchronized by Tweed. He calculated radio cars would be used, that within fifteen minutes other exits would be left unguarded. Even the route he took is significant.'

'Why?' Hendrix asked.

'Because he is heading for where I would head for if I were in his position. Along the Schwarzwaldstrasse – and then deep into the heart of the snowbound Black Forest. We must get on his trail quickly . . .'

Horowitz was walking to the door when Hendrix asked her question.

'But how do we go about it? The Black Forest is enormous – and the snow won't help.'

'The snow *will* help,' Horowitz rasped, showing the first signs of impatience with a mind slower than his own. 'We have one helicopter here. We will bring in more from Frankfurt, from Basle. We will scour the Black Forest from the air. And the snow may well locate Tweed because it will reveal tracks – the tracks of an Audi turning up a side road into the trees, the foot tracks of Tweed and his friend when they leave the Audi to seek shelter. According to the met forecast – which you heard yourself before we came down into the basement – all the roads south from the forest to Switzerland are impassable. I would appreciate it if you would move fast . . .'

'But what are we going to do?' she persisted as she followed him with quick footsteps.

He turned at the bottom of the stairs.

'We are going to ensure Evans provides tracker dogs which are killers. We shall travel in the Volvo with radio contact to all the choppers searching through the night. Must I spell it out in words of two syllables? We are organizing a vast dragnet, a manhunt.'

144

14

Gareth Morgan's Lear jet landed at London Airport early in the evening. He was amiable with Customs and Passport Control and they passed him through quickly. His mood changed as he settled himself in the rear of the waiting limousine and told the chauffeur, Hanson, to make all speed to HQ in Threadneedle Street.

'Those officials get on my wick. They know me but still I have to go through their bureaucratic formalities. Put a man in a uniform and he thinks he's God.'

'Yes, sir,' responded the uniformed chauffeur. Typical of Morgan to overlook the implied insult. But it was Morgan who paid him a fat bonus every Christmas in cash out of subsidiary research. Which meant the money was never accounted for – and that Hanson didn't declare the two thousand pounds for tax.

'What's been going on in my absence?' Morgan demanded of his private spy.

He stared out into the night. It was dry, cold and the sky was studded with huge diamonds. Oncoming headlights had an unusual clarity and power. Morgan lit a Havana while he absorbed the chauffeur's confidential report.

'Mrs Buckmaster has been spending a lot of time in her office checking various files . . .'

'What files?'

Morgan was instantly alert. He leaned forward over his now noticeable paunch. The doctor had said he ate too much and drank to excess. Stuff him!

'Well, sir, I used the duplicate key you had made for me to Mrs Buckmaster's office when she was out to lunch recently. Her desk was covered with files from our companies all over the world. Australia, America, South Africa, various countries in Western Europe. They were full of columns of figures. I took the liberty to use the camera you gave me to photograph some of the pages at random.' The chauffeur handed over his shoulder a plastic box. 'You could see for yourself on the scanner . . .'

Morgan prised off the lid with one hand, clenched the cigar between his teeth, took out the first cut film and inserted it inside the scanner attached to the roof of the rear compartment. He switched on the light, adjusted the focus, turning a small wheel. The figures on the page came up clearly.

He inserted a dozen pages, aware that Hanson was watching his expression in the rear-view mirror. He let nothing of his sense of shock show, but when the last page came up he swore to himself.

'Something wrong, sir?' enquired the chauffeur who had acute hearing.

Hanson was in his late forties. A good-looking man, his voice well-educated, he'd taken on this job after a chance meeting with Morgan in a bar. An excellent driver, he lacked application and had failed to pursue his studies to become an accountant. But he still had the ability to read a balance sheet.

'You looked at these?' Morgan asked in a mild voice.

'Had to, sir – to make sure they'd come out well. Not all of them, but they make interesting reading, I thought. Oh, if you could see your way to increasing my bonus this year. What with inflation, and the mortgage interest payments . . .'

'Consider it done.'

'That's very generous of you, sir.'

Hanson smirked in the mirror and Morgan had an

almost uncontrollable desire to hit him hard. It wasn't the fact that Hanson was driving – although at that moment they were stopped in a traffic jam – which forced Morgan to smile back. He recognized immediately that Hanson had grasped the significance of what he had photographed.

'Not at all.' Morgan smiled again, an oily smile.'You are a great asset to the company. Merit should be rewarded.'

Today's friends are tomorrow's enemies, he reminded himself. One of his favourite maxims. Only trust people for as long as it is in your interests to trust them. Soon he would have to dispose of Hanson. But in a way which rendered him neutered as a potential hostile force. Well, he'd managed that more times than he could add up. He smiled and nodded to Hanson as the car moved again.

'There is one other thing, sir,' Hanson continued, satisfied that he'd made his point about the bonus. 'Mrs Buckmaster has been closeted for hours with Ted Doyle. I don't mean anything naughty,' he added with exaggerated respect.

'Any idea what they've been doing?'

Morgan made his tone casual. He stared out of the window to avoid meeting Hanson's eyes in the mirror, showing too eager an interest. And Hanson was now definitely for the chop – he'd held back this juicy bit until he was sure Morgan would play along on the bonus issue. Which amounted to a devious form of blackmail, the kind of tactic Morgan used on others. He was furious a mere chauffeur should hold him up.

'I've had to take in sandwiches and coffee several times,' Hanson continued. 'Doyle was sitting alongside Mrs Buckmaster at her desk. They had a lot of leather-bound ledgers in different colours in front of them.'

'Doesn't tell me much, Morgan commented. 'Get to HQ fast as you can . . .'

The information told him a great deal and he was even more furious. Leonora had obtained the top secret ledgers showing the financial position of major World Security offices all over the world. And Doyle, who should have kept them hidden, was cooperating with her. Doubtless angling for a seat on the board.

It never occurred to Morgan that Doyle might be honestly worried about the position of Lance Buckmaster's empire. Honesty was a motive foreign to Morgan's way of thinking.

It was nearly 8 p.m. when Hanson drove down Threadneedle Street. No traffic about. Morgan craned his neck to look up at the eighteenth floor. It was a blaze of lights. He frowned. Could Leonora still be in her chairman's office at this hour?

Alighting from the limousine in the underground garage, he told Hanson to wait. Using his special key, he inserted it into the slot beside the elevator. Within seconds the high-speed elevator arrived. He stopped inside, pressed the button, got out at the eighteenth floor and paused as the doors closed behind him. He'd left his case in the car and stood there in his dark overcoat, listening. The silence of an almost empty building at night hit him. He headed for Leonora's office.

He had almost reached the suite when the door opened, Ted Doyle walked out, carrying a red leather-bound ledger, closed it and looked up in a surprise as Morgan waited for him a dozen feet from the sound-proof door.

'Mr Morgan! I had no idea you were due back . . .'

'I guessed that.' Morgan took hold of the red ledger, pulled it from Doyle's grasp, tucked it under his arm. 'What are you doing with this in my absence?'

148

Doyle was a tall, lanky man in his thirties with a lean, clever face and pebble glasses. A top flight accountant and the man Morgan had on his agenda for dismissal under a cloud when the right opportunity occurred. Something to do with money missing and fiddling the figures was needed. Doyle had to be discredited to the outside world when he left. The fact that this would ruin him never crossed Morgan's mind. The world was a jungle; survival of the fittest, the most ruthless, the only law.

'Simply casting an eye over some figures,' Doyle replied.

'Nice to know someone is holding the fort.' Morgan smiled, patted the accountant on the shoulder with his free hand. 'I'll hang on to this for the moment.'

He was walking away when he turned back.

'Oh, Doyle, I may want to chat with you later this evening. So maybe you could wait for me in your office? Get some food sent in to stay the pangs of hunger.'

He smiled again and unlocked the door of his own office. Once inside his expression became grim. Something drastic had to be done about Ted Doyle. And soon. He locked the ledger in his desk after studying at it.

Taking off his coat, he went into his private washroom, cleaned himself up, brushed his thick dark hair, buttoned up his jacket and left his office. He walked slowly towards Leonora's suite. Outside the closed entrance door the red light glowed. *No admittance. In conference.* That had been while she was talking to Doyle. He tapped on the door. The light turned green. He walked inside.

Leonora Buckmaster sat behind her large desk facing him. She sat very erect. The only illumination, a desk light, caught the golden glints in her blonde hair. Her expression was cold and frozen. She gave no sign of being glad to see her managing director. Open in front of her was a green ledger.

'What are you doing here at this hour?' she asked.

Morgan gave her his best smile. 'Just back from touring some of the European offices. Came straight here from the airport.'

'Did you by any chance examine the books at these European offices?'

'I didn't go there for that. I was checking on the latest contracts.'

Including, he thought, the contract with Horowitz to kill Tweed.

'You do know we're pretty near bankrupt?'

It was Morgan's turn to freeze. Inwardly he cursed Doyle for cooperating in his absence. Her statement – the fact that she now knew – was a body blow. He managed to look surprised and pulled a chair up to face her.

'No, I don't know anything of the sort, Leonora. Has that crazy accountant been misinterpreting the figures again?'

'The figures speak for themselves. My father did teach me to read balance sheets – even doctored ones.'

'So, Doyle has been fooling around with the figures . . .'

'Doyle has been showing me the position here, in Australia, the States, in South Africa – and Western Europe.'

'But then he doesn't know about the loan for five hundred mil I'm negotiating. Kind of changes the picture, wouldn't you agree? May I smoke a cigar?'

She was so stunned she didn't object. He clipped off the end, took his time about lighting the cigar with a match, running it round the tip. A display of supreme confidence.

'And may I ask where this gigantic loan is coming from? The banks won't lend us one more red cent. That I *do* know. So what is the source of this loan?'

150

'You will learn in due course. Part of the deal is complete confidentiality . . .'

'It was my money which started this company . . .' Leonora took a deep breath. She had been going to add that she now thought that was why Lance had married her. But she detested Morgan and had no intention of exposing her private life to him. She had successfully concealed her intense dislike of Morgan and forced herself to relax.

Morgan puffed at his cigar. He sensed he had her over a barrel. Once again he'd played his cards right. The ironic factor in the situation was that Morgan had no idea where the loan was coming from. That was something Buckmaster had not revealed during their conversation at Tavey Grange. Morgan's innate cunning caused him to phrase the next phase of their conversation carefully.

'Fortunately we have a brilliant accountant in Ted Doyle. I'm sure he realizes the present problem and will be discreet.'

'I'm sure of it too.' Leonora played with her gold pen. 'Ted is a loyal member of the company. I trust him completely.'

Morgan nodded to conceal the shock he felt. She had just confirmed that Doyle knew World Security was heading for the rocks. Very drastic action would have to be taken. There was now the risk that Doyle would confide in one of his City friends. If he did, that was the end of World Security.

'If there's nothing else to discuss, I think I'll go back to my office, just glance over what came in while I was away. Then I'm off home for some sleep – something I didn't get much of while I was abroad.'

'Those trips are tiring,' Leonora agreed and smiled. 'You push yourself too hard, Gareth. Try to pace yourself a bit.'

'You're probably right.' Morgan held his cigar in his

hand as he stood up, walked round the desk and kissed her on the cheek. She endured his closeness without flinching. 'And maybe you should go home,' he suggested as he walked towards the door.

'I think you're right. It's getting late.'

As Morgan closed the door her pleasant expression changed. I must find a way to dump him overboard, she thought. She was the chairman, after all, she considered as she opened her compact and dabbed on powder furiously where Morgan had kissed her. She slipped on her sable while she continued turning over the problem in her mind.

The trouble was Lance had appointed Morgan as managing director, and Morgan – the son of a coal-miner – had helped to build up World Security from nothing. He knew the organization inside out, including the Industrial Research Division, which he directed personally. She had heard disturbing rumours about that Division which had a secret section inside every HQ across the face of the earth.

I'll talk some more with Ted Doyle, she decided as she checked the contents of her Ferragamo handbag. And we'll look at the red master ledger again. She went to the door, switched off the lights and headed for the private elevator to which only three people had a key – herself, Lance and Morgan.

It always gave her the shivers, leaving the eerily silent and deserted building late in the evening. Her footfalls echoed along the marble-tiled floor. She stood in front of the private elevator, pausing before inserting the key.

She had the uncanny feeling she was being watched. But there was no light under the door leading to Morgan's suite of offices behind her. Staring at the closed elevator door she wondered again whether this wasn't a loophole in security. The elevator could bypass all floors, ending up in the underground garage. She would pass no security guard before getting into her car. When she had pointed this out to Morgan he had dismissed her fears as groundless, reminding her only three top people had a key. She inserted hers, stepped inside when the doors had opened, pressed the button for the garage.

Morgan's right eye was pressed against the spyhole in his door. He squinted like a voyeur at Leonora's legs below her hip-length sable jacket. He'd been waiting for her to leave for ten minutes. She seemed to take for ever before she operated the key and disappeared inside the elevator. He sighed with relief, wiped sweat off his forehead with his handkerchief, switched on his office lights.

He sat for ten minutes behind his desk, quenching his thirst with slugs of cognac from his hip flask while he skimmed through the red master ledger. He couldn't imagine how Doyle could have got hold of it. In his absence the ledger was stored in a special compartment in the vault and he alone had the combination to open it in his head.

Well, there was one person who could enlighten him. And that was the only other person in the building above the ground floor where the security guards watched the main and rear entrances. Ted Doyle.

Hugging the ledger across his broad chest, he walked out of his office and down the long corridor to the room at the far end. He opened the door without knocking. Doyle, seated behind his desk, studying a file, looked up. There was a carton of sandwiches on the desk, another containing coffee. Both were untouched.

'I have been talking about you with Leonora,' Morgan began as he sat in the leather chair facing the accountant. 'I don't think it's too long before you'll be invited to take a seat on the main board.' He smiled, still hugging the ledger.

'That's very gratifying, Mr Morgan.' Doyle peered at

him through the pebble glasses. 'I take it you've been talking things over with Mrs Buckmaster.'

'Exactly.' Morgan's small eyes gleamed with satisfaction. Doyle had gained the wrong impression as planned – that Morgan had been discussing the contents of the master ledger with the chairman. 'One point I omitted to ask her. How did you get access to this ledger when I was the only one who knew the combination?'

'Oh, I see what you mean.' Doyle relaxed, leaning back in his chair. 'She raised the point that there must be a master ledger. I told her where it was kept but only you knew the combination. She very much wanted to see it. So I got her to sign an authorization and we brought in an expert at opening safes. Had to tell him a fib, that we'd lost the bit of paper with the combination on it. With her signature he had no hesitation in opening it for us . . .'

A wave of fury swept through Morgan. He managed to smile and conceal his rage. Doyle had been too clever by half. He had become a more dangerous and immediate menace than Morgan had suspected. Very drastic measures were called for. He checked his watch.

'We actually discussed your joining us on the board in depth. There are one or two questions I'd like to ask. Then, you know me – once I've decided I like to get on with it right away. But would you wait until I get back? I have a call expected in five minutes from New York. You don't mind waiting?'

He smiled again, stood up and padded towards the door. That should hold Doyle in his office for hours if necessary. Back in his own lair he took a deep breath, then picked up the telephone.

Leonora lay in her bed alone in the Belgravia apartment fast asleep when a sound woke her. She sat up, switched on the bedside light. 2 a.m. Oh, Christ!

154

Sleeping by herself was her way of putting pressure on Lance. She had moved into her own bedroom when detectives had reported Lance was seeing his sixth girl friend, a tart of a German girl from Frankfurt. It was the only method she could think of bringing him to heel. His reaction had been disappointing when she informed him of her intention.

'I've decided I want to sleep in the guest room. It will help me to sort things out in my mind.'

'Fair enough.' He'd grinned, waved a dismissive hand. 'You need your beauty sleep and I'm often late dealing with those infernal boxes. Good idea. Then I won't have the added worry of waking you up.'

'Oh, you have other worries?' she'd asked sarcastically.

'Loads of them, darling. Organizing a new Ministry is hardly child's play.'

'I thought you'd done that by now . . .'

'Only just beginning,' he had replied and walked off to the main bedroom.

She heard a creak of wood in the corridor outside. Gathering up her dressing-gown, she threw it on, picked up a heavy silver candlestick and tiptoed to the door. She opened it quietly and stared at Lance creeping towards the main bedroom. He wore his military-style raincoat and there was a hint of moisture on the cloth. He turned as he heard her opening the door.

'Did she keep you up late?' she enquired.

His reaction startled her. He strode towards her, his face distorted with fury. She stepped back a pace and he stood in front of her.

'Don't worry – I'm not coming in there. I thought the idea was you could get some sleep on your own.' His voice rose. 'Do you have to pry into every minute of my bloody life? Have you still no idea of what it means to be a Minister, for God's sake? The hours I have to work? And when you decided to move in here my life became

155

my own.' He paused, his facial muscles working. His tone become cold, arrogant. 'Also don't forget how you savour the reflected glory of being the wife of a Cabinet Minister . . .'

He reached forward, grabbed the handle of the door, slammed it shut with his wife still inside the room. She was trembling. Lance was very fit, very strong. He could have felled her with one blow. She locked the door, went back to bed and lay awake until just before dawn.

At precisely 4 a.m. a patrolling policeman found the body of Ted Doyle sprawled on the sidewalk below his office window eighteen storeys above the corpse.

15

At 6 a.m. Chief Inspector Roy Buchanan of the Homicide Squad stood bent over the slumped figure of Ted Doyle. The skull had been crushed from the immense impact of the fall. Buchanan, a slim man in his forties with a quiet, cynical manner, forced himself to concentrate, to observe by the beams of the flashlights held by detectives. The pathologist, Dr Kersey, stooped alongside the chief inspector, his bag resting on the sidewalk.

'Did he fall or was he pushed or did he jump?' Buchanan commented as he straightened and stared up at the light streaming from the open window on the eighteenth floor. 'That's what it comes to, wouldn't you agree?'

'Gives you plenty of options,' Kersey observed. 'Maybe the clue is up there.'

He gestured upwards and Buchanan crossed the street to get a clearer view of the high window. Not that the different angle helped him at all. He was trying to calculate the angle of a body falling from that height. So far as he could tell it would naturally have hit the outer edge of the wide sidewalk. Exactly as it had done, in fact.

The night guard on duty near the ground floor entrance opened up the building for the Scotland Yard team. Following Buchanan they all crowded into the elevator – Forensic, the fingerprint men, photographers – all the apparatus of trained personnel who spent part of their lives attending the death of men and women they'd never heard of before. It made for a certain outward appearance of callousness, which was really no more than professionalism.

The guard showed Buchanan and his younger assistant, Sergeant Warden, into Doyle's office. Buchanan restrained the guard from entering with a gentle hand on his arm.

'You can leave it to us now. No one else in the building. Only two guards? Tell them to wait until I've interviewed them. Yourself, too, please. Pop off downstairs now.'

'Window wide open,' Buchanan commented as they entered the office. 'Light still on. Everything normal, what I'd have expected. So far.'

'There's a note in that typewriter,' Warden observed.

Both men wore rubber gloves. Buchanan walked slowly across to the machine, his eyes scanning the carpeted floor. He stood looking down at the typed sheet.

No way I can pay my gambling debts. Pressure has become unbearable. Only one way out. Ted Doyle.

'Seems we have everything,' Warden remarked. 'You make a habit of visiting a gambling club. You get in too deep, can't pay your debts. They send along the heavies to persuade you it's serious. You're trapped and decide to end it all.'

'Except we don't know yet that he did gamble,' Buchanan replied. 'And there's something odd about that note. Name typed, not signed in Doyle's hand.'

'We've seen that before,' the phlegmatic Warden recalled.

'But it's all just a little too perfect. Call it sixth sense.'

Buchanan wandered over to the window, examined the ledge which was wide and damp with the drizzle which had fallen since midnight. He'd noticed Doyle's grey suit had been damp. The ledge was clean, no sign of foot-marks, but again he'd observed Doyle had been wearing rubber-soled shoes without a trace of dirt. So he wouldn't expect to find footmark traces.

Supporting himself with one hand, he stared down into the abyss. Plain-clothes men with torches were moving round the corpse. Several flashbulbs exploded, pinpoints of light from that height. Buchanan gritted his teeth: he suffered from vertigo. He turned back into the office to speak to Warden.

'Make sure the fingerprint boys check the keys of that typewriter. And I'd like them to pay particular attention to the edges of the window frame. All against Doyle's fingerprints, of course.'

'Of course . . .'

'And have you found out who is in charge of this organization – as I asked you on the way here?'

'Yes, sir. It came through on the radio while you were on your way into the building before I caught you up. Gareth Morgan is managing director, has a house in Wandsworth. The chairman is something else again – Leonora Buckmaster, wife of Lance Buckmaster, Minister for External Security. She lives in Belgravia. The press could make something big of this.'

158

'Oh, I don't know. They're obsessed with that earthquake which just hit the Soviet Union. I think I'd like to see this Gareth Morgan first. See if you can contact him. Just say a tragedy has occurred at the World Security building and we'd appreciate his presence.'

'Consider it done.'

Warden was walking out to find a phone in another office when Buchanan called after him. 'And the pack can come in here and start their ministrations. I'll wait for Morgan.' Buchanan beckoned to Dr Kersey who had appeared in the doorway, holding his bag.

'The body is on the way to the mortuary,' Kersey informed him. 'You'll want my PM report in due course . . .'

'Yesterday would do nicely.'

'I'll be on my way then . . .'

'Just before you go, Tom. You've seen the corpse. Just for once I'd like you to give me an idea when Doyle died. Off the top of your head.'

'You know I never guess.' Kersey, a portly red-faced man in his fifties, shook his head. 'After the PM I'll know . . .'

'It would help me enormously at this stage of the investigation if I had *some* idea.' Buchanan clasped his gloved hands lightly together. 'No one's asking you to commit yourself.'

'At a wild guess, between midnight and 2 a.m. from the state of Doyle. And that *is* subject to my PM. Yesterday, I think you said. I'd better be going, hadn't I?'

At 7.30 a.m. Gareth Morgan stepped out of the limousine driven by Hanson, showed his identity folder to the uniformed policeman on duty, and walked across the wide marble floor to the private elevator, key in hand.

Sitting beside the security guard, Buchanan observed

him with care. He always attached importance to his first sight of a witness. Jumping up, he joined Morgan as the managing director inserted the key.

'Chief Inspector Buchanan. In charge of this investigation,' he introduced himself.

Morgan let go of the key and stared up at the tall man beside him. His small eyes gazed straight at Buchanan's grey ones which had a remote look.

'Then perhaps you can tell me why I've been summoned here at this hour? All I got out of Sergeant Warden on the phone was a tragedy had occurred. What tragedy? And would it be possible to replace that uniformed policeman with a plain-clothes detective on duty at the front? It's bad publicity for the top security organization in the world to have the police on view. I'd appreciate the consideration.'

Morgan was unsmiling but his expression relaxed as he made his plea. Buchanan nodded, asked him to wait a moment, went and gave instructions for a more anonymous replacement, came back to the elevator.

'This is an executives-only elevator?' he enquired.

'Yes. Only two people have keys. Myself and the chairman.' He turned the key, the door opened and they stepped inside. 'You haven't answered my question,' Morgan persisted as the elevator shot up to the eighteenth floor.

'I see this elevator goes to the basement,' Buchanan replied.

'To the underground garage. We're often in a hurry to get away, to catch a plane. This is an international organization.'

'I'm aware of that, Mr Morgan. I also noticed there were no lights above the doors, indicating the position of this elevator. Presumably the security guard on duty behind his desk at ground floor level has no knowledge of anyone arriving by or leaving by this special elevator?'

160

'His bank of TV monitors doesn't include the garage,' Morgan replied shortly. 'Now will you please tell me who is involved in this so-called tragedy.'

'Oh, it was a tragedy all right for the person involved. Maybe we could go to your office where we can talk in private.'

They had stepped out on the eighteenth floor as Buchanan made his suggestion. He nodded to Warden, standing outside Doyle's office, to join them.

'That is where I'm taking you,' Morgan snapped, opening the door to his office suite. He paused as he saw Warden, wooden-faced, stop alongside Buchanan. 'I thought you said you wanted a private talk.'

'This is my assistant, Sergeant Warden, who will also be present at the interview . . .'

They stood while Morgan took off his black overcoat, checked his appearance in a wall mirror and went behind his desk. He gestured and Buchanan noticed the short thick hand with nails trimmed short. A man possessed of considerable physical power.

'Sit down, gentlemen. Tell me what's happened,' Morgan began.

'I regret I have to tell you that early this morning your chief accountant, Ted Doyle, was found dead on the sidewalk below his open office window.'

Buchanan sat in a relaxed position in his chair, his long legs crossed. His deceptively sleepy eyes watched Morgan for his reaction. The managing director spread his hands.

'This is terrible news. Doyle has worked for us for ten years. What do you mean he was found dead on the sidewalk? A heart attack?'

'Hardly. Perhaps I didn't explain myself too well. His body had fallen eighteen storeys – apparently from his office window.'

'You mean he slipped out of the window?'

'Again, that's hardly likely. You must know his office.

161

Even if he was drunk he would have had to climb up to reach the outside ledge, which is very wide. Did he drink?'

Warden kept his face expressionless with an effort. The cat-and-mouse interrogation was typical of Buchanan. He extracted information like a skilled Queen's Counsel. Morgan opened a box on the table, selected a cigar, clipped off the end and lit it.

'To the best of my knowledge he did not *drink*,' he replied eventually. 'I find all this very upsetting.'

'You look upset.' Buchanan paused and Morgan glanced at him quickly. He had detected the note of irony in the remark. Warden was becoming intrigued: he began to think Buchanan was facing a worthwhile antagonist. 'And', his chief continued, 'I noticed the emphasis you laid on the word "drink". Had Mr Doyle other vices then?'

'We all have something. I expect you have.' Morgan waved his cigar. 'I smoke. You're beginning to make me think poor Doyle committed suicide.'

Buchanan thrust his hands inside his trouser pockets. 'May I ask what gave you that idea?'

'Logic. You pooh-poohed the idea that it was an accident. So naturally – much as I dislike the idea – suicide is the natural alternative.'

'Had Doyle other vices?' Buchanan repeated.

'Well . . .' Morgan hesitated, took several puffs at his cigar, 'I hate to say it, but I had reason to suspect he was a gambler. Very keen on the ponies. Horse-racing.'

'May I ask how you found that out? Not a very desirable pastime for a chief accountant, I'd have thought.'

'I first got the idea into my head about two months ago. I was working here on a Saturday and called him at home to ask about some figures. He seemed irritated and impatient. In the background I could hear the TV going – with a racing commentary.'

162

'Not a lot to go on to jump to the conclusion you did. How many other people like racing, watch it on TV, and never lay a bet in their lives.'

'Exactly the same thing happened on two other Saturdays. I admit the third time I made up a reason for calling him just to see whether it was every Saturday. He always refused to work on Saturdays when we were under pressure. Sundays, yes. Saturdays, no.'

'Still not conclusive, Mr Morgan . . .'

'But what happened last night made me feel pretty certain I was right. And you remarked that it wasn't a very desirable pastime for a chief accountant. You must understand that Doyle had no access to large sums of money. All major cheques here have to be signed either by myself or Mrs Buckmaster, the chairman. Also, the title of chief accountant was really a reward for faithful service. We have a finance director, Axel Moser, who handles the main financial problems. He's in Australia at the moment.'

'What did happen last night?'

Morgan hesitated again, pursed his lips as though reluctant to blacken the name of a dead colleague. 'He asked me for a loan of two thousand pounds in cash. Said it was for the interest on his mortgage. I refused his request point-blank. I guessed its real purpose was to bet on the gee-gees.'

'How did he take your refusal?'

'Rather badly. Said the sum meant nothing to a company our size . . .'

'You had a row then?' Buchanan interjected. His hands were now clasped on his knee and he leaned forward, staring hard at the managing director.

'No. Nothing like that. He just seemed – well, disappointed. As though he'd banked on my agreeing.'

'What time did this conversation take place? And where?'

163

'In Doyle's office. I left the building at 10 p.m. So it must have been about 9.30 when we had this conversation.'

Buchanan relaxed again, changed the angle of the questions without warning. 'How do you know it was precisely 10 p.m. when you left this building? Anyone who can confirm your statement? Just routine.'

Morgan tapped ash from his cigar into a crystal-glass bowl. Giving himself time to think, Warden noted. Morgan was reflecting that this tall lean chief inspector was a formidable opponent. He sat back in his chair, determined to dictate the tempo.

'It's a simple question I asked,' Buchanan said gently.

'I thought it was two questions . . .'

'My apologies. It *was* two questions. By now you should have the answers . . .

'My time is valuable,' Morgan said aggressively. 'I'm being paid a lot of money to use it positively. So I keep an eye on the time. Look . . .' He reached forward and turned round a wide black box so it faced Buchanan. It held various clock faces. The time in London, New York, San Francisco, Frankfurt, Sydney.

'Useful little gadget . . .' Buchanan began but Morgan went on talking.

'I know it was 10 p.m. because I checked that clock just before I went down to the underground garage. My driver, Hanson, was waiting for me. He drove me home to Wandsworth.'

'And you arrived at your home when? I'm sure you know – you live by the clock, you said . . .'

'At 10.25 p.m. I'll anticipate your next question for you. My wife can confirm I didn't leave the house until this morning. In response to your request to see me. Now, if that's all I have an international organization to run.'

'Not quite all, Mr Morgan. You were in this building until ten o'clock. Doyle was presumably in his office after you left. Was anyone else here during last evening?'

'Yes, Mrs Buckmaster. I'd just come back from abroad. So we had a lot to talk about. I'd made a tour of some of the European offices. She wanted to know how I'd got on. That's it.'

'And Mrs Buckmaster was still here when you left?'

Beads of moisture were appearing on Morgan's forehead, Warden noticed. He'd seen this happen so often before. Buchanan going on and on, changing moods, lines of questioning, matching his stamina against that of the witness, but always keeping his temper.

'No,' Morgan replied. 'She left about 9 p.m. I was opening my door to walk around the place, stretch my legs, when I saw her leaving by the private elevator.'

Buchanan stood up and Warden joined him. Morgan also stood up to escort them to the door. Always leave an impression of amiability. Buchanan waited until Morgan had opened the door before he sprang his last surprise.

'Perhaps you'd like to accompany us to Doyle's office? After all, he was your employee for ten years. The place will be a bit cluttered with my men – but that can't be helped . . .'

Buchanan walked down the corridor, Warden stood aside, and Morgan felt obliged to follow. Inwardly he was seething: it was Buchanan's imperturbable manner that had got to him. He stubbed out his cigar in an ash-stand and paused by Buchanan who stood at the entrance to Doyle's office. Suddenly he turned round and asked another question.

'When you came down here to see Doyle did you notice an untouched carton of take-away food and a cardboard container of coffee on his desk?'

'Yes, I did. I simply assumed he was working late and had popped out to the deli round the corner for fodder.'

'You're quite sure about that? That the food and the coffee were untouched?'

'I've said so, haven't I? A security man trains himself to notice details.'

'Thank you. I really think this is a bad time for us to go in there. Too much activity . . .'

'Then, if you don't mind, I'll get back to my desk. This Doyle tragedy is very upsetting but it has to be business as usual for the company.'

'Just before you go, I'll need an office as my temporary HQ here while the investigation proceeds . . .'

'Moser's snuggery. I told you he was in Australia.' Morgan took a key-ring from his pocket, extracted one key from the ring, opened a door, handed the key to Buchanan. 'That's the only key,' he lied, 'so you can have all the privacy in the world.'

'Thank you for your cooperation,' Buchanan said politely. He added, as though an afterthought, as Morgan turned away. 'Oh, there will be more questions I'll have to ask you. But they can wait until I've assembled more data.'

They entered a large office with picture windows overlooking other high-rises. Between two of them a solid curtain of freezing fog was drifting in from the direction of the river Thames. Buchanan stood gazing at the blurred view.

'What was your impression of Morgan?' he asked Warden.

'A strange man. Self-made. Came up from nothing. Glories in his present position.'

'That's all right as far as it goes.' Buchanan rattled loose change in his pocket. 'But his reaction to the news of Doyle's death wasn't quite right. A terrible tragedy and so on – but not a sign of shocked *disbelief* when he was first told.'

'Maybe he thinks only of himself. What do you think happened, sir? Suicide?'

'I might have gone along with that except for the empty

food-carton, the empty cardboard coffee cup in his waste-paper basket.'

'Not quite with you . . .'

'Oh, come on. You're in such a state you're thinking of jumping from an eighteenth-storey window. Morgan replied to my question off guard, I suspect. He said the cartons were untouched when he saw Doyle, refused him the alleged loan. Can you see Doyle – in that frame of mind – waiting until Morgan had gone and then sitting down to eat a substantial amount of ham sandwiches, downed with a cup of coffee? Forensic found traces of ham and crusty bread in that large crushed carton. Plus coffee traces in the smaller carton. Well?'

He swung round and faced his subordinate.

'No, I can't visualize that happening,' Warden said slowly.

'So, if I'm right,' Buchanan continued in the same even tone, 'it wasn't an accident, it wasn't suicide. That means we're investigating a murder case.'

Morgan unlocked the security drawer in his desk, took out the typed list of employees. Each had a number alongside the name. Doyle was 35.

Delving inside his metal box full of keys, Morgan extracted one with a tab carrying the number 35. As a precaution against a possible 'mole' inside the organization, Morgan had ordered the Research and Development Division to make duplicates of all the keys to employees' homes.

If suspicion fell on a man – or a woman – someone could be sent along to wait until the house or apartment was empty. He would then use the key to enter the suspected employee's home to make a careful search. Quite illegal, but this emphasis on total security, regardless of ethics, was one factor which had made World

167

Security the largest and most successful organization of its type in the world.

With the key in his pocket Morgan opened his office door, peered out into the empty corridor and hurried to the private elevator. He found Hanson behind the wheel of the limousine in the underground garage, reading a paperback and munching an apple. He handed him the key.

'You know Doyle's address in Pimlico. You've delivered papers there. He's a bachelor so the place will be empty.'

'I make a search?'

'The reverse. You go to the races. You bet on the Tote?'

'That's right . . .'

'So no one can trace ownership of a Tote ticket. They're anonymous. You usually have some losing tickets . . .'

'Some in here now.' Hanson opened the glove compartment. 'I have another lot in my wallet. Don't know why I keep them – I have a clear-out periodically. Due for one now . . .'

'Which is exactly what you're going to do. Use gloves, wipe those tickets clean, then crumple them up. Drop them inside a drawer in Doyle's apartment. Anywhere will do – don't make them look hidden. And Hanson . . .' Morgan gripped his arm. 'Before you enter that apartment make sure there are no police about. They'll be going there soon. And use the Ford Cortina, not this limo. Too conspicuous. Now, move, man, move . . .'

16

At 10 a.m. Leonora Buckmaster parked her Volvo station wagon at the main entrance to the World Security building as snowflakes drifted down into Threadneedle Street from a leaden sky. The whole of Western Europe was being smothered by the blanket of snow drifting in from the East.

She opened the door, swung her legs out, locked the door and glanced up at the office block looming above her. Her expression was grim as she walked through the door opened by a uniformed security guard. In one hand she held her pass, in the other her elevator key and the car keys. A man in civilian clothes stepped forward to look at her pass which carried her photograph.

'Police, Mrs Buckmaster . . .'

'Then I want to see Chief Inspector Buchanan immediately – that is his name, isn't it?' She handed her car keys to the security guard. 'Keith, could you please park my car inside the garage. Thank you.' She turned to the plain-clothes detective. 'What exactly is going on here? I'm the chairman.'

'The chief inspector is waiting to see you on the eighteenth floor.'

'Is he? How very kind of him . . .'

She crossed the marble floor to the private elevator with long elegant strides. Behind her back the plain-clothes man nodded to his colleague at the reception desk who had taken control of the switchboard. The second man picked up a phone.

When the doors opened at the eighteenth floor Leonora found a tall slim man standing a few feet away. His grey eyes surveyed her, assessing his first impression. A handsome woman in her mid thirties, he estimated. She wore a hip-length sable jacket and relics of snowflakes clung to golden curls in her long mane. It reminded him of the Christmas fairy, a trivial thought he dismissed immediately.

He noted the good bone-structure, the alert blue eyes, the firm but full mouth which suggested a hint of sensuality. A woman who would make an instant impact on most men. She made no such impact on Buchanan. To him she was simply a witness to an as yet unexplained death.

'Mrs Buckmaster? I'm Chief Inspector Buchanan. Could we possibly have a private chat in your office?'

'What the devil is going on? Your men appear to have taken over the security apparatus in this building. Your Sergeant Warden phones me, asks me to come here as soon as I can, says there has been a tragedy, then refuses to elaborate . . .'

As she spoke she was striding along the empty corridor to her office suite. With his long legs Buchanan easily kept pace with her. His manner was neutral, almost everyday.

'I'd prefer to discuss this in the privacy of your office. And Sergeant Warden was acting under my explicit orders.'

She paused before inserting her key, glancing back along the corridor. Men with cameras were emerging from Doyle's office. She frowned, which did nothing to spoil her physical attraction.

'More of your men? What are they doing in Doyle's office?'

Buchanan gestured towards the door. A moment later Warden appeared from the doorway leading to the executive toilets.

'This is Sergeant Warden. If you don't mind, I'd like him to be present at the interview.'

She glanced at Warden, made no reply, unlocked her door and led the way inside. While she took off her sable, shook it, hung it inside a wardrobe with sliding doors, she asked them to sit down.

'Would you like some coffee?' she enquired as she sat behind her desk on which rested only three phones, one red, one blue and one white.

'Thank you, but not for the moment,' Buchanan replied. 'I'm afraid I have some distressing news. Ted Doyle's body was found eighteen storeys below his window during the night.'

'Oh, no. I don't believe it.' Her shapely right hand flew to her throat and held her polo-necked green sweater closer. 'It's not possible. I was talking to him in this office only yesterday evening. He was in perfect shape. I just can't believe it, take it in. Has there been a break-in? Did he disturb an intruder? How is he? From the way you worded it . . .'

All in a rush of words. Her voice was low and husky, throaty. She stared from one man to the other, her left hand clenched into a fist on the desk top. Buchanan spoke quietly.

'Yes, it is the worst news. He's dead. You can't fall from this height and survive. Can you imagine the impact when he hit the sidewalk?'

It was brutally phrased and Warden winced inwardly. At times he felt his chief went over the top. Buchanan's eyes were cold as he studied her. He folded his arms and waited. Either she was an excellent actress or her reaction was genuine. Impossible to say which at this stage.

She fetched a carafe of water from a side table, poured herself a glass, swallowed a generous quantity. Then she sat upright.

'Please tell me what this is all about.'

'You said you were talking with Doyle yesterday evening. What time would that be?'

'Roughly between seven and eight o'clock. I can vouch for the second time. Gareth Morgan, my managing director, arrived back from London Airport. I was surprised to see him. I remember checking my watch when I heard his voice. It was 8 p.m.'

171

'You heard his voice?' Buchanan leaned forward, holding her gaze. 'Talking to who?'

'He bumped into Ted – Doyle, that is – as Ted was leaving my office.'

'And you heard what Morgan said?'

'I'm afraid I didn't. He was speaking in a quiet way. But of course I recognized who it was.'

'And Doyle came back into this office with Morgan?'

'No.' She swallowed. 'I never saw him again.'

'So normally where would Doyle have gone?'

'Back to his own office . . .'

'And had you completed your business with him for the day?'

'Yes . . .'

'So what would keep him from going home?'

Warden listened with increasing interest. Buchanan had built up the tempo, was firing a fresh question as soon as she'd replied to the previous one. She reached for the glass of water.

'Please. It hasn't even sunk in that Doyle is no longer with us. You're going too fast.'

'Perfectly straightforward questions, Mrs Buckmaster. Surely nothing I've asked so far requires thought before you answer. I ask you again – what would keep Doyle from going home? Because', he continued ruthlessly, 'we know he certainly didn't go home.'

'He might stay to work late when there were no phone calls to interrupt him.'

'I see.' Buchanan gazed round the large office as though he'd not seen it until that moment. A smaller desk was angled at a distance to Leonora's. Presumably her secretary's. He looked back at her, spoke suddenly.

'According to what you said earlier you were conferring with Doyle for about one hour. Seven to eight. That's a long time. What were you talking about?'

'Is that relevant?'

172

Her long lashes blinked briefly. For the first time Buchanan sensed a wariness in her. Why? He pressed home his interrogation.

'It could be very relevant. It was the last but one conversation he apparently had before he died. The last one being with Gareth Morgan – after he'd seen you leave at 9 p.m.'

'How could he know that?'

The question slipped out before she realized it. She sat very still and stared hard at Buchanan. He replied offhandedly.

'He said he was opening the door of his office and saw you in the elevator just before it descended. Now, what were you and Doyle talking about for about one hour?'

'We were going over the figures for various European offices. We do have an organization in every West European country. It is one of our major markets. Both in the Common Market and in those countries still outside it. Including Switzerland. So there were a lot of figures to study. It was a matter of comparing the results of one office with another. One point was to see if we could improve our service in any particular area.'

'I see,' Buchanan commented again and paused.

That had been her longest answer yet. Full of unasked-for detail. Almost as though she was covering up what they had really talked about. He attacked from another angle.

'How important is – was – Ted Doyle? He had the title of Chief Accountant. But you have a finance director, Axel Moser. So where does the division in responsibilities come?'

'Ted handled all the day-to-day problems. He had quite a lot of power . . .'

'Including access to all the books?'

Again she blinked. Again she reached for the glass of water, took her time sipping the liquid. Placing it carefully on a mat, she dabbed at her lips with a lace handkerchief.

'Naturally. How else could he do his job? I'm beginning to wilt under this continuous barrage.'

'I apologize. But I'm sure you are as anxious as I am to get to the bottom of why Doyle died. And I'm nearly finished. Was Doyle married? And if you could give me his address it would help our enquiries. My last two questions, Mrs Buckmaster. For the moment.'

She replied as she wrote out the address from memory on a blank card. She handed it across the desk and Buchanan gave it to Warden.

'He was a bachelor. Not from choice, I sometimes thought. But he was very shy where women were concerned.'

Buchanan stood up. He cast a slow glance round the office before he joined her as she escorted them to the door. He asked the question as she grasped the handle.

'How many keys are there to your private elevator? Someone has a spare, I presume? In case of loss.'

'No one has a spare. Bad security. And there are only three keys in existence. I have one, Gareth Morgan has another.'

'And the third key, Mrs Buckmaster?'

She looked him straight in the eye. 'Lance had one, naturally. He was going to hand it in when he was appointed Minister, but found he'd lost it. He never comes here since his appointment, of course. Against the rules.'

'Of course. And thank you for your cooperation, Mrs Buckmaster. I'll keep you informed of progress into our murder investigation . . .'

Buchanan left her staring after him as he walked away with Warden down the corridor.

17

The Black Forest was like a vast icebox. Tweed's hands were freezing as he gripped the wheel. Beside him Newman clapped his hands together to get the circulation moving. In the rear seat Paula pulled the fur-lined coat she had bought in Freiburg closer to her neck.

The hired blue Audi, with chains on its wheels, glided over the icebound surface of the hilly country road. On either side the dense stands of the fir forest walled them in, made for a claustrophobic atmosphere. It was night, the undimmed headlights reflected weirdly off the ramparts of snow lining the road. During the day a snow-plough had obviously fought to keep the route open.

Paula glanced back through the rear window. The lights of the second Audi, a neutral grey colour, driven by Marler, showed as a blur beyond the iced-up window. The temperature outside was way below zero. Above the sound of the engine she heard a crackling noise as their wheels broke the crusted snow ridges.

'Are you sure you know where we're going?' she asked. 'It was a long time ago since you were in Freiburg learning German.'

'I thought you'd grasped I have a photographic memory for routes,' he told her as he drove into a slow skid, then the car came back under his control. 'I drove all over the Black Forest in my spare time. We're heading for a small spa town called Badenweiler. From there we can drive down to the German border with Switzerland. The trick is to cross that border unseen. I think we can do it at a small place called Laufenburg on the edge of the Rhine. Part is in Germany, part in Switzerland. It straddles the river. We have to cross a bridge between the two frontiers. But that's for later.'

'And what's for now?' she persisted.

'We find a refuge for the night when we can. Freiburg was a deathtrap.'

'Maybe then we can talk about what happened back in London,' she suggested.

'Not while Marler is around,' Newman objected. 'And not one word about that *Shockwave* computer on the high seas.'

'You wouldn't be letting your personal dislike cloud your judgement?' Tweed asked.

'No, I wouldn't . . .'

After conducting the decoy manoeuvre planned by Tweed – when Newman had taken over the BMW and driven it on to the autobahn – he had driven back to Freiburg. By then Tweed had slipped the net thrown round the city and was driving to the agreed rendezvous with Newman in the Black Forest.

As they parked near the Colombi Hotel Newman had been in an uncertain frame of mind regarding Marler. Certainly he had cooperated to the full on the autobahn – shooting the tyres on the pursuing Mercedes which had ended up as a fireball. But still Newman had reservations. How far would Marler go to prove a fake loyalty? A long way in Newman's opinion.

Without telling Marler where he had been going, Newman had returned earlier on foot to the Oberkirch. It was there that Tweed had explained his plan to evade the watchers he felt sure would be watching all exits.

'And what about Marler?' Newman had demanded. 'I don't trust him one inch . . .'

'Then this will give you a chance to test him,' Tweed had insisted. 'Take him with you – you may need him. You said he'd collected a rifle from some friend – and he's the best marksman in Europe. If there's an emergency and he backs you up, bring him to the rendezvous – but tell him to hire another Audi. A different colour from the one I'll be driving. Leave the BMW at the car hire agency in Freiburg and you drive Marler to meet us in the Black Forest here . . .'

Tweed had indicated a small village high up in the Black Forest on a large-scale map spread out on the bed. Paula, perched alongside the map, was also worried.

'Marler has always struck me as an unknown quantity,' she commented. 'If he's joining us I agree we should not risk telling him where we're headed for – Switzerland.'

'Then neither of you tell him anything. Leave me to handle Marler . . .'

When Newman and Tweed had eventually arrived at the crossroads just outside the village, Tweed had suggested Newman should transfer to his Audi.

'Marler,' he went on, 'we may need to use the decoy method again. That photograph of Horowitz you took outside the World Security HQ in Freiburg shows me someone will stop at nothing to make sure I don't reach a transmitter alive. So you take over driving the grey Audi on your own from now on. Following me into the forest.' He had smiled drily. 'I just hope you're as good a driver as you think you are. We're driving up into a white hell . . .'

Paula stared out of the window. It was like driving between two giant black tidal waves about to overwhelm them. When Tweed swung the car round a bend the headlights shone over the dense palisade of firs and there was no sign of life anywhere.

'We're close to where we turn off up a wide timber track if it's still there,' Tweed remarked.

They completed the nerve-racking swing round another curve and ahead the country road straightened, marched up a steep hill for about half a mile so far as Paula could tell – it was difficult to estimate distance even by the light of a rising moon. The weird glow reflected off the dangerous sheen of ice on the road, glittered on ice crystals in the ramparts of banked snow. Tweed suddenly reduced speed and then stopped. Lowering his window, he listened. There it was again, the distant chug-chug of a helicopter's rotors.

The sound was approaching fast. At the same moment coming in the opposite direction a car's headlights breasted the crest of a hill, drove down towards them. Behind he heard Marler tooting his horn.

'Marler has switched off all his lights,' he said.

'He's driving close to us,' Paula called out, 'using your lights to guide him. I think he wants us to stop . . .'

It all happened at breathless speed. Tweed slowed, stopped. Seconds later Marler was beside the window he'd lowered. He spoke tersely.

'Chopper with a searchlight approaching from the south-east. I think it's a trap. I'm turning round, driving back with lights full on. I'll act as a decoy . . .'

'Thanks,' said Tweed rapidly. 'When you get clear fly back to London. Organize surveillance on two targets – Ministry for External Security . . . and the World Security outfit . . . I'll leave a number on your answerphone at your apartment . . .'

'After the country code add digits four and five as second and fourth numbers . . .'

'After I've reversed the whole number . . .'

'I'm off. Good luck . . .'

Then Marler was gone. Tweed released the brake, pressed his foot down. The oncoming car was coming

178

much closer. He saw in his wing mirror Marler had already executed a three-point turn, was driving away, headlights blazing. The chug-chug was much louder.

'Watch that vehicle coming towards us,' warned Newman.

Tweed was leaning forward, glancing constantly to his left. 'We've got lucky. Hold on ...' He swung the wheel, turned across the road on to a wide timber track driven through the forest like a great avenue. The wheels began bumping over deep ice-hard ruts. He fought with the steering, felt the wheels slip into wide grooves carved out over the years by timber wagons. He drove on sensitively, feeling his wheels locked in by the iron-hard sides of the grooves. The disadvantage was he was moving along runnels of solid ice. Newman released his safety belt, hauled out the Walther from his hip holster, glanced back through the rear window. No sign yet of blurred headlights, but the oncoming car must have seen them turn off. Of course, it could be an innocent driver. Newman doubted it. Always assume the worst. They hadn't met a vehicle for miles, then one turned up at the same moment the chopper appeared. He looked ahead.

'We're heading for a dead end up here,' he remarked.

'Not necessarily.' Tweed called over his shoulder to Paula who sat tense, frequently looking back. 'When I stop bring the bags out of the car. We may have to run for it.'

'Run where?' snapped Newman.

'There used to be an old hunting lodge hidden in the forest. A winding footpath leads uphill to it. The lodge was for the timber workers who stayed out here. There was an electric cable leading to it which powered the freezer. There may be food and drink still there ...'

'Fat chance ...'

'But we have to hide the car before that chopper finds

179

us. Yes, look! I was right. See that big boulder at the side of the track . . .'

'What about it?'

'That's where the path starts. Fasten your seat belt. I'm increasing speed.'

'God help us . . .'

Tweed pressed his foot down. The Audi slithered and glided over the ice channels but kept moving. Tweed had his window open an inch and cold bitter air was making the interior like a refrigerator. He was listening to the growing sound of the helicopter coming closer. He swung to the left. The wheels rasped and hacked at the walls of the ruts, then broke through. They shot off the track through a narrow opening with the firs pressing closely on either side. They were in the middle of an open space of virgin snow when Tweed doused all the lights, turned off the engine. The bonnet was buried beneath snow-covered undergrowth.

When he leapt out of the car, shoving the ignition key in his pocket, Paula was handing out three small cases to Newman. He plodded back quickly and peered down the track. He wore climbing boots purchased in Freiburg, a dark overcoat and a fur hat on his head. Tweed took his own case as Paula and Newman reached him.

'They saw us turn in,' he commented, his voice calm. His mind was as ice-cold as the night. His instincts for danger asserted themselves. He had mentally gone back years to the days when he operated as an agent in the field.

A few yards from where the track ended at the distant road two small eyes, the headlights of a car, moved slowly towards them.

'We cross the track to the path,' he ordered. 'They're too far away to see us yet . . .'

'You cross with Paula.' Newman's tone was grim. They heard a click as he checked the magazine in his automatic.

180

'I'll come after you. These people have to be stopped . . .'

Tweed didn't argue. He grabbed Paula by her free arm. 'Get moving, they're coming closer . . .'

Crouching down, they stepped carefully over the pit-falls of the timber track. The lights of the car were still too far off to illuminate them. They made their way up the path into the forest.

Inside the Volvo station wagon Horowitz sat beside the driver as the vehicle climbed the road into the Black Forest. Horowitz stared ahead through his steel-rimmed spectacles, his lean face showing no particular expression. His right hand gripped the microphone of the high-powered transceiver installed in the boot. The automatic aerial was extended to its fullest extent. Then the message from the helicopter came to him.

'Elbe Two calling Bismarck. Elbe Two calling . . .'

'Bismarck listening,' Horowitz replied tersely. 'Have you news?'

'Eiger may have been located. A blue Audi proceeding along route . . . Also escorted by a grey Audi following closer behind . . .'

'Continue surveillance. Await fresh instructions.'

Horowitz used a pencil torch to examine the road map spread across his lap. Beside him, the driver, Stieber, a small squat individual built like a barrel, glanced side-ways. 'Keep your eye on the road,' Horowitz said softly without looking up.

'Have we found them?' Eva Hendrix called out from the rear of the car. She was cold and frightened. Behind her was the wire cage hastily constructed at the Freiburg HQ. Inside the cage, far too close for her comfort, five German shepherd dogs were standing up, prowling restlessly. Every now and again one of the killer dogs gave a low snarl and she edged a little further away from

181

the beasts, holding on to the back of Horowitz's seat as the vehicle skidded round a steep corner.

'I guessed well,' Horowitz commented almost to himself. 'You turn left at the next intersection, step on the gas.'

'These bloody roads are like a skating rink,' Stieber growled.

'And', Horowitz continued, ignoring the comment, 'Gustav is driving his Mercedes towards them from the opposite direction.'

'Is Gustav armed?' enquired Hendrix breathlessly.

'Yes, now shut up.' Horowitz called the chopper which had located the target. He now had four helicopters patrolling above the Black Forest. 'Are you there, Elbe Two? Good. Don't lose Eiger or you're out of a job. Next, radio Gustav that the target vehicle is approaching him. Make regular reports of the situation to me. Over and out . . .'

'How long before we reach them?' Stieber asked while he took the left turn at the intersection as instructed. They were climbing a steep hill, driving conditions were becoming worse as they plunged deeper into the Black Forest.

'If you keep this thing moving, less than ten minutes. Then you can do your job – unless Gustav has done it for you.'

Stieber nodded with satisfaction. He was the dog handler and was only really in his element when he was loosing his dogs after a fleeing target. Man or woman, it was all the same to Stieber. He loved his dogs. Human beings he found expendable.

Despite his wool-lined gloves Newman was frozen stiff as he stayed crouched behind a patch of undergrowth. The screen would have been useless except for the thick snow cloaking its branches and twigs. His right hand held the Walther and he'd decided that to fire it he'd have to use his bare hand when the time came.

The time was coming. The beams of the undimmed headlights were already showing on the section of track beyond the small glade. The car's engine was labouring. The vehicle was approaching slowly. Clearly the driver did not possess Tweed's skill in moving up the obstacle course of a track.

Frequently there was a sound of metal grinding against the unyielding ground. The driver wasn't keeping to the runnels: he kept losing them and the chassis was hitting the murderous ridges. Newman wriggled his toes which felt like ice. He hoped he wasn't getting frost-bite.

The lamps of the headlights appeared suddenly. New-man dipped his head to avoid the glare, slipped off the glove from his right hand, gripped the Walther, decided he needed both hands in the dark, slipped off the other glove, gripped the weapon in both hands.

The Mercedes had stopped. They had seen the place where Tweed had turned the Audi across virgin snow inside the glade. How many men? Four at the most, he guessed. And the most dangerous would be those alight-ing from the far side of the car. The Mercedes moved a short distance more and stopped again close to where the Audi was concealed.

The headlights were now angled away from the under-growth and Newman had a better view of the whole car. The rear was empty and in front there was only the driver, a heavily built man wearing a peaked cap. He opened the door and stared round. Newman saw he was holding a gun in his right hand: he thought it was a Luger. If he could take him alive he might extract valuable infor-mation . . .

The man stepped out, stood close to the car, head cocked to one side as he listened.

'Drop the gun!' Newman shouted.

The man swung up his Luger, fired, but in the heavy silence of the forest Newman's voice had echoed. The bullet went wide. Newman fired three times in rapid succession. The man sagged against the car. His fingers lost their grip, the Luger fell into the snow. Its owner slumped slowly to the ground and lay very still.

The silence was broken by another sound. The distant chug-chug of a chopper coming closer. Newman ran forward, felt the neck pulse. Nothing. The gunman was dead. Reaching inside his breast pocket, Newman slid out an identity folder which held the owner's photograph behind a transparent shield. *Gustav Braun. World Security. Industrial Research Division.* All in German.

He slipped the folder inside his raincoat pocket, peered down the timber track where the chopper's rotors sounded much louder. It was flying just above tree level and had a searchlight switched on in the nose. The beam was proceeding up the track.

Newman dashed back for his case, grabbed hold of it, ran across the track before the searchlight reached him. He paused under the trees to insert a fresh mag into the Walther. As the rotors became a roar he vanished along the path in the direction Tweed and Paula had taken.

The moon was a blurred glow from behind a screen of clouds as Marler drove the grey Audi downhill. He was sure that the chopper had seen him but it had passed him and seemed to be concentrating on Tweed's Audi.

Marler drove without lights. The route followed by the road was clear enough in the meagre moonlight. Ahead he saw a bridge crossing the road. Moments later he saw the headlights of an invisible vehicle coming uphill towards him – invisible because immediately beyond the bridge the road, he recalled, turned in a sharp curve.

Apart from the lone car coming downhill towards Tweed's Audi he hadn't seen any form of transport for over an hour. He took his decision on sixth sense.

He had almost reached the bridge when he swung across the road on to the snow-covered verge on his left. He pulled up alongside the bridge – the last few yards he was carried to his hiding place by a skid. Lowering the window facing the road, he switched off his engine, reached for the rifle under a travelling rug alongside, aimed the muzzle through the open window. He sat very still, finger on the trigger.

The Volvo station wagon navigated the turn under the bridge at speed – too much speed for the road surface. The driver was lucky. The vehicle continued up the hill. As it had passed Marler had a glimpse of two men in the front, a girl in the back, and behind her a cage with four or five dogs. No one looked in his direction.

'Oh, Christ!' Marler muttered. 'Tracker dogs . . .'

He decided not to go back. Tweed had given his orders and Newman would have to cope. After all, he'd had training in the SAS for that article he'd written about the elite attack force.

'Elbe Two to Bismarck . . .'

'Bismarck here. Please report present situation . . .'

Inside the Volvo Horowitz held the mike lightly, his body relaxed. Had Gustav Braun rammed the Audi with his Mercedes? Anything to delay Tweed until they caught up.

'Elbe Two reporting. Blue Audi with Eiger has turned off the road you are proceeding along. Look out for wide timber track on your left. Am now flying zero height along track. Braun's car has turned down same track.'

'Continue surveillance. We will be there shortly. Over and out . . .'

Horowitz replaced the mike on its hook. The climax was very close. Tweed had tried to lose himself in the forest. The chopper had frightened him off the road. He was trapped. He glanced at Stieber who was hunched over the wheel, bare hands now gripping it tightly despite the cold.

'Don't miss the turn-off along that timber track.'

'Can't miss it. The chopper's searchlight shows where that track is. Hope we can use the dogs . . .'

Horowitz pursed his lips at the look of eager anticipation on Stieber's face, lips drawn back over his teeth. The man was a sadist. His greatest pleasure was watching his dogs rip another human being to pieces. If he wasn't such a good tracker Horowitz would have dispensed with his services. A job required a professional – a clinical – approach.

Stieber swung the Volvo off the road and bulled his way down the track, moving too fast, relying on the weight of the car to carry him along. It was a recipe for disaster. Horowitz was about to tell him to slow down, when the Volvo slewed out of control, skidded diagonally off the track and stopped. In the headlight glare they saw the Mercedes with one front door open, stopped under the trees.

'We made it,' exulted Stieber.

'Put the dogs on the slip-leashes before I get out,' ordered Horowitz.

There was something disturbing about the parked Mercedes – and now the Volvo's engine had stopped Horowitz realized the Mercedes' engine was still ticking over. The helicopter had flown much further up the timber track, searchlight probing, the rotors a faint chug-chug. 'You stay in the car,' he ordered Hendrix and she was thankful to remain inside.

Stieber was already opening the rear of the cage, leashing the restless animals, telling them to keep quiet. The

186

helicopter was returning down the timber track and it hovered now above the parked vehicles. Horowitz, a Browning .32 automatic held by his side, stepped out of the Volvo. He waved a hand in a downward chopping motion and the pilot switched off the blinding glare of the searchlight.

Horowitz approached the Mercedes cautiously, crouching by the side furthest away from the open door. He peered round the back. It was then he saw the slumped body of Gustav.

Still crouching, he made a quick examination. Two bullets through the skull, a third in the chest. He switched off his pencil torch and thought. No signs of powder burns so Gustav's killer was a first-rate shot. Something to bear in mind for later. Stieber, the five dogs straining on a multiple slip leash, was on the far side of the track.

'Tweed went this way,' he called out. 'They've picked up Tweed's scent.'

'There's more than Tweed to track,' Horowitz warned.

He was recalling the extract from the Tweed dossier he had read. There had been a clear indication Tweed never used firearms. So who was the killer?

'They can't be far away,' Stieber called out impatiently. 'That Audi that's disappeared turned up this track only a short while back . . .'

'Wait!'

Horowitz walked back to the Volvo, settled himself in the passenger seat and called Elbe Two. The radio op responded at once.

'Bismarck here. You know the position of the cars where you hovered. Fly east of that point over the forest. Use your searchlight. I want Eiger – he's now on foot – harassed, kept on the move. Understood? Then get to it . . .'

He walked over to where the five dogs were heaving at the leash, switched on his pencil flash. A clear footpath into the forest showed up. He bent down, found a freshly snapped twig, straightened up.

'Get after them,' he told Stieber. 'Hurry – before those savages lose the scent. I'm not sure how many you're chasing. Two at least. I want them all. I'll follow with Hendrix at a distance.'

'Don't worry.' Stieber grinned, licked his lips. 'They're dead meat.'

18

Tweed led the file up the steep twisting path through the trees. The route was marked by snow-covered boulders of limestone and a small frozen stream ran to their left. Behind Tweed Paula plodded in her knee-length flat-heeled boots. A dozen yards behind her Newman brought up the rear.

Each of them carried their small case and Tweed climbed upwards confidently as though he'd passed this way yesterday. Just enough moonlight percolated through the dense ceiling of forest above them for him to see ahead. And his night vision was now excellent.

The heavy silence, broken only by the soft tread of their feet sinking into the snow, oppressed Paula. They came to a level stretch and she looked round and up. The palisade of endless vertical trunks sheered up like a stockade. The giant firs spread their branches like huge outstretched hands, hands weighed down with frozen snow. She jumped as there was a sound like a rifle shot. Tweed paused, looked over his shoulder.

'That was only an ice-encased branch snapping under

the weight – sounds like a gun going off.'

'It's horribly cold. How much further?'

'Less than a mile,' he lied. He estimated it was much further to the hunting lodge. 'Just keep moving. Don't watch your feet. Keep your head up . . .'

'Then I'll slip,' she protested.

'Plant your feet down flat. Watch the way I walk . . .'

She was amazed by his stamina, by the way he kept up an even pace going uphill. But then for over a year now he had taken to walking between three and four miles every day to and from Park Crescent to his Radnor Walk flat. The thought of that flat – and what had happened inside it – came back to her with a reaction of horror. She must ask him about it when they reached the hunting lodge. That was then Tweed heard the distant chug-chug of an approaching helicopter and a second moon appeared faintly above the tangled mass of branches. Newman came up behind them rapidly, joined them as the machine came closer and closer.

It was after midnight when Chief Inspector Otto Kuhlmann walked into police headquarters at Freiburg. Inspector Wagishauser, the top officer, and a small dapper man with a neat moustache, stared open-mouthed as he automatically stood up from behind his desk and came forward to greet the new arrival.

Kuhlmann, although small in height, reminded him of old movies he'd seen of Edward G. Robinson. Wide-shouldered with a large head and a wide mouth, he radiated a physical aura which made people look as soon as he entered a crowded room. He wore a grey overcoat, which he stripped off, and a cigar was clenched between his teeth.

'Chief Inspector Kuhlmann!' The surprise showed in Wagishauser's tone. 'Wiesbaden asked me to wait, said someone was flying down to see me – but I had no idea it would be you.'

'You should know by now I rarely announce where I'm going,' Kuhlmann growled. As he spoke he padded over to a large-scale wall map of the *Lande* – the state – of Baden Wurttemburg covering south-west Germany to the Rhine and the Swiss border. Various flags on pins had been inserted into the map.

'What's going on?' Kuhlmann demanded.

'There was a terrible pile-up on the autobahn . . .'

'I heard about that. Sorted out the corpses yet? Who was involved?'

'It was all very odd. I'm afraid several of my men died – following that Mercedes as you ordered. Some maniac drove a huge refrigerated truck the wrong way – up the southbound lane. Four of the cars involved belonged to the World Security organization. Nine of their operatives were killed. No survivors . . .'

'What happened to the Mercedes is my main concern.'

'It disappeared. We thought it must have continued on to Switzerland. But I set up a road-block and it never appeared. I called our frontier control at Basle and they hadn't seen a car with the registration number you—'

'Sounds like my man. You'd expected him to drive on to the Swiss border. He never does the expected. My bet is he took the next turn-off, drove back up the northbound lane. Any other developments?'

'Only that patrol cars have reported unusual aerial activity over the Black Forest – still going on . . .'

Kuhlmann swung round, removed his cigar. 'What unusual activity? Spit out the details, man.'

'Several choppers are criss-crossing the Forest. We think they belong to World Security. The airport tower reported two had flown in from Frankfurt, one from Basle. They refuelled and took off immediately . . .'

'And they're still flying over the Black Forest on a night like this?'

'So it would seem . . .'

190

'You have a police Sikorsky at the airfield, I noticed when I came in. It's still there?'

'Yes, Chief Inspector . . .'

'I wanted it equipped with a swivel-mounted machine-gun inside thirty minutes.' Kuhlmann was slipping on his overcoat. 'And the machine must be fully fuelled. By the time I get there. Thirty minutes from now . . .'

The helicopter was hovering just above them as Newman stood with Paula and Tweed. They were sheltering under an enormous overhang of snow perched on the lower branches of a huge fir. The invisible machine was slowly rotating its searchlight over the forest below.

'He'll spot our tracks in the snow,' Paula whispered and then wondered why she was whispering. The beat of the rotors would have drowned a shout.

She pointed to the path alongside the frozen stream they had walked up. In the snow their footsteps were clear imprints and there were gaps in the tree cover. Tweed put his arm round her shoulders and gave her a reassuring squeeze. She smiled gratefully. The raw dry cold was penetrating her coat and her feet felt like blocks of ice.

'Keep still,' Newman warned in his casual voice.

He had taken off his gloves, tucked them under his arms. He held the Walther ready for use. There didn't seem to be anywhere the chopper could land but he wasn't taking any chances. The probing searchlight passed slowly across the platform of snow hiding them. Seconds later Paula nearly shrieked, clapped a hand to her mouth with fear.

It was probably the proximity of the vibrating rotors which caused the near catastrophe. Without warning the platform of snow collapsed, covering them with snow, exposing them to view. Newman repeated his warning and stood like a statue, staring upwards. He could see the faint outline of the chopper now.

It appeared to be poised just above the treetops, a long luminous shape as the moon reflected off its fuselage. He could even see the dizzying blur of the whirling rotors. Paula had clenched her teeth tight. Tweed was gripping her more firmly to keep her still. Their cases, which they had placed on the ground, were mounds of snow. The stream, about two feet wide, was frozen solid where it had once tumbled downhill over and between rocks. In places the moon gleamed on pure ice which made her feel even colder. Oh, God, she thought, how much more of this nightmare can I stand?

The helicopter began to ascend and then flew slowly away. As its chug-chug faded they heard another sound as they were on the point of continuing their trudge uphill. Tweed heard it first and placed a restraining hand on Paula's arm as she stopped to dig in the snow to locate the handle of her case. She straightened up, her gloved hand gripping the handle. It felt heavier – the snow was freezing solid on the suitcase.

'What is it?' she whispered again.

Then she noticed Newman had turned his head in the direction they had come, listening intently. He lifted his ear flaps from his fur hat, cocked his head sideways. Tweed stood like a waxwork figure, his expression grim, staring down the path. Then Paula heard it.

'Oh, God, no!'

'Tracker dogs,' Newman said tersely.

'And coming this way,' Tweed commented.

Newman glanced all round, stared at the frozen stream, then looked up. He delved into the snow, found Tweed's case, handed it to him. As he burrowed for his own case Tweed knocked the snow from the surface of his case and Paula automatically cleaned off her own.

The eerie howl of the pursuing dogs echoed weirdly in

the white wilderness. They seemed terribly close to Paula, a whole tribe of the ghastly hounds. Newman stood up, holding his case and looked at Tweed, speaking quickly.

'You head for the hunting lodge with Paula. I'm staying here. We can't out-run those beasts. No argument. Just one thing. How can I be sure to find the hunting lodge on my own?'

'Follow the stream, Tweed told him quickly. 'Higher up it flows past the side of the lodge . . .'

'I want you both to leave this path,' Newman snapped. 'The only way to kill your scent is to make your way up that icy stream. Can you manage that?'

'We'll have to. You have a plan?'

'Yes, but for Christ's sake get moving . . .'

Both Tweed and Paula wore footwear with crêpe soles, but Tweed's boots were corrugated. He took a long stride, gripping Paula by the arm, placed one foot on the stream, felt the snow holding him steady and started moving uphill fast. Several times Paula slipped, but always Tweed held her up, saved her balance. In half a minute they were out of sight. The banshee-like howling of the dogs was much closer. Newman bent down, opened his case.

Horowitz, his eyes calm and cold behind the steel-rimmed spectacles, trudged at a steady pace up the path as Hendrix struggled to keep up with him. He noted the muddle of footprints in the snow – the many small impressions of the paws of the dogs, the broad marks of Stieber's footprints and other footprints. What worried him was he could hear the dogs growling in blood-lust fury and the sound was close and stationary. He walked round a dense strand of trees and found Stieber holding the multiple leash, staring back at him.

193

'Why have you stopped?' he demanded. 'And quieten those savages.'

Stieber gave an order and the dogs fell quiet, circling each other in frustration. Hendrix caught him up, breathless, as the two men faced each other.

'You heard the dogs?' Stieber asked.

'I could hardly fail to hear them. Why were they suddenly making such a terrible row?'

'Because the meat is close,' Stieber gloated. 'Very close. They can sense it. I waited for you to get your agreement.'

'Agreement to what? Get to the point . . .'

'To release the dogs. Let them go on ahead by themselves – finish the job.'

'I don't want to see it,' muttered Hendrix.

Horowitz considered the request. 'How far away do you calculate the targets are?' he enquired.

'No more than half a mile.'

Not only the dogs were straining at the leash. Horowitz sensed Stieber couldn't wait to bring the hunt to its bloody and final end. He brushed snow off his sleeve, spoke quietly.

'Release the dogs . . .'

The snapping, snarling animals, freed from the leash, bounded forward, leapt up the path, vanished from sight. Slipping and slithering all over the ice, Stieber followed, far behind his creatures.

Newman sat about ten feet above the ground, his legs dangling over the branch of the giant fir they'd sheltered under. His case was perched in a crook of the tree. Lying in the snow directly below him was a soiled shirt he'd extracted from the case. In his right hand he held the fully loaded Walther.

The sound of the baying dogs had changed, was coming

194

nearer much faster. He guessed the handlers had released their charges. Almost frozen stiff, he flexed each arm, transferring the weapon from one hand to the other. He waggled his legs backwards and forwards to keep the circulating moving. Fortunately when the platform of snow had collapsed it had left the thick branch bare so he sat on wood but he could still feel the cold infiltrating his clothes. The joyous barking was much closer. He saw movement lower down the path. He gripped the Walther firmly in both hands, aimed it.

'Come and get it,' he said to himself.

The unknown factor was how many there were. He had eight shots in the gun and hoped he wouldn't have to reload. He could have perched higher up, but they would be moving targets. He wanted point-blank range. The first hound came into view, a massive beast, mouth open, sharp teeth showing. Newman remained quite still.

The dog was faster in its reactions than he'd expected. It sniffed briefly at his shirt, stared round, looked up, saw him. It gave a deep-throated growl as four more dogs joined it, then it crouched and sprang upwards. Newman whipped up the Walther, shot it through the head, slicing off the right side. A second dog made the leap, almost reached his feet. He shot it in the chest. It hung in mid-air for a fraction of a second, collapsed as a still heap in the snow. A third dog leapt for him. It rose so high its head was level with his feet, inches away. He fired twice. The dog fell like a stone, lay on its side. The remaining two beasts paused, circling the bodies. He fired twice more and they sagged, one lying twitching.

A heavy hush descended on the forest. Newman stared down the path as he reloaded, throwing the rejected magazine as far as he could. No sign of the handlers yet. The dogs would have outpaced any human being.

He took hold of his case, leaned down, dropped it on a pile of snow which cushioned its fall. Shinning down the tree, he approached the animal which was still twitching, aimed the muzzle, pulled the trigger. The dog jerked convulsively, lay still.

Newman walked away from the tree across the snow to the south, a different direction from that taken by Tweed and Paula who had climbed east. He came to a bare patch of moss-covered ground where the snow hadn't penetrated, walked a few more paces. Then he slowly walked backwards, placing his boots in the footprints he'd already made until he reached the tree.

Picking up his case, he took a long stride, placing one foot on the frozen stream. Then without a glance back, he plodded on upwards, out of sight.

Horowitz, followed by Hendrix, heard a howl compounded of fury and misery echoing through the forest. Not the sound of a dog. The sound of a human being. He climbed higher and walked slowly round a stand of trees, the Luger in his hand and concealed behind his heavy raincoat with a belt and epaulettes.

Stieber stood looking down at the carnage of his destroyed animals. He swung round as he heard Horowitz and his face was contorted in such rage he reminded Horowitz of one of his charges when alive. Shaking, he pointed.

'They killed my dogs, the bastards . . .'

'The dogs were trying to kill them,' Horowitz reminded him in a mild tone.

Stieber stared wildly at the Hungarian, his right hand slid inside the lapel of his own raincoat. Horowitz whipped up the Luger, aimed the muzzle at Stieber's chest.

'Take your hand out slowly. There had better be nothing in it. Now, that's more sensible. Feeling calmer now? Good. Oh, while I remember it, Stieber – if you ever threaten me again I shall shoot you. Understood?

Now let's fix our concentration on the job in hand . . .'

'There's a trail of footprints heading to the south. I'm going to check them . . .'

Horowitz stood quite still as Stieber trod through virgin snow, walking alongside the footmarks. Behind Horowitz Eva Hendrix shivered, tore her eyes away from the corpses.

'I don't see how they managed it,' she gasped. 'Five dogs attacking at the same time.'

'Oh, it wasn't Eiger. He never carries a gun. But someone with him does.' He looked up. 'And that someone is clever and dangerous. You see that bare branch? He cleared off the snow, then waited – out of reach of the dogs but in an ideal position to pick them off. Hence the shots we heard.' He used one foot to poke at a crumpled shirt on the ground. 'The gunman even left one of his used shirts – to make sure the dogs would pause beneath where he waited. Eiger has a formidable protector. Ah, here comes Stieber with nothing.'

Stieber looked depressed. 'The tracks disappear. They went on over bare ground.'

'I wonder.' Horowitz made an impatient gesture. 'We can't waste more time here. I have an ace to play. The helicopters. We must return to the Volvo so I can re-establish contact.'

19

Aboard the police Sikorsky Kuhlmann stared down at the endless sea of the Black Forest as the machine headed towards the small spa town of Badenweiler. They were flying five hundred feet above tree level. From that height the forest was a criss-cross of black and white. Black where snow had fallen from the firs, white where it clung frozen to the treetops. The moonglow cast a ghostly light on the empty world below. Kuhlmann glanced up, stiffened.

Maybe half a mile away on the port side flew another chopper. It appeared to be skimming the treetops and from its nose a searchlight was angled downwards, turning slowly as it scanned the forest.

'See that chopper over to port?' he growled into the mike attached to his headset, addressing the pilot in the control cabin for'ard. 'Reduce height, fly towards it, when you're within forty yards of it fly on a parallel course.'

'Forty yards?' the pilot almost yelped. 'That's too close.'

'Which is what that other pilot will think . . .'

'Chief, my co-pilot has been watching it through night glasses. It's a World Security machine.'

'Pull alongside it. That's an order.' He addressed the gunner who was seated in front of him next to the door. A swivel-mounted machine-gun had been secured in front of him. 'When we're in position,' Kuhlmann continued, 'they may need to be persuaded to obey my orders. When I tell you, open fire, give them a burst a dozen yards ahead of their control cabin. That should prove an effective persuader . . .'

'It's illegal,' the gunner protested.

'If I say so, it's legal.'

The machine had altered course, was losing altitude, as Kuhlmann wrenched off his headset, stood in the narrow passage-way and held on to the backs of seats, making his way towards the pilot's cabin. Entering it, he held himself upright with one hand; with the other he reached towards the co-pilot and grasped the night glasses. The co-pilot was also acting as the radio op. He glanced up nervously while Kuhlmann splayed his feet, angled his back against the side of the entrance, focused the glasses. The co-pilot glanced at the pilot, raised his eyes to heaven. Kuhlmann's reputation for taking chances had preceded him.

Within minutes the police chopper was flying alongside the World Security machine, which still had its searchlight on. Through his glasses Kuhlmann was now scanning the forest beyond the second chopper. He suddenly switched them back. Yes, he'd been right. In the middle of a clearing on top of a peaked hill stood a snow-covered mountain lodge. No sign of life. No smoke from the chimney. He didn't think the other chopper had seen it yet. He handed back the glasses, reached for the microphone in front of the co-pilot.

'Calling World Security chopper 4902. This is the police. I am ordering you to return to base immediately. Return to Freiburg airfield immediately. Kuhlmann of Kriminalpolizei speaking . . .'

The co-pilot was gesturing, pointing north. Kuhlmann gazed in that direction and saw three more machines with searchlights spread out over the forest. The co-pilot, who had been staring through his night glasses, handed Kuhlmann a spare headset.

'They're all World Security machines. What's going on?'

'That's what we're here to find out.'

They were still flying parallel to the other chopper, which continued on course. Kuhlmann gestured for the mike, gripped it tightly.

'Calling World Security chopper 4902. Chief Inspector Kuhlmann here again. I repeat – just once more. Return to base immediately. Return to Freiburg airfield . . .'

There was a lot of atmospheric crackle and then a reply this time. The voice of the radio op aboard the other machine was disjointed.

'4902 calling. Kuhlmann, I can't hear what you said . . .'

Kuhlmann handed back the mike, spoke into his head-set mike, his tone grim. 'Hans, I said give them a burst. I'm still waiting. That's an order.'

Nothing happened. 'God Almighty,' Kuhlmann muttered to himself. The co-pilot caught his expression, looked away. Kuhlmann swung round, re-entered the passenger cabin. Hans sat frozen, holding the machine-gun. He looked up, shook his head with a gesture of hopelessness. Kuhlmann reached down, grabbed his arm, tugged. Hans tore off his headset, scrambled out of his seat, the chopper wobbled, Hans fell into the seat opposite.

Kuhlmann was already easing his bulk into the gunner's seat. He fastened his belt. He used both hands. One pressed down a lever, slid open the door. Ice-cold air rushed inside the cabin. Hans shuddered with shock. The drop in temperature didn't seem to affect Kuhlmann. He swivelled the barrel of the gun, peered through the sight, fixed the crosshairs on a point about thirty feet in front of the other chopper's nose, pressed the trigger. One short burst, one much longer . . .

The World Security climbed vertically, turned through one hundred and eighty degrees, headed back towards Freiburg airfield. Kuhlmann leaned forward, grasped the door handle and hauled it shut. He felt like a block of ice. He rammed the headset in position again, addressed the pilot.

'Escort him back to Freiburg. Now patch me through to police HQ, same place. Ask for Inspector Wagishauser . . .'

He waited, rubbing his large, stubby-fingered hands together. Jesus, it was a cold night. A few minutes later Wagishauser came through. Kuhlmann began speaking rapidly.

'Arrange for a reception committee at Freiburg airfield. And three more World Security choppers are flying over

200

the forest. Order them to return yesterday to Freiburg. I'm escorting a fourth machine back. I had to fire a burst of machine-gun fire across his nose to persuade him to obey my recall order.'

'You did what?' Wagishauser sounded appalled.

'You heard. Now contact those other three choppers. They have to be grounded. And that's an order. Any difficulty, get off your butt, drive round to World Security HQ, locate their communications room, pressure them to recall the other three choppers. OK?'

'But what is this all about? What are the charges?'

'Suspected involvement in drug-trafficking, of course . . .'

Sitting in front of the stationary Volvo, Horowitz couldn't contact the chopper, Elbe Two. No reply. He had a moment of inspiration, sensing trouble, and switched to the police radio band. He was just in time to hear the latter part of Kuhlmann's transmission:

'Arrange for a reception committee . . . I'm escorting a fourth machine . . . I had to fire a burst of machine-gun . . .'

He shushed Hendrix, again sitting in the back, while listening to the rest of the transmission. Beside him, Stieber, still fretting over the massacre of his precious dogs, showed alarm. As Kuhlmann signed off, Horowitz turned off the radio and gazed ahead in silence.

'Shit!' Hendrix called out. 'That's torn the whole ball game wide open . . .'

'We'd better get out of here,' Stieber snapped. 'Once I was interrogated by that bastard, Kuhlmann. He's no feelings at all.'

Horowitz was secretly amused at Stieber concerning himself with other people's feelings. He looked over his shoulder – Hendrix was shredding a lace handkerchief between her teeth.

'You two are easily disturbed,' he remarked. 'A couple of setbacks is nothing in my business. Eiger is still a target. I'm convinced he will run for the Swiss border when the roads south are open. The latest met report forecasts milder weather. We have to be patient. Meanwhile I'll organize a fresh team of World Security operatives . . .'

'At least eight have already been killed,' Stieber interjected, 'in that autobahn pile-up.'

'Please listen. They were all British. This time Evans must supply German operatives – men who really know the area.'

'Which area, for God's sake?' Hendrix asked.

'The Swiss border-crossings, of course. Basle, Konstanz, etc. When Eiger tries to slip over the frontier we'll be waiting for him.'

Landing at Freiburg airfield, Kuhlmann climbed into the car he'd radioed to be waiting for him. He was driven straight to police headquarters. Behind him followed a convoy of two police vans bringing in the crews of the four WS choppers.

Inspector Wagishauser greeted him with the news that the Minister had called him three times from Bonn.

'He sounded agitated. News of the aerial activity over the Black Forest has reached him. He sounded very upset . . .'

'His permanent state of mind. Can I use your desk and phone?'

The two men were alone as Kuhlmann put in the call to Bonn. As he expected, the Minister was still up, answered the phone himself on his private line.

'What is going on down there, Kuhlmann? I've had a

complaint from a man called Evans, managing director . . .'

'I've met the crook. Interrogated him over that business of a truck with high-tech equipment trying to slip over into East Germany . . .'

'Case not proven . . .'

'If you'd listen to me, Minister, I might save you a whole heap of political embarrassment. This thing could go up to the Chancellor. He might be asking *you* some pretty loaded questions.'

A long pause. 'Go on,' the Minister said, and Kuhlmann knew he'd got him.

'First, the original request was for us to locate Tweed. But they didn't tell us they were hiring a British outfit – World Security – to hunt him down and liquidate him on Federal territory. At least that's the way it's beginning to look. How well do you think that would go down with the Chancellor?' He didn't wait for a reaction. 'It's all wrapped up with four WS choppers patrolling the Black Forest in the middle of the night. They've already tried to kill Tweed once, hence that pile-up on the autobahn when eight plain-clothes men ended up on slabs. Maybe you'd prefer to let me go on handling things?'

'What does it all mean?' bleated the Minister.

'If Tweed is caught and taken back to Britain, imagine the public scandal. A quiet death over here would solve the problem nicely, thank you,' Kuhlmann continued smoothly.

'I'm more than happy to leave the case in your hands.'

I thought you would be, Kuhlmann reflected to himself and grinned at Wagishauser who stood listening with fascination.

'One more problem I'm not sure of handling – it might affect how you deal with the problem.' The Minister paused again. I really have you on the run, Kuhlmann thought. 'Lance Buckmaster, their Minister for External

Security, has been on the line to me. He wants to know how we're progressing in the search.'

'Tell him the hunt is continuing. But Tweed is a fox – he'll appreciate that phrase – and difficult to locate. We are now narrowing the search area. No specifics. And ask him if he's questioning our ability to cope.'

'That's a good ploy. Leave it all to you. *Carte blanche* to solve the problem . . .'

Kuhlmann grinned again as he put down the phone. The best detective in the whole of Germany, Kuhlmann was also past-master of the art of handling the politicians he despised. Wagishauser sat down in the chair facing his visitor.

'I'd never have dared talk to him like that, Otto.'

'Which is why you're here and I'm sitting behind my desk in Wiesbaden.'

Kuhlmann lit a cigar and reflected for a moment on the present situation. He was convinced Tweed was the last man to be involved in a murder and a rape, for Christ's sake. And he'd had enough experience weighing up criminals. There had to be a conspiracy. He couldn't actively help Tweed, but he would put roadblocks in the way of his discovery. Give his old colleague time. That, he guessed, was what Tweed needed: time. He looked at Wagishauser.

'The next move is to put the squeeze on Evans and his hirelings. Call Evans, get him out of bed, I want him here in thirty minutes. Counting from now.'

20

The hunting lodge was perched high up on top of a small peak with a clear view from the upper-storey windows over the Black Forest which lapped the sides of the peak like a sea. Standing shivering by a window she had opened, Paula gazed down, searching for any sign of a helicopter. The moonlit sky was empty. She closed the window and made her way down the wooden staircase of the timber-built structure.

'It's all right,' she informed Tweed, 'I can't see any sign of life on the ground or in the sky.'

'Then we'll light this up and get some warmth before we perish.'

He was crouched in front of a huge brick fireplace piled up with logs. While she was upstairs he'd found some old newspapers inside an airtight chest and tucked sheets among the logs. He used his lighter to ignite the paper and within minutes the logs were flaming.

They had reached the lodge to find it closed and shuttered. Tweed had picked up a short straight branch on their way up the mountain: he had seen it as a crude makeshift weapon and had used it as a walking stick up the final steep ascent. After walking all round the large lodge, he had utilized the stick as a crowbar to prise open one of the shutters. Hitting the exposed glass window beyond with his gloved hand, he had reached in through the hole and turned the handle to gain access.

The interior was ice-cold and had a musty odour. Paula had caught whiffs of pine cones scattered over the log fire.

The power had been turned off, the freezer and the fridge were empty. Tweed had grimaced at her discovery.

'So, we go hungry.'

'Hardly. Isn't it a good job that I did some shopping while I was out in Freiburg on my own.'

'What shopping?'

'At a supermarket.' She perched her case on a heavy wooden table, fumbled it open with her gloved hands, started taking out supplies. Two cans of baked beans, two of canned meat, two camping gas canisters with metal frames and grids, two cans of coffee, one of powdered milk, two loaves of bread and a wrapped pack of butter. 'We should survive on that – but not for long,' she warned.

'I should have thought of all that myself.'

'Men!' she chided him with friendly contempt. 'They assume food appears out of thin air.'

'I'm afraid I assumed the power would be switched on for lost travellers – with frozen food in the freezer.'

'But did you ever come up here in winter?'

'No,' he admitted, 'It was in autumn. Now, I'd better get that fire going before we freeze to death.'

'The smoke will show for miles coming out of the chimney,' she warned.

'So you explore upstairs where you get a panoramic view – check if there are any signs of life. Meantime I'll prepare to get the fire going – when you've made your check . . .'

When she ran down the wooden staircase and reported to him she repeated her warning. 'We're perched in the open on top of the highest point for miles. The smoke could locate us.'

'We'll have to risk it – otherwise we freeze to death,' he'd repeated before he set light to the paper.

Paula explored the ground floor, found a modern kitchen with a Calor gas stove – but no Calor gas. The lodge was furnished with rough-hewn wooden chairs and tables and cupboards. In one cupboard in the main living-room she found a stack of sleeping bags. Tweed, still crouched over the fire, using an ancient pair of bellows to fan the flames gently, looked up.

'So, we have something we can sleep in.'

'Just dive inside one of them, you mean?' she suggested.

'Why not? We need sleep . . .'

'Men!' she said again as she sniffed at a sleeping bag and held it to her face. 'They're damp, need drying out.'

She hauled chairs in front of the fire, opened one sleeping bag and looped it over a chair. That was when Tweed stood up suddenly, put a finger to his mouth with one hand, grabbed her with the other, gestured towards the kitchen.

'What is it?' she whispered.

'Someone coming. I heard a faint crunch of feet on crusted snow. No noise. Get into the kitchen . . .'

Moving silently, he picked up the heavy stick which would serve as an effective club, then took up a position on the opposite side of the front door he had unlatched earlier. He was pressed against the roughened wall away from the hinged side. Paula had disappeared. He took a firm grip on the club, waited.

The door moved a millimetre. Tweed would never have noticed had he not been watching it. Seconds later the heavy door was thrown inwards as though struck by a hurricane, slammed back against the wall. Newman dived inside, crouched low, Walther gripped in both hands, swinging the weapon in a wide arc.

'Relax, Bob,' Tweed said in a quiet voice, staying pressed against the wall.

'You might have put out the welcome mat.' Newman slid the gun inside its holster. Tweed closed the door quickly to shut out the cold as Newman went on talking. 'I arrived and saw footprints leading up to this place. No guarantee they were yours.'

Paula appeared from the kitchen. 'Bob! What happened to those horrible dogs we heard coming?'

'Meat for carrion-eaters. Five of them. I shot the lot, then hoofed it up here over that frozen stream. Where does it end? We seem to be on top of a small mountain.'

'I'll show you,' said Tweed. 'It's remarkable.' He paused. 'Any chance you were followed?'

'Oh, come off it. I left the hounds at the foot of that big fir we sheltered under, then trudged up the stream for a short distance. Next move, I climbed another tall tree from where I could just see the corpses. I watched the area with these.' He took a small pair of binoculars from his pocket. 'Two men and a girl arrived. They spent about five minutes there – one of them followed a false trail I'd laid and then came back. Brief discussion. They all went back downhill the way they'd come. I continued on up the stream. What did you want to show me?'

Tweed led the way through the front door on to a wide verandah, walked down the steps and, with Newman and Paula following, took them round the side of the lodge where the frozen stream ran. He pointed to a snow-covered mound.

'That's the origin of the stream, frozen solid now. A very powerful spring gushes up there normally. After winter the stream becomes a rushing torrent when the snow melts.'

'Could you melt it now?' Paula asked. 'That would give us fresh water for our coffee. I have a plastic bottle of water but fresh would taste much better.'

'It would be a cold job,' Newman commented, crouching down, moving layers of snow until he exposed a thick jet of ice.

'So', Paula told him, 'get on with it while I prepare us all a meal under conditions I regard as somewhat

208

primitive. And, Tweed, you keep an eye on that fire . . .'

She left them. Newman glanced at Tweed. 'Ever occur to you that women can be pretty bossy?'

They ate their meal off cardboard plates on the table, which had been hauled near the blazing fire. The pine logs oozed resin, sputtered and crackled, but Paula welcomed the sound. It helped to counter the brooding silence which pressed down on the isolated lodge.

She had served them meat and baked beans cooked on the camping gas, crusty bread and butter. They used plastic cutlery and at one stage Newman made the mistake of cracking a joke.

'This is just like a meal served by an airline – even down to the plastic knives and forks.'

'Really?' Paula folded her arms. 'Maybe you'd have preferred metal cutlery? But then I'd have had to carry it. The weight of my case was quite something coming up through the forest.'

'I assumed it just contained a few clothes. Sorry, I was just trying to lighten the proceedings.'

Tweed intervened. 'Difficult to do that. Under the circumstances. We're all – including Paula – feeling the strain.'

'Then if it's all right by you,' Newman said soberly, 'I'd like to hear what happened when all this started – back at Radnor Walk. I walked in on it and no one has told me much so far.'

'Hardly been time, Bob. But you're right,' Tweed agreed. 'And this is as good a time as any. So this is what happened . . .'

Newman listened in silence as Tweed recalled the late phone call allegedly from Klaus Richter asking Tweed to meet him urgently at the Cheshire Cheese pub in Fleet Street on the fatal night. Tweed gave a concise account, omitting no relevant detail. Paula watched him anxiously, wondering how re-telling the grim story might affect him in his state of near-exhaustion. Newman nodded as he completed his story.

'It all fits with what I observed while I was in your flat. Down to that damning detail of your half-smoked pipe in the ash-bowl. But what about this Klaus Richter? You said he lived at the edge of Freiburg.'

'In an apartment in a new development at the very end of Schusterstrasse . . .'

'But that's where we stayed the night,' Paula burst out in surprise. 'The Hotel Oberkirch was in Schusterstrasse – so why didn't we visit Klaus Richter to find out what was going on?'

'Because I'm sure it would be a death-trap,' Tweed assured her. 'Work it out for yourself. Richter was the bait to lure me away from going home to Radnor Walk until very late. To give someone time to strangle and rape that poor unknown girl. So, either Richter phoned me under pressure – maybe with a gun pressed to his skull. Or if someone else did a good job of imitating him they would still put a close watch on Richter's apartment in Freiburg – especially when they realized I was heading in this direction. Which they obviously did – hence the assassination attempt on the autobahn. No, Richter's apartment was the last place I was going to call on. He's probably dead, anyway.'

'I still think it should have been checked,' Newman commented.

'Oh, it is going to be checked. One of the special instructions I gave Marler when I was alone with him at the Oberkirch was to visit Richter's place. He'll be very careful.'

'Marler?' Newman queried. 'You still trust him?'

'I have to, I'm short of personnel. I need you, Bob, to protect me. I'm the only one who knows about the secret project *Shockwave* I was working on.'

'Care to enlighten me?'

'Now is as good a time as any . . .'

Tweed repeated what he'd told Paula in Brussels about the new computer which was the key to a viable Strategic Defence Initiative. The computer travelling aboard the freighter *Lampedusa* and bound for Plymouth by a devious route.

'Devious?' repeated Newman.

'Yes. It is following a course which avoids all the major shipping lanes.'

'And you have the code book for contacting the *Lampedusa* – with two trick questions to check all is well. Apart from the ship's radio op, does anyone else have the code book?'

'Only the Minister – Lance Buckmaster. He'll carry on making contact with the ship in my absence. From a room with radio equipment at the Admiralty. But he doesn't know about the trick questions. Like the radio op, I have them in my head. Not in the book.'

'What I want to know,' Paula said in a low tense voice, 'is who killed that girl at Radnor Walk?'

'Which is another mission I gave Marler, who is returning to England after checking Richter in Freiburg. You have to grasp the fact that all this was carefully planned by the opposition well in advance. Every contingency was foreseen. And Marler is rather good at unravelling other people's plans.'

'But who is the opposition?' Paula protested vehemently. 'We are working in the dark, on the run, getting nowhere.'

'I think I can answer your question about the identity of the opposition,' Newman replied. 'Someone tried to shoot me from the Mercedes down on that timber track. I shot him instead. I searched him and came up with this.'

He produced a folder from his pocket, threw it on the table. Paula picked it up, examined it, then stared at her two companions.

'Gustav Braun. An employee of World Security & Communications.'

'That's the opposition,' said Newman. 'I've heard rumours of WS using some pretty ruthless tactics in business – but this is the first time I realized they operated murder teams.'

'It could be for a very special operation,' Tweed mused.

'It is. For hunting down and killing you. The big question is who is running the operation? Gareth Morgan, Lance Buckmaster – or Leonora Buckmaster, now chairman. It has to be one of those three. Only power at the top would dare risk going so far.'

'What was your impression of Gareth Morgan when you confronted him over breakfast at the Colombi?' asked Tweed.

'Tough as granite, wily as a cobra, the biggest liar since Baron Munchausen. Very ambitious.'

'So the motive might be complicated – if Morgan plans to take over the whole organization. His first move would be to discredit Lance Buckmaster.'

'How would he do that?' Paula asked.

'By compromising him – maybe to the extent of having him convicted of murder. And if that's the case Morgan is using me as his cat's paw. Marler may uncover a nest of vipers.'

'He'll have his work cut out – considering what you've sent him back to do,' Newman commented.

'Oh, he has a lot to do,' Tweed agreed. 'One line of enquiry he will pursue is to try and obtain the findings of the Special Branch pathologist who conducted an autopsy on the body of that girl. There were traces of blood on the girl's wrists and on the sheet. I think she was tied up before she was foully assaulted – strangled and raped. So identification of the blood groups becomes important. The pathologist's report will record them.'

'You should have left Marler to protect you,' Newman told him. 'Sent me to London instead to dig up all this stuff . . .'

'Except that Marler is a member of the Service and can walk into places you'd never be admitted to. I know you're fully vetted, Bob – but it was always on my say-so that they let you travel to top secret establishments. Now I'm disgraced, to say the least. You'd also be suspect.'

Tweed has really foreseen all the problems, Paula reflected. She asked the question which had been bothering her for days.

'But why did someone go to all that trouble to set you up – have you suspected of this awful crime, go all the way by committing the crime. Why?'

'When we know the answer to that we'll know who murdered the girl in Radnor Walk,' Tweed replied. 'I think we're all at the end of our tethers. We need sleep. We'd better arrange a roster of guard duties – someone must be awake upstairs to watch the approaches to this lodge. I'll take it in turn with Newman. Two hours on, two hours off.'

'Not on your life,' Paula said firmly. 'I thought I was a member of the team. I'll take my turn. But what do we do next – in the morning? It would be dangerous to stay here too long.'

'Which is why we won't stay beyond the morning,' Tweed decided. 'We'll have to try and make it to Switzerland in one day. Move faster than anyone will expect.'

'With no transport?' Paula pointed out.

'There's the blue Audi still hidden inside that copse near the timber track,' Newman reminded her. 'And Tweed drove it deep into the undergrowth, which should give some insulation for the engine. I predict it will take me a while to get it going, but get it going I will.'

'Agreed,' said Tweed.

PART TWO

The Assassin – Horowitz

21

During the night after the abortive hunt for Tweed in the Black Forest, Horowitz had slept soundly for several hours in his bedroom at the Colombi. At precisely 5 a.m. the automatic alarm clock inside his head woke him. He got out of bed, immediately alert, washed, shaved and dressed swiftly.

Wrapped against the cold in a thick scarf and an overcoat, he told the night porter he hadn't been able to sleep and was going for a walk. The porter shook his head.

'It's bitterly cold out there, sir. And watch your footing. The sidewalks and streets are like a glacier   '

Horowitz thanked him for the warning and made for the Altstadt. The street lamps threw an eerie glow over the snow and no one else was about as he headed up Schusterstrasse, continued along Munzgasse to a T-junction where Konvikstrasse crossed it.

His breath created small puffs in the sub-zero air and from the roof gutters on either side hung rows of icicles. He had reached the edge of the town and ahead a flight of concrete steps led upwards. To their left was a colony of new houses, their architecture carefully designed to merge with the medieval dwellings facing them.

They had steep-tiled roofs and large dormer-windows projecting from the roofs. Beyond them in the near distance rose a wall of dense forest. Several of the houses – all of them divided up into spacious apartments – had pleasant gardens in summer with trees and shrubs and plants. Horowitz looked round one last time, then gently prised up the latch of the grille gate leading into a courtyard. Despite his care the ice splintered under the pressure of his gloved hand and the sound was like a pistol shot.

He closed the gate behind him, walked up to the house, peered inside an uncurtained window. Klaus Richter sat upright in an armchair facing the TV set. Horowitz went back to the front door, rapped on it with a certain irregular tattoo, turned the handle and walked slowly inside. A wave of warmth met him.

'Keep your hands where they are or I'll disembowel you,' ordered a throaty voice.

Horowitz froze, turned his head slowly. Stieber sat in a chair against the wall, a sawn-off twin-barrelled shotgun aimed at Horowitz's stomach.

'Oh, it's you.'

He sounded disappointed. Horowitz remained perfectly still as he spoke in his soft voice.

'First, point that thing away from me – at the far wall.' When Stieber had obeyed he spoke again. 'Now put the safety catch on and place the gun on the floor, muzzle aimed at the wall.'

Stieber grinned unpleasantly as he obeyed the order. 'Nervous, aren't we?'

'Just cautious. You have been here all night? Good. At least I find you alert. Has anyone been near the place? Eiger might have come back to contact Richter – or he might have sent the girl.'

'You see no bodies,' Stieber answered truculently. 'No, no one has been here so far,' he replied quickly as he saw Horowitz's expression. A night spent in the dark had done wonders for his night vision.

'You'll be relieved soon after daybreak. Meantime, stay here.' He glanced at Richter and now an unpleasant stench assailed his nostrils. He wondered how Stieber had stood it through the long hours, then remembered his other profession was that of pig farmer. Richter had been killed by the simple process of injecting air into his veins. Morgan had said something about his first making a phone call to London. Horowitz calculated Stieber had killed him well over twenty-four hours before. He was about to leave when Stieber made the remark.

'I wonder whether anyone has been blown to pieces by the bomb you placed under that blue Audi we found hidden near the timber track?'

'We can always hope.'

'Gives me quite a kick thinking about that bomb. Helped to pass the time while I was sitting here with Zombie over there. The idea of Eiger coming back for his transport, turning on the ignition time and again to get the frigging motor going. That should have set off the bomb – the vibrations. Or maybe he'd got it going and was backing on to the track when – *Boom!* I'd like to have been there to see that – from a distance, if you see what I mean. It would have given me a real kick . . .'

'I'm going now,' Horowitz said. 'Tell the man who relieves you to stay inside here on duty until nightfall, then leave. No one will come after that.'

Horowitz was glad to leave the house. The reactions of the toad he'd left behind filled him with distaste. And he doubted if anyone would come near the apartment to check on Richter.

Marler, who had driven back to Freiburg the previous night in the grey Audi as soon as the chopper disappeared, also slept at the Colombi. The alarm clock on his bedside table woke him at 5.30 a.m.

'You're the second guest to brave the elements this morning,' the night porter remarked.

Marler paused at the front entrance. 'Really? Perhaps that was my friend who also likes fresh air before breakfast. What did he look like?'

'Tall, thin chap. Older than yourself. Maybe forty. Hard to tell. And he wears steel-rimmed glasses. Got a very deliberate walk. He'll need that this morning. So will you. Bloody ice all over the place. Was he your friend?'

'No. The description doesn't fit. I'll heed your warning.'

And that, Marler thought, as he walked through the eerily silent town, was more of a warning than the night porter could ever have guessed. The description fitted perfectly the photograph he'd taken the previous day of one of the men entering WS headquarters. A perfect word description of Armand Horowitz.

Why would Horowitz be prowling Freiburg so early? Marler noticed the single file of footprints leading from the Colombi imprinted in the snow. It was a long shot chance but he followed the footmarks to see where they led.

His suspicions strengthened as he followed them along the street called Schuster, continued along Munzgasse. They were leading him to the address of Klaus Richter, 498 Konvikstrasse, given to him by Tweed. Was it possible that Horowitz was waiting at Richter's address, foreseeing someone would sooner or later arrive to question Klaus? He decided it was not only possible – it was probable. Horowitz never missed a trick.

As he approached the long flight of concrete steps leading to the colony of new houses, eventually to the footbridge which crossed the ring road, he put his hands inside his trench-coat pockets, checked their contents. A .32 Browning automatic, a knuckleduster – and an aerosol filled with Mace gas. The last weapon was quite illegal.

He paused outside the shuttered café called *Wolfshohle* – the Wolf's Lair. Appropriate enough if Horowitz was in the vicinity. To his right was a fountain which would normally project water into the stone basin surrounding it. The jets were frozen solid, the water in the basin a sheet of ice. And still he had seen no one.

He strolled slowly up the steps, noted that Konvikstrasse

498 stood to his right, the way into the courtyard barred by a small grille gate. He also noted the footmarks leading inside, the fractured ice on the latch. He continued higher up to look the place over from the back.

There was a small rear garden enclosed by walls. Bare-headed, his hair gleaming under a lamp, Marler could stand up to any amount of cold weather. He thought for a moment.

At the main entrance lower down the flight there had been a second trail of footmarks, leading *away* from the apartment, continuing along Konvikstrasse towards the Munster. Marler was puzzled. Was the place empty now? A dangerous assumption.

He climbed over the wall, dropped into a heap of snow which broke his fall, made no sound. He approached the rear door. No lights inside the place. Extracting a leather pouch from his jacket pocket, he studied the lock, chose a pick-lock, inserted the instrument inside the lock, fiddled gently. He felt the lock turn. He slipped the pouch back inside his pocket, took out the Mace gas aerosol, slowly turned the handle of the door, pushed it inwards with great care. Well-oiled hinges. No sound. Warmth rushed out to meet him. He stiffened.

The central heating was turned on. Why – if no one was inside the apartment? He half-closed his eyes, blinking in the gloom. He was in the kitchen. He sniffed. A faint aroma of coffee recently made. He closed the rear door with equal care. His eyes were becoming accustomed to the dark.

The inner door was open and beyond was a straight passage which presumably led to the living-room at the front. He'd been puzzled on his arrival by the fact that no net curtains were drawn across the front windows down-stairs, no curtains at all – unlike all the other apartments.

The passage was tiled, which was fortunate. Less risk of giveaway creaks. He walked slowly down the passage,

221

holding the Mace aerosol at chest height like a gun. The door to what he felt sure was the living-room was wide open. He listened. A quiet creak, like someone changing position in a wooden chair. His nerves went like steel, as they always did at the moment of crisis.

He reached the doorway, peered through the gap between the door and the wall. One man, facing him, sat rigidly still in an armchair. Too still. Against the inner wall by the passage a second man sat, short, squat, with a rounded head. Across his lap rested a sawn-off shotgun. Charming.

Marler retraced his steps silently to the kitchen. A can of coffee stood on a wooden working surface. There had been a peculiar smell drifting from the living-room. To Marler it had been the smell of death, decomposition. He lifted the can of coffee, made sure the lid was pressed on tightly, then knocked over the can. It rolled, rested against the rear wall.

Marler was now squeezed against the wall alongside the door and opposite the hinged side. From the living-room came the sound of the same creak, but louder. Like a man slowly getting up. The man moved so quietly Marler's first intimation that he had reached the kitchen was when he saw the barrel of the shotgun poked through the opening. The squat man took two more paces. Marler took a deep breath, held it, squirted a limited jet of Mace into the jowly face.

Everything after that happened very quickly.

Stieber gasped, staggered into the kitchen. His left hand flew to his eyes, blinded temporarily by the gas, groaning with the pain. His right hand still gripped the shotgun. Marler moved behind him, his crooked right arm looped round Stieber's neck, jerked it backwards, just short of the point where it snapped.

'Just a little more pressure,' he hissed in German, 'and your neck snaps like a stick of celery. Put the safety catch on that gun. Now!'

In agony, Stieber grasped the message from the chilling voice of his unknown assailant. He fumbled with the shotgun. More by luck than judgement he found the safety catch, put it on.

'That's better,' Marler told him. 'Now we're going to walk back into the living-room. Shuffle with your feet. I'm not relaxing my hold. But I might take it that extra inch tighter . . .'

Stieber was disorientated, in a state of shock. Awake all night, he was in no condition to resist, even to think clearly. One emotion dominated his mind. Fear. He turned round, shuffled slowly along the passage in Marler's grip, clawing at his eyes with his left hand. The smarting sensation was growing worse.

Marler guided him through the doorway into the living-room, told him to place the gun on a table. *Very carefully*. He then guided him to the carver chair where Stieber had been sitting – probably to keep himself awake – and sat him in the carver. Stieber sagged, used both his hands to rub his eyes while Marler patted him all over for other weapons. Nothing.

The dead body of Richter had been propped up inside a chair to give him a lifelike appearance from the window. Marler stopped several feet away from the corpse, wrinkled his nose. He turned his attention again to Stieber.

'I'm going to ask you questions. I know most of the answers. Lie to me once, I'll know, I'll break your neck. Play along with me and you'll live to see another day. Understood?'

Stieber nodded. His right hand massaged the back of his neck which was aching horribly. But his vision was coming back. To protect himself, Marler had used only a small quantity of Mace. Stieber could now see him as a blurred silhouette. He was careful not to stare at the silhouette. His eyes fell on the outline of the shotgun, a few feet from where he sat.

'Understood,' he replied in German, the language this bastard had addressed him in from when he first spoke.

'Klaus Richter made a telephone call to London. You forced him to make that call. How?'

'I held a knife across his throat . . .'

'The call was made from here? From that telephone over there?'

'Yes . . .'

'I warned you.' Marler's voice was cold, detached. 'The man who took the call in London heard a lot of noise in the background . . .'

'Tape recorder . . .' Stieber's throat hurt and he was croaking. He pointed. Marler noticed the finger pointed straight at the recorder perched on a sideboard. Stieber's vision was clearing.

Marler, watching Stieber, crossed to the recorder, switched it on. The sound of voices with music in the background filled the room. That was how they had made it sound convincing to Tweed: noises like a pub. He switched off the recorder.

'Name of the man Richter called? Don't hesitate . . .'

'Tweed, whoever he may be—'

'When Richter ended the call someone killed him.' He aimed his Browning. 'I don't give a damn who. Just tell me—'

'I did. Injected air into a vein with a hypodermic—'

'Who ordered you to do this?'

A long pause. Stieber stirred restlessly. Marler holstered the Browning, flexed his hands, approached Stieber.

'Horowitz,' Stieber croaked quickly. 'Armand Horowitz. And don't ever let him know I told you, for God's sake.'

'Or for yours. I won't. Where is Horowitz now?'

'No idea.' Another pause. 'He came here about half an hour before you showed – to make sure I was waiting in case Eiger came here to check on Richter like you've done.

224

Then he left. I don't know where for. I don't think he'll come back. Hope to God he doesn't – my neck must be bruised and he'd notice that.'

'Show me the hypodermic you used on Richter. I need proof of that part of your story.'

Stieber stumbled to his feet, staggered to a sideboard, opened a drawer. 'In here—'

'Show it to me,' Marler ordered.

Stieber picked up the hypodermic out of the drawer. Marler nodded. That ensured the instrument carried his fingerprints.

'Put it back in the drawer. What is your name?'

'Helmut Stieber.'

'Who do you work for?'

'World Security in town here. As a guard. Richter was a freelance job I did on the side . . .'

I'll bet, Marler thought. Stieber was swaying about, having trouble keeping his balance. He staggered back towards where he'd sat, then lunged suddenly for the shotgun. Which was the move Marler had been expecting. Before Stieber reached the weapon his crooked arm closed round his neck for the second time. Stieber yelped with frustration and terror, sagged like a sack of potatoes.

'Stand up straight or this is it,' snapped Marler.

Stieber forced himself upright. Marler tightened the death grip, then released a little of the pressure. Stieber croaked out the words, his voice trembling.

'I've told you the truth.'

'I'm sure you have. But it was naughty trying to reach that shotgun. A good try, I'll give you that. Now, I'll tell you what I'm going to do. I need to get away from here . . .'

'I won't say a word. I'll stay here as long as you—'

'Yes, you will do just that. Why? Because we're going up that staircase to one of the bedrooms. Then I'm going to use adhesive tape to tie your wrists behind you, and I'm going to tape your ankles. You'll be left on one of the beds.

225

When I'm a long way from here I'll phone any friend you name to come and release you. Got any friends, Helmut?'

He was guiding Stieber into the hall as he spoke. He looked round the room and everything was perfect. Stieber's fingerprints on the shotgun; more important – Stieber's prints also on the hypodermic. The police should be able to work out something. At the foot of the stairs he used his left hand to take out the Browning. He thrust it against the German's back, then released his grip. 'This is a Browning. Walk slowly upstairs.'

Stieber climbed the treads one by one. Marler had released his grip, but the muzzle of the Browning was pressed hard into Stieber's back.

Marler ordered his captive to lie face down on a bed in a room at the back. Taking a small reel of adhesive tape from his pocket, he bound Stieber's wrists together behind his back, then performed the same action with his ankles.

'I have a friend—' Stieber began, turning his round head on the pillow.

'So have I,' Marler informed him.

Closing the door, he slipped on a pair of surgical gloves, ran downstairs and picked up the phone in the living-room. The lifeless Richter stared at him as he dialled police HQ.

'I'm reporting a murder in Freiburg. I have to speak with Chief Inspector Kuhlmann. No, no one else will do. And I'm going off the line if he doesn't come to the phone in thirty seconds. If he's sleeping somewhere else I want the number now . . .'

'He's here. Hold on—'

'For thirty seconds.'

Kuhlmann, freshly shaven, had been up all night and was in the canteen, drinking a cup of black coffee. He had got nowhere interviewing Evans. The Welshman insisted he had just returned from a conference at their Basle headquarters in Switzerland. He knew nothing of recent operations and was only prepared to talk with his lawyer present.

'Kuhlmann followed the uniformed policeman who had told him he was needed on the phone. No, the man at the other end had given no identification. Another crank call, Kuhlmann thought.

'Kuhlmann here. Who am I talking to?' he asked in German.

'A friendly informant,' the voice replied in the same language. 'Konvikstrasse 498. A case of murder. The murderer is still on the premises. So is the victim. That's it.'

Marler put down the phone quietly. His acute hearing caught the sound of footsteps approaching the front, crunching the snow. The sound of the grille gate being opened.

He walked rapidly back down the hall into the kitchen, shut the door, opened the back door, shut that door. Ice-cold air hit his exposed face. He ran to the wall, climbed it, hanging on to the metal rails at the top for support. He had changed his surgical gloves for his leather pair. He hauled himself over the rail, peered down the deserted staircase.

A fresh trail of footsteps were planted in the snow, footprints which stopped at the entrance to the house. He crept down until he could see the front of the house. A familiar figure stood with his back to him outside the front door, a tall thin man. Armand Horowitz had returned for some reason.

Marler waited until Horowitz had disappeared inside, then he ran down the remaining flight, turned left and walked along the Konvikstrasse towards the city gate, the Schwabentor. It was going to be a race against time. Kuhlmann might arrive soon enough to trap both men. Horowitz might move swiftly enough to free Stieber and both men might escape. That was Kuhlmann's problem.

Marler's problems lay much further away. In England.

22

It was 7 a.m. in London. Buckmaster sat behind Morgan's desk at World Security HQ in Threadneedle Street. He had driven early from the Belgravia apartment in Leonora's Volvo – one advantage of her insistence on sleeping in her own bedroom. He could come and go without her knowledge. The Volvo was parked in the underground garage.

Morgan, wearing another dark suit buttoned tight over his ample stomach, sat in a chair facing his chief. He felt sleepy from the flight during the night in the Lear jet from Freiburg but his eyes were alert, like two blackcurrants.

'So, Tweed is still on the loose.' Buckmaster ran a hand through his unruly hair, leaned back in the swivel chair and placed one foot, shod in a handmade shoe, on the desk top. 'I thought you'd have cleaned up that little problem by now,' he said sarcastically, and clasped his hands behind his neck.

'Not so little.' Morgan toyed with a long cigar without lighting it. 'We have made great progress. We know he's somewhere in the Black Forest area—'

'*Was*,' Buckmaster snapped. 'What guarantee have you he's there now?'

'One attempt was made on him along the autobahn—'

'No details, please. When are you going to complete the job?'

He spoke in his bored voice, the one so often used

addressing an idiot questioner in the House. He had the satisfaction of seeing a flash of resentment in Morgan's eyes. Keep them on their toes. Especially the top people.

'The snow will help,' Morgan said emphatically. 'There has been a heavy fall in that area. Which means a car can be spotted more easily. He has to move out of the area soon – and we know the car he'll use.'

'I want him kept on the run.' Buckmaster leaned forward and slapped the flat of his hand on the desk. 'I want him harassed to death. Literally. I want him so confused he can't think. I want him driven out of his mind with terror. Maybe the best route to get at him is through Paula Grey.' He smiled sadistically. 'You do get my meaning?'

Morgan had always prided himself he could stand up to any pressure. But during his ranting Buckmaster had raised his voice until he was almost shouting. His expression was vindictive, his complexion red with fury. There were times when Morgan had wondered whether he was close to the edge – of insanity.

'I get your meaning,' Morgan said slowly. 'We've been faced with problems like this before. We have the apparatus to solve them—'

'*You* have the apparatus!' Buckmaster's voice rose to a manic shriek. He leaned across the desk, hair awry. 'I want this man destroyed. You can't do it sitting on your fat backside here in London. You said Freiburg, the Black Forest. So that's where you should be. Leading the manhunt.'

'I'll fly back today. Leave it all to me. You've never known me to fail . . .'

'There's always a first time . . .' Buckmaster's tone dropped to a sibilant hiss. 'This had better not be it.'

He used both hands to straighten his tie, tucking the end back inside his trouser top. Then he gave a broad smile, steepled his hands in a praying-mantis gesture, elbows rested on the desk.

'I do have every confidence in you, Gareth. Without you I'd never have built up this organization. You're the one person in the world I really trust.'

Morgan nodded while he thought. He'd just witnessed a typical Buckmaster performance. First, the use of threats and a mood of almost uncontrollable rage. Then, a swift change of mood to sweet reasonableness. He was familiar enough with the technique. But always before it had been practised on minions. He didn't appreciate being the recipient. He changed the subject.

'The killing and rape at Radnor Walk. Has anyone identified the victim yet? I might be able to use it in my pursuit of Tweed. The Special Branch net closing in – that kind of tactic.'

'Not a clue yet.' Buckmaster was relaxed again, hands behind his neck, legs stretched out under his desk. 'The Chief Inspector in charge of the investigation thinks she was probably a foreign girl. Tweed travelled abroad a lot.'

'Why foreign?' Morgan couldn't conceal the anxiety in his voice.

'Because all the makers' labels had been removed from her clothes. Her underclothes were newly bought – probably the first time she'd worn them. Same with her handbag, shoes and her tights. Inside her handbag was a bill listing the purchase of some of those items from Harrods the day of the murder. No credit cards. Only fresh bank-notes in her purse.'

'All of which must have made her appear to be very English,' Morgan ventured.

'Too English for the Inspector's liking. More like a foreign girl who had been equipped with everything English.' Buckmaster yawned. 'You seem very interested in her identification.'

'I just told you why.'

'I must go.' Buckmaster stood up, straightened his jacket, reached for his overcoat. 'Before Leonora arrives.

230

She gets in early sometimes. How are you coping with her?'

'I can handle her. She's a woman. They're all subject to becoming emotional, even hysterical. That's why they make lousy top executives.'

'God! Look at that weather.' Buckmaster had wandered over to the window. The panoramic view was blotted out by a curtain of thick snowflakes drifting steadily down. Buckmaster spun on his heel. 'I'm off. I was never here.'

'Of course.'

Half an hour later, as Morgan checked through recent contracts, the summons came over his intercom.

'Gareth? Could you pop along to my office? For a short chat?'

He was startled to hear Leonora's voice. His first thought was Buckmaster had left just in time. His second thought was to wonder what she was up to. Her voice sounded very husky, very appealing. The tone she adopted when she wanted to throw someone off balance.

She was sitting behind her desk, dressed in a Chanel suit. Her blonde hair gleamed in the desk lamp she'd switched on: outside it was like night. As he settled himself in a chair on the opposite side of her desk she stood up, hauled a stiff-backed chair round the end, sat beside him, crossed her shapely legs.

'Lance has been here to see you, hasn't he? This morning.'

'No,' Morgan lied smoothly. 'As a Minister he can't . . .'

'I know. He's not supposed to have anything to do with the running of the company.' She had been tapping her perfect white teeth with a pencil. Now she used it to tap the knuckles of his stubby-fingered hand resting on his knee. 'But I can keep a secret. Come on, Gareth, give.'

And I can keep a secret, Morgan thought. 'I was here at

231

7 a.m.,' he told her. 'I've been working in my office on my own.'

'So why did he take my Volvo early this morning? I had to be driven here in the Daimler by Hanson.' Her blue eyes gazed into the distance. 'Still, if he wasn't here he must have been visiting a friend. Feminine sex. The stamina of the man. At this hour of the day. I ask you!'

'He's Minister for External Security,' Morgan persisted. 'He could have gone anywhere in that capacity – maybe somewhere it wasn't good policy to be seen. Hence his taking your Volvo.'

'Gareth, if he's fooling around, I want to know who with. I'm putting a first-class detective agency on his track. Sooner or later I'll know who she is.' Her tone became coaxing. 'You know, I haven't many people I can trust. I'm not such a fool as to confide in women friends. I need someone I can talk to. You fit the bill.' She tapped his knuckles again with the pencil. 'You do know, I hope, that Lance has plans to ease you out of the company?'

Morgan stirred uncomfortably in his chair. This was a dangerous situation. Which was the best way to play it to his future advantage? Leonora had dumped a time bomb in his lap.

'No, I didn't know that,' he said eventually.

'It doesn't mean he'll succeed,' she continued. 'Provided you have me on your side.'

'I'm grateful for your support,' he said quietly, wondering how he could bring the conversation to an end.

'We'll talk some more later, Gareth.'

She gave him her winning smile, stood up, walked back behind her desk and waved a slim hand at her in-tray. He stood up, said he also had a whole load of work to get through and left her office.

He locked the door of his own office, went to his desk, pressed the button which lit up the red *Do not disturb* light outside and sank into his chair. He mopped his damp forehead and hands with a handkerchief, took out his hip flask and swallowed a large slug.

He was badly shaken. Was it possible that Buckmaster was planning to get rid of him? Or was Leonora playing some devious game of her own. His second worry was her idea of hiring some detective agency to follow Buckmaster. Sooner or later the detectives were bound to come up with evidence of dalliance with some attractive female.

Should he warn Buckmaster? He decided he'd better leave the whole thing alone until he saw how it developed. Either way lay a trap. If he didn't warn Buckmaster and he found out about what Leonora had said, then he was out. And these fools of women had a habit of losing control in an argument and telling their husbands about things they shouldn't. But if he did warn Buckmaster, and Leonora won in a battle for control of the company, her first executive decision would be sack Morgan.

Inside her own office Leonora studied her appearance in a wall mirror, searching for traces of the dreaded wrinkles. She was satisfied she had planted doubts in Gareth's mind. He might even play along with her. She smiled at her image. Morgan had no suspicion that if she gained control her first pleasant task would be to throw him into the street.

Walking briskly to her desk, she took her notebook from her handbag, checked the phone number Marler had given her during their ride back to London from Dartmoor. Her slim fingers dialled the number and she soon grasped she was in touch with one of those beastly answerphones. Marler's voice came over the line.

'This is . . .' He gave only the number. No name. '. . . I am not available at the moment. Leave a message when you hear the tone . . .'

She thought quickly, worded her response carefully: she never trusted recorded phone calls.

'This is the lady you gave a lift to from Dartmoor. Please

call me at the office as soon as possible. At the office,' she repeated and broke the connection. A call to their Belgravia apartment could be dangerous; Lance was so often there.

What a wicked web I'm weaving, she mused. The thought gave a lot of satisfaction.

Marler took a cab from London Airport to the address of a man who ran a picture library of well-known people. He obtained the picture he wanted – a better photograph than he'd hoped for – and paid the large fee. He next took a cab to his flat in Chelsea, dumped his bag, checked the answerphone.

Leonora had made her voice sound very sexy in the few words she had spoken. Marler listened twice to the message before he put down the phone. I wonder what you're up to my devious lovely, he was thinking. He made himself a cup of black coffee, using the percolator in the tiny galley kitchen, and drank the whole cup in two swallows. Before leaving the flat he rammed a peaked check cap over his fair hair, took a cheroot from a packet, tucked it in his breast pocket. Clutching the cardboard-backed envelope containing the photograph, he left his flat.

The next cab took him to Wardour Street in Soho. He paid it off and walked the half-mile to his real destination, a first-floor office in Greek Street. The area was a mix of respectable restaurants, recording studios, and less respectable sex shops.

'Grubby' Grundy, as he was known in the trade, worked inside a small fortress. Running up the greasy staircase, Marler used the metal speakphone attached to the door above a plate which read J. GRUNDY, PHOTOGRAPHIC AGENCY.

'Grundy? This is Freddie Moore. Got a job for you . . .'

'I'm pretty busy now. Wait a minute,' a gravelly voice replied through the grille.

Marler lit a cheroot. He knew he had plenty of time. He could hear the grind of the steel inner door beyond the wooden one he faced, opening on its hinges. Then came the sound of bolts being drawn, three locks being unlocked. Marler pulled down the peak of his cap. He had the appearance of a racecourse tipster.

The wooden door opened on a heavy chain and a face like a wrinkled walnut peered through the gap. Impossible to guess Grundy's age. Wearing an old-fashioned waistcoat over a soiled shirt, his hooked nose supported a pair of *pince-nez*. The cuffs of his shirt were worn and hadn't seen a laundry for a long time.

'It is you,' Grundy commented and released the chain.

'You should be able to recognize my voice,' Marler commented.

He spoke again with the cheroot in his mouth, which altered his voice.

'Can't be too careful these days,' Grundy mumbled. 'Folks can mimic voices. Come in. Like I said, I'm pretty busy so you'll 'ave to wait for a few weeks, whatever it is you're wanting.'

Marler said nothing as Grundy went through the process of reconstructing his fortress. All this gab was an attempt to put up the price. Grundy shuffled over to a wooden work-table covered with photographs, a pot of glue, various photographic mounts in different sizes. All window dressing.

'What is it you be wanting?'

Grundy drank some liquid which looked like stale tea from a chipped mug. The large room overlooking Greek Street had the musty odour of an office which hadn't been polluted with fresh air for weeks. Marler opened the envelope, placed the photograph upside down after clearing a space on the table.

235

'I want one of your famous artistic fake-ups with some girl. Not a tart. Someone who looks classy, even if she isn't . . . No, don't touch!' he warned as Grundy reached for the photo. 'There's a little matter of the price to decide first. The girl will have to be reclining . . .'

Grundy snickered. 'Ah! A dirty picture. That comes very expensive . . .'

'How much? Just one copy. And I'll collect it this afternoon.'

'Don't know if I could manage that . . .'

'Then I'll go elsewhere . . .'

Marler was reaching for the print when Grundy's gnarled hand slapped down over it. He shook his head, his expression resigned.

'You always want everything yesterday on the few occasions we've done business. Five hundred nicker . . .'

'Five hundred pounds!' Marler took the cheroot from his mouth, flicked ash on the floor, replaced it between his lips. 'You are out of your crazy mind. One hundred is my price. For one photo.'

'You don't know what skill I 'ave. I 'ave to make two master prints – one of your pic, one of the girl. Then I 'as to merge the two, make another master print. I then 'as to take another master – after the retouchin' to hide the linkin' of two pics into one—'

'I do know,' Marler snapped. 'And since I'm in a generous mood I'll make it a hundred and fifty.'

'Two hundred,' Grundy snapped. 'And that's my final offer – the door is there.'

'Done. Two hundred. And that includes the negatives. You forgot to mention them.' Marler reached up with both hands, grasped Grundy by his waistcoat and shook him, his ice-blue eyes staring at the photographer. Feeling the slippery texture of the waistcoat he wished he'd been wearing gloves. 'I wouldn't like to have to call back for a missing negative, so be a good lad. Now, show me the girl.'

He released his grip and Grundy was trembling. Mumbling to himself, he took a key-ring from his trouser pocket, shifted a pile of framed blow-ups leaning against a wall and exposed a safe. Squatting on his haunches, he opened the safe, riffled through a pile of glossy prints, selected three, closed the safe and stood up.

'One of these should do you. They're all nudies . . .'

'Show me.'

Marler studied the three prints Grundy spread out over the table. They were mildly pornographic, showed three girls in the act of making love to a man. One was a blonde whose appearance surprised Marler – surprised him that she would permit such a photo to be taken. She was sprawled sideways.

'That one, I think. If you can marry it up.'

Grundy grinned lecherously. 'Oh, I bet I can marry them up all right . . .'

He reached for Marler's print, turned it over. Buckmaster fully clothed, had been photographed sprawled on his back along a couch, hands clasped behind his head. Grundy swore foully, glared at Marler.

'Moore, that's Lance Buckmaster. The bloody Minister. If I'd known you wouldn't 'ave got it for a penny less than the five hundred nicker I asked . . .'

Marler lifted a hand as Grundy crouched over the table and pressed his fingers hard on a certain muscle. Grundy yelped with pain. Marler's voice was quiet, sinister.

'One other thing I'm paying for. You've a bad memory. If I hear you've been talking about this I'll be back.' He looked round at the messy room, the shelves stuffed with a collection of brown folders. 'Some people might wreck this room, but it's a wreck already. You talk, I'll hear about it, and you'll be the wreck.' He let go of Grundy. 'You *can* marry them up?'

'They're both in a perfect position. The subject will be 'avin' the time of his life when I've finished my work.'

237

'I'm off. I'll be back at five this afternoon. And you've a job to do. Make it perfect. I have an artistic eye and I'm expecting a masterpiece. Go to it, Grundy.'

Marler stood on the pavement in the middle of Waterloo Bridge, the collar of his trench coat turned up against the bitter wind. Snowflakes were drifting down again.

He had given Leonora precise instructions when he called her from a public phone. She was to borrow a car from one of the directors, drive south of the river, head for Waterloo, then turn north along the bridge, *crawling*. She had told him she'd be inside a silver Mercedes after she'd asked him to hold on while she checked which car was available. Now he saw a silver Mercedes crawling towards him. A cab driver overtook her, shouted at her as he passed. She continued her crawl.

Marler stared hard at the vehicles behind her, checking for a car following her. There wasn't one. She pulled up alongside him. He opened the front passenger door, glanced back, dived inside, slammed the door, reached for the seat belt.

'Move! Now! And head down the Strand underpass and keep going north . . .'

'Anything you say. My, you can be masterful. I like masterful men . . .'

While she flattered him she did as he said, swinging across into the next lane skilfully and speeding up. Then they were disappearing down inside the underpass and, with a clear road ahead, she roared, pressing her foot down.

'Mind if I smoke?' he asked, glancing in the wing mirror.

'Of course not. You can light me one.'

He lit a king-size cigarette, passed it to her. She inserted it between her lips, took a long drag. Glancing at him, she smiled.

'That tastes especially good.'

'Keep your eye on the road. I want us well away from here in no time. We could have been followed. You could, that is.'

'Who would do that?'

'Morgan – or, rather, one of his minions. If he's in town.'

'He is. He came into the office early this morning. Just back from abroad some place. You know Europe well, Marler?'

'Funny question.'

'I don't see why. You told me you were with an insurance company which covers VIPs against kidnapping all over the world. Plenty of them in Europe. I need someone who's an expert investigator to find out what's going on inside the World Security offices on the Continent. I've heard some strange rumours about the Research and Development Division. That's under Morgan's direct control.'

'What sort of rumours? Keep straight on.'

For a change traffic was light. They were driving towards Euston Station.

'Rumours that we're mixed up in industrial espionage action. That's strictly between you and me. I don't want any nasty surprises. That division makes money – but as chairman the responsibility is mine.'

'You want to hire me?' Marler enquired.

'Yes. The fee would be thirty thousand pounds for starters, plus expenses. If you insist, we could draw up a secret contract.'

'No contract. No money. Not until I've sniffed around a bit. I'll see what I can do for you. And when I contact you at your office it will be Freddie Moore calling. Now, drop me off by Euston Station.'

'You don't take long to make up your mind. I like that. I like the idea of dealing with you. When you get back maybe we can have dinner to discuss what you've found out?'

'We can decide that later . . .'

Marler climbed out of the car when she'd stopped it in front of the station entrance. He gave her a little salute and she drove off. Marler bought a paper from a newspaper stand, pretended to read it while he watched the traffic. No one was following Leonora. He wondered what she'd think if she knew his next meeting was with Lance Buckmaster.

23

Seated behind his desk, Morgan braced himself. The guard at the main entrance had phoned to announce the arrival of Chief Inspector Buchanan. Morgan pressed the button which converted the light outside his door to green. He would have liked to say he was not available, that he was in conference, but felt it would be unwise not to show willing.

The door opened, his secretary, Melanie, ushered inside the tall policeman. Once again he was accompanied by his assistant, Sergeant Warden. Morgan remained seated, waved a pudgy hand.

'Please make yourselves comfortable. Coffee? Tea?'

'No, thank you, sir,' Buchanan replied as he took one of the two chairs facing Morgan. He hauled it back a couple of feet so he could cross his long legs.

Morgan shook his head at Melanie, who left, closing the door behind her. He clasped his hands on the desk and waited for Buchanan to speak. The Chief Inspector took his time.

'We are definitely treating the death of your accountant, Ted Doyle, as a murder enquiry.'

'May I ask why?' Morgan asked.

'Certainly. Suicide is out – lack of motive. The post-mortem showed no traces of alcohol in his system. That rules out an accidental fall – especially from that window. Which only leaves murder.'

'But I thought . . .'

'If you don't mind, I haven't quite finished, sir.' Buchanan's tone was firm, his grey eyes steely. 'I think you were about to say Doyle was a gambler. We have visited his flat. We did find some betting slips tucked under a coffee pot in the kitchen – tickets bought at the Tote . . .'

Buchanan, his right hand resting inside his trouser pocket, paused, but Morgan had learned his lesson. He remained silent, clasping his hands a little more tightly. Buchanan resumed what he had been saying.

'One odd thing about those tickets was they were completely clean of fingerprints. If Doyle had handled them I'd have expected to find some of his prints. You don't go round wiping useless tickets – or any kind of tickets, for that matter.'

Buchanan paused again. Morgan felt obliged to react. 'It does sound odd,' he agreed. 'What was the other odd thing?'

'I beg your pardon?'

'You did say *one* odd thing. That implied something else was odd.'

'Sorry, sir.' He glanced at Warden who sat quite still, staring at Morgan. Buchanan turned back to face his host. 'I was just coming to that. We have a witness.' For the third time he paused. Morgan's knuckles were white. 'The other odd thing was what this witness saw. She lives opposite the entrance to Doyle's ground floor flat. A reliable witness – we don't get too many of them . . .'

Morgan was beginning to feel the strain. This bastard was playing cat-and-mouse with him. He ignored the drops of moisture forming on his high-domed forehead.

Buchanan again continued after the pause.

'This woman saw a man entering Doyle's flat. Dark trousers – the type worn by a commissionaire . . . or a chauffeur, and a hip-length suède jacket. Any idea who that might have been?'

'None at all,' Morgan lied. 'Was this before Doyle . . . died?'

'No, afterwards. Later that day, in fact. He stayed inside for no more than a few minutes. When he left our witness had a good view of his face. It puzzles me considerably.'

'Perhaps he had a friend,' Morgan suggested.

'A friend with a key to Doyle's flat?'

'Sorry. I'm not following you.'

'I just explained. The woman saw this unknown man entering Doyle's flat. He used a key to unlock the door. According to the woman, who knew Doyle, he was a bachelor whose main interest was listening to classical music. Mainly Wagner. By himself. He had a fairly expensive hi-fi system in his living-room. Or perhaps you know that, sir? Ever visited him at his flat?'

'Never!' Morgan's reply was swift. 'Why should I?'

'I thought maybe because of his position you might sometimes have called on him after office hours to discuss some knotty accountancy problem.'

'I'd discuss that with our Finance Director. He's abroad at the moment . . .'

'So you told me during our previous interview.' Buchanan uncrossed his legs, took his hand from his pocket and leaned forward. 'Would you know who might have had a spare key to Doyle's front door?'

'No one here, I'm sure,' Morgan lied again, then clamped his lips close together.

'You can see where all this is leading, sir?'

'I'm afraid I don't.'

'An unknown man enters Doyle's house with a key. In the living room, as I mentioned, is a hi-fi system worth

242

several thousands pounds. Just the kind of thing a burglar would whip. So this mysterious caller didn't go there to take anything. Maybe he went there to leave something. Betting slips with no fingerprints. Incidentally, he wore gloves. I told you the witness is unusually reliable.'

Morgan shrugged his heavy shoulders and made no comment as though it was all beyond him. Buchanan stood up and Warden jack-knifed erect at almost the same moment.

'I think that's all, sir. For the moment.' Buchanan gave one of his rare wintry smiles. 'I thought you'd like to be brought up to date with the present stage of our investigation.' He turned towards the door, then swung on his heel. 'Oh, you weren't thinking of leaving the country, were you, sir?'

'What the devil does that mean?' Morgan glared malevolently at the Chief Inspector. 'I'm managing director of an international corporation. I happen to be flying over to the Continent later today.'

'Anywhere we could contact you?'

'The Basle office should be able to locate me. In any case Mrs Buckmaster is here all the time if you need someone.'

'Of course. She would do very nicely. Excuse me, I'd overlooked her. Better not let her know – ladies don't like to be overlooked, do they? We'll be going now. Have a good trip . . .'

Buchanan said nothing as they left the building, a frown of concentration on his face until they were inside their car. Warden took the wheel, Buchanan sat beside him.

'What do you think, Sergeant?'

'He was very tense, sir. Very keyed up. His hands gave him away. He clenched them tighter when you mentioned the betting slips, tighter still when you told him about having a witness.'

'Yes, I noticed that. It doesn't necessarily mean anything. People get nervous when they're talking to the police. And I'd just told him it was a murder case.'

'And later he had beads of sweat on his forehead.'

'Again, could be natural tension. He's still in a neutral zone as far as I'm concerned at this stage of the enquiry. Let's get back to the Yard.'

Morgan was in a cold fury. Hanson had allowed himself to be seen while entering Doyle's flat to plant the betting slips. He'd even been wearing his dark chauffeur's trousers. At least he'd had the sense to wear a suède jacket.

Morgan decided to tear a strip off Hanson at the first opportunity. And to warn him never to go anywhere near that district again. Morgan was also worried about Buchanan. A sly piece of work; full of little verbal tricks. For the first time Morgan felt he had met his match when it came to low cunning. No time to dwell on that now.

Riffling through the dial-card index box, he extracted the card for Freiburg, slipped it into the phone slot. Then he pressed the button which lit up the red light outside. He didn't want to risk intrusion while he made this call. The phone began ringing.

'World Security, Freiburg? Put me straight through to Evans. Morgan here. Make it fast . . .'

'That you, Evans? Now listen carefully. I'm only going to say this once. I'm flying to Basle today. That will be my HQ for the next few days. Any news of the target?'

'No more than when you left,' Evans reported.

'He's making for the Swiss border. This is what you have to do. Send men to watch every frontier crossing from Germany into Switzerland. Along the Rhine from Basle to Konstanz.'

'I haven't the manpower,' Evans protested.

'Do I have to teach you how to tie on your bib? The best operatives you do have should be stationed at the major

244

crossing points. For the smaller ones hire outside help. Tell the people you hire to take cine-cameras. They're to station themselves where they can watch – from the Swiss side – and use the cameras to record everyone crossing.'

'And just supposing the target does put in an appearance?'

'They play it off the cuff. If they have a car or truck at their disposal they use it. Providing they can make it look like a genuine accident. Do I have to spell it out in two-syllable words?'

'Understood . . .'

'And once you've organized our watch on the Rhine you fly to Basle. I'll expect you to be waiting for me at our HQ when I arrive.

'Understood . . .'

A thought struck Morgan. 'This conversation isn't being recorded, I take it?'

'Well . . . as a matter of fact, it is. You've always insisted every conversation *should* be recorded.'

'Heaven save me from professional idiots. Evans, your first job when this call ends is to erase the tape. You heard me? *Erase the tape* . . .'

'Will do. Personally.'

'And now, set in motion the manhunt. The target must be found within the next twenty-four hours.'

24

A major weather change over the Black Forest. The morning sky was a dazzling blue. From the verandah of the lodge Tweed half-closed his eyes against the blinding glare.

The sun was reflecting off the snow, the ice crystals clinging to branches of immense firs. The temperature was still below freezing but the air was crisp, invigorating. Behind him Newman and Paula emerged with their own cases. Tweed had taken the decision as soon as they woke.

'We're moving south soon after daylight – heading for the Swiss border.' He had a map spread open on the table. 'We are close to Badenweiler – that's a spa inside the forest. There will be few people there at this time of the year – and a good road leads south through Kandern. Then we're out of the forest. From there we make for the A 98 autobahn which runs east close to the Rhine. Our objective is Laufenburg, a small town which I know. I told you earlier it straddles the Rhine – at that point the river is the frontier. We have one bridge to cross and we're in Switzerland.'

'Where are the checkpoints?' Paula had asked.

'On either side of the bridge.'

'Isn't it risky?'

'Of course it is.' Tweed had spoken with relish at the prospect of action. For the first time since they'd fled from England he seemed his normal resourceful self, calm, determined. 'It will be risky wherever we try to cross. But it's far more risky hanging about here. Horowitz knows we're in this area. Those tracker dogs Newman shot last night prove that.'

'That Horowitz frightens me.' Paula had shivered.

Before they had gone to sleep Newman had produced the two photographs Marler had taken outside the Freiburg HQ of World Security. The photos showing Gareth Morgan and Armand Horowitz entering the building. Tweed had recognized the Hungarian.

'Only one other photograph has ever been taken of that man. Pierre Loriot of Interpol showed me it. He's the most dangerous assassin in Western Europe. Morgan certainly has some peculiar contacts for a so-called respectable businessman . . .'

That had been a few hours earlier. Now, as they prepared to leave, Paula asked another question.

'And what are we going to use for transport? We're marooned.'

'Not necessarily,' Tweed had replied as they ate the breakfast she had cooked. Tinned meat and toast. 'The Audi we travelled in from Freiburg may still be down that path we came up. Let's hope so. We did conceal it in the undergrowth – and when our pursuers arrived they'd be taken up with the abandoned Mercedes and the guard, Braun, Bob shot . . .'

'Could be tricky. I'll lead the way back, arrive first,' Newman had commented.

Before they left he helped Paula to clean up the lodge. He emptied the Elsan bucket they'd used as a toilet down a crevasse in the snow, then had sprayed it with a can of disinfectant Paula found in a cupboard. To lighten their load, the rest of the uneaten food went down the crevasse.

'No sign – or sound – of a chopper,' Newman remarked as he followed Tweed down the slippery steps from the verandah. 'And everyone had better watch their footing – a twisted ankle we don't need . . .'

Then he went on ahead, holding his case in his left hand, the fully-loaded Walther in his right. The going was very treacherous once they disappeared inside the trees, following the path of the frozen stream. Muffled up with a scarf over her head, Paula shivered as she followed Tweed. Not from the penetrating cold. The atmosphere of the dark and silent forest closed round them like a vast tomb. The only sounds were the crunch of their boots on crusted snow, the crackle of ice. Newman had disappeared below them, making greater speed.

'I wonder if they've identified that poor girl they found in your flat?' Paula mused.

'I doubt it. I think someone – the murderer – brought her in from outside Britain. To cover his tracks.'

'Any ideas yet as to who the murderer could be?'

'I think I know now. Either Lance Buckmaster or Gareth Morgan.'

'My God. What makes you think that? Wouldn't they bring in a minion, maybe even a hired killer?'

'No. Too great a risk. Whoever killed and then raped her was going to be sure no one else could point the finger. The idea was to get me out of the way, which they have done.'

'Why do you also suspect Morgan?' she asked.

'Keep your voice down. Sound travels a long way in this silence. Why Morgan? Because of that folder Newman extracted from the pocket of the man who tried to shoot him by the Mercedes. The folder which identified him as Gustav Braun, member of World Security. Braun was small fry, would never dare use a firearm without backing from the top man. Gareth Morgan. I hope to God Arthur Beck is friendly – I need to have the use of a long-distance transmitter as soon as possible. To contact the *Lampedusa*.'

They reached the bottom of the path and Tweed peered out along the timber track they'd driven down the night before. No sign of anyone, not even of Newman. Paula gave a sigh of relief as she ran across the track. She could just make out the snow-covered silhouette of the blue Audi where they'd left it concealed in the undergrowth.

'Stop! Don't move one inch further. Don't touch that car.'

Newman's voice. Paula turned round and he emerged from behind the trunk of a massive fir. She heard a soft *plop!* She stared round to locate the source of the sound as Newman walked towards her. He waved her back across the track to where Tweed still stood.

She had recrossed the track when she saw a solid wedge

of snow slide from a fir's branch. It made the same *plop!* sound as it hit the ground. Newman gestured towards the fallen snow.

'The temperature has risen above zero. There's a snow melt. Both of you go back a dozen yards up that path while I check that Audi.'

'Check it?' Paula queried.

'Look round you. There are the ruts under a film of snow where they turned the Mercedes and drove off – with Gustav Braun's body in the boot would be my guess. I've been waiting to make sure they hadn't left behind a couple of men in ambush. Not a sound. But even in the dark they may have seen the Audi – and left us a birthday present. A final birthday present.'

'He means a bomb,' Tweed said quietly and, taking her by the arm, led her back up the path.

Newman walked all round the white mound which was the Audi. He walked slowly, placing each foot carefully. He doubted whether they had planted landmines but World Security was capable of any devilry – especially if Horowitz had been with the pursuers.

He studied the bonnet. Using his gloved hand he whisked some of the snow off it. The front of the bonnet was sealed with a coating of ice. Unlikely that the engine had been tampered with.

He continued his circuit. On the driver's side snow had drifted against the lower side of the chassis. Except in one place. There was a gap about eighteen inches wide – the width of a man's body. He stooped down, used his gloved hand to whisk away more snow.

Lowering himself to the ground, he eased his way slowly under the body of the car, feet first. He paused to extract a pencil flash from his trench coat pocket, then vanished underneath the Audi. Sprawled flat on the snow, he hauled the glove off his right hand, switched on the flash, moved the beam round slowly. *Bingo!*

*   *   *

The explosive device was a slim black metal box attached to the underside of the Audi by small protruding legs. Newman remembered his training with the SAS in Wales when he'd been writing a series of articles on the outfit. The man in a Balaclava helmet whose face he'd never seen. The man known as 'Sarge'. He could hear his voice now on the bomb disposal course.

'So, you've been smart, you've found the bomb. Take it easy, lad. Locating the bastard is only the first step. Check it for booby traps, you stupid bugger . . .'

Newman swivelled on his back, aiming the flash along the edges of the device. Looking for tell-tale wires. None. At one end a metal lever protruded a quarter of an inch, something he'd never have seen without the flash. He clenched the flash between his teeth, reached up with his bare hand, took hold of the box and pulled gently. It remained solid as a rock.

He was pretty sure the four small legs at each corner which clamped it to the car were magnetic. That the protruding lever controlled the magnetic system. Press the lever in and the box would be released. He suddenly realized he was sweating despite the cold. If he was wrong, if the lever was a trap, this would be the end of Bob Newman.

But they needed the car. He took a deep breath. His right hand reached up again, index finger extended close to the lever. You bloody idiot! He dropped his hand, took off the glove from his left hand and cupped that beneath the box to hold it when – *if* – it fell away from the chassis. Another deep breath. Get on with it. You're either right or wrong.

His right index finger tip touched the ice-cold metal of the lever. He paused. Again he examined it with the flash and was no more certain of its function. His index finger pressed the lever. The metal slid inside the slot, the box

250

dropped free into his extended left hand.

He let out his breath. Easing his way back into the open – holding on to the box – was an endurance test of nerve. He stood up slowly, walked back into the centre of the timber track. He shouted up to Tweed and Paula hidden on the path.

'Wait for one bloody great bang. I'll be OK. I'm going to hurl a bomb.'

He turned to face along the timber track away from the main road. Like a cricketer bowling, he threw the container overarm with all his strength, then dropped flat in the snow. The device described an arc in mid-air, curved down and landed at the base of a fir tree. The tremendous boom of the explosion nearly cracked his ear-drums. A cascade of snow plunged down from the nearby trees.

Newman watched grimly as he saw the tree the bomb had landed nearest sway. There was a wrenching, cracking sound. The big fir tilted, toppled, fell across the track, tearing up its root system. Then an eerie silence descended. The tree lay across the track, barring the way. Newman thanked heaven he'd had the sense to throw the bomb away from the main road.

'Oh, my Lord!'

Paula had run down the path, slipping and sliding. Now, seeing Newman was safe as he climbed to his feet, she was gazing at the stricken fir. As Newman slapped the front of his coat to clear it of snow she used her gloved hands to brush it off his back.

'So, they did leave us a goodbye present,' Tweed commented.

'The car is safe now, anyway,' Paula said. 'I'll be glad to get inside it. I'm frozen stiff.'

'You'll have to freeze a bit longer,' Newman warned. 'I want to check it further . . .'

It was half an hour before he had used his gloved hand to de-ice the bonnet, to lift it cautiously and check the engine.

251

Then he had to use his gloved hand again to de-ice the lock before the key would turn. Still cautious, he made them stand well away while he tried the ignition. The engine fired at the twentieth attempt. Paula gave a muted cheer.

They dumped their cases inside the boot. For ten more minutes they sat inside the car while Newman turned on the heaters and waited for everything to warm up. Eventually he turned to Tweed who sat beside him.

'We're ready to go.'

'Then let's get moving. Head for Badenweiler and then south for the border.'

The Audi slithered all over the place as Newman drove back along the timber track, skidding over solid ice from one rut to another. He drove at a slow speed, expertly following the skids, then turning the vehicle back to the centre of the track. Paula said something to keep her mind off the ordeal: she was scared stiff the car would stop, that they'd be trapped in this awful white wilderness.

'That bomb you found, Bob. How did it operate?'

'My guess is it had a trembler mechanism. Anyone starting up the car, causing vibrations, would have detonated it.'

'Thank God you found it. We seem to be up against some grim people. Worse than the opposition from the Soviets in the old days . . .'

She relapsed into silence as Newman reached the end of the track, turned on to the main road away from the direction leading back to Freiburg. The road climbed steeply, began following a series of bends, and again the dense wall of fir trees hemmed them in on both sides. The road surface was virgin snow; no other traffic had passed this way since the previous fall of snow.

Whenever he arrived at a level stretch Newman braked, lowered his window. Icy air dispersed the warmth instantly. He leaned his head out and listened. The heavy silence was broken only by the occasional *plop!* of melting snow sagging to the ground.

'What are you listening for?' Paula asked.

'Something I can't hear, fortunately. The sound of a chopper. They don't seem to be out this morning. Odd.'

'Unless Kuhlmann has grounded them,' Tweed suggested. 'Last evening I heard the faint sound of a machine-gun when two choppers were in the air.'

'That would make sense,' Newman agreed. 'Kuhlmann is tough and independent-minded. But to cover himself he'll still warn the frontier posts to look out for you. When we get there I'll spy out the land first.'

'You won't be with us,' Tweed informed him.

'What's the plan?'

'You drive us to the German side of Laufenburg, drop us there, then drive back to Basle. I want you to check on the World Security HQ in that city. It's a big one. Time we began to hit back, to find out exactly what kind of outfit it is.'

'And how do I go about that? Just walk in and ask? I think not.'

Tweed was scribbling on the one-time pad he always carried. He tore off a sheet and handed it to Newman. 'Contact that man. Use my name as reference. He'll get you inside.'

Newman read what Tweed had written. Alois Turpil. An address in Berne. A phone number. He looked at Tweed.

'That World Security HQ in Basle is probably a fortress. How can this Turpil character help? Who is he anyway?'

'One of my underworld contacts. And the most professional safe-cracker in Europe. Also an expert on security systems. He'll get you inside – and out again – and no one will know . . .'

'You hope . . .'

'If you find interesting data, call Arthur Beck at Federal

253

Police headquarters in Berne. That's the second number I've added at the bottom of the sheet, the one without a name. You'd better call him in any case. As I said, let's hope he's as friendly as Kuhlmann. If you run into a road block, make for Zürich. We'll be staying at the Hotel Schweizerhof, facing the main station.

'If you ever reach Switzerland.'

'You have a point,' Tweed agreed. 'A few miles after we've driven through Badenweiler we descend to Kandern – and then the forest has ended. We'll be completely in the open.'

'And that sounds like running a gauntlet. Especially if this clear weather lasts, which I think it will.'

Horowitz stood next to Evans, looking out of the first-floor window of the Basle headquarters of World Security. Below the Rhine flowed swiftly westward, a river as wide as the Thames even at Basle, hundreds of miles before it flowed into the North Sea. A huge barge, its hold covered with canvas, coated with snow, surged past. Horowitz peered down to where a narrow stone promenade followed the river bank.

'Are all the watchers in position along the frontier?' he enquired, adjusting his steel-rimmed glasses higher up his nose.

'They should be,' Evans replied. 'It was a devil of a rush to get them in place. I phoned instructions from Freiburg before flying here.'

'What about the more obscure crossing points – like Konstanz where you can walk over the border. Or Laufenburg where you stroll over a bridge and you're in Switzerland?'

Evans looked surprised, glanced at the motionless thin man. 'You seem to know the area very well. Are you by any chance Swiss?'

'That is something I never discuss,' Horowitz responded in his slow deliberate way. '. . . my origins.'

He turned to gaze at his companion. Evans again felt uneasy as the eyes stared at him unblinking behind the lenses. An aura of deadly purpose, ice-cold control, emanated from this strange individual.

'And you haven't answered my question,' Horowitz reminded him.

'I called the Zürich office for reinforcements. They, too, were short of manpower. They've hired other operatives to cover the smaller places. Not that I'd expect Tweed to know about the obscure crossings.'

'If I were Tweed it is exactly one such place I would choose to slip across the border.'

'What do we need that girl for?' Evans asked to change the subject. He gestured with his head to Eva Hendrix who was sitting out of earshot at the far side of the large office, drinking a cup of black coffee.

Horowitz glanced round. Hendrix was reading a German fashion magazine. She raised both hands and ran them through her titian hair. The curls fell back into the same place: it was an unconscious mannerism she practised frequently.

'She may come in useful at some stage of the operation,' Horowitz told him and left it at that.

He saw no reason to inform Evans that he hoped to infiltrate her alongside Tweed. He had already drilled into her the story she should tell him, a story Horowitz felt certain would convince Tweed of her innocence. The phone rang and Evans picked it up off a nearby table. He spoke briefly in German, put it down, and looked smug as he reported what he'd heard to Horowitz.

'That was the two men who have arrived at Laufenburg. One called to tell me they are in position overlooking the bridge you mentioned.'

'Then now we must wait.' Horowitz turned away from

255

the window to join Hendrix. 'Waiting is the key to success in such a task as we are engaged on. Moving around a lot is a mistake. I only move when I have located the target and *he* has stopped moving.'

Due to the altitude, the air in the small spa town of Badenweiler was mountain fresh. It was deserted at that time of the year as Newman drove slowly along the curving roads. On either side trees and shrubs laden down with snow increased the atmosphere of a town from which the inhabitants had fled, as from some dreaded plague.

They drove past great hotels half-hidden by the foliage, all unoccupied with the shutters closed. Tweed peered out of the window as they glided past the sign for one hotel. The Romerbad. He had once had lunch in summer there in a restaurant at the back overlooking a distant view of hills towards the French Vosges beyond the Rhine.

'The whole town is like a great garden,' Paula whispered.

'And someone I talked to in the Oberkirch at Freiburg told me that during the season the police close certain roads from 1300 to 1500 hours,' Tweed remarked.

'Why?'

'So the rich who come here in summer to take the waters can have their afternoon nap undisturbed by vehicles.'

'They must have been joking,' she protested.

'No, it's that kind of town. A haven for the rich . . .'

Tweed took his decision on the spur of the moment as they approached a signpost. He leaned forward to read the directions, than spoke quickly.

'Don't take the Kandern turning, Bob. Drive straight on.'

'Anything you say. May I ask why?'

'It's a more devious route, takes us right up into the forest before we emerge into the open. If Morgan and

256

Horowitz have people watching for us they'll be more likely to assume we'll take the direct route for the border via Kandern . . .'

They left the small town behind quickly. They drove past a few splendid private villas – again shuttered – and suddenly civilization vanished. Newman was driving up a steep, winding and lonely road where again the surface ahead was virgin snow. The dense palisade of firs on both sides turned the road into a dark corridor, a tunnel of white. The road seemed to climb forever and Newman was constantly turning the wheel to negotiate a chilling series of dangerous zig-zag bends, praying he wouldn't meet a snow-plough coming from the opposite direction. To his left were the trees, but to his right the ground now fell away like a precipice. One skid and they would dive into eternity.

'You've been driving a lot,' Tweed remarked. 'Want me to take over the wheel?'

'I think I've got the feel of the ice. It's just below this coating of snow.'

'Can we just stop talking about it and just get on?' Paula said through her teeth.

It was the first display of nerves she'd shown so far. Newman looked briefly at her in the rear-view mirror and grinned. She managed a wan smile in return and eased herself across to the left side of the car. Away from that awful chasm. Couldn't bear to watch it any longer . . .

'We're close to the summit,' Tweed reassured her a little later. 'I remember this road in summer.'

'But now it's winter,' Paula replied. Then, 'Sorry, I'll keep my big mouth shut.'

The precipice had disappeared. They were driving uphill along a winding avenue lined with the forest on both sides. Paula wiped her damp hands with her handkerchief. Newman had increased speed, and then they reached the crest and the whole world changed.

257

Newman slowed, swung the car off the road on to a vast platform of land. He put on the brake, left the engine running, leaned back in his seat. Tweed opened the door and got out followed by Paula and Newman. Paula gasped.

'It's like being on top of the world.'

'We are,' Tweed agreed. 'At least in this part of the Black Forest. Look at that board.'

The sign read: *Waldparkplatz Kreuzweg 1079 m*. They were perched over three thousand feet up. In the distance an endless valley spread away to the south, a valley without trees. The descending plain was a blanket of snow and the intense glare of the sun off the whiteness was almost painful. Paula took in a deep breath of air and then spluttered. It was very like breathing in liquid ice.

Tweed had taken a pair of compact binoculars from the pocket of the sheepskin he'd bought in Freiburg. He stood on the eminence scanning the vast panorama. Newman, shielding his eyes against the glare, was also gazing all round.

'What are you looking for?' Paula asked, banging her gloved hands together.

'Movement,' Tweed replied. 'On the ground, in the air. It looks deserted.'

'Agreed,' Newman commented, 'so let's get back to the car and head for Laufenburg.'

'There's a ski-lift up that slope . . .'

Paula pointed to their left. A small closed-up cabin stood at the base. The cables shone like silver wires, encrusted with solid ice. They climbed back into the car and Paula relaxed: they were leaving behind the claustrophobic forest, the dreadful ascent alongside the precipice. Minutes later as Newman drove at controlled speed downhill her nerves were twanging again.

The steeply descending road between vast open fields was a crazy and dangerous route. Newman was guiding the Audi round endless spirals, ferocious hairpin bends. Paula braced herself as they swung and skidded round yet

258

another hairpin which turned through a hundred and eighty degrees to the level below.

'Aren't we going rather fast?' she ventured.

'We're in the open,' Newman said tersely. 'The sooner we're clear of this lonely area and hit the autobahn the better.'

If we ever reach it, she mumbled under her breath. They drove past isolated farmhouses and steep-tilted rooftops over barns with ramps leading up to them. They passed through a series of deserted villages. Kalbelesch. Schinau. Neuenweg. Burchau. Then they were down in the plain as they reached Tegernau and a crossroads.

'We drive straight on for the autobahn,' Tweed warned, the map open on his lap.

An hour later they reached Laufenburg, a small medieval town toppling down the side of a hill to the Rhine. Newman parked the car and turned to Tweed.

'I could drive you over to Switzerland, risk it,' he said.

'Too big a risk. We've been travelling in this blue Audi ever since we left Freiburg. Paula and I will walk from here. There used to be a guest-house perched at the end of the bridge over the Rhine. I hope it's still there. We'll use it to spy out the crossing. And, if you can, I'd advise you to turn in this car for another vehicle before you cross the frontier at Basle.'

Their parting was brief. Newman gave the thumbs-up sign, drove back westward. Tweed stood in the snow, holding his case, and smiled at Paula.

'It's not far down this hill. Watch your footing.'

'And you watch yours.'

She trudged after him, placing her booted feet carefully. No one about. The town seemed uninhabited. They turned a corner and Tweed walked faster, then stopped, waiting for Paula to catch up.

'There it is. The border crossing. And the guest-house is still there.'

She stood looking down the hill. At the bottom was a small single-storey building with parking lots in front of it. Outside stood a German guard in a blue overcoat and a peaked cap. The frontier post at the end of the bridge. Facing it was a colour-washed building with a legend in ancient German script inscribed on the wall. GASTHOF LAUFEN.

25

Basle. The German checkpoint was located north of the main part of the city and north of the Rhine. Uniformed guards were stopping cars, asking for identification, taking a good look at the passengers inside each vehicle.

Stieber, his round head leaning forward over the wheel, had parked his Mercedes close to the checkpoint and was watching each approaching car. Beside him sat another security guard from the main HQ at Basle.

'Don't forget, Klaus,' he rumbled in his throaty voice, 'we are looking for a blue Audi. Maybe with three people inside. We see it, we follow it into the city. At the first chance we take them.'

'You've told me all that before,' Klaus, a six-foot giant remarked. 'And let's hope no one checks us with the armoury you've brought.'

'The guards know me,' Stieber snapped, 'know I'm from World Security. They just wave me on without a second thought.'

The armoury Klaus referred to was a pair of knuckle-dusters Stieber carried in his jacket pocket, the 9-mm. Luger tucked inside a shoulder holster and the hand grenade hidden inside the glove compartment. They sat and waited. It was mid-morning and a glorious sunny day. The snow was melting to slush.

It was mid-morning as Newman drove towards the Basle checkpoint. Now that he was well clear of Laufenburg he began to worry about Tweed and Paula. Could they really slip over the frontier unseen? Was the border being watched?

He was driving through the suburbs of Basle and in the distance he could see the checkpoint. He carried no weapons. He'd dumped the Walther – minus the magazine – out of the window into a deserted field. Without the magazine in case some child picked it up. Later he'd thrown all the mags one by one into another field ten miles further along the highway. There was a queue of vehicles at the checkpoint.

Unusual. He slowed down, stopped behind a Volks-wagen Passat. While he waited he studied the road beyond the checkpoint. A Mercedes was parked by the roadside, facing his direction. Two men inside, one round-headed character leaning forward over the wheel, taking a great interest in the queue.

'Amateurs,' Newman thought. 'Too close to the frontier. Too obvious. Definitely not Kuhlmann's men. Which only leaves the World Security thugs.'

He worried a little more about Tweed and Paula. Then decided he was being silly. Tweed was one of the most experienced field agents in the world. And spending several years behind a desk at Park Crescent hadn't dulled his tradecraft. In any case he'd broken with tradition on several occasions and gone back into the field in recent years.

The round-headed man was staring at Newman's vehicle now. He said something to his companion and lit a cigarette. Then he slumped behind the wheel. As the queue moved forward Newman felt relieved he'd seen a car-hire agency on his way in to the city. He'd told them he didn't like the Audi, had shown his international driving licence, had changed the Audi for a cream BMW which he was now driving. The queue moved faster. Newman, keeping his eyes off the parked Mercedes, looked at the frontier-control guard.

'Papers, please.'

Newman produced his driving licence, his passport.

The tall guard glanced at the licence, took a few seconds longer to look at his passport, handed everything back and waved him on. Newman drove on into the centre of the city. The Swiss control-point officers didn't even stop him.

Back at the German checkpoint, the guard waited a few minutes, examined the papers of several more vehicles, then spoke to his companion.

'Take over, Hans. I have to make a phone call.'

Inside the cabin he called Police HQ at Freiburg, asked for Chief Inspector Otto Kuhlmann. He had to wait a few minutes before a voice growled.

'Yes, what is it?'

'Frontier Control, Basle, sir. Sergeant Berger speaking. Robert Newman, the foreign correspondent, crossed into Switzerland a few minutes ago. Driving a BMW. Registration number—'

'Don't bother about that. Who was in the car with him?'

'No one, sir. He was alone.'

'Thank you for the information. No report necessary. I want no written record of this incident. That's all.'

Kuhlmann put down the phone, chewed on his cigar, walked over to a wall map of Southern Germany and Switzerland. 'You're being clever, Tweed,' he said to himself. 'But I'll bet my pension you'll be back. And then the people after you had better look out.'

*　　　*　　　*

Gareth Morgan landed at Basle Airport and a waiting limo drove him straight to World Security headquarters. He showed his pass to the guard and took the elevator to Evans's office. It was late afternoon and already night was falling and they had the lights on. Evans stood up from behind his desk and on a couch Horowitz sat with Hendrix while he worked at a crossword puzzle. Stieber was staring out at the Rhine and turned round, giving Morgan a little salute.

'Well?' demanded Morgan, dumping his case on the couch next to Hendrix. 'What's happened? Where are we? What is the latest situation report?'

Always let them know the boss had arrived. His manner was aggressive, his mouth a tight line. Horowitz finished writing a word on the crossword, laid the newspaper carefully aside, glanced up.

'Nothing has happened.' He smiled grimly. 'We are in Basle. The latest situation report from Stieber is that no one has passed through the Basle checkpoint. Not that I ever expected a man of Tweed's experience to come that way.'

Morgan glared at Stieber. 'What are you doing here? You've left the Basle border crossing unwatched – when Tweed might try to slip across after dark?'

Horowitz answered in the same deadpan tone. 'Other guards took over the watch when Stieber came off duty. You know, Morgan, you really must learn to wait . . .'

'I make things happen . . .'

'Then make Tweed cross the Rhine. We have men with cine-cameras observing the minor crossing points. Couriers are standing by to collect the films. By tomorrow afternoon I'll be sitting in your cinema in the basement, watching those films.' He picked up his crossword. 'Patience is the maxim for the moment.'

'I don't pay you to sit around doing crosswords . . .'

Horowitz's pencil was poised to write a fresh word. He

263

raised the pencil, pointed it like the barrel of a gun. 'You pay me to get results. In my own way. In my own time. Understood?'

Morgan's eyes flickered away from the eyes behind the steel-rimmed glasses. He twisted his lips and transferred his gaze to Evans. 'We'll go to the accountant's office. I want to check the books. Now.'

Horowitz had already resumed filling in his crossword. Beside him Hendrix let out her breath, unnerved by something in the tone of Horowitz's voice.

Tweed had reserved two rooms at the Gasthof Laufen. He had asked for his room to overlook the Rhine and from his window he gazed down on the bridge dividing the two countries. Beside him Paula stared through the heavy net curtains at the far end of the bridge, at Switzerland.

Swiss Laufenburg also clung to the side of a steep hill dropping to the river. To the left of the bridge ancient houses, rooftops weighed down with snow, fell sheer to the Rhine like a cliff. Tweed scanned the crossing through his binoculars, then let them hang from a strap round his neck.

'So near, yet so far. How long do we wait here?' Paula asked.

'The rest of today, all night, then tomorrow we attempt our move into Switzerland. From here I can see what the form is, whether people are stopped at either – or both – ends. It's an ideal observation post.'

Paula walked across to Tweed's bed, perched herself on it and crossed her legs. She picked up a German fashion magazine to pass the time.

Tweed had raised his binoculars again. The sun was shining brightly, had moved round a fraction. It was reflecting off something which glittered in one of the houses to the left of the bridge. A car from Germany arrived at the checkpoint below him. The German guard stopped it, examined the driver's papers, walked round to the back, opened the boot, glanced inside, slammed it closed and waved the car on to Swiss control. Arriving at the other side, the driver was waved on without examination.

The sun had moved another fraction. The glittering reflection in the window of the house perched high above the Rhine vanished. Tweed focused his glasses, gazed through them for several seconds, grunted.

'Something catch your attention?' Paula enquired.

'Yes, I've found what I was looking for. Someone in one of those houses across the bridge is operating a cine-camera, photographing everything that crosses.'

'Oh, my God!' She dropped her magazine and rushed to join him. 'Where? Who do you think it is? The Swiss police?'

'No. They could check people at their frontier post. These are clandestine watchers. Undoubtedly men sent from World Security – and waiting for us.'

'Had we better find some other place to cross?'

'No, this will do very nicely. It's all working out according to plan. We cross here tomorrow morning.'

And with this cryptic remark Tweed lapsed into silence and Paula couldn't get him to explain any more. She was left wondering why he was in such a good humour, even humming a little tune as he continued to survey the bridge.

Once inside Basle, Newman had driven to the best hotel in the city, probably one of the best in Switzerland. The Drei Könige, The Three Kings. It had the advantage of being situated overlooking the Rhine less than a mile east of World Security HQ.

He parked the BMW a short distance from the hotel, collected his bag from the boot, walked into the large reception hall he remembered from previous visits. The concierge greeted the foreign correspondent warmly.

'It's a little while since we've had the pleasure of your company . . .'

Newman asked for a double room overlooking the river, registered, left his bag on the bed with the lid open, left the hotel and took a tram to the main station. He called Alois Turpil in Berne from a phone booth in the station. The mention of Tweed's name acted like magic.

'What can I do for you, Mr Newman?' a guttural voice asked in German.

'I have a job requiring your professional services in Basle. I know your fee. Tonight, if you can make it. You can? Good. I can meet you off the express from Berne if you let me know when you're arriving. 1800 hours? Yes, that would be convenient. I can explain the details over dinner. Too complicated for the phone . . .'

'Of course,' the voice purred. 'We meet on the platform at the *Hauptbahnhof* when my train arrives?'

'Agreed. I'll be wearing a blue suit with a chalk stripe, a pale trench coat and carrying a copy of the *Financial Times*.'

'Mr Newman, I've seen your picture in the papers. It's part of my profession to recognize international VIPs. I'd know you if you were naked.' The voice snickered.

'It's a bit cold for that. See you at 1800 hours. And don't forget your equipment.'

'And don't you forget the fee for my consultation.'

Newman broke the connection and frowned. There had been a touch of flattery he hadn't liked. And the snicker had an unpleasant flavour. He picked up his executive case, which he had wedged against the rear of the phone booth. He recalled what Tweed had said while he sat in a huge restaurant inside the station and drank coffee.

'You may not take to Turpil. He's not my favourite person, but his skill is extraordinary. As to his fee, you'll have to negotiate. He'll be nervous about operating inside

266

Switzerland – against his normal rules. He'll make a big thing about his objection to drive up the price. He'll probably demand thirty thousand Swiss francs. Haggle. You'll get him down to twenty thousand. Especially when you show him the cash. He's greedy for money, is our Alois . . .'

Tweed had then opened his own executive case and handed Newman several stacks of high-denomination Swiss banknotes at the lodge high up in the Black Forest. Only then had Newman realized why Tweed had instructed him to buy his own executive case in Freiburg.

Newman decided he wouldn't let Turpil know where he was staying, that he would take him to dinner at the Merkur restaurant he'd noticed from the tram on his way to the station. He would, in fact, remain as anonymous as possible. He just hoped that when he did meet Turpil he liked him better than he had talking with him over the phone.

When he did meet Turpil he took an instant dislike to the safe-cracker. Worse still, he mistrusted the man.

When Marler phoned the Ministry for External Security, asked for Buckmaster, identified himself, he was transferred three times to different girls before he reached Miss Weston. She sounded as though she'd swallowed something unpleasant and her tone was falsetto.

'Mr Marler, you said?'

'That's right. For the third time. The Minister knows me – I'd like a word with him.'

'The Minister left a message in case you called. He's driven to his home in the country. I can't give you the address.'

'Thanks a lot,' Marler snapped and rang off.

He thought it unwise to tell her he knew that meant Tavey Grange on Dartmoor and he swore as he walked back to his mews flat in Chelsea. Inside five minutes he had backed his second-hand Porsche into the cobbled yard and was driving west.

The journey to Devon was uneventful but when he turned on to the moor for Moretonhampstead the snow was much deeper. The white ridges were stark against the clear blue sky like a series of tidal waves frozen in mid-air. Another red Porsche was parked in front of the main entrance in the cobbled courtyard.

The surface was icy. He nearly skidded as he pulled up. He almost sprawled on the ground as he walked to the arched porch. Why did the English love leg-breaking cobbles? José, the butler, opened the heavy door in response to his jerking the chain-pull bell.

'Ah, Mr Marler. Please come in, sir. The Minister is expecting you.'

'He is?'

'Indeed, yes, sir. Miss Weston phoned from London.'

Marler mentally revised his impression of Miss Weston and was glad he'd told her nothing. He stepped into the warmth of the centrally-heated hall and Lance Buckmaster ran down the massive staircase. Clad in hip-length, fur-lined driving jacket, the uniform for the upper-class driver in winter, Buckmaster was on top form, began talking before he'd reached the bottom tread.

'You made good time. It's a marvellous day for a spin over the moor. You can wait for refreshment until we get back, I'm sure.'

It would have been nice to have the option, Marler thought, but he followed the tall agile figure back through the doorway. Buckmaster halted suddenly when he saw Marler's car.

'So you run to a Porsche as well.' He sounded aggrieved. Behind them the door closed as José disappeared inside the mansion. 'We'll take mine. Give you a few tips on how to drive the beast.'

'Yours is new,' Marler pointed out as he climbed in beside the Minister. 'I couldn't run to this on my salary.'

'Let's get away from here before you give me your report,' Buckmaster snapped as though addressing the foreign housemaid.

He drove straight out on to the main road between the gates of the lodge, tooting his horn, not pausing to check whether anything was coming in either direction. Marler adjusted his seat belt and made no comment on the atrocious behaviour.

He was capable of racing along himself but as Buckmaster took his Porsche across the moor the experience was hair-raising. They drove past a field where a small frozen lake lay beyond it. Buckmaster gestured, driving with one hand.

'That's the Miniature Pony Centre. Fascinating to see them in summer. They're rather like big dogs. Very sweet.'

'Mm,' responded Marler.

It was beyond the steep hill leading down into Postbridge, a tiny hamlet, and the equally steep hill leading out of the place, that Buckmaster let rip. There were wheel ruts in the snow-covered road, just a few. Soon they were climbing higher into the vast openness, swerving round murderous bends at high speed. There were patches of ice gleaming on the road, Marler noted. Buckmaster had his window open and a blast of Arctic air filled the interior. Marler buttoned the collar of his topcoat. Buckmaster glanced at him and gave his braying laugh.

'Invigorating, isn't it? Blow the cobwebs out of your system.'

'We just passed a dangerous-curve sign.'

'I know this road like the back of my hand.'

'But we're not driving on the back of your hand.'

'Insubordinate bastard, aren't you, Marler? They said that in your file – or words to that effect. In the usual Civil Service jargon . . .'

He stopped talking. The Porsche was sliding into a skid. They were very high up, no other traffic, sweeping views and, on Marler's side, a sheer drop into a chasm as Buckmaster fought for control, just managed to ease the Porsche round the bend. Marler looked down into the abyss. A massive rock shaped like the snout of a shark loomed up below.

'That's Shark's Tor down there,' Buckmaster shouted breezily. 'Enjoying the spin? Not frightened, I trust?'

'Just cautious.'

They were on top of the moor and to the south in the sunlit distance the moor rose to a ridge topped by a huddle of rocks which Marler guessed would be huge seen close up. Buckmaster gestured again.

'Haytor there in the distance. Really makes you glad to be alive on a day like this.'

'Just so long as we stay that way.'

The braying laugh again. Buckmaster was getting a kick out of playing on his passenger's nerves. Just like a bloody great schoolboy, Marler was thinking. And naturally the choice for a Minister of the Crown.

'Give me your report,' Buckmaster said suddenly. He fished a cassette out of the glove compartment, rammed it inside the slot, turned a switch. Nothing happened. Not a sound. Buckmaster shrugged. 'Should be playing Stravinsky's *The Rite of Spring*. That's the third time the cassette player has gone on the blink. Pay a small fortune for this tin can they call a car and nothing works. That building on the right we are approaching is an inn – the only habitation for miles. Now, get on with it. Give me your report.'

The inn, half-submerged in snow which had drifted up to the height of the ground-floor window sills, had an abandoned look. Who the devil would visit a place like that for half the year, Marler wondered.

'Tweed is alive and well,' he began. 'I located him,

270

talked with him, in Freiburg on the edge of the Black Forest.'

'You did what! You actually had him under your gun and you tell me he's still alive and well. What the bloody hell do you think you're playing at, Marler? Didn't I make my meaning clear before you flew to Europe?'

Buckmaster's voice had risen to a shout closely verging on a shriek with the last sentence. His gloved hands slipped on the wheel. Now the road fell away sheer to their left into a rocky valley. Marler's hand moved, gripped the wheel and turned it towards him a fraction, then released it.

'Don't you ever dare touch the wheel again when I'm driving,' screamed Buckmaster, his face contorted with rage.

'You were within an inch of the edge – and there's ice under this snow.' Marler's voice was cold, terse. 'Concentrate on your driving and keep quiet until I've finished . . .'

Buckmaster struggled with his emotions, startled and sobered by something he had never heard before in Marler's tone. He reduced speed as his passenger continued.

'You don't try to assassinate a man when he's surrounded with armed bodyguards. There were three other men in the room at the Hotel Oberkirch on Schusterstrasse. And Tweed thinks I'm on his side. That's a big plus. At the moment he's somewhere inside the Black Forest. His objective is Switzerland. Probably it's that country's neutrality which appeals to him. I'm going back there shortly and I'll find him again. So not to worry . . .'

'I am worried. I *shall* worry.' Buckmaster's mood changed to one of near-petulance. 'Until the problem of Tweed is solved. Permanently. If there was a trial on a charge of rape and murder the scandal could bring the government down.'

'Murder and then rape . . .'

'Whatever.' Buckmaster was pressing his foot down again suddenly. Marler watched the speedometer climb.

Forty-five m.p.h. Fifty. Sixty. On a snaking road coated with snow and ice. The only thing which had saved them so far was the lack of any other traffic. Buckmaster glanced quickly at Marler. 'How do you know which came first at Radnor Walk? The murder or the rape?'

'Tweed talked about what he alleged he found when he arrived back at his flat. Few signs – if any – of a struggle by the unknown girl victim. Some blood on a sheet. Traces of skin under her right index finger. It looked like she had known the murderer, wasn't frightened of him. To start with.'

'Alleged is the word. So that's the story he's going to relay – if he ever reaches the witness box alive. That's your job, Marler. You suggested it was the solution when you came to see me at Tavey Grange last time.'

'I did?'

'We're coming in to Princetown. I'm turning back here. I have to be in the House this afternoon. Answering a lot of damnfool questions.'

'You're driving back to London?'

'Lordy no. The chopper is standing by. I never liked this town. The prison may be on the other side but the whole place reeks of it.'

Which was a graphic description, Marler thought. The houses where the warders lived with their wives were long bleak stone terrace blocks. They passed a building with a sign, *Prison Officers' Association*. Something like that. When they'd left Princetown behind and were back in the open Buckmaster opened up the engine. Marler braced himself for yet another endurance test.

The sunshine had now gone, the sky was a ceiling of leaden clouds full of snow to come. As they ascended back on to the moor Marler stared at the bleak aspect, the tors rising up like prehistoric sentinels. This was Doomsday country.

'I don't think Howard is up to the mark,' his companion

272

said suddenly. 'I may have to ask for his resignation – and that would leave the post of Director General vacant.'

Another sprat to catch a mackerel, Marler thought, and I am the mackerel. No commitment, just a devious hint. Buckmaster's unstable temperament bothered him. When he'd told the Minister Tweed was alive and well Buckmaster's reaction had been beyond all reason, a near-manic fury. His most public posture was of the commanding ex-Airborne Division officer. But Marler had seen a very different side to the man.

'That pathologist who conducted the autopsy on the murdered girl is coming to see me,' Buckmaster remarked, going off at another tangent. 'A boring chap, this Dr Rose.'

They were approaching the dangerous bend with the steep hill beyond it, the precipice now on Marler's right with Shark's Tor spearing up out of the snow. He spoke in the cold tone he'd adopted earlier.

'You slow down here. If you want to commit suicide wait until you're on your own.'

'Damn your impudence . . .'

But Buckmaster reduced speed as he negotiated the diabolical bend. He was descending the hill when Marler leaned forward, pressed the eject lever for the cassette, grabbed it with his left hand and hurled it out of the window he'd lowered a few minutes earlier. It sailed over the drop towards Shark's Tor.

'What the hell did you do that for?' Buckmaster demanded.

'You inserted a cassette with nothing on it – to record our conversation. *My* conversation mainly. I don't like tapes existing which can be held over my head.'

Buckmaster grinned wolfishly. 'You must admit it was a good try.'

273

26

At Park Crescent in London, Howard's first question to Marler showed him which way the wind was blowing.

'What have you been up to – or shouldn't I ask?'

Howard was sitting in Tweed's office, but, significantly, not in Tweed's chair behind his desk. He occupied the armchair, his legs crossed, wearing an expensive grey Chester Barrie suit from Harrods. For Howard it was the only shop in town. Marler thought Howard's plump pink and well-fed face showed signs of strain.

Tweed's faithful, long-time assistant, Monica, sat behind her own desk, watching Marler like a hawk. She fiddled with her bun of grey hair. Without Tweed, the familiar office had a ghostly feel of no one being there.

'May I smoke, sir?' Marler asked.

Howard waved an indifferent hand, then gestured towards the hard-backed chair close to him. 'Sit.'

Marler perched himself on the chair, lit one of his king-size cigarettes. He threw the question at Howard, studying his reaction.

'You're convinced that Tweed is guilty of that murder and rape at his Radnor Walk flat?'

'Are you?' Howard flashed back, one leg waggling up and down.

It was a stand-off, an *impasse*. It was Monica who broke it, her voice accusing.

'The whole idea is just damn ridiculous. What I'm trying to find out is who really did it – and why.'

Howard turned to Monica. 'Do you believe in him?'

274

'Probably . . .'

'Thanks for the vote of confidence,' Marler snapped. 'But I have to believe the two of you. I do. Probably.'

Howard stirred. 'We're talking in Tweed's office because Harry Butler has just flashed this office for listening devices. It's clean now. He's checking my office at the moment.'

Marler was stunned. 'What's going on, for God's sake?'

'Harry found this phone was bugged. He's just called me before you breezed in to tell me my own phone was also bugged. Last night someone broke in here in the early hours, bashed our guard, George, over the head. He's at home, slightly concussed. A clumsy attempt had been made to break open one of the filing cabinets,' Howard continued. 'I wasn't satisfied that was the real purpose of the visitation. Hence my getting Harry to check the whole building, room by room. The intruder was bugging the place. Identity unknown.'

'Could you guess?'

'I never guess,' Howard replied stiffly.

'I do,' interjected Monica. 'Buckmaster wants to know what's going on here. His authority over these premises, the SIS, is limited – thanks to a directive from the Prime Minister. So who has the expertise? We've heard some funny rumours about an organization called World Security.'

'No proof, Monica,' Howard warned. He pouched his lower lip over his upper. Marler waited. Howard was on the verge of a decision. He reached for a green file on Tweed's desk.

'Might as well tell you. In complete confidence. I found out from Special Branch the name of the pathologist they used on the autopsy of the murdered girl. Identity also unknown as yet. Pathologist is a Dr Rose. He doesn't like Buckmaster – who has been badgering him for the report on the post-mortem. He also doesn't like the fact that the

275

Minister asked for only one copy of the report to be typed and brought to him. He sees his lordship this afternoon. But Dr Rose was here this morning at my request. Secretly.'

'What does his report reveal?'

'An interesting fact.' Howard opened the file, riffled the typed sheets. 'On this page he confirms the victim was first strangled, then raped afterwards. Underneath the right index finger of the girl's hand he found traces of skin and blood. Rose believes – although there were no other signs of struggle – that she managed to claw her murderer's naked back while he was throttling her.' Howard looked up. 'Are you sure you're convinced of Tweed's innocence?'

'Oh, for God's sake, what do you want from me? A sworn affidavit?'

'Fair enough. Now we come to the interesting fact. The blood type under the girl's fingernail corresponds to a patch of blood which stained the sheet. She was blood group O Positive.'

'Do keep me in suspense. No hurry at all . . .'

'The blood group of the stain and under her finger was a rare blood group. AB Negative. The murderer's blood group.'

He closed the file, replaced it on the desk, and paused. Howard was not averse to a little drama. His tone was grim when he continued.

'Tweed's blood group is A Positive. That lets him out. You see how vital the Rose report is? Lucky I have this photocopy.'

'Could I have a copy of that photocopy?'

'No,' said Howard.

'Oh, give it to him,' Monica interjected again. 'I can make a copy for him and no one will be any the wiser.' She glanced at Marler as Howard handed her the file. 'You must promise not to lose it.'

'Promise.'

Marler gave her a mock salute, waited until she had left the office. 'You said that lets Tweed off the hook. You're not suggesting it would be safe for him to surface, to come back?'

'No. Definitely not. Buckmaster is trying to push me out, to take over the SIS by remote control. I'm fighting him tooth and claw. He demands a file, I provide only a doctored extract – just one example of the battle that's raging. The PM is adopting a neutral stance. So far. How is Tweed? Does he want to get back here quickly? He had some secret project on the go. I didn't know a thing about it. Resented the fact to start with. Now, after what's happened . . .' he waved his manicured flipper in a dismissive gesture.

'Tweed's OK,' Marler replied after a long pause, 'I doubt if he's in a hurry to return. He's up to something. They tried to kill him on the autobahn near Freiburg . . .'

'Good God! I didn't realize it had come to that. Now tell me, who are "they"?'

'Difficult to be sure.' Marler blew a perfect smoke ring, watched it float up, disintegrate after forming an oval shape. 'World Security has a big office in Freiburg.'

'You mean that fat toad, Gareth Morgan, is going into business on his own account?'

Marler was surprised at Howard's swift reflex. He was equally surprised at the transformation in Howard's character. The SIS chief who had spent half his time at his club had become a tiger: there was the light of war in his blue eyes. Buckmaster had performed a miracle – had turned Howard into a gut fighter.

'Could be Morgan, I suppose,' Marler replied. 'He was present in Freiburg when a noose was thrown round the city to trap Tweed. He slipped through it, of course. Bob Newman is with him. Paula, too.'

'I was going to ask where she was. Does Tweed need

back-up? I could fly out Harry Butler and Pete Nield at an hour's notice.'

'Hold them in reserve – until you get a phone call saying we need a butler and an assistant for a banquet.'

'And you're going your own way, of course, as always?'

'Of course.'

By arrangement Marler met Leonora at the World Security HQ in Threadneedle Street at nine o'clock that night. She was waiting for him in her office. By the side of her desk stood a silver bucket filled with ice on a tripod. A bottle of Bollinger champagne protruded its head above the ice as though signalling, 'I'm chilled. Rescue me . . .'

'Anything to tell me?' Leonora asked as Marler extracted the cork, poured the liquid into two tulip-shaped glasses perched on her desk. She was wearing a form-fitting N. Peal polo-necked sweater, a mid-length pleated cream skirt slashed to her thighs. Marler speculated whether she was wearing anything else except her tights. She tucked a blonde curl into the corner of her red-lipped mouth and reached out the other hand for her glass.

'To us.'

'Down the hatch,' responded Marler.

It was very quiet in the building on the eighteenth floor. He had the impression the only other people in the tower were the guards at the main entrance. Ignoring the chair drawn close to hers, he sat facing her with the desk between them like a frontier pole.

'I have something to show you,' he began. 'But before I show you it might be better if you had a refill.'

'That's what it's for.'

She extended her glass and looked up at him as he leaned to pour more champagne. She nodded to a large couch beneath a window. Marler had noted all the curtains were drawn shut. He carefully avoided following her gaze.

'We might be more comfortable on the couch,' she suggested, and drank half her glassful.

'Might be safer sometime when I visit Tavey Grange when Lance is up in town,' he parried.

'No.' She shook her head and her blonde hair swept across her face. 'José, the butler, is a creep. Reports everything to the boss, Lance. We're far more likely to remain alone and intimate here.'

'I'd better show you what I've brought you,' he said quickly. Lifting the cardboard-backed envelope off his lap he took out the glossy print he'd collected from Grubby Grundy. Holding the print so it faced him, he made a performance of hesitating.

'Oh, come on, Marler. Show me, whatever it is. And why are you still wearing those kid gloves? It's warm enough to fry an egg in here.'

'Which is what I was doing – or trying to – when I badly burned my hands. One of those cheap pans which conduct heat up the handle. Bit unsightly. Here you are. Brace yourself.'

She took the print with one hand, her lips tightened, she drank the rest of her champagne, held out the glass as she went on staring at the photo: the picture Grundy had created of Buckmaster sprawled, fully clothed, on a couch with a nude girl lying on top of him.

'I don't know her,' she said eventually.

'Sorry. It's a bit pornographic.'

'He's found a new way of doing it. He's fully dressed – and she's starkers. Maybe he's found he enjoys them undressing him.'

'Maybe.'

'Who is this particular cow?'

'No idea,' Marler lied.

'And may I ask how this came into your possession?'

'You just did.' Marler sipped more champagne. 'A detective – private – I know who is a whizz with a zoom lens

279

took it. You won't expect me to supply his – or her – name and address.'

She had put her glass on the desk, was handling the print and plastering it with her fingerprints. When she threw it down on the desk he whipped it up with his gloved hands, slipped it back inside the envelope, then leaned forward to pour more champagne in her glass.

'I'd like to keep that photograph, Marler,' she said.

'I'll get you three more prints. I need this copy for the photographer to select the right negative.'

'He takes so many? Of that kind of picture?'

'I told you, he is a detective.' He raised his glass to her, took a sip. 'Lord knows how many he takes in a year. And not necessarily of that sort. Often a picture of a man and a girl entering a flat is sufficient.'

'Then get me three prints.' She frowned. 'If Lance goes on the way he's doing he's going to end up with a nervous breakdown – what with his big job and his women on the side. Talking about women on the side, it really would be more comfortable on that couch.'

'Next time, if you don't mind.' Marler checked his watch and stood up. 'I have exactly ninety minutes to catch a plane.'

'Be like that. You can find your own way out?'

'I can . . .'

As he drove through the night to London Airport Marler reflected that by showing the photograph he'd laid the groundwork for a lot of aggravation for Lance Buckmaster.

The Minister made the call from a public phone-box inside the Post Office off Trafalgar Square. He got through to Freiburg and they told him Morgan was at the Basle HQ. He dialled the Swiss number and caught Morgan just before he left for the company flat.

'You know who this is,' Buckmaster said. 'No names, no pack drill.'

'What can I do for you, sir?'

'I have obtained the pathologist's report. Only one copy in existence.'

In Basle Gareth Morgan sighed with relief, but not audibly. He made no comment, waited for the next instruction.

'I'm worried about a Dr Arthur Rose,' Buckmaster continued. 'I think he's accident-prone. He has a consultancy at St Thomas's Hospital on the Embankment.'

'I know the place. You want me to send someone to attend to him?'

'Under the circumstances, don't you think it would be wiser?'

'Agreed. Consider it done . . .'

Buckmaster broke the connection and in his Basle office Morgan turned to Stieber, who spoke pretty good English. The German looked expectant as Morgan opened the wall safe, took out several bundles of bank-notes, tossed them on his desk.

'You're paying a visit to London. Catch the plane tomorrow morning. A Dr Arthur Rose, consultant at St Thomas's Hospital. Near Waterloo – on the Thames Embankment and facing Parliament. The good doctor is accident-prone. Be careful but make it a quick job. You know your way round London.'

'These for me?'

Morgan nodded and Stieber picked up the banknotes, stuffing them into his jacket pockets. He was leaving the room when Morgan called out to him.

'And the first thing you do when you reach London Airport is to change those Swiss notes into pounds sterling. The lot. Anything left over, change it at another bank back into Swiss notes before you fly back here.' His voice became menacing. 'Don't forget, change the lot into pounds sterling.'

'Will do.'

And that, Morgan thought as the door closed, will eliminate my fingerprints from any money he has on him if he botches the job. He mopped his moist forehead. This Tweed business was getting complicated. Morgan always worried if operations became complicated.

Arriving in London the following day, Stieber changed the banknotes, then took the Underground into the city. Cab drivers had good memories. He eventually emerged from the mole world at Regent's Park station. Ironically, when he stepped out of the elevator and walked east he crossed one end of Park Crescent, which meant nothing to him.

His destination was the street leading down into Fitzroy Square which is lined with used-car dealers and their dubious wares. Stieber's knowledge of London was mostly confined to the less salubrious areas.

He decided on a Ford Escort, which had seen better days, on the basis of the price, the vehicle's anonymity. He insisted on driving the car a long distance north with the dealer, a cunning lout with a soiled open-necked shirt.

'Petrol costs money, mate,' the dealer informed him as they turned back.

'So does this heap of scrap metal.'

Stieber was wearing an outsize pair of dark glasses and a cap he had brought with him, a piece of headgear purchased on a previous stay in the British capital. It gave him the look of a wide boy who might have had something to do with horse racing which the Jockey Club would not have approved of.

Parking it back at the kerb in the same street, Stieber

spent another half hour haggling over the price. It was expected. The deal concluded, he drove straight to St Thomas's, being very careful to obey the regulations. Especially to drive on the wrong – the left – side of the road. Stieber wanted to leave no official record of any kind of his lightning visit to Britain.

Morgan had trained him to operate in this manner abroad. If he ran into trouble he had in his memory the name and phone number of a lawyer who specialized in 'difficult' clients.

Driving to the hospital, he crossed Westminster Bridge from the north side and automatically registered there was a pedestrian crossing near the southern end. He drove slowly and found an empty parking slot nearby. Another car was about to occupy it. Stieber accelerated, drove across its bows, forcing the other driver to pull up with an emergency stop. As he slid inside the slot the competing driver jumped out of his vehicle and strode over. A City gent, wearing a bowler hat. Stieber didn't know there were any of them left.

'You've taken my slot,' Bowler Hat fumed. 'And you nearly caused an accident.'

'You are correct.' Stieber leaned out of his open window, extended his large paw. 'Shake.'

Bowler Hat was taken aback, uncertain how to react. Assuming that Stieber was giving way, he extended his own hand. Stieber grasped it, squeezed hard, almost crushing Bowler Hat's fingers. He yelped with pain as Stieber released him and spoke.

'Don't push your luck, matey.'

Stieber was reproducing the vernacular of the used-car salesman back near Fitzroy Square. The other man swore, retreated to his own vehicle, decided not to mix it with this brute and drove off.

Feeding the meter, Stieber collected the cardboard-backed envelope he'd bought at a stationer, an envelope crammed with sheets of blank A4 paper. Adjusting his tinted glasses, tilting his cap at a rakish angle, he walked to the entrance to St Thomas's.

He knew Dr Rose was on duty with his consultancy somewhere inside. He'd phoned from a call box on the way after buying the Ford Escort. He entered, spoke to the nurse on reception duty. This was the tricky part.

'I have some important papers for Dr Arthur Rose. Not urgent.'

'You can leave them with me . . .'

'Can't do that. I've been told to hand them to him personally. Like I said, it's not urgent, but he needs them by the end of the day.'

'He's in conference . . .'

'Then I'll come back. Any idea when he'll be leavin'?'

'About seven this evening.'

'I have a parking problem,' Stieber continued. He stared at the receptionist through his glasses. 'If I may say so, you look very smart in that uniform. Really suits you . . .'

The girl, very plain, coloured, then resumed her posture of the correct receptionist as Stieber continued.

'So if I could just get a glimpse of Dr Rose? Then I'll recognize him, hand him these important papers and dash back to my car before I'm nicked for a ticket.'

'I think I can arrange that.' She called out to a nurse hurrying across the lobby. 'Susan, could you take this gentleman to the third-floor conference room where Dr Rose is addressing the symposium? He just wants to be able to recognize him later.'

Stieber said nothing to the stern-faced nurse who accompanied him in the elevator. She led him down a corridor, then paused by a large window. A dozen or so men in white coats were seated, listening to a man in outdoor clothes standing on a dais.

'That is Dr Rose. On the platform.'

A well-built man of about forty, chubby-faced and wearing rimless glasses. Hair greying at the sides. Clean-shaven. The nurse stood on guard and wasn't going to leave him. Stieber didn't want to depart by the main entrance, to be observed more closely a second time by the receptionist.

'Thank you . . .' He suddenly put his hand to his mouth. 'Lord, my stomach. I'm going to throw up. I thought that hamburger tasted funny . . .'

'Toilet through this door,' the nurse said briskly. 'You know your way out? Good.' She held the door open. With all she had on her plate she could do without a mess on the floor to clear up.

Stieber disappeared inside, walked into a cubicle, locked the door, sat on the seat, clutching his envelope. He waited several minutes, flushed the toilet and peered out into the corridor. Empty. He walked quickly to the door marked *Fire Exit*. Beyond a flight of iron steps led to the ground.

No one was about as he left the hospital by a rear entrance and made his way back to the car. He drove off into Lambeth, found a pub with a free parking slot, walked inside and ordered a ham sandwich and a mild and bitter.

When in London pubs were his favourite haunt. Not for the beer, which tasted awful compared with its German counterpart, but for the conversation which he eavesdropped on. It was the perfect place to polish up his English, absorb the accents, note the colloquialisms which were the passport to acceptance.

'Are you a cabbie?' asked the barman as he brought the second half-pint. 'It's a hobby of mine – guessing my customer's profession.'

'No. I'm on the dole.'

'Bad luck. A lot of people are. Been out of a job long?'

'Only a month. Seems like a year . . .'

Fortunately another customer came up to the bar.

285

Stieber had removed his glasses and stuffed his cap into the pocket of his windcheater before entering the place. Like cab drivers, barmen had good memories.

He killed the rest of the day visiting two more pubs, where he drank orange juice – no point in being stopped by the police and being breathalized. Then he drove round south of the river, noting the layout of the streets. He had to circle the area close to St Thomas's several times before he found a parking slot.

It was dark now. Six o'clock. Three slots became vacant all at once. The British were going home early. Trains were late due to iced-up rails, frozen signals. Stieber had read about weather conditions in a newspaper he'd bought before entering another pub. The temperature had nose-dived, there was a sheen of ice on the streets. The lack of people and the ice would help. Stieber had a feeling this would be an easy one. Unlike the Tweed problem. But that was his experience – jobs were either a piece of cake or bloody difficult. A piece of cake. That was a phrase he'd picked up in one of the pubs: at first he'd thought they were talking about their favourite food, but the subsequent chat had given him the real meaning of the phrase.

He was parked where he had a good view of the main entrance to St Thomas's. He'd arrived an hour early to be on the safe side. He just hoped that Rose would leave the place by himself.

As he sat with his gloved hands on the wheel – he had worn gloves ever since leaving the plane that morning – with the engine ticking over, he thought about the British. They did not work like the Germans did. And they spent so much time in their awful pubs, chatting or just sitting alone, maybe reading one of their boring newspapers. Stieber's idea of relaxation was to visit a blue movie, watch a couple of girls frolicking.

At seven on the dot Dr Charles Rose, wearing an overcoat and carrying a briefcase, emerged by himself. As

286

Stieber backed out of his slot, Rose walked towards Westminster Bridge, placing his feet flat on the treacherous
surface. Stieber couldn't believe his luck.

He checked ahead, behind him in the rear view mirror.
Not a soul in sight. Not even a car. He drove slowly
towards the bridge. Then he blinked. What incredible
luck. A piece of cake. Rose had stopped by the pedestrian
crossing, pressing the button and waiting.

The light turned red for traffic and Rose stepped off the
kerb. Stieber gunned his engine, raced forward. He saw
Rose turn at the sound, saw his horrified face, then the car
slammed into him at speed. Stieber felt the soft thud of
metal meeting flesh and bone. Rose's body was lifted off
the ground, arms flailing, briefcase describing an arc in
mid-air. The body fell back, sagged on the road. Stieber
kept up his speed, felt the vehicle wobble as the tyres rolled
over the corpse. Best to make sure, Stieber thought, and
sniggered.

He drove through central London to Finchley where he'd
had a bed-sit during the three months he'd once spent in
England at Morgan's suggestion to polish his English.
Moving slowly down a suburban side street he spotted a
house in complete darkness. He drove on, parked round
the corner.

Walking back, he studied the semi-detached house
again, then pushed open the gate and made for the side
entrance, creeping over a mossy path. There were no lights
at the back. He pressed the bell, ready to run if he heard
sounds inside. Nothing.

It took him five minutes to break a glass pane in the back
door, reach in and turn the key, enter the kitchen, close the
door behind him. A cloth was laid over the table. He
whipped it off, tucked it under his arm and went down the
hall into the front room. A pair of silver-plated candlesticks

and a silver-plated bowl were perched on a table. He grabbed them, wrapped them in the table cloth, left the house by the way he had come in.

Snow had begun to fall again in the eerily silent street when he reached his car. He opened the boot, shoved the wrapped articles he'd stolen inside, closed it quietly. Half an hour later he abandoned the car five miles away and close to an Underground station.

One hour later Stieber was alighting from the Underground carriage which had transported him to London Airport. There were no flights until the following morning so he booked a room at the Penta Hotel and after dumping his case in the bedroom he went to the restaurant.

As he ate he checked over the details of his brief visit. He had used no car hire, no taxis. Of course the police would, sooner or later, possibly connect his abandoned car with the murder of Rose. The front of the car was bound to carry relics of its encounter with the doctor. But it would all look like the work of a petty thief, an accidental killing of a pedestrian. The 'loot' found in the boot would confirm the theory. The work of what they called a 'lager lout' these days. No fence would look twice at silver plate.

Stieber enjoyed his meal, treated himself to a bottle of German Riesling. He'd earned it. Tomorrow he'd fly back to Basle, congratulating himself on a very neat job.

27

At the Gasthof Laufen Tweed was out of bed as soon as it was daylight. He washed, shaved, dressed and packed his night things inside his case in ten minutes – an exercise he'd learned years ago as an operative in the field. You always had to be ready for a swift departure in an emergency. Then he stood by the window, binoculars pressed to his eyes. He dropped them to hang suspended from the loop round his neck.

He was gazing down at the bridge, where the red-and-white striped frontier poles were raised on both sides, when Paula tapped on his door. He unlocked it, let her inside, relocked it and joined her by the window. He could sense the tension inside her.

'Shouldn't we wait a day or two longer?' she suggested.

'No, we cross mid-morning. We've been in the same place for one night. That's long enough. We have to keep on the move.'

'You sound horribly fresh, horribly confident. I wish I did. What's happening?'

'It's a good job I took this room to observe that bridge. I know their routine now.'

Paula compressed her lips, stared at the bridge and the river. At this point the Rhine curved in an S-bend. On the German side officers clad in green overcoats and peaked caps stood by the frontier control building. On the far side their Swiss counterparts wore blue overcoats and blue peaked caps. All their coats were buttoned to the neck against the cold.

'The routine is important?' Paula queried.

'Vital. They stop all cars on this side, check drivers, their papers and their vehicles. They even stopped girls going over on bicycles. But they don't stop people on foot. That's the point. So, we have to get rid of our suitcases. Even on foot I think we'd be checked.' Tweed's voice was terse, fresh. 'It means we have to transfer our few clothes to plastic bags – several people have walked over with them and no one bothers.'

'I remember there was a supermarket, a small one,

where Newman dropped us. I could go there, buy a few things, collect some plastic bags.'

'After breakfast . . .'

'But what do we do with the cases?'

'Shove them in here. I've been exploring.' Tweed led her to a small door under where the roof sloped. He opened it, shone his pencil flash inside while Paula peered in. She stood up.

'Won't the chambermaid find them?' she objected.

'Not immediately. I'll hide them under those two spare duvets on that shelf. Before I do that I'll break the locks. That will give a reason why they were left. But when they discover them we'll be long gone.'

'Will we?' She wandered over to the window again. 'Are those men with the cine-camera still watching from that house?'

'Of course.'

'They'll photograph us then . . .'

'I hope so . . .'

She spun on her heel. 'Another cryptic remark. What the hell does it mean?' she flared. 'And I hate these clothes. Do I pass inspection?'

Paula was clad in worn blue jeans and a padded wind-cheater. Her feet were shod in trainers. She had bought this clobber, as she called it, at Tweed's insistence in Freiburg.

'You look fine. You look like everyone else. It's a uniform these days. So you merge into the background. Now, breakfast. You'll feel better on a full stomach.' He smiled. 'So will I.'

'I'm sorry', she said, and hugged him impulsively, 'for that attack of nerves. I'll be all right when we're on the move – really I will.'

'I know. A good breakfast. Now . . .'

*   *   *

Tweed walked down the hill to the German frontier post first, followed by Paula, a dozen yards behind him. He'd insisted on this sequence, partly to steady her nerve, but he'd also issued a stern instruction.

'Nothing is going to happen to me – but if it does you keep walking and you go up to that Swiss police car parked near their border post.'

As he came close to the frontier post the blue-coated guards stopped a BMW. In each hand Tweed carried a plastic carrier-bag containing the contents of his suitcase. Paula also was similarly burdened. They looked like two people who had completed their shopping, two people who had nothing to do with each other.

Tweed paused at the edge of the kerb, looked back as though to check no car was coming, saw Paula stepping it out, her head high. He walked past the post at his normal pace. The sun was again shining brilliantly, reflecting a hard glare off the chrome of the BMW.

He was on the bridge now, moving along the left-hand sidewalk, his pace steady. He had passed the German cabin without anyone taking any notice of him as they checked out the driver of the BMW, opening his trunk. Tweed was half-way across, the Rhine flowing swiftly below him, when he paused and stared straight at the house concealing the cine-camera.

Paula was appalled. It took all her determination to keep moving. What the devil was Tweed up to? It was almost as though he'd deliberately challenged the invisible watchers behind the curtains. Then he was walking again, approaching the Swiss control.

'It's going to go wrong where we least expected,' Paula said to herself. 'The Swiss guards will have the description sent from London . . .'

She gritted her teeth as Tweed drew closer and one of the Swiss officers walked across the road. He was going to intercept Tweed. It was all over. After they'd

291

gone through so much already . . .

The officer stood on the sidewalk, hands on his hips, facing Tweed, who continued walking towards him. The officer gazed over the parapet of the bridge as a police launch passed beneath it, shouted something down to the men aboard, waved his hand, crossed back to the post and began talking to his companion. Tweed walked past and began climbing the hill where the road turned off the bridge.

He would have given anything to look back to see how Paula was faring but he resisted the temptation. He went on climbing the road which curved round to the right past the ancient houses. The railway station was less than ten minutes' walk from where he was now.

He knew he was out of sight of the bridge when he heard the crunch of feet coming up fast behind him. Still he didn't turn his head. Paula drew alongside him, breathing heavily. It was so cold that, like Tweed, her breath was coming out as puffs of white vapour.

'Don't you think we might co-habit now?' she enquired.

'Depends what you mean – it's a bit public here.'

She dug him affectionately in the ribs with her elbow. 'You know what I mean! And look at that sign. We've made it.'

By the roadside a large sign pointed back the way they had come. DEUTSCHLAND. Tweed grinned at her as they continued trudging uphill over the icy slope.

'Want to go back for a second look?'

'Not bloody likely. Eliza Dolittle in Shaw's *Pygmalion*.'

'I have seen a few plays in my time, I'd have you know . . .'

They were joshing each other like a couple of school-children. It was for both of them the release of tension after their ordeal. They passed several expensive-looking villas with grey colour-washed walls, then they were on

292

the level. At an intersection was another road sign. *Altstadt*. The Old Town.

Tweed nodded his head to the right. 'It's a wonderful example of an old medieval town. Pity we haven't time to explore it. Ah, there's the station. We turn left here.'

Paula glanced to the right. A straight cobbled street led to an old tower. The arched entrance to the Old Town was cut out of the base of the tower. Below the sloping roof was a clock with roman figures painted in gold. It was so large she saw the minute hand jerk forward.

Normally she'd have loved to explore, but she was frozen and couldn't wait to get far away from the border. As they turned left she saw the *Bahnhof*. Laufenburg's rail station was a compact two-storey building with coral-washed walls and shuttered windows. More like a private residence than a station.

Tweed entered the booking hall, studied the timetable on the wall. He walked up to the ticket window, put down his plastic bags as Paula stood alongside him, then he stared at the clerk.

'I – want – two – top – tickets – to – Zürich. Single . . .'

To Paula's astonishment he spoke in English, spoke to the clerk as though addressing a mental idiot. The clerk looked at him, nodded, produced two tickets from the machine while Tweed was fiddling with Swiss banknotes. Then he examined the tickets and stared again at the clerk.

'These – are – first – class?' he mumbled.

'I beg your pardon,' the clerk said in perfect English.

Paula's patience snapped. 'Erste Klasse fahren,' she said.

'Ah, first class? I did not hear you friend clearly . . .'

The clerk changed the tickets, sorted out the banknotes Tweed pushed under the window, gave him half of them back, leaned forward, spoke slowly and clearly.

'For Zürich you change at Eglisau. The train is due in five minutes. The next train.'

'I eventually worked that out from your timetable,' Tweed grumbled. 'British timetables are much better than German.'

'Swiss,' the clerk corrected him. 'You are in Switzerland.'

'I know that. You think I am stupid?'

On the deserted platform Paula, still suffering from the reaction of crossing the bridge, exploded.

'Have you gone mad? Half-way across that bloody bridge you stopped and stared up at the house where they have a cine-camera. Now you make a scene with that ticket clerk, you talk in English when you could so easily have spoken in German. That clerk is going to remember us, if someone enquires after us.'

'I hope so.' Tweed's mood had changed. He was his normal alert self. 'I am springing a trap.'

'What does that mean? Sometimes I feel humiliated by the way we keep on running, running, running. It's not our style.'

'So,' Tweed repeated, 'I am springing a trap. Laying a powder train in our wake, if you like – a powder train which in due course will blow up in the face of our pursuers.'

28

Newman used the same phone at the main station in Basle to call Alois Turpil. The idiot hadn't kept his appointment the previous evening. Newman had met the train arriving at 1800 hours. Passengers had alighted as he stood with his copy of the *Financial Times*. Then the platform was deserted, the train moved out, and no one had approached him. He swore, went into the restaurant and ordered a large Scotch.

'Who is this?' the same voice as previously enquired in German at the other end of the line.

'You should bloody well be able to guess. You never came to Basle last night. What the hell are you playing at?' Newman responded in the same language.

'If you had told me where you are staying, given me a phone number, I would have called you,' Turpil purred. 'Something most urgent, most unexpected came up. I couldn't leave here. Where are you calling from now?'

'A public box at the *Hauptbahnhof*, of course . . .'

'I can meet you tonight. Most definitely. At the same time and the same place.' The tone had become deferential.

'Let me tell you something, Turpil. Stand me up again and I am going to report your behaviour to our mutual friend. You won't ever get another commission from him again. Or from me. No, don't interrupt. Just listen. 1800 hours this evening. On the platform where your train arrives. Look for the *Financial Times* under my arm. It's pink in colour . . .'

'I know that . . .'

'Glad to hear you know something. Last chance, Turpil . . .'

Newman slammed down the phone and walked away.

'Wake up. We're at Laufenburg.' Horowitz, dug his elbow into Morgan's overweight bulk settled in the seat beside him.

'Where are we?'

Morgan had eaten a large lunch with all the trimmings. An aperitif for openers. White wine, then red wine with the four-course meal. Followed by a large cognac with coffee. He blinked. They were seated in the dark in the

295

cinema in the basement of World Security HQ in Basle.

More pictures were being flashed on the screen, films projected from the cine-cameras which had photographed the more minor Rhine crossings the previous day. It was mid-afternoon. The films had been brought in fast by couriers on motor-cycles. They had watched eight films from eight different crossings before Morgan fell into a deep sleep.

'I just told you,' Horowitz said quietly. 'This is Laufenburg.'

'Another negative result,' grumbled Morgan, reaching for his cigar case. He extracted a cigar and twirled it between pudgy fingers. If he lit it that puritanical bastard, Horowitz, would object. He forced himself to concentrate. More people crossing the bridge. Another blank . . .

Horowitz leaned forward. Morgan sensed his companion was coiled like a steel spring. He blinked again, yawned, sat up more erect to keep himself awake.

'Freeze that frame!' Horowitz called out to the projectionist behind them. 'That's it. Now, zoom it up. That man crossing and carrying two plastic bags . . .'

Morgan frowned, stuck the cigar in his mouth, chewed on the tip as the frame froze, the picture became enlarged, showing the head and shoulders of the hatless man trudging across the Rhine. Horowitz's voice was a sibilant hiss.

'That is Tweed. When was this picture taken?' he called out.

'Yesterday morning.'

The projectionist's voice was a weird disembodied echo. There were only two other people watching. Horowitz and Morgan. The Welshman stared hard at the frozen face which was looking straight at the camera with a grim expression. The image was blurred but, now Horowitz had pointed it out to him, Morgan felt sure it was Tweed. Horowitz was calling out to the projectionist again.

'There may be a girl with him. Continue running the film now.'

The blurred image vanished, the screen went white for a few moments, then the focus was back to normal, taking in most of the bridge. Morgan settled back, but Horowitz still leaned forward, motionless. His deliberate voice broke the silence again.

'That girl – also carrying plastic bags – in denims and the windcheater. 'Freeze *that* frame. Zoom it up. Quickly!'

Morgan sucked at his wet cigar end. Another head-and-shoulders image filled the screen. Again the image was blurred but her features were clear. Horowitz sank back in his seat and turned to Morgan.

'I studied the photos closely enough to be sure. That girl is Paula Grey. The two of them have crossed over into Switzerland.'

'Well, he'd want his girl friend with him,' Morgan commented. 'All home comforts on tap . . .'

'According to the file Grey is his trusted assistant. There was nothing said about an intimate relationship.'

Horowitz sounded severe, as though he found Morgan's attitude to life repellent. Yes, a ruddy puritan, Morgan reflected, and a cold-blooded assassin into the bargain. Who is he to come out with moral lectures? Instead he said:

'Well, there's your target. What's your next move?'

'Where is Stieber?'

'He won't be back till tomorrow,' Morgan replied quickly. 'I sent him to check something for me in Germany.'

'Then I need a car immediately. To drive me to Laufenburg. It will only take a short time and I wish to question the men who filmed those shots. Also I may make further enquiries in Laufenburg. I wish to leave at once. With a print of both those frames.'

'I'll come with you.' Morgan heaved his bulk out of the chair. 'I'll tell the projectionist to provide the prints within five minutes. And there's a Merc waiting in the car park. Which should get us there fast.'

'You can stop wasting any more film,' Morgan told the operator of the cine-camera as they entered the room of the old house perched above the Rhine. 'You filmed the target, Stutz. And is there an ash-tray in this dump, Jost?' he asked the other man, waving his lighted cigar.

'Mr Stutz,' Horowitz began more politely as the operator pressed a switch, stood up from behind his camera and stretched his arms. 'Mr Stutz, this is a frame of a man you've filmed crossing the bridge. Yesterday, I understand. Do you by any chance remember this man? You are concealed behind net curtains – hence the blurred image – but the strange thing is he appears to be looking straight at you.'

Stutz, a small lean-faced man, studied the print, scratched his head. He handed back the print and slipped a peppermint in his mouth.

'Oddly enough, I do remember him. And I had the weird sensation that he *was* looking at me. Which is impossible.'

'Not necessarily. He is a very clever man. And this print of a girl – you remember her?'

Stutz reacted more quickly, glancing at the print before he returned it. 'No. I don't recall her . . .'

'She was walking not a dozen metres behind the man,' Horowitz insisted.

'Then that explains it. I was so startled by the man staring straight up at me I don't think I took a lot of notice of what I was filming for the next few minutes.'

'Thank you, Mr Stutz. Incidentally, what time of the day was it when the man crossed?'

'Mid-morning. Maybe a bit earlier. Hard to be exact.'

'Thank you again, Mr Stutz. One final question. In Laufenburg is there a car-hire firm, even a small outfit?'

298

It was the other member of the team, Jost, small and stocky, who answered. 'No, there isn't. Quite definitely not.'

'You sound very certain, Mr Jost.'

'I spent a holiday here last year. Which was one reason I was chosen for this assignment. I knew where we could site the camera for a fee. No car-hire people in Laufenburg . . .'

Morgan waited until he was alone with Horowitz back in the icy street, standing by the parked Merc, before he asked his question.

'You think they hired a car to make their getaway after they'd slipped over the border?'

'I don't now.' Horowitz gave Morgan a glance verging on the contemptuous. 'Not when there's no place to hire a car. So, we have two people on foot, carrying heavy carriers in each hand. The bags sagged, I noticed. And in this weather. They need to leave here quickly. They have overcome a nerve-racking hurdle – crossing the frontier. They would wish to leave this town quickly. How? The railway station is our next visit . . .'

Once again Horowitz slipped quickly behind the wheel. He had noted Morgan's reaction to too large a meal. Sluggishness. Driving needed swift reflexes, especially in these conditions. His judgement was confirmed when he started the engine and the wheels spun futilely on ice. He released the brake, let the car slide back a few feet, braked on packed snow. The car moved forward up the curving hill.

In the front passenger seat Morgan glanced to his right as they reached the level area at the top of the hill. He gestured with his cigar.

'There's a Hotel Bahnhof over there. They could be sitting inside that place while we drive past.'

'No.' Horowitz crawled forward, saw the station to his left, turned the wheel. 'I am beginning to think myself inside the mind of this Tweed. He is a clever and resourceful opponent. He knows when to wait. He must have spent one night inside the Black Forest at least, maybe two – before he drove here. And he must also have detected the bomb I attached to the Audi we found in the undergrowth off the timber track. You have your World Security pass for Switzerland with you?'

'Yes. Why?'

'I am going to question the station staff. All you have to do is to flash your pass, say "Police", and then leave me to do the talking. That pass looks very like a Swiss detective's identity pass. Which, I suppose, is why you had it designed like that. One day the police will complain.'

'We do a lot of business in Switzerland. They don't bother us.'

'That won't influence the police in this country. Ah, here is the station . . .'

Morgan did as instructed. Standing beside Horowitz in front of the ticket window, he flashed his pass. '*Polizei.*'

'We think you may be able to help us,' Horowitz began in his soothing voice. 'We are looking for a dangerous criminal. A German who can pass for an Englishman. He may have been accompanied by an attractive girl. Here is his picture. It is a little fuzzy, but still a good likeness. Have you ever seen this man?'

'Yes,' the ticket clerk said promptly. 'I'm hardly likely to forget him . . .'

'Oh! Why is that?'

'He was very aggressive, talked to me like a schoolboy and was rather stupid in the way he asked for the two tickets to Zürich. I don't think he knew Switzerland at all well – he spoke in English word by word, and of course I know the language well.'

'Of course,' Horowitz agreed amiably.

'He was so muddled,' the clerk continued, 'that I gave him two ordinary tickets and he wanted first class. The girl

300

with him had to say "first class" to me in German. Then I got it sorted out for him.'

'Two return first-class tickets to Zürich?' Horowitz enquired.

'No. One-way. He did know he had to change at Eglisau.'

'And can you recall about what time of day this was?'

'In the morning.' The clerk reflected. 'Sometime about mid-morning. Has he done something awful?'

'Possibly a question of taking money which doesn't belong to him.' Horowitz smiled. 'You have been most helpful. I thank you.'

Morgan stamped his feet to clear his shoes of snow before he climbed back into the Mercedes beside Horowitz. Then he clasped his gloved hands together to get the circulation going.

'So now we know. It's Zürich.'

'I find the behaviour of Tweed very curious,' Horowitz commented. 'It bothers me more than a little.'

'What behaviour? Seemed pretty clear to me.'

'I said earlier I was beginning to know Tweed, how his agile mind works. First, while crossing the bridge, he gazes straight at the camera. A coincidence? I think not. I believe that somehow he knew that camera was there. Then when he reaches the station he makes a great fuss, goes out of his way to draw attention to himself so he will be remembered. Why? We will drive back to Basle now. Later I will go to Zürich, perhaps with Stieber. But Zürich worries me. I shall tread very carefully, I promise you.'

301

29

Newman had spent some time parked in a slot opposite to the entrance to the eight-storey modern building overlooking the Rhine which was World Security HQ. He had then parked his car in another slot out of sight and had explored on foot.

Six steps led up to the large plate-glass entrance doors. Beyond them uniformed guards with dogs patrolled. He walked down the side street next to the building and came to the river. A flight of steps led down to the Rhine near one of the bridges spanning the wide river.

At the bottom was a pedestrian walk alongside the Rhine. He looked up as he strolled along with a bitter wind blowing in his face. More snow on the way. There were plenty of footprints in the snow covering the promenade and under them the snow was packed hard. Above him on each floor windows gave a view across to the opposite bank. Attached to the river wall was an iron-rung ladder leading down to a mooring point for boats.

The rest of the day he was careful not to go near the building. It began to snow heavily in mid-afternoon. Would that help or hinder their entry into the building? That was assuming Turpil turned up this time.

At 1800 hours, having eaten an early dinner at the Hilton, he was standing on the same platform as the train glided into the *Hauptbahnhof*. Passengers again alighted, girls clutching scarves close to their throats as they left the warmth of the coaches and the icy air hit them.

Newman stood well back, the *Financial Times* tucked

under his arm. All the passengers disappeared down the exit steps, the train moved out, leaving a deserted platform except for Newman. He swore.

'All right, Turpil,' he said to himself, 'that's it. And thank God I didn't tell you where I was staying . . .'

'Mr Newman? Mr Robert Newman?'

The guttural voice was familiar. Newman swung round. A man had emerged from the top of the nearby steps, had moved with the silent tread of a cat. A small man, inches shorter than Newman, slimly built, but with a remarkable face. Very strong bone structure, his nose hooked, a wide thin-lipped mouth and a pointed chin. His eyes, a pale luminous blue, stared hard at Newman.

Alois Turpil wore denims, the bottoms nipped tight to his ankles with bicycle clips, a close-fitting dark wind-cheater buttoned to the neck. Perched on his head above a high forehead was a woollen pixie cap. He reminded Newman of a pixie, a formidable pixie.

'You came this time,' Newman remarked in German.

'I explained that on the phone, Mr Newman,' Turpil replied in English. 'Shall we go into the restaurant out of the cold so we may talk?'

'Where did you spring from?' Newman asked as they walked towards the restaurant. 'You didn't alight from that train.'

'Always do the unexpected. That is the only way to survive. I drove here by car, parked it. I have been watching you from the opposite platform – from behind that trolley of luggage. I wished to make sure you were alone . . .'

They chose a table in a corner. Probably it was the weather, the time of the year, the time of day – the place was three parts empty. A waiter wearing a white apron arrived.

'You'd like something to drink?' Newman suggested.

'Nothing alcoholic. Coffee would do nicely.' Turpil, still

303

wearing his woolly cap, waited until they were alone. 'I never drink alcohol when I'm working. It muddles the brain. Now, Mr Newman, what is it you wanted me to do for you?'

Newman shifted his executive case more firmly between his legs under the table, offered his cigarette pack, took one when Turpil shook his head. The direct approach, he decided.

'We have to break into World Security HQ down by the Rhine. I want to photograph their most secret records. I'd guess in the so-called Research & Development Division section – wherever that may be. I have a camera. You get us inside, open up filing cabinets, any safes you can locate. I photograph certain documents, you replace them exactly where you found them. When we leave I don't want them to know we've paid them a call. Especially I don't want them to know that we've copied some of their records.'

He paused as the waiter brought coffee. They drank it in silence while Newman waited for Turpil to react. He guessed his age as about fifty, maybe a little older. Hard to tell, he was so slim. The silence went on. Turpil frequently gazed at Newman with his strange luminous eyes. The Englishman was not happy about the eyes – they had a remoteness which hinted at a man who cared not a fig for his fellow human beings.

'This place is too public,' Turpil said after finishing his coffee. 'Surely there is somewhere else where we can discuss this problem more privately?'

Newman sighed, paid his bill, led the way out of the station to where he had parked the BMW. He saw Turpil glance at the front number plates and congratulated himself on his precaution. Before leaving the car he had scooped up handfuls of snow in his gloved hands and plastered it over the registration. Both front and rear plates.

Turpil settled himself in the front passenger seat. Newman climbed in behind the wheel, turned on the engine and both heaters. The interior was like the inside of a refrigerator. Ice had formed on the windscreen.

'What you propose is a dangerous operation, very dangerous,' Turpil began. 'World Security is an unpleasant crowd. If we were caught we'd be liable to end up floating in the Rhine, unconscious.'

'So, you know the building,' Newman said with a flash of insight.

'I didn't say that. You've told me the problem. Now I need to know the fee for my services.'

'Fifteen thousand Swiss francs . . .'

'Ridiculous. I've wasted my time coming here. Your friend, Tweed, would know better.'

'I'm talking about cash, Turpil.'

Newman rested the executive case on his lap, unlocked it and raised the lid. Turpil glanced at the neat stacks of banknotes inside and for a second Newman saw a flash in the pale eyes. He closed the lid.

'And I only deal in cash,' Turpil replied. 'We're wasting time. What time were you thinking we'd make the break-in?'

'Around midnight . . .'

'No. Three o'clock in the early morning. The morale of the guards, their alertness, will be at the lowest ebb.'

'You do know the building,' Newman persisted. 'I'll raise the fee. Twenty thousand francs. My last offer. In fact it's all I've got in this case, all I can afford.'

He omitted to tell Turpil that for his own travelling expenses he had deposited ten thousand of the francs Tweed had provided in the safety deposit at the Drei Könige. He snapped the catches shut on the case, lit a cigarette and stared out at the bleak deserted street.

'I make a rule of never operating inside Switzerland,' Turpil informed him in his quiet purring voice.

Newman didn't reply. He glanced at his watch. 6.30 p.m.

'You drive a hard bargain,' Turpil commented, and Newman knew the fish had taken the bait. It had been the sight of all that cash. Turpil's next remark confirmed he'd assessed the man's character correctly.

'Do you mind if I look inside that case for myself?'

'Be my guest . . .'

After checking the contents and handing back the case Turpil sat silent for several minutes. Newman was catching on to his tricks, mannerisms. He also said nothing. Then Turpil tapped the closed case resting on Newman's lap.

'I normally receive an advance before I do the job. Fifty per cent of the agreed fee.'

Newman shook his head. It wasn't only letting go of so much money: Turpil would have thought him a soft touch if he'd let him get away with it. They were conducting a ritual dance and Newman's patience was wearing thin.

'What is the next move – between now and target time?'

'You amuse yourself on your own until 2.30 a.m. Then I pick you up from your hotel . . .'

'The Hilton,' Newman said promptly. He turned to face his passenger. 'Let me ask you a couple of questions before you disappear into the wild blue yonder. Where is your equipment? And what are *you* going to be doing?'

'My equipment is in my car, parked not a dozen yards from where we're sitting. It's an Audi with a souped-up engine. I shall be checking the World Security building again thoroughly.'

'Again?'

Turpil smiled for the first time. 'My earlier profession was security expert. I installed the security system inside that building. I know my way around it better than I do the inside of my own apartment.'

So, all that talk about how tough the job was going to be was pure sales pitch, Newman thought. But he was

306

relieved that Turpil would be working on familiar territory so he said nothing as Turpil opened the door. He leaned inside before he closed it.

'The main entrance to the Hilton just down the road. 2.30 a.m. prompt. Timing is everything.'

He slammed the door shut before Newman could reply.

Tweed had phoned his old friend Arthur Beck, Chief of the Federal Police in Berne, from a call box in the main station as soon as they reached Zürich. Paula stood a few feet away, guarding the plastic bags. It was a tense moment for both of them. How would Beck react?

'Arthur Beck here,' the familiar breezy voice came over the line. 'Who is this?'

'Tweed speaking . . .'

'Give me the name of that lovely girl assistant of yours – it sounds like you, but . . .'

'Paula Grey. And last time we were here you held a plane *en route* to Athens while we talked at Kloten Airport.'

'That's enough. Excuse the precaution. Where are you calling from?'

'A public call-box . . .'

'I have been waiting for this call ever since you crossed the frontier over the bridge at Laufenburg, my friend.'

'And how the devil do you know about that?'

'Oh, I had Howard's report about your unconventional behaviour in London, plus photographs of yourself and Paula flown to me. I circulated copies to the frontier posts. Surely you noticed the Swiss official who stood staring at you on the bridge and then went back to a police car? He recognized you from your picture, reported back to me over his radio. Now, where are you?'

'Zürich. I need to get to a high-powered transmitter

very quickly, to use it in secrecy. I may tell you why if – when – we meet.'

'Oh, we must meet. I'd arrange for a car to bring you here from Zürich police HQ but I think you should keep under cover. Do you mind taking an express to Berne? No? Good. Get a cab from the station. I suggest you enter the Taubenhalde by the rear entrance. Remember where it is? Then when may I expect you? Give me time to get out the welcome mat.'

'It will be a few hours yet. We have to eat and then take an express to Berne.'

'Good. Arrange it so you arrive after dark. When we meet you can tell me who has gone stark raving bonkers in London. Not Howard, from what I read between the lines. Take care.'

Tweed smiled as he replaced the receiver, partly with relief, partly at the English colloquialism – Beck prided himself on his use of the English language.

'He seems friendly,' he told Paula. 'Now, first we must buy two suitcases to pack our things. Then lunch.'

'I know just the place in the Bahnhofstrasse to get suitcases. There's a café over there where you can get coffee. Wait for me. I'll be as quick as I can . . .'

Horowitz sat alone with Morgan in the latter's office in Basle. He had sent Hendrix back to her apartment in Frankfurt after paying the girl a large fee. He now saw no opportunity to infiltrate her into Tweed's company.

'The time has come for me to fly to Zürich,' he announced. 'I wish to take Stieber with me. When is he due back – from Germany you said?'

'Any minute now.'

'You must alert as many operatives in Zürich as possible about Tweed and the girl. They have photographs, I assume?'

'Yes. I'll phone, tell them to run off more copies.'

'Those operatives are reliable, I hope? They can throw a dragnet through as complex a city as Zürich?'

'Of course.' Morgan was indignant. 'I have an old woman on a cycle who can cover an incredible distance. We have motor-cyclists, men on foot who look like young louts. We have men selling toys and balloons at strategic points no one would suspect. We can scour Zürich . . .'

'Send two top operatives, a man and a girl, to the main station. Tweed and the girl probably arrived there. Check all the hotels. Give them a cover story for when they show their photographs of Tweed. I suggest they say he has to fly urgently to New York. His wife is seriously ill. They can pretend to represent some big insurance company and Tweed is one of their top executives. The Prudential. Have you the facilities to print fake Prudential visiting cards?'

'Yes. On the premises in Zürich.' Morgan suppressed his resentment at this stream of instructions. 'You're flying to Zürich today?'

Horowitz stood up. 'No, tomorrow. That gives you time to get your people in Zürich moving . . .'

'Manpower will be stretched to the limit,' Morgan protested.

'Send men from here. The focus has switched to Zürich. I'll see you later.'

Horowitz left the office without another word and walked back to the Drei Könige where he was staying. Morgan sat fuming, puffing his cigar, when the phone rang. It was Buckmaster. The pressure never eased up.

'Just a brief word,' the lofty voice told him. 'I'm sorry to have to tell you Dr Rose met with a fatal accident. A hit-and-run driver according to the papers. Sorry to be the bearer of ill tidings. Must go.'

Morgan sank back in his chair and sighed with sheer

309

relief. At least that call counter-balanced his conversation with Armand Horowitz.

Newman drove back to the Drei Könige for dinner when he had watched Turpil leave his parking lot inside his Audi. From what Turpil had told him he seemed to be making careful preparations for the break-in at World Security. He parked the BMW near the Drei Könige, walked into the lobby, acknowledged the concierge's greeting, went up to his room and had a quick shower.

The drive through the night from the station had been short but a gruelling experience. It had stopped snowing but the temperature had nose-dived. The tram-lines were bars of ice, there had been shot ice as he turned the bends and twice he had skidded.

After the refreshing shower, which warmed him up, he changed into a heavier suit for the night's work and went down to the dining-room. The promenade deck overhanging the Rhine where tables were laid in the open in summer was closed and ankle-deep in snow.

There were very few people in the dining-room. The head waiter was leading him towards a table when Newman spoke quickly.

'I think I'd like that table for two by the wall, please.'

'But certainly, sir . . .'

Newman sat down with his back to the wall. Pretending to examine the menu, he watched the tall thin man with steel-rimmed glasses seated four tables away, providing Newman with a three-quarter view of him. Newman had had a bad shock.

He recalled the photographs Marler had taken of the men entering the World Security Building in Freiburg. The turnip-figured man Marler had identified as Gareth Morgan. His tall companion, Marler had explained at greater length, was one of the top assassins in Europe. And now,

310

apparently like Newman, Armand Horowitz also considered the best hotel in town was good enough.

30

Latitude 30. 10. N. Longitude 41. 0. W. The mid-Atlantic south-west of the Azores. Captain William North, American skipper of the *Lampedusa*, a 20,000-ton freighter with a single smoke-stack, gave the order to heave to. Hundreds of miles away from the well-used sea-lanes, he was worried about the stricken vessel half a mile to starboard. His First Officer had just reported to him on the bridge.

'Radio op reports a Mayday signal from that ship, sir. I gather they have a sick woman aboard. Fell down a companionway and broke her left leg. Compound fracture. They've no doctor. They also have engine trouble. Permission to take the lady aboard?'

North stood, feet splayed, binoculars pressed into his eyes while he scanned the vessel. It was motionless, swaying on the gentle swell. He then swept the horizon and, as he had expected, there was no other vessel in sight. It was broad daylight and the sun rippled off the wave crests.

'We do have a doctor,' his officer persisted. 'If she is left there and they can't repair the engine trouble she could be in real trouble.'

'Let me think.'

North lowered the binoculars. He had a lot to think about. The stricken vessel was the *Helvetia* and flew the French flag. About twenty thousand tons, he estimated. It

311

could have drifted a long way south if the engines had broken down a while ago.

Yes, he had a lot to think about. In the hold of the *Lampedusa* rested the giant computer, *Shockwave*. So enormous it almost filled the large hold. North had a crew of twenty American seamen, all of them armed. Underneath the canvas-covered erection on the foredeck was concealed a high-powered machine-gun. Seen through his glasses the *Helvetia* had a frail look as she rolled helplessly.

'Supposing we just sail on,' North suggested, thinking out aloud. 'Get the hell out of it and continue *en route* for Plymouth. Then we can hand over that lump of hi-tech to the Brits, go ashore, try out the Limey beer.'

'Then I wouldn't sleep too well for the rest of the voyage,' his officer replied.

'Don't suppose I would either,' North agreed. He took his decision. 'Tell the radio op to signal them to send the lady over to us in one boat. Repeat one boat. Warn Dr Schellberger he has a patient coming aboard. Wait! Also tell the radio op to report what we're doing to Langley on the agreed waveband. I presume you've checked with the sonar team that there are no subs in the area?'

'I did that before I came to the bridge. Normal procedure in an emergency.'

'Well, OK. Get it moving. We can't hang about here for the rest of the year. And, just to make assurance doubly sure, tell the gun team to stand by their weapon. But don't take off the canvas. We don't want to give that skipper of the *Helvetia* a heart attack. That would make for another patient for Schellberger . . .'

North stood, hands on his hips, staring at the other vessel, then called back his officer who was running off the bridge.

'Another precaution, Jeff, warn the guard crew to be on the alert. Assemble them close to the foredeck. Get to it.'

North, a six-footer, wrinkled his forehead. Why was he

taking all these precautions? Because something about this goddamn situation bothered him. Couldn't put his finger on it. Everything looked peaceful enough. He checked his watch. Should take them about a half-hour to get the lady aboard the *Lampedusa*. The *Helvetia* crew was white, European. Something he'd checked when he'd scanned the deck of the vessel.

He glanced over his shoulder as a short heavily built man heaved himself up the ladder. White-haired, Dr Schellberger was very spry for his age, his weight.

'Hear I've got work to do, sir,' he remarked. 'A hip fracture and a broken leg. That will make for a deal of pain.'

North nodded. Then another possible solution occurred to him. He suggested the doctor could go aboard the *Helvetia* to tend to the patient. Schellberger shook his head.

'With a compound fracture you never know. I'd prefer to have her aboard here to keep an eye on her.'

North nodded agreement. The First Officer reappeared, reported. 'The radio op is sending your signal to the *Helvetia*. He was delayed responding to a signal from London. Then he'll be contacting Langley.'

'Thank you. I guess we'll be under way in the next half-hour.'

Several thousand miles away to the north-west Lance Buckmaster left the special room at the Admiralty which had been put at his disposal at the specific request of the PM. Inside the room, for which he had the only key, was a high-powered transmitter which he had no trouble operating by himself. They had similar advanced transceivers at all the main headquarters of World Security & Communications.

He returned through the dark to his office at the Ministry

313

for External Security. Alone, he sat down before a type-writer and tapped out a brief memo to the PM. He read it once, initialled it with a flourishing 'B', put it inside an envelope, sealed it, addressed it *Highly Confidential. Personal attention of Prime Minister*, called a messenger, gave him the envelope and told him to hand it direct into the hands of the PM.

Alone again, he clasped his hands behind his neck, stretched and yawned. Now all that remained to be done was to work his way through his red despatch boxes. As suited the PM, the memo had been brief.

1810 hours. Contacted North. Cargo proceeding according to schedule.

On the bridge of the *Lampedusa*, Captain North watched the activity aboard the *Helvetia* through his glasses. A staircase had been lowered, the platform resting just above the lapping waves. A large boat had also been lowered from its davits and was being brought alongside the platform. Two crew members ran down, tied up the boat securely fore and aft to the platform.

More crew appeared at the top of the staircase, men moving slowly as they handled a stretcher, manoeuvring their burden down the platform at an angle. Inside the stretcher North had a glimpse of a girl with long dark hair splayed, a girl who lay very still and appeared to have a piece of wood strapped to the side of her left leg.

North lowered his glasses, checked the situation on his fore-deck. As ordered, several seamen stood round the canvas-covered machine-gun. Others, their hand-guns concealed, lounged at the port side, gazing at the *Helvetia*. Because his vessel was riding the sea with the bow pointed towards the stricken ship, North felt he had made his dispositions. No need to waste manpower at the stern.

*   *   *

Aboard the *Helvetia* ex-Sergeant Greg Singer, late of the SAS, stood at the head of the staircase, checking the operation. A six-foot-tall man, he was heavily built, his large head was like a sculpture carved out of teak. His dark hair was cropped close to the skull and he wore a pea jacket and denim trousers.

Thirty-three years old, he had been drummed out of the Special Air Service for brutality in his treatment of young recruits. His CO had been sorry to lose him.

'Singer is as tough as a rock,' he'd remarked. 'Pity that he went too far on that training course . . . He has brains . . .'

Too far had been British understatement for the incident when Singer broke the jaws of two trainees climbing the Brecons in Wales. They hadn't been trying hard enough, according to Singer. Now he glanced at the stop-watch held in the palm of his large hand. Timing was everything in this operation. Seconds counted. And his fee of £100,000 was at stake. For that kind of money he was prepared to go the limit. And that was exactly what he was going to do. He slid his right hand inside the jacket, felt the butt of the Luger shoved down his leather belt. The skipper, Captain Hartmann, born in Austria, appeared alongside Singer.

'Radio op reports they've given permission for us to move the wounded passenger aboard.

'Time to start the jamming,' Singer snapped, his expression a graven image.

'We've already started that. No further signals from the *Lampedusa* will go anywhere. What about the frogmen?'

'They went over the port side five minutes ago. They'll reach the stern about the time our boat arrives . . .'

Singer ran down the steps, leapt into the boat. The stretcher had already been carefully laid inside near the bow. Five men were aboard, including Singer, when they cast off. Rolls of canvas were littered untidily inside the large boat as Singer gave the order and the engine fired.

The mooring rope was unhitched, thrown on the platform, and the boat headed across the gentle swell for the *Lampedusa*.

The attention of all the men on deck aboard the vessel was concentrated on the approaching boat, a factor Singer had banked on. Nothing like insatiable curiosity to bugger up security. He checked his stop-watch again. 'Slow her down a bit,' he ordered.

It was all a question of synchronization. The five frogmen under the waves had to reach the *Lampedusa*'s stern about one minute before Singer's boat hove to under the staircase North had now lowered over the side of his vessel. Three minutes was the maximum period Singer had planned for completion of the operation.

It was a peaceful scene, North thought, arms folded as he waited on the bridge. The clearest of blue skies, the sun gleaming off wavelets, the approaching boat now close enough to see down inside it. The injured woman would be in her twenties he estimated. Her suède jacket was open, exposing her tight sweater, the two mounds of her breasts thrusting against the wool. Her denims seemed pasted to her long shapely legs. Several members of the *Lampedusa*'s crew gave wolf whistles. The girl smiled briefly, waved her right hand. North stirred restlessly. The wolf whistles irked him.

'Cut that out!' he shouted. 'Prepare to bring the casualty aboard . . .'

At the stern of the *Lampedusa* something like a nightmare was appearing. Hands grasped the gunwale, bodies heaved themselves over and on deck. They were clad in frogmen's suits, which masked their faces, and as they came aboard they carried waterproof bags which they dumped on the deck.

They moved silently and with great speed. Unzipping the bags, they wrenched off their flippers from their feet, their masks from their faces. From inside the bags they

316

hauled out gas-masks and breathing apparatus. Fitting them over their heads, they hauled gas pistols from the bags and ran along either side of the deck. A crew member of the *Lampedusa* appeared suddenly at the top of a companionway. He stared in amazement at the hideous figures running towards him, reached for his gun inside his holster. One of the masked intruders aimed, fired his gas pistol. The seaman clutched at his throat, gave a horrible gurgling sound, collapsed backwards down the companionway. He was dead before he reached the bottom.

The invaders fanned out, one group diving down the companionway, a second couple ran up towards the bridge, another man dived up the port side. They paused at the top behind the bridge. One man crept forwards and peered round the corner.

The boat from the *Helvetia* was now moored to the platform of the *Lampedusa*. Crew members had run down the platform and were lifting the stretcher, easing it carefully on to the platform. Singer grabbed something from under a roll of canvas, fitted the gas mask on swiftly, bent down again and hauled out a Uzi machine pistol. He ran up the staircase and was on deck before North realized anything strange was happening.

'Man the gun!' He shouted. 'Open fire on the terrorists . . .'

He broke off in mid-sentence as a short burst from the Uzi cut his body in half. Singer swung the barrel towards the crew manning the machine-gun. They had ripped off the canvas, were swivelling the muzzle under the instructions of the First Officer. Singer fired several more short bursts. Four men slumped to the deck. Blood began to seep from the corpses, staining the woodwork. Singer pressed a lever, put his weapon on single shot, fitted in a fresh magazine.

He ran from his bridge, down a companionway below decks, still wearing his gas-mask. The cyanide gas was lethal at one sniff. Two of his masked men were moving further along the corridor. He jumped over two bodies, heading for the wireless room. Automatically he made a body count. Seven so far. Including North, the captain, there was a crew of twenty to be accounted for. He burst into the radio cabin.

The operator, an American called Hoch, held a clutch of code-books in one hand. With the other he was fumbling to open the porthole. Singer raised his mask clear of the lower part of his face, pressed the muzzle of his Uzi against Hoch's skull.

'Put those bloody books down on that table. There's a good boy. Now, I'll ask you once only. You contacted Langley?'

Hoch, a tall, very thin man, opened his mouth and nothing came out. Then he swallowed, tried again.

'I tried to do that. No dice. A lot of interference – you know, atmospherics. No contact . . .'

Singer experienced a wave of relief. The jammer aboard the *Helvetia* had worked. He stepped back a few paces, gestured at the floor.

'You're the one who may survive. We need you, *Kamerad*. Lie flat on the floor. No, on your belly.'

Singer fished a pair of handcuffs from his pocket, jammed the Uzi muzzle into Hoch's neck to scare him a bit more. He laid the Uzi on the floor, stooped over the prone figure who was shaking with fear. Wrenching both hands behind his back, Singer attached the handcuffs. Hauling the American to his feet, he clenched his huge right hand, hit his victim on the jaw. Hoch fell down unconscious. Yes, they'd need Sparks, Singer was thinking. For radio transmissions. At the other end they'd be familiar with Hoch's 'fist' – his touch when he tapped out a signal.

Singer picked up his Uzi, adjusted his mask, opened the door, jumped into the corridor, swinging his weapon in both directions. One of his men, gas-mask in place, kicked

318

open one of the cabin doors. From inside there was a crackle of gunfire. As his man was hurled back against the other side of the corridor he performed a reflex action, pressing the trigger of his pistol. A gas shell hurtled into the cabin. Silence.

Singer approached slowly, waited by the open door, peered inside, a quick jerk of the head forward and back. Then he stood in the doorway. Six crew members of the *Lampedusa* lay piled on top of each other, still clutching guns in their lifeless hands. One man's face was already turning a bluish colour. Cyanosis.

Singer heard a muffled groan, swung round. His man lying in the corridor was shot but still alive. No time to waste on looking after casualties. Singer glanced up and down the deserted corridor, slipped inside the cabin, pulled a Smith & Wesson .38 from a dead hand, went back into the corridor and bent over the badly injured man. He placed the gun muzzle against his skull, pulled the trigger. The fallen man gave a convulsive jerk, lay still. Singer replaced the gun in the hand of the dead American.

No point in letting his team know what he had done. Bad for morale. His memory made another body count. Twenty aboard the *Lampedusa* – including Hoch. That left nineteen. So far he made the body count thirteen. Another six to be accounted for.

Emerging up the companionway on to the aft deck, he found one at the foot of the companionway, two more on deck. That left three. The engine-room. Had the bloody fools checked there? He doubted it. He went down more steps, stopped in front of a steel door, turned the handle, opened it and stepped on to the metal grille beyond. A ladder led down into the works of the tub.

Three engine-room men stared up, paralysed by the sight of the apparition. He picked them off one by one.

319

Nineteen. A clear field. He ran back up on to the bridge. There was a lot to do.

Singer, minus gas-mask, stood on the bridge and sucked in good fresh sea air. The Swedish girl, Ingrid, who had acted as decoy, had been freed from the stretcher, had removed the dummy splint from her leg, and was leaning over the rail.

'Naylor,' he called out to a seaman from Liverpool. 'Put on your mask. You know the layout of this tub. You damn well should, you studied the layout along with the rest of us back in Antwerp. Go right through her, open up every port-hole. I want the ship clean in one hour. Get rid of all traces of cyanide gas. We're going to have to sleep and eat aboard this vessel.'

'On my way, Sergeant.'

'Lapointe,' he called out to the Frenchman. 'You put on your mask, too. But first assemble a working party. I want all the bodies transferred to the *Helvetia* within an hour. Dump them in the engine-room. And don't forget – every body must be handcuffed to a metal support. You'll find one of our own – Johnson – in a corridor. They shot him. Take him with the rest. We can't afford incriminating evidence. You all want to be hanged in Turkey? No, I thought not.' He smiled grimly. Nothing like a little joke to release the tension.

'On my way,' reported Lapointe, and hurried down the companionway off the bridge.

'Next the second funnel . . .'

Singer joined Ingrid by the rail. The launch which had transported them from the *Helvetia* had returned to berth alongside the freighter. An immense cylindrical object was being loaded on the motor-boat, roped securely. It was so large it projected over the bow and the stern. As he watched he saw through the binoculars he'd hauled from

320

round Captain North's corpse, that they had completed the job. Lapointe and a helper had now moved the body close to the step-ladder still slung over the side.

'Everything went well, then, Sergeant?' Ingrid enquired, as though referring to a banquet.

'So far, so good.'

Singer glanced at her, then looked away. He had found her running a small brothel in Rotterdam. She was expendable – before they reached their destination she'd have to be dropped overboard one night with heavy weights tied to her ankles. Women were a nuisance aboard a ship crewed by so many men. And women couldn't resist opening their big mouths.

Singer had recruited his team by travelling round all the ports of Western Europe – from Oslo to Marseilles. He was very choosy. No prison record and the potential candidate must know his job.

Captain Hartmann was a case in point. A first-rate skipper, he had almost lost his ticket when drugs had been found on board his ship. The charge had been dismissed for lack of positive evidence, but afterwards Hartmann had trouble finding employment.

'What are you thinking about?' Ingrid asked and pressed her arm against his. He shifted further along the rail. Singer was a clever organizer and was constantly checking in his mind the next steps in the programme.

'Pearson,' he called out half an hour later, 'stand by to erect the funnel. Got your tools ready? I want a reliable but quick job.'

Pearson, a ship's carpenter, bent down to his tool bag and came up with a power drill. He brandished it and grinned.

The boat had arrived and men were slowly hauling up the considerable weight of the dummy smokestack. It was Pearson's job to fix it to the deck behind the existing funnel. Other men were already slung over the ship's side in a cat's cradle, painting out the name *Lampedusa*, substituting *Helvetia*, the name of the vessel still floating half a mile away.

'Everybody give Pearson a hand,' Singer ordered. 'That metal funnel is bloody heavy.'

He made his second trip to the hold which he'd visited after checking the body count. All the corpses had been transferred to the *Helvetia* by fast motor-boat making several trips. Descent by ladder into the huge hold was a tricky operation. There was so little space between the ladder and the cargo.

Singer, smoking a cigarette, once again gazed up at the computer, *Shockwave*. He felt dwarfed by a small building. A monster of a computer, so he'd been told by the voice on the phone which gave him all his instructions while on the European mainland.

Looking up, he thought the description good. There was something frightening about its sheer size, by the thought of the vast number of circuits packed inside its metal coat. I am earning my money, Singer thought, and then hurried back up the ladder. More jobs to do: he had to check everything himself.

On deck he climbed over the side, ran down the staircase to the motor-boat moored to the platform. Naylor, who had reported all portholes opened, that the gas was clearing, was sitting by the engine which he started up when Singer gave him the nod.

A few minutes later Singer was climbing aboard the almost deserted *Helvetia*. The abandoned ship had an eerie feel. Alone, Singer made his way to the engine-room. Only one live man awaited his arrival. Marc, the Belgian explosives expert. Short and stocky, he was his usual passive self.

'Where is the bomb?' Singer asked.

'Behind you, against the bulkhead. That large black box.'

Singer turned round. 'And that will send it to the bottom? You are certain?'

'No, sir,' Marc replied in his polite way. 'It will blow it sky-high. That is the expression?'

'It is . . .'

Singer was touring the nineteen corpses which had been put aboard, each handcuffed to a steel upright, each with a rope attached to its ankles, a rope also attached to a huge metal ring. Even so far from the shipping lanes Singer wanted no risk of a body floating to the surface. Satisfied, he asked one more question before leaving the ship with the Belgian.

'You said you could detonate with that radio gadget. Can you be certain it will work from the *Lampedusa* – that is, from the *Helvetia* as we must now always call it.'

'It will blow sky-high,' Marc repeated, showing no resentment at this checking of his skill.

'OK. Let's move it . . .'

Singer paused on the deck before running down the steps to the motor-boat. He was gazing at the other ship where they had now erected the dummy funnel. It was extraordinary how convincing the addition looked. They had done their research well – checking the precise measurements of the real funnel from Lloyd's shipping records. The height, the diameter, the colour.

'That's it . . .'

Five minutes later Singer was on the bridge of the other vessel with *Shockwave* in its hold. Still he hadn't finished checking as he talked to the skipper, Captain Hartmann.

'You did bring with you all the papers? The manifests showing we're transporting bauxite from Jamaica to Turkey?'

'In my cabin, Sergeant.'

Everyone had been trained to call him by his rank. It made for good discipline. Singer scratched his stubble, thought of one more point.

'You know we're heading for the eastern Med to make the rendezvous. But you must pass through the Straits of Gibraltar during the night.'

'I have timed it for that. Our course is planned.'

Singer turned to Marc who stood holding a small gadget like a camera. 'Blow her!' Marc turned to face the original *Helvetia*, paused, then pressed a button. Like the eruption of a volcano, the *Helvetia* exploded into an inferno of flames and smoke. The bow section soared into the air, turned in an arc, plunged bow first down into the ocean like a gigantic torpedo, vanished. Amidships the vessel lifted clear of the water, shattering into a thousand fragments which showered back into the water. The stern split in two, rode the waves for a short time, then dived deep down towards the ocean bed.

The destruction of the *Helvetia*, an awesome spectacle which caused Singer's crew to freeze, gazing motionless, was accompanied by an ear-splitting *boom*! Then a small tidal-like wave swept towards the *Lampedusa*. Men gripped the rail and waited for it to reach them, still hypnotized by the power of the explosion, by the sight of a large freighter disappearing completely. The wave rolled majestically forward. Singer splayed his feet, took a firm grip on the rail. The wave reached them and the freighter rolled at an angle close to forty-five degrees. Next to Singer, Ingrid was petrified, sure their vessel was going to capsize. The vessel righted itself, the wave rolled on beyond the starboard side. The relics of the *Helvetia* sank and the sea resumed its normal appearance. Singer turned away from the rail, looked at Captain Hartmann.

'That's it,' he said laconically. The thought that nineteen men had been cremated never crossed his mind. With Singer it was always the next step to take.

'OK, Skipper,' he called out. 'Make your own waves. Head for Gibraltar. How long before we get there?'

'Several days. Depends on the weather conditions.'
Hartmann gave the order to start up the engines.

31

During the few hours they spent in Zürich Tweed and
Paula were very active. Paula bought two suitcases in the
Bahnhofstrasse, returned to the main station with them.
Tweed took one case and they visited the public lavatories.
Inside a cubicle Tweed perched his case on the toilet seat,
quickly transferred his belongings from the two plastic
carriers inside the case, locked it. He stuffed one bag inside
the other, flushed the toilet and met Paula by the refreshment counter.

She was also carrying her case and had screwed up the
plastic carriers. They dumped the carriers in a litter bin.
Paula looked at Tweed.

'What's next on the agenda?'

'We book two rooms at the Hotel Schweizerhof across
the *platz*. Remember, I told Bob he could communicate
with me there.'

'Of course. I'm not quite myself yet. Can I show you
something really interesting in a shop before we go to the
hotel? It's only a short distance down the Bahnhofstrasse,
just round the corner from the hotel.'

'Why not?'

Tweed thought it best to humour her. She had been
under pressure ever since they arrived in Brussels, which
seemed a year ago. Paula led the way down an escalator
into Shopville, the shopping precinct beneath the *platz*.
They crossed the large complex, past shops selling fruit and

chocolates and mounted a second escalator, emerging at the beginning of the Bahnhofstrasse.

It was only a brief walk down the great banking and shopping street before Paula stopped in front of a shop window. Tweed gazed at the display. The shop sold Walkmans. Slung across the inside of the window was a hammock and inside it sprawled a large toy monkey. On its head was attached a Walkman and the toy had an expression of pure bliss.

'Isn't it sweet?' said Paula.

'Very comic,' Tweed agreed. 'But those things are the instruments of the devil. Half our young people are going to end up deaf . . .'

Inside the Schweizerhof Tweed reserved two rooms for a week. He insisted on paying for the rooms in advance after registering.

'We'll go up to our rooms,' he explained, 'but then we have to visit a business associate in Interlaken. So we'll leave a few of our things in the rooms, then take our cases with us. We may be kept in Interlaken overnight. But we'll know our rooms are waiting for us when we do get back.'

'That's perfectly satisfactory, sir,' the girl receptionist assured him in English.

'Now, a word with the concierge . . .'

Tweed explained the situation briefly again. 'The point is I am expecting a message from one of my staff. Could you please hold any messages until we get back?'

He handed the concierge a banknote. 'Certainly, sir. Thank you. All messages will be carefully recorded . . .'

Inside his corner room overlooking the main station and the Bahnhofstrasse, Tweed took out a few clothes, stored them in drawers. In the bathroom he left a spare toothbrush and tube of toothpaste, then rejoined Paula who had just arrived back in the lobby.

'We could have lunch here,' she suggested. 'Remember?

The restaurant on the first floor is elegant, the food excellent, the service very good.'

'No, not here,' Tweed whispered, clutching his case. 'They have us recorded on the register. We'll eat at the first-class restaurant in the station. More anonymous. Safer.'

'I'd really better get a grip on myself,' she commented.

They had a late and leisurely lunch at the station, lingering over their coffee. It was well after dark when they caught the 1710 express for Berne. The journey through the night took a little less than an hour and a half. They stepped down the steep drop to the platform in the large cavern of Berne *Bahnhof* at precisely 1829.

Outside the station Tweed fiddled with his suitcase until two other passengers had taken the first two taxis, then he told the driver of the next cab to take them to the Bellevue Palace Hotel. It had started snowing again as he paid off the cab, waited for it to drive away and then picked up his suitcase.

'A bit of a walk, I'm afraid,' he warned. 'We go up this side street to reach the back entrance to the Taubenhalde, Federal Police HQ.'

'I'll have to wear a heavier coat,' she said, buttoning her hip-length suède jacket at the neck.

'And mind your footing,' he warned as they started walking up the hilly side street alongside the Bellevue Palace.

'Where does this lead to?'

'The famous *Terrasse* above the river Aare. In good weather you get a marvellous view of the Bernese Oberland range . . .'

'This is hardly good weather . . .'

'The *Terrasse* runs past the Parliament building. There's a small funicular, the Marzilibahn, which we can take down to the lower level.'

A bitter wind raked their faces as they plodded through

the snow. Tweed glanced up and swore briefly. 'Looks as though the funicular is iced up. *Kaput.* That means a dicey walk down a steep path.'

'Great!' she commented and left it at that.

Workmen with lamps and wearing orange boiler suits worked on the iced-up rails and the funicular cabin, perched at the top, was in darkness. Slithering down an icy path they reached the bottom and Tweed headed for the entrance to a modern building. At reception inside he presented his passport to the uniformed police guard.

'I have an appointment with Arthur Beck. He is expecting us.'

Paula revelled in the warmth inside the building while Tweed waited, the guard used the phone, spoke briefly in Switzer-Deutsch, which she didn't understand, then handed back the passport to Tweed.

'You know the way, Mr Tweed? To the Taubenhalde – it is rather complex.'

'I've been here before. Ready, Paula?'

Paula was fascinated as she followed Tweed through a long subterranean passage and then ascended an 80-metre-long travelator to the main entrance inside the Taubenhalde. Another uniformed guard escorted them inside an elevator to Floor Ten. The door remained closed until the guard inserted a special key inside a slot. Arthur Beck was waiting for them when they stepped out.

'You arrived safely. Good.'

Beck hugged Paula, kissed her on both cheeks, said she was very welcome, then turned to shake hands with Tweed.

'I suppose you're welcome, too. Come to my office.'

Beck, in his forties, was plump-cheeked; his most arresting feature was his alert grey eyes under dark brows. Of medium height, he moved his hands and feet quickly, his complexion was ruddy and he wore a smart grey suit, a blue-striped shirt and a blue tie which carried a kingfisher emblem woven into the fabric. Inside his large office overlooking the front street he took their coats, hung them on hangers, and offered them coffee.

'Or something stronger after your long and arduous journey?'

They both asked for coffee when he had stored their cases in a corner. Beck used the intercom on his desk, ordered coffee for three, ushered them to armchairs and joined them. Typically, his first question was direct.

'How urgent is it, Tweed, that you have the use of a transceiver? The communications complex is in the basement.'

'Very urgent. And I have to request that I be permitted to use it on my own.'

'Within ten minutes he'll have taken over the Taubenhalde – he'll be sitting behind my desk,' Beck joked to Paula, who smiled. She liked Beck, the man Tweed had once called the cleverest policeman in Europe.

Beck's manner changed as he gazed at Tweed. 'Before I let you inside our sophisticated communications apparatus I have to know who you are calling – and why.'

Tweed nodded and paused. He had expected this and now he had reached his Rubicon. He either had to reveal top secret information, known only to Buckmaster, the Americans, the PM, Newman, Paula and himself – or sacrifice the opportunity to call the *Lampedusa*. He waited until a uniformed girl brought in the coffee on a tray laid with a cloth, supporting a silver pot and Meissen china, placed the tray on a table Beck had hauled forward, then left the room. As they drank the steaming liquid, he told Beck about *Shockwave*.

'I know Swiss colonels who would give an arm and a leg to have this information,' Beck observed.

'I warned you it was in complete confidence.'

329

'Agreed. But you explained this *Shockwave* computer has made the Strategic Defence Initiative a reality, that it would defend not only England against all Soviet-launched rockets, but also Western Europe. That means Switzerland also would be protected by this extraordinary scientific umbrella.'

'That is so.'

'Then I suggest I entertain the delightful Paula while you work away in the basement. I will have to accompany you to the complex.' He turned to Paula. 'I will be back in three minutes. While I am away please be thinking of what you would like to eat. A nice steak, well done? Some river trout? It is an important decision. Ponder it . . .'

Beck left Tweed alone in a room in the basement after asking him if he could operate the model of the transceiver resting on a steel slab projecting from the wall. Tweed said that he was familiar with the machine, omitting to say it was exactly the same model they used in the communications complex in the second building they occupied at Park Crescent.

Adjusting the headphones, he turned to the correct waveband. It took him ten minutes to make contact with the vessel he was calling. The codename for the *Lampedusa* was *Valiant*.

'Monitor calling,' he began, using his code-name for this operation. 'Are you proceeding on schedule?'

'We are on schedule. We are on schedule,' the answer came back.

'Is the cargo is good condition?' he asked, making it sound as though the vessel was carrying perishables. No one expected eavesdroppers on this waveband but it was a precaution.

'The cargo is in excellent condition,' the reply came back.

'Are the weather conditions clement and is Tray in good health?'

330

Tweed tensed after he'd made the reference to Tray. The first trick question known only to himself and the radio op aboard the *Lampedusa*.

'Weather conditions clement so far. Atmospherics garbled the rest of your signal.'

Tweed froze. His mind went as cold as ice. He sent a fresh signal, including the second trick reference.

'Is the crew in good health? Give my regards to White.'

'Crew all well. Transmission not perfect. Again the rest of your signal was garbled.'

'Signing off, I will call you again as arranged. My regards to North . . .'

Tweed sat for several minutes in front of the transceiver like a waxwork. He had received a nasty shock. The second trick question had also not been responded to correctly. The reference to White should have been answered by a reference to Cowes in the Isle of Wight. Some such statement as, 'White was taken sick before we sailed, was sent home to Cowes.'

Now he had to decide whether to tell Beck the real situation. He weighed up the pros and cons quickly. He was on the run, a fugitive. Only Beck could help him now. And he already knew about *Shockwave*.

He stood up, altered the waveband he'd transmitted on, then he pressed the bell by the door Beck had locked. The Swiss came down in the elevator quickly to release him, locked the door. Tweed was silent as the elevator ascended. When he re-entered Beck's office he saw Paula was sitting up to a table covered with a spotless cloth. She was devouring the last of an omelette.

'You also would like some sustenance?' Beck suggested.

'I think I'd like a drink. A stiff cognac.'

Two pairs of eyes stared. Tweed rarely drank. On the few occasions when he imbibed it was always wine, never spirits, except to fight a cold. Beck nodded, went to a cabinet, poured a tot into a balloon glass, handed it to Tweed without a word.

Paula swallowed the last of her omelette, drank coffee quickly, dabbed her lips with a napkin, and swung round in her chair, crossing her shapely legs as she studied Tweed. Beck sipped at a glass of beer, leaning back in his chair, eyes half-closed while he waited.

'Someone has hi-jacked *Shockwave*. It's a disaster area,' Tweed announced.

32

'We've pin-pointed Tweed already in Zürich.' Morgan stabbed at his blotter with a paper knife as though spearing Tweed to its surface.

He was leaning back in the chair behind his desk in his office at World Security HQ in Basle. On the other side of the desk, summoned from the Drei Könige, sat Armand Horowitz and by his side in a hard-backed chair was Stieber. Morgan puffed his cigar with satisfaction and then continued.

'He's staying at the Hotel Schweizerhof. We've got him.'

'That hotel is opposite the main station,' Horowitz observed with a frown. 'He draws attention to himself in Laufenburg, buying tickets for Zürich. Now you tell me he walks out of the station at Zürich and books in at the nearest large hotel.'

'That's about the size of it. He's not so smart as you make out. Maybe he's exhausted. How would I know? You want me to hand him to you on a plate? Well, I've done just that.'

'I'll take him before sunset tomorrow,' Stieber interjected. 'Just leave it to me.'

'Like we did in Freiburg?' enquired Horowitz. 'I go back to Richter's house on Konvikstrasse and find you trussed up like a chicken. Lucky I had a hunch about that place.'

'That was a nasty experience,' complained Stieber. 'That English bastard who ambushed me in the kitchen was as cold as ice. A pro to his fingertips. He scared the guts out of me – and I don't mind admitting it.'

'What's your beef?' Morgan demanded, staring at Horowitz.

'It's all too easy. The trail from Laufenburg was too easy to follow. Now he chooses the obvious hotel. How did you find out so quickly?'

'Because my apparatus is organized. I told you I was sending people round to check the hotels with Tweed's photo and a phoney story. They started with the major hotels first. Bingo! One team calls at the Schweizerhof and hits pay dirt. And that's not all.'

'What else?'

Horowitz sounded weary. He also sounded troubled and unconvinced by Morgan's flamboyant confidence.

'I told you I was well-organized. I'm using the Walkman technique of observation and communication. You know what I am talking about?'

'No, I don't.'

Morgan leaned over his desk and pointed with his cigar, a mannerism Horowitz found irritating. 'You know those Walkmans all the kids walk about with, listening to pop music from one of those gadgets clamped to their heads and ears. They even ride bikes wearing them, which is damn dangerous . . .'

'Yes, I understand now. Please explain further.'

'So, I've trained a large team of youngsters – in their early twenties. Don't worry, they've no idea they're employed by World Security. They think they're working for a debt collection agency. We train them in a building we hired for the purpose in a Zürich back street.'

'Maybe we could hear what they do?' Horowitz suggested.

'They have these gadgets – headsets – strapped to their skulls with a wire leading to a jacket pocket. Looks just like one of the musical Walkmans. Actually they're disguised walkie-talkies – high-powered and good for operating over a radius of two miles. They can take instructions from the communications vans located carefully to cover the city. And they can communicate back by talking into a concealed mike. Get the idea?'

'Go on, please.'

'They have been shown a blow-up picture on a cinema screen of Tweed, another of the Grey woman. They'll be patrolling the streets until they spot one or both. They report back to the nearest communications van the moment they spot one of them. The stage is set for the final denouement.'

Morgan waved his cigar in a grand gesture and settled more comfortably in his chair.

'It's all too straightforward,' Horowitz commented. 'Tweed is one of the wiliest and most dangerous opponents I have ever been up against. He avoided the bomb I attached to the Audi in the Black Forest.'

'It probably failed to detonate . . .'

'When I place a bomb it detonates,' Horowitz told him. 'I am going to earn my fee with this one, I can sense that already.'

'I don't know why you've got an attack of nerves,' Morgan responded, and studied the tip of his cigar.

'My nerves are in perfect condition,' Horowitz said in such a cold voice that Morgan blinked. 'I am flying to Zürich and I will take Stieber with me. I want to study the situation on the spot, see for myself what is really happening. Phone Zürich, tell your managing director there that he will take all his orders from me.'

'If you insist . . .'

'I do insist.'

'Then you'll be dealing with Evans. He's already aboard a flight for Zürich.'

Horowitz nodded, picked up his suitcase, left the office without another word, followed by Stieber. Morgan sat frowning behind his desk. Why did Horowitz always leave him with this worried feeling, verging on fright? He checked his watch. It was 6 p.m. Time for a snifter. He reached for his hip flask.

Inside his office at the Taubenhalde Beck had listened with great attention, his eyes never leaving Tweed's, while the latter gave him a summary of what had happened from the moment he'd discovered the unknown girl's body in his flat in Radnor Walk.

Paula was puzzled by how much Tweed omitted from his account. No reference to the attempt on his life on the Freiburg autobahn, nor to the bomb attached to the Audi in the Black Forest. But he had talked about Bob Newman and Marler. Newman knew Beck, had once sat in this very office.

'That's about it,' Tweed concluded as he finished the story of their flight across the Rhine at Laufenburg, their arrival in Zürich, their reservation of rooms at the Schweizerhof.

'I see,' Beck said eventually. 'That murder in your apartment is most mysterious. Who has a motive for such a brutal killing?'

'I'm not sure yet.'

'Come, you must have some suspicions. And it's a very odd factor that the girl has still not been identified.'

'You know that? How?'

'Simple. I phoned Howard in London to ask him how the case was progressing.'

335

'And didn't he express an opinion?'

'No, he didn't. He seemed completely mystified. And rather worried about you, to use British understatement.'

'What do you know about an organization called World Security?' Tweed asked him suddenly.

'One of the West's great conglomerates. While he was running it Buckmaster made takeover bid after takeover bid, bringing many smaller security outfits into his fold. Sometimes using very aggressive methods. But that seems to be the way of big business now.'

'Is that all you know about them?' Tweed persisted.

Beck drank some more coffee. Tweed waited, glanced at Paula. She sat with a wary expression. Beck put down his cup.

'The man to put that question to is Colonel Romer, Director of the Zurcher Kredit Bank. You remember Romer?' Beck took a pen and began writing on a pad of headed notepaper as he continued. 'At one time you suspected Romer of being mixed up in criminal activities. Wrongly, as it turned out. He has now moved to their headquarters in Zürich. In Talstrasse. Give him this letter from me.'

Signing what he had written, he folded the sheet, wrote the address on an envelope, slipped the sheet inside, tucked in the envelope flap without sealing it, handed it to Tweed.

'Thank you. Now, I said I needed a hideout, some remote refuge where I can ponder my next move in comparative safety.'

'I've been thinking about that. Brunni is the answer. A nowhere place up in the mountains of Schwyz canton. Beyond the town of Einsiedeln. There is a chalet a friend of mine has for the summer, at the very foot of the Mythen, a dramatic mountain. You should be safe there.'

'And a means of radio communication with the outside world?'

336

Beck looked at Paula and smiled. 'He doesn't want much, does he?'

'*Shockwave* is at stake, the salvation of the West, including Switzerland,' she told him.

'But you said this great god of a computer has been hi-jacked, Tweed. What do you think is its ultimate destination now?'

'Russia,' Tweed said promptly.

'Does such an act fit in with *glasnost*, *perestroika*?' Beck asked cynically.

'Gorbachev is in deep trouble,' Tweed replied. 'We know he is up against both the Left and the Right in his country. Both factions have formed an unholy alliance. They think they are the guardians of Leninism. So, news reaches Moscow that they can lay their hands on *Shockwave* – which will protect Russia from any missile attack by the West. The Red Army generals are already restive because Gorbachev is clipping their wings. How can he reject the chance of acquiring this marvellous machine? If he did so it could cause his instant downfall. God knows there are enough hardliners praying for just that to happen.'

'You are guessing,' Beck suggested.

'Yes, I'm guessing,' Tweed admitted. 'Theorizing might be a better word.'

'We have talked enough. Paula looks tired.' Beck stood up. 'You both need a good night's sleep. I have reserved two rooms for the night in false names – at the Bellevue Palace.'

'False names?' Tweed was puzzled. 'The Swiss registration system at hotels is very strict.'

'But I am accompanying you there. I will deal with the paper work. Give me your passports. I will flourish them. I have a car waiting.'

'It's only a short distance. We could walk,' Tweed suggested.

'But then you might be recognized. Tomorrow, have breakfast brought up to your rooms. I will call for you both at ten, if that is all right. Another car will drive you to Zürich. An unmarked car.' He paused by the door as Tweed and Paula collected their cases after slipping on their coats. 'And a plain-clothes guard will be placed outside both your rooms. I trust you do not object?'

'Have we an option?' Tweed enquired with a wry smile.

'No, you haven't . . .'

Paula tapped on the interconnecting door between their bedrooms. Tweed, unpacking his case, walked over, drew the bolt on his side. Paula stormed into the room with an expression like thunder.

'We're prisoners,' she protested. 'Guards on our doors. An escort from a building five minutes' walk away from this hotel. And another escort tomorrow morning in a car to Zürich. Beck doesn't believe you.'

'Calm down. He's cautious. I had rather a dramatic story to tell him. He's had this report from London about murder and rape in my flat. He's just taking no chances. Can't say I blame him.'

'And', she fumed, 'you left out the terrible incidents which might have convinced him. No mention of the attempt to kill you on the autobahn. No reference to the bomb Bob found beneath the Audi . . .'

'Deliberate omissions,' he told her. 'They would have made my account of events even more dramatic. I foresaw all this from the moment we arrived at the Hilton in Brussels. So I worked out a plan to convince him in due course. Remember, this is a neutral country.'

'What plan?' she demanded.

'You'll see what I mean as events develop. The opposition is going to help us.'

33

Basle. 2.45 a.m. It was snowing again as Turpil drove the Audi through the deserted streets of the centre of the city. By his side Newman peered out at the medieval buildings. He caught a glimpse of the Munster rearing up and then it was gone as they headed down towards the Rhine. The rear seats were empty, he had noted.

'Where is your equipment?' he asked.

'In the boot of the car, of course. If we're stopped by a patrol car I have in my pocket a typed phone message from a doctor saying my sister is ill. You're a close friend of the family.'

'What's your sister's name?'

'Klara. She's had a bad fall down a staircase. Lives on St Johannsplatz. That's not far from the World Security HQ.'

'This Klara, I take it, doesn't exist?'

'Of course not.' Turpil waved a small hand. 'But it's the best excuse for being up at this hour.'

Newman settled down to watch the snow falling. Turpil had planned the operation better than he'd expected. They turned down a side street and Turpil stopped the car. He lowered his window, listened, then raised it.

'I can hear a footfall half a mile away, let alone another car. Here, take this. Put it in your ear when I tell you after we get inside. It's an ear-piece.'

'For what purpose?'

Newman examined the small pink-coloured cylinder which was like a small sweet with a tiny grille at one end.

'To increase your hearing powers. Be sure to insert it in your ear so the grille projects outwards. That's the microphone.'

'I've never seen anything like this before . . .'

'I should hope not. I invented it myself. I used to be a watchmaker – precision work. Don't lose it. Now, we'll collect the toolkit.' Turpil produced another of the tiny gadgets, grinned as he inserted it in his own right ear. 'I'll hear anyone coming with my ear-drummer.'

Opening the boot, he hauled out a slim rectangular canvas holder, handed it to Newman. 'You start working for your loot.' Taking another smaller leather hold-all out, he closed the boot. The snow was falling less heavily now as Turpil extracted a pair of rubber overshoes from the holdall, slipped them over his shoes. 'Gives a firmer grip.' He looked down at Newman's footwear. 'I hope those don't slip on ice.'

'Rubber-soled, corrugated with a grip surface.'

'Then let's march.'

They emerged on to a wide street and to his right Newman saw the entrance to the World Security HQ. He could hardly avoid it – overhead searchlights illuminated the plate-glass doors. No sign of life inside, but he was viewing the interior from an oblique angle.

'Guards walking about inside,' Turpil whispered.

'I can't see them.'

'No, but I can hear them – their footfalls on the marble floor. With my ear-drummer. Now, down to the river . . .'

Newman recognized the side street he had walked down when he had checked the geography of the area. They were close to the Rhine and Turpil went ahead, running nimbly down the six ice-covered steps. Newman paused, inserted the ear-piece, turned sideways. The sudden deafening sound almost made him lose his balance. It was like the surge of a great ocean. It took him a moment to realize he was listening to the flow of the Rhine, enormously magnified. He snatched out the ear-piece, put it in his trench-coat pocket as Turpil peered round the corner at the bottom, then gestured for him to follow.

Newman trod carefully down the steps to the prom-enade, holding the canvas carrier by the handle. A raw breeze raked his face as he turned the corner. There were no footprints on the promenade beyond where Turpil had walked. How was he going to enter the building from the back, Newman wondered. The first row of windows were a good twelve feet above them. Turpil was gazing up, waited for Newman to join him.

'No danger of early morning lovers in weather like this,' he commented, his left ear bent towards Newman.

'They come along here?'

'In summer you step over them. The Swiss youth has developed uninhibited habits. Give me your satchel.'

Turpil unfastened the straps, hauled out what looked like an aluminium grid with large rubber suckers along one rung. He extended it, section by section, and Newman realized it was a ladder at least fifteen feet high. Perching it against the wall, Turpil adjusted the height, swung it sideways and rubbed handfuls of snow against the suckers, then melted it with the warmth of his gloved hands.

'Now it will be firmly attached to the wall,' he explained, and hoisted it again, positioning the top carefully just below a window sill before he pressed hard against the whole ladder.

'This is World Security,' Newman reminded him, bend-ing to speak into his left ear. 'Those windows probably have the best alarm systems in the business.'

'They do,' Turpil assured him. 'But for summer ventil-ation they can be lifted sixteen centimetres before they contact the alarm bolts. Inside on the right is a switch. You lift it once, then down, then up, and the alarm is cut off. In

341

hot weather they can then lift the window up wide open. It's just a precaution. They considered it impossible for anyone to get inside this way.'

'And how can you be certain they haven't added refinements?'

'Didn't I tell you?' Turpil grinned slyly. 'They called me in a couple of months ago to repair a defect. I checked the whole system and they haven't changed a thing since I installed the original system.'

'That was a couple of months ago. Let's get on with it.'

Newman, always careful, wasn't completely reassured. Morgan's organization might well have its own security specialists who had added a few booby traps. Alarm systems of which Turpil had no knowledge existed.

'Use your ear-drummer,' Turpil told Newman. He pointed along the promenade. 'Then you can check no one is coming along by the river while I go up the ladder. I'll wave when I'm inside the building. Then you follow me up the ladder. Ready? I'm on my way . . .'

He was climbing the ladder, holding on with one hand, the other clutching his hold-all, while Newman adjusted his ear-piece. The roaring surge filled his head until he grasped his gadget was beamed towards the Rhine. He faced the wall, aiming it along the promenade. The deafening surge was replaced by a curious swishing sound. Startled, he looked quickly along the promenade, moving his head only slightly.

The breeze was blowing swirls of light snow along the surface of the frozen promenade, a sound he'd been unable to hear before. It made him realize how sensitive the instrument was. He looked up.

The snow had almost stopped falling. Perched at the top of the ladder, Turpil was brushing his clothes clean of snow with one hand. He raised the window a few inches, reached inside with one hand, held it there a few seconds, then lifted the window wide open. Climbing in over the sill, holding his satchel, he peered out and waved.

Newman listened for a short time, heard only the swish of the swirling snow. He extracted the ear-drummer, slipped it into his pocket and shook the ladder. The base remained firm, the rubber-covered legs now held fast by the frozen snow. He began the ascent.

Heavier than Turpil, he felt the ladder whipping under him as he pressed his feet carefully into each icy rung. The higher he went the stronger the breeze became, flapping his trench coat. The intense cold began to penetrate his gloves, freezing his hands.

He resisted the temptation to hurry, to look down, staring at the wall as he continued his ascent. One foot slipped off a rung. He gripped the ladder more tightly, ignoring the bitter cold. Recovering his balance, he climbed higher. He reached the level of the open window unexpectedly. Turpil reached out a hand, placed it on Newman's shoulder and pulled, indicating he should climb inside quickly.

Newman needed no encouragement. Swinging one leg over the sill, he dipped his head under the open window, heaved himself inside. Despite the open window warmth met him and his fingers began to tingle.

'Now we must haul up the ladder,' Turpil told him.

'Why? We need that to escape . . .'

'No! No! We use another method. We may be here some time. Someone may see the ladder. Don't argue. Help me haul it up.'

They both took hold of the top rung and heaved with all their strength. The feet embedded in the frozen snow came loose suddenly and the ladder was free. As they hauled it up Turpil telescoped it until it was converted to the grid Newman had carried in the canvas container. Turpil slid it back inside the container he had carried up with his tool-kit.

'I'd just like to know how the hell we *do* get out of this place,' Newman snapped.

'Everything is prepared – for an emergency . . .'

Turpil produced a pencil flash after drawing a curtain over the open window. He handed another flash to Newman, who was beginning to be impressed. Turpil seemed equipped for the job.

'But how do we get out of this place?' he repeated.

Turpil lowered the beam of his flash. Coiled on the floor was a mountaineer's rope, knotted an intervals. One end had a large rubber-sheathed ring. The ring was attached to the steel leg of a large table. Newman stooped to examine it more closely.

There was a join where the ring was looped round the table leg, rather like two claws meeting. And a wire was wrapped round the full length of the rope, a wire which had a small handle at the other end of the rope.

'That table is screwed to the floor,' Turpil explained. 'It is used for computers and other machines, so they need good stability.'

'I still don't see how this rope works. We throw it out of the window in an emergency, I assume, and then abseil like a mountaineer down the wall. Why can't we use the ladder?'

'You said we shouldn't leave any traces of the break-in. It would take too long to remove the ladder. When we've both gone down the rope I operate that handle. The two claws round the table leg open and we can haul it out of the window. Another of my inventions. Now, we're wasting time – so what is it you want here? We're in the main Research & Development room, as they like to call it. The dirty tricks set-up. Plus confidential records . . .'

'Dirty tricks? What do you mean?'

'In a few words, blackmail and sabotage. They're bidding to take over another company. Right? So they sabotage their security trucks, tip off the underworld, and the contents of the truck are grabbed. The target company's reputation is ruined. I'll tell you about the blackmail later. What do you want?'

'Evidence of illegal – criminal – activity . . .'

'Now you're talking. First, I de-activate the whole alarm system. Then I'll open the wall-safe I installed. Of course, sometimes they play clever, hide something important in an unlocked drawer under a pile of notepads. So if you want to ferret around wear these.' He handed Newman a pair of surgical gloves, then slipped another pair over his own hands.

He opened the control box attached to a side wall, holding his pencil flash gripped between his teeth. Inside was a complicated arrangement of coloured wires and plugs inserted into sockets. Turpil went on talking as he began moving plugs from one socket to another.

'Don't smoke in here. Smoke lingers. Later I'll want you to open the door into the passage – after you've inserted your ear-drummer. Beam it down the passage to the right where the elevators and the staircase are at the far end. You'll hear anyone coming a mile off. And when you open that door don't put a foot in the passage. There's a pressure pad outside. Not one of your crude mats – it's part of the woodblock floor.'

Wearing the surgical gloves, holding the pencil flash in his left hand, Newman began opening drawers quietly in a large desk. He'd found nothing when he came to the last drawer at the bottom on the left. A pile of printed memo pads, A4 size.

'Alarm neutralized,' Turpil whispered. 'If I've made a cock-up the alarm will sound in their Zürich HQ. The systems are linked. Added precaution. The Zürich guards find nothing, phone this place.'

Turpil removed a large grid chart hanging from the wall which was headed *Gross Turnover*. The line on the chart climbed to new heights of business activity. Behind it a

345

large safe was embedded in the wall. Turpil inserted his ear-piece. Newman glanced up, expecting the little man to produce a stethoscope.

'No stethoscope,' he called out quietly.

'You've been watching too many films. My ear-piece picks up the fall of the tumblers.' Turned sideways, his ear close to the safe, his gloved hand turned the combination slowly. Newman went back to checking the drawer. Carefully lifting up another pad he found a desk diary for the current year. Why conceal that?

Underneath at the very bottom of the drawer was another desk diary. For the previous year. He flicked through the pages from the beginning. Full of appointments. What attracted his attention was certain days which had an initial letter prominently written in with a felt-tip pen – unlike all the other entries inscribed with an ordinary pen. The initial letter was 'M'.

Alongside each initial there was a time. Always late in the evening, 9.30 p.m., 9 p.m., 10 p.m., 9 p.m., 10.30 p.m. All the dates were between January and April. He double-checked. No date later than April 25.

Newman flicked over the pages of the current year. January and part of February. More appointments at intervals but no more 'M' entries. He was intrigued, partly by the fact that no name was given alongside the times for these entries, unlike every other appointment noted which *did* have a name.

Newman looked up, saw that Turpil was opening the large wall safe. He walked over and Turpil dived a hand inside his hold-all, brought out two wash-leathers which he gave to Newman.

'Now, all the snow has melted off our shoes. Could you clean up the floor? No traces that we've been here, you said . . .'

Newman swore inwardly. But Turpil was right: Newman had noticed the pools of liquid from the melted snow on the woodblock floor and had been going to mention them. He crouched down, used the wash-leathers vigorously. One to mop up most of the water, the other to polish the surface. Finishing the job he gave the leathers back to Turpil who put them inside a plastic bag, then shoved the bag into the hold-all. Turpil gestured towards the open safe after checking his watch.

'Up to you now. Remember exactly how everything was stored.'

The wall-safe was shoulder high. Newman used his flash to check the contents. To the left several wads of bank-notes tied together with elastic bands. He ignored them. In the middle were piles of large envelopes. He lifted the top one out carefully, took it over to the desk, extracted the sheets inside.

Records of income and expenditure for the company the previous year. Certain items were underlined in red ink; all for the sum of 6,000 Swiss francs. Alongside each was the same phrase. *One-time cost.* Bribes? Newman glanced down all the sheets, then went through them a second time, again to double-check.

He frowned. Certain sheets carried a flourishing initial at the bottom and all were dated. The initial was a 'B'. He examined other sheets with references to 'Sab.' and names of companies taken over by WS & C. The German for 'sabotage' was the same as the English word. Newman looked round. Turpil had opened the door to the corridor. He closed it, came across to Newman.

'Not a sound. We have to be careful now. The time element.'

'Turpil, take these sheets and photograph them. You said you had brought a camera.' The little man felt in his pocket, produced a compact horizontal-shaped camera with a flash-bulb attached.

'Won't there be a danger the flash will be seen?' Newman asked.

'Curtain is drawn. There's no window on to the passage. I'll lay them out on the desk . . .'

'And while you're at it, there's a last year's desk diary I've left out. Photograph five pages. January 15, January 28, February 16, March 4 and April 25. And just inside the front cover you'll find the owner's name. Morgan. Photograph that, too.'

Newman turned back to the safe. He found nothing that interested him until he came to the sixth large envelope. Inside were four glossy prints of different girls. All attractive, all a head-and-shoulders picture, all in colour, all the girls in their late twenties or mid thirties.

A titian-haired beauty, a blonde and two brunettes. All had a provocative smile and half-closed eyes behind long lashes. Again Newman frowned as he studied the blonde-haired girl. Memorizing the sequence, he took them over to Turpil, glad that he he'd checked about the camera. The room had been lit up time and again with flash-bulbs going off. Turpil worked at great speed. Newman placed the photos on the desk top.

'I'd like good copies of these,' he said. 'They'll have to be black-and-white, I suppose?'

'I'm using a colour film . . .' Another flash. 'Only way to record the red underlines. I'll leave you to put the desk diaries back – you know how they were stored.'

Turpil glanced at the four photos Newman had spread over the desk. He paused as he saw the picture of the blonde-haired girl, then looked at the other two and nodded, continuing to photograph the last two cost sheets. He glanced at his watch as he turned to the photographs.

'You've got three more minutes to look for anything else. Then it gets dangerous.'

Newman walked back to the open safe, carefully piled the other envelopes in the sequence he'd found them ready to go back into the safe. Reaching inside, he drew out a thick red master-ledger. Full of figures, it meant little to him.

On an impulse he turned to the last page where the balance was drawn up. He carried the ledger over to the desk, open at the last page.

'Last item. A copy of this page. Then maybe we'd better call it a day . . .'

'A night.'

Newman collected the five cost-sheets, arranged them in the original sequence with the rest, slid them inside the envelope and carried them back to the safe. He dealt with the photos when Turpil handed them to him. Finally he slid the ledger back into its place at the bottom. When he turned round Turpil was by his shoulder.

'I have to close the safe, turn the combination to its original setting, then reactivate the alarm system. Go to the door, use your ear-drummer, listen to the right down the passage. We have to be careful but quick. Don't forget to slip those diaries away first . . .'

Newman dealt with the diaries, placed the notepads on top and crept to the closed door. Inserting the ear-drummer, he opened it and thrust his head only outside. No sound of movement.

When it happened Newman nearly jumped out of his skin. He was almost deafened with the sound of ferocious dogs snarling, followed by several pairs of footsteps, then more dog sounds. Had he not been staring down the endless passage he would have sworn they were almost outside the door.

He turned to warn Turpil. The little man had closed the safe, was replacing the alarm system plugs. Some instinct made Turpil glance over his shoulder. Newman crept across to him.

'Big trouble. I can hear guard dogs and men's feet. They sound to be very close, coming this way . . .'

'Keep calm. They're a long way off and they'll be

checking each office. Close the door quietly.'

Turpil had even produced a large waterproof for New-man to slip on over his dried-out trench coat. Despite the open window the air-conditioning inside the building was almost tropical. Turpil had earlier pulled aside the curtain for a few seconds. It was snowing heavily.

Newman was tense as Turpil coolly handed him the canvas carrier containing the telescoped ladder, advising him to fix the handle firmly to his belt. Then Turpil pulled back the curtain, picked up the coiled rope, leaned out of the window to check the promenade and dropped it.

'I'll go first. You watch how I go. You can abseil down a cliff, I assume?'

'Just get on with it . . .'

Newman couldn't get out of his mind how close the guard dogs had sounded. Turpil reminded him to pull the window down, to turn the alarm switch on from outside.

'Press it down once, then up, then down. The alarm is then active. The reverse of what I did before I entered . . .'

'Got it! Now, move! They could be here any minute.'

Turpil had attached the handle of his hold-all to a belt he'd taken from inside it and wrapped round his waist. He tugged at the rope, climbed over the sill, disappeared. Newman peered out.

Turpil had rammed his woolly hat over his head before leaving and from above he looked like a gnome as he descended, using his feet to kick himself away from the wall. Newman was surprised at the speed of his descent. Reaching the promenade, Turpil gestured for him to follow.

Newman had already tucked the surgical gloves inside his coat pocket with the ear-drummer and was wearing his leather ones. Grasping the rope, he heaved himself over the edge, remembered just in time the window and cursed. Holding on with one hand above a knot, he reached up, hauled down the window to within a few inches of the sill, reached inside, fumbled around for the bloody switch which seemed to have moved, found it, operated it and closed the window to within inches of the sill.

By now, supported only by his right hand and arm, his whole body was feeling the strain. Thankfully he gripped the rope with his left hand and began his descent. The knots were a godsend: they prevented rope burn from a prolonged slide. The snow was not a godsend – getting in his eyes and penetrating down behind his collar as he abseiled down the wall, kicking his feet against it, arching his back outwards, hoping the damned thing would support his heavier weight. It seemed to take an eternity before his feet slammed into the promenade.

'We must be quick,' Turpil hissed.

'Now he agrees on the need for speed,' Newman thought bitterly, but he kept his mouth shut.

Turpil told him to move well up the promenade, then stooped to grasp the handle at the end of the wire. Looking up, he turned the handle, rammed it upwards, hauled on the rope. Newman realized the claw apparatus at the other end had got trapped behind the sill. He stamped his feet as the cold seeped into him. Turpil, still staring up, hauled with all his strength. The claw shot out of the window and Turpil ran towards Newman, dropping the rope end. The claw ring hammered into the snow. Turpil ran back, coiled the rope swiftly as Newman joined him.

'Back to the Audi?' he asked. Turpil shook his head, slung the rope over his shoulder and went to the edge of the river.

Newman waited for him to slip over the edge. Turpil gestured for him to follow, knelt down and then disappeared. Newman glanced up at the building, walked to the gap in the railing and looked down. Attached to the river wall was an iron ladder leading to a small landing stage. A boat was moored to a bollard and Turpil was stepping aboard.

Newman took a deep breath, clenched his fingers, and with his back to the Rhine descended the ice-coated rungs. Turpil beckoned to him to hurry. The motor boat had a canvas awning protecting the wheel and the controls. Newman stepped aboard, Turpil reached out, untied the mooring rope, hauled it on to the deck and the swift flow of the Rhine swept them out towards mid-stream. Seated under the awning, Turpil made no attempt to start up the engine as Newman sat beside him and released the canvas container from his belt.

'What's the idea?' he said.

'If there's an alarm in that building they have a drill. A number of the guards immediately rush outside, men carrying secret guns, and surround the whole building. Look, there are lights.'

Newman stared back at the building receding in the distance. The curtain had been pulled back from the window they had left by. Powerful torches shone down on the promenade and searched from left to right. The motor boat was already too far away for them to have any chance of seeing it and soon the flashlights were blotted out by the snow. Above them, the awning sagged under the weight of snow it had already collected.

'Too early to start up the engine?' Newman enquired and shivered.

It was incredibly cold as they drifted fast into mid-river. A cutting wind penetrated Newman's waterproof and his trench coat under it. The boat was moving much faster as the main current caught it up in its westward flow.

'Too soon,' Turpil agreed. 'They might just hear it from the building. In any case, we don't want anyone to hear us at this hour. Don't worry. We are heading for where the Audi is now parked.'

'Impossible,' Newman protested, 'we're drifting miles away from the *platz* where we left it.'

'But it is not there,' Turpil explained, as though to a

352

child. 'Shortly after we walked to the building Klara, who has a key, drove the Audi across the Rhine and parked it on the opposite bank. We are close now, so I will start up the engine.'

'Just a second. Who is Klara? Not your imaginary sister?'

'My real sister from Berne. Earlier she parked her own car at the same spot, took her bicycle from the boot, cycled to that *platz*, and as I have just said, drove the Audi to the same secluded spot.'

He was starting the engine when Newman stood up to stretch his aching legs and wandered out towards the stern as the boat rocked. Turpil shouted to him before starting the engine.

'Better give me back that ear-drummer while we remember it.'

'Got it in my pocket.' Newman pulled out the surgical gloves, transferred them to his other pocket, brought out the ear-drummer, appeared to lose his balance and grabbed the edge of the gunwale.

'Sorry, Turpil, I've dropped it overboard.'

He palmed the ear-drummer and slipped it inside his trouser pocket. A useful little gadget, which you couldn't buy in the shops.

'I'll have to charge you for that,' Turpil shouted and fired the engine.

Newman hurried back under the awning, sat down. 'How long before we reach the parked Audi?' he called out.

'A matter of minutes.' Turpil glanced over his shoulder as he held the wheel and began to steer the boat towards the eastern bank. 'It's awhile since I've seen Tweed. Maybe I could meet him soon? Say "Hello", and all that . . .'

Newman was frozen, the back of his neck was damp with melted snow, he was aching in every limb, but his mind was

353

still alert. There was something a shade too casual in Turpil's reference to Tweed. He made a vague gesture with his hands while he thought.

They were close to the high river embankment on the east, heading for a mooring landing with a flight of steps leading up to the promenade, when a searchlight came on, began probing the chopping surface of the Rhine. Turpil reacted instantly.

Turning the wheel, he headed back for mid-stream, out of the range of the searchlight, then he cut the engine and let the boat drift again. Once again the boat was caught up in the powerful current of the Rhine. Newman stood up as Turpil beckoned and joined him by the wheel.

'We cannot use the Audi,' Turpil told him, his teeth chattering. 'The police have found it. We have to change our plans.'

'I thought that searchlight was mounted on a patrol car,' Newman commented. 'Start the engine up and make for the nearest landing stage on the west bank. We must get ashore as fast as we can.'

'If you say, so but why?' Turpil fired the engine.

'Because,' Newman explained patiently, 'the men in the patrol car will radio for a police launch to come and find us. The nearest landing stage. Then we push the boat out, let it go downriver, drift with the current.'

The sudden crisis had made Newman forget the cold, his aches, and he automatically took charge. Within a few minutes they found a landing stage, Turpil moored the boat, they climbed out. The only sounds were the surge of the river, the thump of the boat against the landing stage. It had stopped snowing.

'What do we do next?' Turpil asked.

'Walk. Back to where I've parked my car. You can wait inside it while I pay my hotel bill. Is there anything inside that boat which could identify you?'

'No. I stole it earlier this evening . . .'

'Then set it loose. Quickly.'

Turpil unlooped the rope from the bollard, threw it on to the deck and the boat slid away, moving out towards the centre of the Rhine. Newman was still carrying the canvas carrier containing the ladder. Turpil's toolbag lay on the wooden platform.

'It's not safe to walk through Basle in the middle of the night carrying incriminating break-in kit,' Newman warned.

'I suppose you're right . . .'

Turpil picked up the hold-all and hurled it out over the river. It hit the water with a splash, sank immediately. Newman threw the container with the ladder after it as Turpil produced the camera from his pocket. Newman grabbed it off him, tucked it inside his trench-coat pocket.

'That is more dangerous evidence,' Turpil protested.

'So why should you worry? I'm carrying it. And we worked damned hard to get it. I can see a launch coming downriver with a searchlight. Let's get back up the steps. And', he added as an apparent afterthought, 'we'll drive to Zürich and you can meet Tweed.'

As they mounted the steps and disappeared into a side street Newman was convinced he had fed the bait well – with the promise to Turpil to meet Tweed. That remark aboard the boat had definitely been more than a shade too casual. Newman was determined not to let Alois Turpil out of his sight.

34

All roads led to Zürich.

The following morning Tweed and Paula had breakfast

early in their rooms. When they left they found new plain-clothes guards had taken up duty in the corridor outside. One of them came forward, showed Tweed his police identity card.

'We have to escort you to the car. Your bills have been paid. The Mercedes is waiting at the front entrance.'

'Nice to be treated like royalty,' Paula joked.

'Or like prisoners,' Tweed whispered.

Beck was waiting for them in the rear of the car, perched on a flap seat. He gestured for them to enter quickly and they climbed inside clutching their suitcases. The door was shut, the driver, also in plain-clothes, operated the central locking system. Tweed looked at Beck as the car moved off.

'Worried we're going to dive out at a traffic-light stop?'

'It's security,' Paula said quickly.

'Paula is right,' Beck agreed.

Tweed stared out of the window as they were stopped by traffic lights. The glass was amber-tinted, which neutralized the sun glare. As they'd walked down the hotel steps the sunlight reflecting off the snow-covered street had been blinding. And, Tweed reflected, it made it more difficult for anyone to see who was inside the car.

To his right a long bridge spanned the Aare. A tram trundled across it, passed in front of them. Why didn't the British go back to using trams? The car moved, turned left past the Casino. As they drove on through the ancient city the Mercedes bumped over the exposed cobbles where the snow had melted.

'We want to go to the Schweizerhof Hotel in Zürich,' Tweed remarked. 'We left some of our things in the rooms I reserved.'

'The driver can collect them . . .'

'No, Beck, we'll collect them ourselves. Get the driver to park near the hotel when we arrive, not outside.'

'As you wish . . .'

356

'And Bob Newman may want to contact me. He'll probably call you to find out where we are. It's essential that I see him.'

'As you wish . . .'

'I do wish.'

Tweed settled back in his seat and said not one more word until they reached Zürich.

Newman made no attempt to break any records as he drove the BMW through the night towards Zürich. Alongside him Turpil clasped and unclasped his hands in his lap. Well away from Basle they stopped at an all-night café for truckers.

'We'll get some coffee and something to eat,' Newman said.

'I am hungry after what we've been through,' Turpil grouched.

It had been a long walk back to the Hotel Drei Könige. Newman had taken Turpil to his car, told him to sit in the rear seat and had given him a notebook taken from the glove compartment. 'If a patrol car spots you, tell them you're waiting for Newman, the foreign correspondent. You've been into France? Good. To do a few jobs, I expect. So scribble a few notes in that book about Albert Leroux – tell them I am writing a story about him. There's been enough in the papers about Leroux and his suspected embezzlement for you to make something up . . .' Newman had then lowered a rear window a few inches and locked Turpil inside the car.

Driving the BMW into the car park at the back of the eating place, Newman alighted with Turpil and went inside. Several huge ten- and twelve-wheeler juggernauts were parked near the BMW. At the plastic-topped tables rugged-looking men wearing leather windcheaters sat talking, eating ham rolls, drinking coffee.

'Tweed is in Zürich?' Turpil asked as he devoured a ham roll.

'Say that again. Can't hear you with a mouthful of food . . .'

It gave Newman a few seconds to think up an answer. Intriguing that once again Turpil was showing interest in Tweed's whereabouts. Turpil repeated the question, then drank more coffee greedily.

'I didn't say that,' Newman replied. 'But when we get there I'll know how to contact him, find out where he is, go to see him.'

'On his own, is he?'

'No idea.' Newman grinned. 'You know Tweed, a regular will-o'-the-wisp.'

'I'd like a bath when we get there. Where will we be staying? And I'm short of clothes.'

The hook-nosed little man began destroying a third ham roll. As he asked the questions his ferret-like eyes watched Newman.

'We'll put up at a hotel I know. You can get your bath there. And you can buy some new clothes anywhere. I have a question for you.'

Turpil hooded his eyes, looked guarded. 'What is it?'

'In the camera I've got in my pocket there are pictures of four attractive girls. I've got an idea about them – how they make their living. It's the blonde-haired beauty I'm really interested in.'

Newman drank coffee from his mug and waited. A knowing gleam came into Turpil's eyes. He smirked, waited until he'd finished his roll before he spoke.

'Fancy the lady, do you? Well, why not? Mind you, she's expensive. But you can afford her. That huge fortune you made out of that big bestselling book you wrote. Sold all over the world. What was it called?

'*Kruger: The Computer That Failed,*' Newman said shortly. 'Get back to what we were talking about. This highly expensive girl. 'What exactly does she do for a living? What's her name? Where does she hang out?'

'Information costs money.'

Turpil made a gesture, rubbing his thumb over the tips of his fingers. Newman, about to explode, thought again. If he paid, Turpil was less likely to get restive in Zürich – hoping for more loot.

'How much money?'

'A thousand francs will give you the answers – and the girl.'

'You don't come cheap, do you?'

'She doesn't come cheap.' Turpil leered. 'Very classy . . .'

'I'm talking about *you*,' Newman snapped. It would be a mistake to agree too easily. 'A thousand francs is too much.'

'Then let us talk about something else.'

'No, let's talk about this girl, about . . .'

What he was going to say was muffled by the sudden boom of twin exhausts outside. One of the big diesel trucks was leaving. The atmosphere inside the canteen was over-heated, polluted with the stench of cheap cigars mingling with the smell of cooking. Newman shrugged his shoulders, drank more coffee. Turpil leaned forward.

'You were going to say something?'

'I've lost interest. I don't think you know anything about the girl.'

'But I do! I have used her.' He saw the expression on Newman's face. 'No, you misunderstand. Not in that way. She has provided me with information. For a fee. She is English. She came to Switzerland to work as a secretary in Geneva. It was not long before she saw how she could make much more money, a great deal of money. There are wealthy Swiss who feel taking a mistress, setting her up in a flat in a different city from where they live, is a constant expense. Bankers and businessmen. So they hire her

359

services for a night, pay her the fee in cash, and there is no more expense. She also services wealthy Frenchmen and Germans across the borders.'

'A high-class call-girl.' Newman sounded as if he had lost interest. 'You said you used her. How?'

Turpil hesitated, then couldn't resist showing Newman how clever he was.

'I have an arrangement with her. She is going to visit some German in Stuttgart. His wife is away but he does not risk using his apartment – in case the neighbours see his friend. A banker, let us say. He meets her at a hotel in Ulm. She tells me this and I know I can enter his apartment safely. It is amazing how much money some of these Germans keep in cash.' He winked. 'The tax inspector never knows.'

'I've grasped your system,' Newman commented. 'How long is it since you last used her?'

'Oh, several months. The opportunities only crop up occasionally.'

'And her name? And where does she live?'

Turpil went quiet. He made the same gesture with thumb and forefingers, then took hold of his last ham roll.

'Stop eating,' Newman snapped, and handed him a folded banknote. One thousand francs.

'Her name is Sylvia Harman. She lives in the Altstadt in Zürich. An expensive apartment. Her address is Rennweg 1420.'

'And what does she charge for the pleasure of her company for a night?'

'Six thousand francs.'

Horowitz caught the 1055 flight from Basle Airport for Zürich. Alongside him sat Morgan and several rows behind them Stieber sat alone. The aircraft was three-quarters empty so they could talk freely.

360

'I've been up half the night,' Morgan grumbled. 'I was called out of bed by an alarm at HQ. Funny business. The alarm went off at the Zürich HQ. When they found no signs of trouble they phoned Basle. The alarm systems sometimes cross.'

'What did you find?' Horowitz asked to be polite, his mind on something quite different.

'Panic stations. And no sign of forcible entry. I can't put my finger on it, but the incident bothers me.'

'Better tell the police,' Horowitz suggested ironically, wishing his companion would keep quiet.

'You have to be joking. Now, what are your plans when we get to Zürich?'

'Oh, I'll prowl around certain districts, ask a few people I know certain questions . . .'

'Time is running out. I had a call from London while I was in my office. London wants results.' Morgan paused. 'If you move fast, get the job over with, there could be a bonus for you.'

'London can wait.' Horowitz's tone was chilling. He turned to face Morgan who had the corridor seat. 'Now you listen to me, Morgan. The fee for my services, plus expenses, has been negotiated. I do not work on bonus systems. I regard the word – bonus – as an insult. You're not hiring a hoodlum to put sand in the gear boxes of a competitor's vehicles . . .'

'It was just a suggestion,' Morgan said hastily. 'Well-meant but . . .'

'I loathe the little people of this world who mean well.'

There was a long silence while Horowitz stared out of the window. Morgan fiddled with his cigar, twirling it between his fingers. A stewardess bent over him.

'I'm sorry, sir, but smoking is not allowed in this section. And, as the captain announced earlier, pipes and cigars are frowned on even in the smoking section.'

Morgan glared up at her. 'Something wrong with your

361

eyesight, little lady? This cigar is not lit. May I suggest that your first call when you leave the aircraft is to an optician to get your eyes tested.'

'I'm very sorry, sir. I mistakenly thought you were about to light it. Could I fetch you something more to drink?'

'A large cognac to get over the lousy service . . .'

Morgan sat fuming as the stewardess hurried away to fulfil his order. It was Horowitz who had insisted they sat in the non-smoking section. Morgan struggled to control conflicting emotions. He was furious with his companion but aware that Horowitz was not a man to get on the wrong side of.

The stewardess brought his drink. Morgan took it from her without a word of thanks. He swallowed half the contents at a gulp. Horowitz spoke, still staring out of the window as the machine began its descent.

'I really can't think of any better way in which you could have ensured her attention was drawn to us, that she would remember us after we've left the flight.'

'OK. You're right. You always are. It's the lack of sleep which made me blow my top. No excuse. When we get to Zürich I'll take you straight to our HQ – if that suits you. A car will be waiting for us. Then after we've arrived you can hear all the details of the dragnet we've thrown out. Anything you don't like, change it. I won't say a word. You're the boss.'

'That is the way to handle it,' Horowitz responded and lapsed again into silence as the captain announced they were landing and the *No Smoking* and *Fasten Seat Belts* signs were illuminated.

35

On the outskirts of Zürich Beck had argued with Tweed, but had eventually given in. Reluctantly. He was still very unhappy with the risk element involved.

'I want you to drop us both immediately outside the *Hauptbahnhof.*' Tweed had insisted. 'Paula and I will then go across to the Schweizerhof and pick up our things.'

'And then do what?' Beck had demanded.

'Why, come back to join you,' Tweed had responded as though surprised at the question.

The Mercedes was now parked outside the main station by the cab rank. Beck had left the rear of the car and sat next to the driver as he picked up the radio microphone and used the agreed call sign.

'Commander speaking to all cars. Which of you is closest to the main station?'

'Car Nine responding. We are just crossing the *Bahnhof* bridge in the direction of the main station . . .'

'Pull up by the cab rank. I'll come and see you.'

Beck returned the mike to its cradle and spoke to the driver.

'Keep your eye on the entrance to the Schweizerhof. You know what our two passengers look like. If the man comes out you follow him. I can contact you from the other radio car.'

'What about the raving beauty of a girl?'

'Watch it, Ernst. Remember, you're a married man,' Beck replied with mock severity. 'If she's with him, so much the better. If she comes out on her own, ignore her.

It's the man we have to keep under surveillance. Back in a minute.'

As Beck walked past the huge station he wondered again what he should do. Tweed had spun a plausible story, had told him about his escape route from England via Brussels and the Black Forest. But Beck was convinced Tweed had left out a great deal from his narrative. It seemed impossible that he could have murdered and then raped a girl in his flat in London. The trouble was Beck had experienced many shocks in his career as a policeman. There was no certainty about Tweed's innocence. The only answer was to watch him closely.

To reach the Schweizerhof after leaving the car Tweed and Paula had descended one of the escalators into Shopville, the shopping precinct beneath the Bahnhof-platz. There were many exits and Beck recalled his anxiety when they had seemed to take too long to appear at the entrance to the hotel. Then, to his relief, they *had* appeared.

Car Nine was parked at the end of the cab rank. An unmarked car. He was glad to see the two plain-clothes men in the front seats were Tanner and Graf, two very reliable detectives. He stopped to speak to Tanner in the passenger seat.

'A man and a girl have gone into the Schweizerhof. Leave the car here and tag them. The man is medium height, medium weight, mid forties, wearing a pale grey suit and he has horn-rim glasses . . .'

As he gave the description it crossed his mind how easily Tweed could pass unnoticed in the street. Normally one of his virtues, but damned inconvenient now.

'And the girl?' Tanner enquired.

'About thirty, a mane of raven black hair, good bone structure, also of medium height but slim – a good figure. Dressed in denims and a windcheater. Pale grey.'

'We're on our way, Chief . . .'

Beck returned to the Mercedes to resume his own watch. Now nothing could go wrong.

Walking across the lobby with Paula by his side, each carrying a case, Tweed approached the concierge, who handed him their room keys.

'I have a message for you. And something else to tell you.' As he spoke the last sentence the concierge leaned over the counter and lowered his voice. He passed a folded sheet of paper to Tweed. The message, dated and timed earlier that morning, was simple.

Am at the St Gotthard with a friend. Bob.

'Thank you,' Tweed responded, 'and the other thing?'

'Two men called earlier this morning asking if you were staying here. They even had a photograph of you. One of them flashed an identity card inside a plastic folder and he said, "*Polizei*". Something about their manner, about the card, made me suspicious. I told them you were staying with us but you had gone to Interlaken. I also said it was not certain when you would be back, maybe a few days. You will excuse me for changing your message about your return, and I should have examined the card more carefully . . .'

'That's all right,' Tweed said easily, 'they sound like business rivals.'

He handed the concierge another banknote, refused the aid of a porter and they went up in the elevator to their rooms. Tweed waited while Paula unlocked her door, told her to dump her case and come along to his room. She waited until he'd closed and locked the door.

'Someone knows we're here.'

'They do,' Tweed said grimly.

He handed her Newman's message.

'Bob has been clever. He knows I normally stay here

365

when I'm in Zürich, so he avoided this hotel. The St Gotthard is just behind us on the Bahnhofstrasse . . .'

'And this reference to a friend?'

'My guess is it's Alois Turpil, although why he brought him here I've no idea. We must move fast. Go back to your room, change into quite different clothes . . .'

'Thank God for that. I hate these denims . . .'

'Make yourself look as different as possible, but hurry it up. I'm also changing and I'll come along to you when I'm ready . . .'

'I can always change quicker than you,' she said with an impish smile and left the room.

When Newman drove into Zürich the city was just going to work. Streets and trams thronged with people. He parked near the St Gotthard, locked Turpil inside the car after taking his passport off him, went into the hotel. He reserved two rooms, took his suitcase to his room, left it there and called the Schweizerhof to leave a message in case Tweed turned up.

The first part of the morning was taken up with furious activity. Returning to the car, he threw the question at Turpil.

'The films in this camera. I want them developed, printed, and fast. Also discreetly. An ordinary shop won't do.'

'I do have a contact.' Turpil paused. 'It will cost money.'

'You should have that phrase printed on a card. How much – and how far away is this friend?'

'He is very close. Also very discreet. To develop and print those films? Two thousand francs . . .'

'Not on your life! Don't waste my time . . .'

'Well, as a special favour I might persuade him to do the job for a thousand francs . . .'

'Which includes your commission?' Newman said cynically. 'So let's get moving. Where to?'

'Lindengasse 851. I'll guide you there. It's near the Sihl and difficult to find . . .'

Following Turpil's instructions, Newman drove down the Bahnhofstrasse. The city was ankle-deep in a mush of well-trodden snow and overhead leaden clouds drifted so low Newman felt he could reach up to touch them. More snow on the way, a lot of it.

He turned right into the Pelikanplatz and then Turpil was constantly instructing him as he drove through a maze of backstreets. The snow was deeper here with fewer footprints. He parked outside a villa near the end of Lindengasse. Newman realized they were close to the Sihl, the second river of Zürich which joined the main river, the Limmat, near the *Hauptbahnhof*.

To his surprise Turpil's 'friend' was a stooped old crone who was introduced to Newman as Gisela. A forbidding woman, her first question showed the sort of business she was involved in.

'These are dirty pictures?'

'No, they are not,' snapped Newman and glanced round at framed photographs on the walls of nude girls in provocative poses.

'A thousand francs is the fee,' Turpil said hastily.

'Only because you give me other business,' Gisela replied and took the films Newman handed her.

'And that includes the negatives,' Newman told her. 'Also I will be present when you do the work.'

'You don't want much, do you . . .'

But inside the dark-room she was skilled at her work. Newman watched the prints of the four girls emerge as clear images. He had asked for two copies of everything. She took time with the girls' prints and then dealt rapidly with the documents. When they were dry she inserted them inside two cardboard-backed envelopes with no printed indication of their source.

Newman returned to the St Gothard with Turpil.

*   *   *

Inside the World Security HQ in Zürich on Belle-rivestrasse Morgan glowed with triumph. He sat in a large black leather executive chair facing Horowitz and Stieber, seated on a couch.

'We have located Tweed, gentlemen. Here, in this city. I know the hotel he is staying at. Opposite the main station where, undoubtedly, he alighted from the train he travelled on from Laufenburg.'

He puffed at his cigar and glanced out of the window. The modern building looked across towards a park, and beyond, the Zürich See – Lake Zürich – was like a plate of molten lead. His office was on the fourth floor. He switched his gaze to the other two men.

'The Hotel Schweizerhof,' he told them.

'Are you sure of that?' Horowitz asked.

'Of course I'm sure,' Morgan rapped back. 'You're always asking me that question. Two of my men report he is registered there.'

'But has anyone actually seen him?' Horowitz persisted.

Morgan controlled his temper with an effort. The hired assassin wasn't a man at all: he had a mind like a Swiss watch with his obsession with precision.

'Not yet,' Morgan replied. 'Are you never satisfied?'

'I find it most peculiar. The location,' Horowitz continued. 'As you say, the main station is probably where he got off on his way from Laufenburg. But look how easy it has been to follow him. The way he stared up at the man supposedly filming him in secret as he crossed the bridge. That absurd fuss over buying the tickets at Laufenburg station. Now, in Zürich, he stays at the nearest large hotel to the *Hauptbahnhof*. I told you before, I am beginning to know my opponent. His behaviour does not equate with his record of cleverness.'

'So he's scared witless. Loses his judgement. Goes to earth like a rabbit in the nearest burrow. And I have my

368

lads with Walkmans on patrol. It is only a matter of time before they report a sighting.'

'It is not Tweed's normal pattern,' Horowitz insisted. He stood up. 'I think I will take a tram to the Schweizerhof to see for myself what is going on.'

'Suit yourself. Why a tram? I can give you a limo . . .'

'Because a tram is one of the most anonymous forms of transport.'

Inside his corner room at the Schweizerhof Tweed was very active. First he changed from his plain grey suit into a navy blue business-suit with a grey chalk stripe. He left the grey suit on a hanger in the wardrobe.

Next he sat at a desk, took a sheet of headed hotel paper and wrote a note to Beck. He slipped it inside an envelope and wrote on the outside. *A. Beck.* It was a common enough name.

It was exactly midday by the station clock when he dialled the St Gotthard and asked to speak to Mr Robert Newman. In less than half a minute the familiar voice answered.

'You know who this is, Bob,' Tweed began. 'I'm at the Schweizerhof with Paula . . .'

'Your timing is perfect. I've just returned with my friend.'

'Good. We must meet urgently. On our own, if you get my meaning. Without my protector, or maybe my escort would be a better word.'

'Understood.' Newman lowered his voice. 'Can I bring my friend with me – I don't want to leave him on his own. If you get my meaning . . .'

'By all means bring him. You know the Hotel Baur en Ville? Good. They have a small and very good restaurant – a café – which you enter from the side. You do know it? Splendid. It is a split-level layout – on three levels. I will be at a table on the top level. Say in fifteen minutes from now.'

'I'll have certain things to show you. Bye,' said Newman and rang off.

Tweed was changing his tie when someone tapped on the door to the small lobby. He unlocked the door on the chain, saw it was Paula, let her in. She wore a light raincoat over a sweater and had tied her hair into a pony-tail, which completely altered her appearance.

'Told you I'd be ready first,' she joshed him. 'Men take for ever . . .'

'We're going to lunch to meet Newman. I've just called him and we meet at the Baur en Ville. He has someone with him. It could be Turpil. If it is, occupy the little man's attention so Bob and I can talk in private. Now to slip out of here without Beck knowing.'

'Which I'd have said was well nigh impossible . . .'

Tweed had also substituted a blue topcoat for the raincoat he'd worn earlier. He paused in the hotel lobby, had a further word with the concierge, handing him the sealed envelope.

'I want you to send that envelope by a porter over to the silver Mercedes parked outside the station. But please wait five minutes until after we have left. Here is the tip for the porter, and this is for your help.'

'Please wait just a moment, sir.'

The concierge strolled towards the entrance, looked at his watch as though waiting for a taxi he had ordered, then came back to Tweed.

'I've seen the car. Please leave it to me . . .'

Paula, puzzled, followed Tweed as he crossed the lobby towards the bar, glancing across the *platz*. Then he changed direction, walked towards the entrance and turned left as the automatic doors opened leading to the small café attached to the hotel. Paula followed him, saw a stationary bus was blocking Beck's view, and went down the steps inside the café. At the front it was open to the

370

public and several smartly-dressed Swiss women were eating omelettes. The bus was still stationary as Tweed slipped out of the front door and turned left, away from the Bahnhofstrasse.

The *platz* was choked with a traffic jam and every vehicle was stationary as Paula followed Tweed down a side street alongside the hotel. She caught him up.

'Keep at least a dozen yards behind me,' he ordered. 'And when we reach the Bahnhofstrasse walk on the opposite side to me. They'll be looking for two people.'

Reluctantly she dropped back, wishing to God she had her Browning automatic in her handbag. Tweed was in danger: she sensed it. That was why he was distancing himself from her.

Walking three-quarters of the way round the block, Tweed entered the great banking and shopping street of the Bahnhofstrasse and turned right along the wide sidewalk, away from the Schweizerhof and the station. His rubber over-shoes sloshed through the snow mush as he walked slowly, glancing round as though it was the first time he'd seen this street. Paula waited for a tram to pass and crossed to the other sidewalk.

A youth clad in the usual uniform of jeans and windcheater, a Walkman attached to his head, pushed in front of Tweed, glanced at him, apologized in German. Tweed, shoulders hunched, gloved hands inside his coat pockets, trudged on. A girl on a bicycle, moving in the same direction, stopped and gestured with her head for a couple to cross. She also wore a Walkman headset. Over-polite, Tweed thought: she'd had plenty of time to cycle past without inconveniencing the couple.

He looked across the street where Paula was stepping it out. Another youth equipped with a Walkman turned his head away, stopped to stare in a window. The display was of ladies' underclothes. Not his scene, Tweed thought, unless he was kinky. An attractive girl, braving the elements in a

371

short skirt, walked towards the lad who had resumed his stroll. The girl had excellent legs. The lad turned to watch her as she passed. Definitely not kinky. Tweed suddenly recalled the window Paula had shown him – the shop display with the monkey sprawled in a hammock, a look of bliss on its face, the Walkman clamped to its head.

Tweed came to a tram stop. Feeling in his pocket for a one-franc coin, he inserted it into the machine, took his ticket and waited. The youth who had walked in front of Tweed was trudging behind him. He went to the machine and collected a ticket for himself.

Tweed stared at him. The youth looked away, shuffled his trainers in the snow, building a ridge of snow, then looked around vaguely. In every direction except where Tweed stood.

There was a whining noise as a tram approached. Passengers moved forward, ready to board. Tweed glanced at the destination plate, took two paces back. The youth leaned against the machine. The tram, a heavy blue juggernaut with three coaches linked, stopped.

The automatic doors opened, the passengers on the pavement waited as people got off, then climbed aboard. Everything was automatic – the doors, the platform step which dropped and then was raised as the tram moved off. The tram was still stationary. The doors began to close. Tweed leapt forward, just escaped being caught by the closing doors.

As it moved off he sat down and looked out of the window. The youth had jumped forward too late. His expression was one of fury and frustration. The tram glided on. The girl on the bicycle with the headset pulled alongside, pedalling vigorously. She glanced up. At the wrong moment. She failed to see the patch of ice in the road. The cycle toppled, dropped her into a pile of snow swept up earlier by road cleaners.

Tweed stayed aboard until the tram reached the stop

before the lake, then alighted. He crossed the street, bought a fresh ticket, boarded another tram coming in the opposite direction.

36

'Blast it!' said Beck.

Sitting in the passenger seat of the Mercedes he read again the note which had just been handed to him.

My dear Beck: I am so sorry to absent myself for a few hours. Urgent business which must be attended to. I will contact you at police HQ in Zürich. Please excuse my playing truant!
Tweed.

He dived out of the car, threaded his way through the stationary traffic. Wandering inside the lobby, the concierge saw him leave the car, recognized him as the man Tweed had asked to have the envelope delivered to. He was behind his counter when Beck strode in, his manner brusque.

'You have a Mr Tweed and a Miss Paula Grey staying here. I have an appointment with Mr Tweed.'

Could this be the husband of the girl who called herself Paula Grey? – wondered the concierge. He liked Tweed, and not only for his custom and the generous tips.

'Maybe he is in his room,' he suggested. 'I will call him.'

'No reply,' he said a little later, 'and now I see his key is missing. He may be in the restaurant . . .'

'I'll check for myself,' Beck snapped and ran upstairs. The next place he checked was the bar, and finally the small café. He walked out in search of Tanner, who stood a few yards to the right of the exit, pretending to read a newspaper. Beck was told he had not seen Tweed, but the pavement had been crowded. Beck checked with Graf who had taken up a position round the corner in the Bahnhof-strasse. No luck there. Beck said, 'Blast it!' again and went back to his car.

'Hell's teeth!' said Morgan and slammed down the phone. The report had just come in from the communications van parked near the Quai-brücke, the bridge where the Lim-mat ran out of the lake. He glared at Stieber, as though it were his fault.

'They had him – Tweed – in the palm of their hands.'

'What happened?' enquired Stieber cautiously.

'They picked him up walking down the Banhhofstrasse. Would you think anyone could give them the slip once they'd seen him?'

'But he did?'

'Oh, yes, he did. He tricked them. Oldest ploy in the world. Pretended not to be boarding a tram, then he dives on to it at the last moment. Vanishes into thin air. Why do I employ such idiots?'

Stieber was careful not to reply as the phone rang. Morgan snatched it up.

'Yes? Who is it?' he rasped.

'You know who it is. You sound agitated. Something gone wrong?'

There was no mistaking Horowitz's quiet sibilant voice. Morgan gripped the receiver more tightly. He'd better own up.

'We have located our target,' he announced.

'You have? Where is he?'

374

'Well, he was spotted in the Bahnhofstrasse, walking towards the lake. Then he disappeared. We have to start again, which we are doing, of course.'

'Of course.' The tone was mocking. 'Precisely where and how did he *disappear*, as you put it? Vanish in a cloud of blue smoke, did he?'

Morgan explained, Horowitz listened, then put down the phone. Horowitz had been calling from the main station. Patience. He would travel round this area on trams until he saw Tweed.

Tweed walked into the Baur en Ville café-restaurant and found Paula waiting for him inside. He took her by the arm.

'We'll go up to the top level – you can see everyone coming into this place from there . . .'

He asked the head waiter to reserve an extra table across the aisle, explaining that two more people were arriving to join them. The café had dark wooden walls and when they sat down with their backs to the wall they had a good view of the entrance from their elevated position at the third level.

'Are you all right?' were Paula's first words. 'I saw you dive aboard that tram at the last moment. Is there trouble?'

'There was.' Tweed picked up the menu. 'I'll tell you about it later. Here comes Newman with friend Turpil. What I want you to do is to entertain Turpil at that other table. He was once a watchmaker . . .'

He broke off as the two men arrived. Tweed noticed that Newman was shepherding Turpil in front of him. The little man greeted Tweed like a long-lost friend.

'How wonderful to see you again. It has been too long since last we met. You remember Geneva?'

'Of course.' Tweed shook his limp hand. 'Now, I have some business to discuss with Mr Newman. This is Paula.

She will keep you company. You'll enjoy being with her more than you would with us.'

'Yes, indeed . . .'

Paula had hung her coat up and Turpil stared at her figure with interest. She shook hands with him and guided him to the other table. Turpil offered her the inside seat against the wall but she demurred.

'Please. I'd much sooner sit on the outside. More legroom.'

Tweed smiled to himself. She had manoeuvred the seating so that Turpil was penned in. Also he was too far away to catch any of the conversation between Tweed and Newman. They both ordered veal paillard and mineral water.

'What happened when you crossed the frontier at Basle?' Tweed enquired.

'Someone was waiting for you. Two men parked in a car close to the frontier post. Not police. The driver was a round-headed thug – like a football.'

'He spotted the Audi?'

'It wasn't there to spot. I'd changed it for a BMW on the outskirts of Basle. Since then I've been busy with Turpil – breaking into World Security in Basle at dead of night. I've things to show you, but how have you got on? You made it here, thank God.'

'Zürich is a trap,' Tweed replied, coming straight to the point. 'On my way here I noticed a lot of youths with Walkmans. The only trouble is they're not genuine Walkmans – they're mobile radio communication gear. I saw one talking into what looked like a microphone after he'd spotted me.'

'That's a diabolically clever idea . . .'

'The idea is. The operators aren't, fortunately. Amateurs. When we leave here you know what to look for.' He paused as the food came, then switched the subject. 'I keep telling myself the key to this business is who killed that girl in my London flat. And the identity of the girl. You've something to show me?'

Without saying a word, Newman glanced at the table across the aisle. Paula had Turpil engaged in conversation, had asked him about his days as a watchmaker. The little man clearly loved having an attractive girl as an attentive listener. Newman extracted one set of photographs of the four women, spread them out in front of Tweed.

'Copies of photos we found in a safe at the Basle HQ,' he said and started his lunch.

Tweed's eyes swept across the display, then stopped. He was staring at the blonde-haired beauty. He tapped it with his finger, looked at Newman with a frozen expression.

'This is the girl who was murdered in my flat. Who is she?'

'A Sylvia Harman, according to Turpil. English. Lived here in Zürich. Address, Rennweg 1420 . . .'

'A stone's throw from where we're sitting,' Tweed commented.

'She was a high-class call-girl . . .'

Newman described the information Turpil had given about her. Tweed listened, watching Newman, eating automatically. He put down his knife and fork as Newman said this wasn't all, extracted from the cardboard-backed envelope the copies of the cost sheets and the pages from the desk diary, and handed them across the table.

'Items of income and expenditure and pages from last year's desk diary. Also from the World Security HQ in Basle. I had to search to find the diary.'

Tweed scanned the copies quickly, then at Newman. 'You said she charged six thousand francs a night for her company.'

'That's right. Over two thousand pounds. Expensive, wasn't she? You see the point?'

'Yes. The item, *One-time cost*. Always for six thousand Swiss francs – Sylvia Harman's nightly charge. Also the five dates from January to April in the diary with an appointment marked with the initial "M". They are the same dates as the *One-time cost* items. It forms a pattern of liaisons between someone inside World Security at Basle and Sylvia Harman.'

"And "M" suggests Morgan . . .'

'That could be a cover for Buckmaster. The dates for last year are January to April. He vaulted from the back benches to be appointed Minister for External Security in June last year.'

'I find that too subtle.'

'Whatever you find it, I congratulate you. You see what all this means – at one blow you've achieved something I thought we'd never manage. You've identified the dead girl in my flat. And these sheets give us a direct link between her and World Security. After all, you found her photo in the company's safe.' Tweed gave a sigh of sheer relief. 'I congratulate you, Bob,' he repeated. 'The next move seems obvious.'

'It does?'

'Yes. We break in to Sylvia Harman's flat on Rennweg.' He glanced across to where Turpil was still chattering away non-stop to Paula, who kept nodding her head, bobbing her pony-tail up and down. 'And we have the means to do that at the next table. Friend Turpil . . .'

The argument which raged for some time was vehement. Tweed and Newman had joined Turpil and Paula, sitting opposite them while they all drank coffee.

Tweed proposed the break-in to Turpil. There was the normal haggle over the fee until Tweed, who sat facing Turpil, agreed a generous amount. Newman had just volunteered to accompany Turpil when Paula spoke.

'It's no good your searching that apartment. You've no idea where a girl would hide something. Only another woman knows where to look. I'll go with Turpil . . .'

'Out of the question,' snapped Tweed.

'Oh, stop being so macho,' Paula burst out. 'I've been trained to be careful,' she said, phrasing it carefully in front of Turpil. 'I repeat, only another woman knows where to look.' She flared up with a pretended burst of temper. 'Or is this your way of saying I haven't got the bloody nerve? If so, I would greatly appreciate it if you'd come straight out with it . . .'

They talked about it for several more minutes and Paula refused to give way. It was Newman who cooled the argument as he turned to Tweed.

'She is right, you know. And I can go with them and act as lookout. So if something goes wrong and a little muscle is called for I think I can provide it. Unless you're going to argue about that?'

Tweed threw up his hands. 'Outnumbered, out-voted, talked down. You're a couple of rogues and rebels . . .'

'But at long last you agree?' Paula said and smiled. She turned to Turpil. 'You said you knew the flat, that you'd been there, so you know how to get in, presumably?'

'Easy as jumping a low hurdle,' the little man agreed.

'So', Paula continued, 'wouldn't it, on balance, be safer if we did the job in daylight? You said she lived alone? You're sure about that?'

'Positive. She had the money. She didn't need to share the expenses with another girl. She didn't like the idea of sharing. She lives alone. All I have to do is to make sure she isn't in. She usually exercises about this time of day. A great one for keeping fit. Can't guarantee she will be out, of course.'

'Yes, we can.' Newman had been puzzling over how he could reassure Turpil without letting him know the girl was dead. 'I'll tell you now, while you were using the bathroom in my room at the St Gotthard I called a friend in need of some feminine company, gave him Sylvia's phone number out of the directory. He called back and said she'd agreed to go with him back to his hotel this afternoon.'

'Then what are we waiting for?' Turpil asked. 'I carry a portable kit which will get us inside that place in just a few minutes.'

Tweed noticed Turpil had been eyeing him furtively at intervals during the long argument. He leaned forward.

'We may have another job for you later. But you'll have to come with us to a place in the mountains where I'll be resting up for a few days. In the canton of Schwyz. Near the town of Einsiedeln.'

Newman stared across the table at Paula in blank amazement at this extraordinary breach of security. Paula had trouble not showing her alarm and incredulity. Tweed said he would meet them at Sprüngli, the chocolate shop with a tea-restaurant on the first floor further down the Bahnhofstrasse. He nodded towards Turpil.

'Don't forget to bring our friend back with you.' He stood up, then bent down to whisper in Newman's ear. 'I'm trusting you to take very good care of Paula.'

It was still light when they made the break-in at Rennweg 1420. Renneweg was a street of small shops which branched off Bahnhofstrasse at an angle and led to the section of the Altstadt on the west bank of the river Limmat.

Newman was glad to see there were plenty of shoppers moving up and down the street. The entrance to Sylvia Harman's apartment was a straight staircase open to the street. The door was latched back and Newman assumed it was locked after nightfall.

Turpil disappeared off the street and Paula followed him up the steps. He paused in front of a heavy door on the first landing, then pressed the bell and waited. He looked at his watch to time three minutes. Then he took a bunch of keys from his overcoat pocket and began trying one after another.

It was very quiet inside the building and Paula found herself glancing at the upper flights in case someone was descending. On the pavement below Newman was leaning against the side of the entrance, smoking a cigarette.

'It's open,' Turpil whispered.

Paula stood looking down a narrow hallway, listening for the sound of a shower gushing, a bath emptying of water. Then she strode inside and Turpil followed, closing the door behind him. Paula was very suspicious Turpil had the key to the heavy door and had performed a pantomime to conceal the fact.

She checked the layout of the flat. There was a living-cum-dining-room, one large bedroom, the kitchen and the bathroom. She had the impression of an expensively, tastefully furnished apartment. Opening a wardrobe door in the bedroom she surveyed a quantity of fashionable clothes that also suggested good taste. On the floor rows of good shoes were neatly arranged.

Neatness, tidiness, expense and taste were the words she used mentally to sum up the occupant. She heard the squeak of wood being moved, returned to the living-room to find Turpil starting to search through a sideboard.

'Don't you touch anything,' she snapped. 'You've no idea as to the best places to look.'

'I'm a pro—' he began indignantly, then broke off in mid-sentence.

He closed the drawer and Paula sent him back into the lobby to stand guard in case Newman came rushing up the stairs. It took her ten minutes to find the inconsistency she was looking for. In the bathroom stood a laundry bin. She lifted the lid and stared.

Inside used clothes were crammed higgledy-piggledy. A mess of clothes hastily shoved into the bin. She bent forward, began to sort through the clothes. She found the diary for the previous year at the bottom.

'I want to phone my sister, Klara,' Turpil said.

They were walking down a side street leading to Bahnhofstrasse. Paula had slipped the diary into her shoulder bag after a swift examination. On their way to the break-in Newman had quietly told Paula the sort of thing she should look for. Lists of phone numbers with names; any kind of financial record; diaries, especially for the previous year.

'You should have phoned her from the St Gotthard,' Newman told Turpil. 'We're on our way to Sprüngli . . .'

'And when did I have the time?' Turpil demanded. 'I have to call her before we go to the cake shop.'

'Why the urgency?'

'I want to make sure she got back safely.' Turpil glanced at Paula as they emerged on to Bahnhofstrasse, a sneaky look. 'You understand, I'm sure. And Klara may have a business message for me.'

'Business messages can wait . . .' Newman began, then he swore under his breath.

Turpil had darted from his side, had run to a ticket machine. Newman was moving after him when Paula grabbed his arm, warned him to be careful. A police patrol-car, which Turpil had undoubtedly spotted, was parked nearby and the two uniformed men inside were looking their way.

Newman ran to the ticket machine as a tram approached the stop, moving towards the main station. He bought two tickets as the tram stopped and Turpil scrambled aboard a coach. Newman ran for the same central door with Paula by this side and passed her a ticket.

'Something funny going on,' Newman said quickly. 'He

gave two reasons for making a call. Keep an eye on him . . .'

She mounted the step to the interior of the coach, saw that Turpil was occupying a seat near the door, walked past him as the doors closed and sat down a few seats in front of the little man, choosing a divan seat with its back to the side of the tram. She could now keep him under observation.

Newman went in the opposite direction from the central doors, occupied an outer seat next to the aisle. They had him in a pincer movement. The tram stopped again, several passengers alighted, but a whole crowd boarded the coach, most of them standing. It was now difficult for Newman to see Turpil.

The next stop was close to Globus department store on the other side of the street; close also to the *Hauptbahnhof*. Newman stood up as a lot of people alighted. He caught a glimpse of Paula who was leaving the tram, beckoning to him furiously. Newman managed to leave the coach just before another horde came aboard. Rush hour was starting and now it was dark. He stood on the wide pavement, looking in all directions. Turpil had vanished.

Paula ran up to him, her coat flapping. She was out of breath and couldn't speak for a moment.

'I saw him,' she gasped out. 'Heading for the *Hauptbahnhof*. I think I saw him going down an escalator. Into Shopville. I'm not certain it was him . . .'

'You walk round the *platz*. Watch all the exits from Shopville. If you spot him grab him by the arm, tell him you'll accuse him of trying to interfere with you, call the police, unless he comes back with you to Sprüngli. I'm going down into Shopville . . .'

Paula was away, walking briskly as Newman reached an escalator, descended into the underground shopping precinct. He slowed down inside Shopville, looking everywhere. The bloody place was like a labyrinth. Plenty of people down here, men and girls hurrying back and forth.

Newman kept walking slowly, scanning the whole area. He saw Turpil's back suddenly. There was a row of telephones under perspex hoods. Turpil was using the phone at the end of the row. Newman started walking forward, then remembered the ear-drummer.

Taking it out of his trench-coat pocket he inserted it inside his right ear, which was turned towards one of the escalator exits. A deafening growling rumble followed by a high-pitched whine filled his ear. A tram was turning round off the *platz* down Bahnhofstrasse.

Newman swivelled his stance, standing opposite the phone compartment where Turpil was making his call. The sound of footsteps clacking like hammerblows on the floor; then, quite distinct, Turpil's voice.

'It's taken me long enough to get through to you. Morgan. You want to know where a man called Tweed is to be found soon? I know. Twenty thousand francs? Agreed. He's going to hole up in the mountains, in the canton of Schwyz, near Einsiedeln . . .'

The connection was broken as Newman's left hand wrenched the phone out of Turpil's hand, replaced it. His right hand gripped Turpil by the forearm, just above the elbow, on the nerve. Turpil yelped with pain as Newman hauled him out, turned him towards the escalator leading to Bahnhofstrasse.

As they walked side by side, with Newman holding on to the elbow, Turpil began to babble.

'I had to speak to Klara . . .'

Newman showed him the palm of his bare left hand, the ear-drummer resting inside it, then put it back in his coat pocket. Turpil swallowed several times before he spoke again.

'You dropped that in the river . . .'

'Pretended to. Is Morgan your pet name for Klara? Who is she?'

'My mistress. She looks after me. Cooks for me.

384

Manages the apartment in Berne . . .'

'But you were talking to Morgan of World Security. Selling Tweed for thirty pieces of silver. No, for twenty thousand francs. You're a lump of dirt. How did you know Morgan was interested in Tweed?'

'They've spread the news on the grapevine, the under-world. A reward of twenty thousand francs for news of his whereabouts. I'm getting old, Mr Newman. I'm getting near retirement. I need every franc I can lay my hands on . . .'

They were on the automatic escalator now, standing together as it carried them up towards the Bahnhofstrasse exit. No one behind them. No one in front. After the warmth of Shopville the icy temperature of night met them.

'And you were supposed to be a friend of Tweed's,' Newman commented. 'With friends like you who needs . . .'

They had stepped off the escalator. The temperature had dropped rapidly. Newman didn't see the patch of ice, slipped on it, loosened his grip. Turpil snatched his arm away and ran.

He ran across the street without looking. He tripped almost as soon as he'd left the kerb. He never saw the great hulk of the blue tram swinging round the corner into Bahnhofstrasse. He sprawled forward full length over the track. The tram driver jammed on his emergency brake. The rails were coated with ice. Too late. The tram slid forward a few more feet. There was a screech. Which could have been Turpil. Or the tram grinding to a halt. The wheels sliced through the prone body like a mincing machine. Spurts of liquid gushed from under the tram. Splotches of deep carmine splashed on the white snow. Blood. A woman began screaming. A crowd was gathering.

Newman walked further down the street. He saw Paula's

horrified face on the other side and crossed to join her.
'We must get to Tweed quickly. It's an emergency.'

37

At a corner table inside Sprüngli on the first floor Tweed listened while Newman tersely reported their experiences. Paula sat beside Tweed staring out at the leafless skeletal trees lining Bahnhofstrasse. A tram appeared. She looked away. Tweed squeezed her hand.

'Would you like a cake?'

'I couldn't face anything to eat. More black coffee please.'

Tweed gave a waitress the order and glanced again at two men sitting at separate tables a few yards away. One was a poker-faced man in his thirties, wearing a business suit. The other, who sat closer, was a youth eating a cake, a Walkman clamped to his head. Newman drank coffee: he had finished his story. He put down his cup, said quietly to Tweed:

'What I don't understand is why you let Turpil know you were heading up into the mountains, to this place in the canton of Schwyz, Einsiedeln.'

'The plan is working,' Tweed replied. 'Although I didn't foresee it would have such grisly consequences.'

'Turpil asked for it,' Newman told him. 'He set out to betray you for money. To some pretty grim people. Don't forget the bomb I found under the Audi back in the Black Forest.'

'True . . .'

Tweed was thinking that Newman had grown harder

since his ordeal travelling secretly in East Germany a few years earlier. Not less human, but tougher.

'What plan, for God's sake?' Paula burst out, still shaken.

'We need Beck's full cooperation. As I realized before we ever reached Switzerland, it would be difficult to convince him completely of my innocence, that we are being hunted by professional killers. We have to *demonstrate* the situation to him, bring the enemy out into the open.'

'In the . . . excitement . . . I forgot to give you this diary. I found it hidden in the linen bin in Sylvia Harman's apartment,' said Paula and handed the book to him.

'Last year's diary.' Tweed riffled through the pages, stopping briefly at certain dates, then he looked at Newman. 'A further link in the chain linking World Security with the girl I found dead in my flat. The same dates as those in the desk diary you found in Basle, Bob. January 15, 28. February 16. March 4. April 25. Alongside each date is the initial "M". Even the times are the same in both diaries. 9.30 p.m., 9 p.m., 10 p.m., 9 p.m., 10.30 p.m. I remember them distinctly.'

'But how would Sylvia Harman turn up in London?' Paula asked.

'Easy,' Newman replied. 'Whoever used to spend the night with her – Buckmaster or Morgan – could fly her in by the Lear jet. For six thousand francs she'd fly there without a second's hesitation . . . What's the matter?'

Tweed had slipped the diary into his pocket and was staring behind Newman as the poker-faced man approached their table. He drew up a chair at the end, next to Tweed, sat down. He showed Tweed a folder in the palm of his hand.

'Norbert Tanner, Federal Police. Working for Arthur Beck. I don't know whether you realize it, Mr Tweed, but you're being followed. That youth sitting by himself with the Walkman. He tagged you here from near the Baur en Ville. Shall I take him in with us?'

'No. Leave him alone. Pretend you haven't noticed him.'

'If you say so. And now, if you don't mind, I'd like you all to accompany me to police headquarters. Orders of Mr Beck. There's a Merc waiting outside, the one with amber-tinted glass . . .'

'We've got Tweed this time,' said Morgan, standing by the window of his office on Bellerivestrasse, staring out into the night. 'He's headed for Einsiedeln, a nowhere place up in the mountains in the canton of Schwyz. All I have to do is to send my Walkman lads up there ahead of him in a bus.'

The only other occupant was Armand Horowitz who sat in a hard-backed chair. He'd refused the offer of an armchair: they relaxed you, made you less alert. And Morgan had the heating turned full up, compelling Horowitz to remove his raincoat. He wore a drab grey suit, but it was well cut and fitted his thin tall frame perfectly.

'Might I enquire how you know this?' he enquired.

'You might!' Morgan, his turnip-shaped bulk emphasized by the thin stature of his guest, was in flamboyant mood. He walked back to his desk, settled himself behind its vast size. They laid a lot of emphasis on status symbols, the size and quality of the desks, Horowitz was thinking.

'Then get on with it,' he said.

'A little turd called Alois Turpil – we've used him occasionally for break-in jobs – phoned me. Tweed himself must have told him . . .'

'Another out-of-character action,' Horowitz observed.

'Can it!' Morgan burst out. 'This is the real McCoy.'

'Describe this Turpil.'

Morgan was thrown off balance. 'A small man,

mid-fifties, a hooked nose, looks a bit like a gnome . . .'

'Looked,' Horowitz corrected him.

'What's that?'

'I spent the afternoon travelling on trams round the station area and the immediate vicinity. Sometimes the long arm of coincidence reaches out to help persistence. Was it a lengthy phone call?'

'No. As a matter of fact he broke off in mid-sentence. I don't know why. Maybe the connection was broken accidentally . . .'

'Or by someone else.' Horowitz had an amused look in the eyes watching Morgan. 'This time I believe you. I was on the tram which mowed Turpil down, turned him into goulash.'

Morgan paused in the act of placing his cigar between his lips, held it in mid-air like a conductor grasping a baton. 'What are you talking about?'

'Turpil – from your description – is very dead. He came up from Shopville on an escalator with a man who was holding him by the arm. Turpil broke free at the top. He ran into the street and my tram rolled over him.'

'I see . . .'

'No, you don't. I have a photographic memory and the man holding on to him was the foreign correspondent, Robert Newman. His picture has appeared in the papers often enough. More to the point, in Basle the arm of coincidence was stretched to breaking point. Newman was dining in the restaurant of the Drei Könige when I was staying there. And you said something about an alarm going off here in Zürich for no reason.'

'Oh God! Was there a break-in at Basle? I'll have to get them to double-check nothing is missing. Turpil was an expert break-in artist. For hire by anyone who had the money.'

'That's your problem. Mine is Einsiedeln. Cancel that fool idea of sending up those Walkman louts. They'll stand out like clowns in a small town.'

389

'Someone has to go there,' Morgan objected.

'Someone is going there. I am. With Stieber. At once.'

Police headquarters on Lindenhofstrasse is a four-storey old block of grey stone. One side overlooks the river Limmat which divides Zürich into two separate districts. Through the net curtains masking Beck's office window on the third floor Tweed could see the dim bulk of the university perched high up on the opposite bank.

'You've got a nerve – wandering round Zürich.' Beck said to Tweed. 'And in your present position I suspect you need it. *If* you are being followed.'

'Mr Tweed *is* being followed, sir,' interjected Tanner. 'No doubt about it. I picked him up near the Baur en Ville and he walked to Sprüngli. During that short distance I spotted three of them. Two youths on foot and a girl on a bicycle. All equipped with fake Walkmans.'

'Fake?' Beck queried. 'A bunch of kids has you worried?'

'It's the equipment, sir. It has to be very sophisticated. I saw two of them reporting to someone through concealed microphones. You called them a bunch of kids, but whoever has organized them is pretty professional. With equipment like that. And another one on a motor-cycle followed us to here. A man. He could still be outside, waiting for Mr Tweed to leave the building.'

Beck looked bleak. 'I don't like that. Go down and see if he's still there.'

'And if he is, permission to bring him in for questioning downstairs? I think I can persuade him to talk.'

Newman and Paula, sitting on chairs close to Tweed, stared at Tanner. Yes, Newman thought to himself, you'll make him talk if you get your hands on him.

'Agreed, Tanner,' Beck decided. 'And I do want to know who his employer is.' He waited until Tanner had left the office. 'Tweed, while you've been running round Zür-ich I have been to see Colonel Romer of the Zurcher Kredit in Talstrasse. He has now been waiting all after-noon and part of this evening to see you.'

'Something I said caught his attention?' Tweed suggested.

'Yes, it did.' He looked at Newman before turning his attention back to Tweed. 'All of this is highly confidential – but I know you've been fully vetted. Now, Tweed, you can be awfully frank with Romer. He carries a lot of clout in military circles in this country.' Beck checked his watch. 'Romer has gone out to get something to eat. He'll be back in three-quarters of an hour. Meantime, who wants some refreshment?'

Tanner returned half an hour later. 'He talked – the motor-cyclist. There's a control communications van parked near the Quai-brücke.'

'Is there now? Tanner, send a patrol car to check it out. It will have an aerial – so our men can say it is interfering with the police radio band.'

Beck waited until Tanner had gone. 'Who do you think these people are, Tweed?'

'World Security.'

'I see.' Beck thought about it. 'Even if it is, it would be logical for Lance Buckmaster to pass the word through to his organization to keep a lookout for you, to back up the continent-wide alert Howard sent to police chiefs.'

'I see,' Tweed replied tersely.

'Now,' Beck continued. 'Colonel Romer will be back at Talstrasse. I'm sending you there in a car. Whatever you say to him, he is totally trustworthy and discreet. He will discuss the matter only with myself. He might just hold the key to this weird business.'

Colonel Romer was a tall, well-built man with a trim moustache who held himself erect and was in his early fifties. He wore a dark grey business suit. His thick brows and hair were grey and there was a hint of humour in his blue eyes.

His office, overlooking a narrow side street, had stripped pine panelled walls, the furniture was English antiques. He had drawn up an armchair alongside Tweed's and had two glasses of Montrachet and the bottle on the low coffee table near them.

'I am a good listener, Mr Tweed,' he said and smiled. 'I recall our rather tense meeting in Basle a couple of years ago. Since then I've become chief executive of Zurcher Kredit – it simply means more work.'

'And you're a colonel in the Swiss Army,' Tweed commented.

'Correct. And as such much concerned with national security,' Romer responded in English. 'I am also a good listener . . .'

Tweed had already decided Romer was as discreet as Beck had indicated. He began. He started with the discovery of the dead girl in his flat. But he was careful not to refer directly to the Strategic Defence Initiative. Instead he used the phrase, 'The most advanced hi-tech system of defence for the West ever invented . . .'

'And you say that when you contacted this vessel, the *Lampedusa*, from Beck's communications complex in Berne, they did not know the replies to the two trick signals? So the ship *has* been hi-jacked?'

'I'm sure of it . . .'

'And only two people in England check its progress – yourself and the Minister for External Security, Lance Buckmaster?'

'That's right.'

Romer sipped his wine, looked grim as he put down the glass. 'What I am going to tell you is highly confidential. In my position I hear a lot on the international financial grapevine which never gets into the papers.' He paused. 'World Security is bankrupt. Buckmaster is a megalomaniac. He went on borrowing vast sums for expansion to further his ambition to build one of the ten top companies in the world. He has over-reached himself. He needs about five hundred million pounds to save his company from going under.'

'Where on earth is he going to lay his hands on a sum like that?'

'Not from any of the major banks. They have loaned him too much already.' Again Romer paused, sipped more wine. Tweed remained silent. 'There is one intriguing development, some people might call it sinister.'

'And that is?'

'Through the Narodny Bank, which is, of course, the Russian bank operating in the West, the Soviets have placed in reserve, ready for some huge business deal, the equivalent of five hundred million pounds in gold bullion. The transfer will take place in Switzerland – not through this bank. I just wonder what the Kremlin is buying for such an amount.' Again he paused. 'Unless, in view of what you have told me, you could guess?'

Tweed sat very still. Romer *had* given him the key to the whole bizarre sequence of events. He now knew positively who was behind the murder and rape of Sylvia Harman in his London flat – to get him out of the way. The only question was which of the two men had committed the crime. But for the first time he now knew the *motive*.

38

A world of snow and ice. Horowitz, wearing knee-high fine leather boots, a fur coat and a Russian-style fur hat, walked slowly through the small town of Einsiedeln. High up in the mountains, the old buildings crowded in on the narrow streets. On one side of him walked Stieber, on the other he had Morgan, who had insisted on accompanying them in the car.

'It's bloody cold,' grumbled Morgan and shivered.

The temperature was well below zero. From the roof gutters of the buildings long spear-like icicles were suspended. The snow underfoot was a foot deep, hard-packed by the tread of the locals. A bell began to toll, a sound laden with doom. It was four in the afternoon.

'What the devil's that?' asked Morgan.

'You'll see when we turn this corner,' Horowitz told him.

Women shoppers, well muffled, some with only the top halves of their faces showing above woollen scarves, shuffled along with plastic bags. Turning the corner, the street opened out into a large space with the ground rising behind it steeply. Perched on top was a vast and ancient façade with twin towers.

'The Benedictine monastery,' said Horowitz as the bell continued its mournful dirge.

Morgan suddenly had the premonition of something awful. Around this part of the town the dense forest closed in, branches bent under the weight of frozen snow. Away from the shopping street, it was very quiet, the grim solitude of an Arctic wilderness.

'That is one of the most famous monasteries in all Europe,' Horowitz continued. 'In summer, pilgrims come from everywhere to visit it. The area inside its wall is immense, like an enclosed town cut off from the world.'

A woman dressed in black, her head covered, had climbed the slippery path and pushed open one of the huge double doors. From inside came the sound of singing, again a dirge-like sound. Morgan shuddered again. He hated the atmosphere of this place which reminded him of some huge tomb.

'What is that yodelling?' he asked.

'Not yodelling,' Horowitz chided him. 'That is the monks' choir which sings at this hour each day.' He stooped down to pick up his case from the snow. 'Wait here, Morgan. We are going to reserve rooms in the Hotel St Johann. Unless you are going to stay with us?'

'No,' Morgan said hastily. 'I have to get back to Zürich. I have an international business to run. In case you'd forgotten . . .'

But he was speaking the last sentence into space. Horowitz and Stieber were plodding away with their cases through the snow. Swearing to himself, stamping his frozen feet, Morgan watched them disappear inside a small five-storey building with a grey slate roof. The St Johann.

It was ten minutes before they returned without their cases. In that time Morgan watched a monk emerge from the monastery, a figure clad in a black robe with a cowl pulled over his head to protect himself against the snow which had begun to drift down.

'I have phoned for a taxi to take you back,' Horowitz informed him. 'It should be here soon.'

'A taxi? I'm going back in the Mercedes we parked in the main street . . .'

'No.' Horowitz's tone was firm. 'We need transport when Tweed arrives – so we can follow him.'

'You're confident he will do that?' Morgan demanded while he brushed snow off his coat, his fingers frozen inside his gloves.

'You were, back in Zürich,' Horowitz reminded him. 'And I sense this is the kind of place he has been making for – a remote refuge.'

'Well, enjoy yourselves . . .'

Morgan took a step forward, slipped on a patch of ice which nearly upended him. Recovering his balance, he swore again as a Mercedes taxi stopped close to them. Horowitz handed him a brochure of the St Johann.

'I did a sleight of hand with my passport when registering. I'm staying under the name of Anton Thaler. If you want to call me the phone number is there. You were lucky with the cab – the company they phoned radioed to one just on its way back to Zürich. And you can see why I told you not to bring your Walkman louts up here – they'd stand out like clowns.'

'See you,' mumbled Morgan, 'and I'll collect the chauffeur from the parked car on the main street.'

He collapsed into the rear seat of the taxi, sighed with relief at the warmth, and thanked God he was returning to Zürich from this benighted wilderness.

Horowitz smiled as the taxi departed. 'I think our esteemed friend is glad to be on his way to civilization. What is it, Stieber?'

The German was staring at several monks leaving the monastery clad in their black robes and cowls.

'I just had an idea,' he said. 'Doesn't matter now. What do we do next?'

'Wait for Tweed.'

At police headquarters in Zürich, after listening to Romer's call to him, Beck put down the phone and looked at Tweed as he stood up.

'I'm going downstairs to make arrangements for transport to take you up to Einsiedeln – and then on to Brunni. That was Colonel Romer, and you convinced him at least.'

'But not you?' Tweed commented quizzically.

'I'll be back in a few minutes . . .'

'Could we use your phone? To call London?'

'Go ahead . . .'

'And,' Newman interjected, 'where is this place, Brunni?'

'At the end of the world,' Tweed told him.

'In that case,' Newman continued, gazing at Beck, 'I'd like a weapon to guard Tweed. There have already been two attempts to assassinate him. A juggernaut tried to drive him down on the autobahn near Freiburg. Then a bomb was placed under his car in the Black Forest.'

'And I can confirm both attempts,' Paula said. 'Because on both occasions I was there.'

Beck's expression froze. 'Why on earth didn't you tell this to me earlier?'

'Would you have believed it in Berne?' Tweed challenged him. 'I thought it would have sounded too dramatic, that I was bolstering my story.'

'What weapon had you in mind?' Beck asked Newman.

'Something like a Magnum .45. Preferably just that. With plenty of spare ammo.'

'And I'd like a Browning,' Paula chimed in. 'You know I've experience with the gun.'

'Plus temporary permits to carry the weapons,' Newman added.

'I'll have to think about it. I'll be back within ten minutes . . .'

Tweed drank more coffee. It will be coming out of my ears, he thought. He looked at Newman.

'It's time we had back-up. I sense a climax is coming. Up in the mountains. Can you call Howard? Ask him to fly out Harry Butler and Pete Nield to Zürich immediately? They

397

can take rooms at the Schweizerhof, wait there for further instructions. They may catch the last flight tonight.'

'I'm sure Howard will play. I talked about using them when I saw him in London. I'll call him now – before Beck gets back.'

While he made the call Paula moved closer to Tweed.

'Surely with that evidence you told me about in Sprüngli that Bob found in Basle – plus the diary I took from the flat in Rennweg. And plus the fact that we've now identified the dead girl in your flat – and can link her with World Security. Surely with all that we could return to London and prove your innocence?'

'It's all circumstantial. And I have to solve the problem of *Shockwave*. That takes priority over everything. Beck has now agreed to provide a mobile transmitter. I have to contact the *Lampedusa* again, make sure she's been hijacked.'

'Can't that wait until we reach London?' she persisted.

'It cannot! I'm convinced that vessel with its vital cargo is on its way to Russia. We're racing against time to stop it.'

'And how are you going to do that?'

'I have no idea yet,' he admitted as Newman put down the receiver.

'Butler and Nield will be on the first flight here,' he reported. 'Officially they'll be helping to track you down. Howard is playing it clever with Buckmaster . . .'

He broke off as Beck entered the office, carrying a large hold-all. He dumped it on his desk, thrust his hand inside and it came out holding a Browning .32 automatic. He handed it to Paula who checked that the safety catch was on, released the magazine and checked that there wasn't one up the spout. She shoved the magazine back inside the butt, slipped the weapon inside her shoulder bag. Beck had watched her.

'If you hadn't done that I'd have taken it off you,' he said with a wintry smile. 'Here are spare mags.' He reached inside the hold-all again, brought out a Magnum .45, gave it to Newman.

'Here's your cannon. Plus spare ammo. And for each of you a temporary permit to carry firearms.' Beck leaned against his desk and looked severe. 'I may tell you I wouldn't have supplied weapons, but I made a quick call to Chief Inspector Otto Kuhlmann. He confirmed that there was a pile-up on the autobahn outside Freiburg. Tweed, what was the name of the informant you said lured you to the Cheshire Cheese pub in London?'

'Richter. Klaus Richter. Lives in Freiburg . . .'

'Kuhlmann also told me they found the body of a Klaus Richter – in his Freiburg apartment. A case of murder.'

'I see. And the mobile transceiver?' Tweed prodded.

'Already on its way to Einsiedeln. Concealed inside a plain van carrying on the outside the name of a Zürich builder, Ingold. The driver will park outside the monastery and wait for you. I thought it wiser if you travelled up there in a car without the van tagging on. The codeword for contact with my driver is simple – Limmat. He'll then go where you tell him to.'

'And where is this Brunni you mentioned earlier?' asked Newman.

'A tiny summer resort at the end of a remote valley. Brunni,' he repeated, 'not Brunnen, which is near the capital of the Schwyz canton. We have a chalet there where we have kept key witnesses in hiding. The driver of your car, Georg, will unlock the place for you.'

'What about food and tea and coffee – provisions to keep us alive?' asked Paula.

'I was coming to that. You won't get anything in Zürich now. In any case I don't want any of you wandering around the city again. There are good cooking facilities at the chalet which is regularly cleaned. And only a very few locals live there in winter.'

'The food,' Paula persisted.

'As you drive into Einsiedeln there's a small super-market to your left – it stays open late and you'll be able to get anything you need there.'

'Then what are we waiting for?' Tweed asked.

'Nothing more. The car is waiting for you outside. Tanner is downstairs and will escort you to it. There's a phone in the chalet. Keep in touch. This whole business worries me.'

'And what do you think it does to us?' Paula asked.

Horowitz stood by the window of the room he'd reserved at the St Johann. He'd asked for a room at the front and now he stood with Stieber alongside him, a pair of night binoculars pressed against his eyes. His steel-rimmed spectacles rested on top of a chest of drawers as he examined the van which had parked opposite the monastery.

'It's a builder's van,' he remarked. 'Some Zürich company called Ingold. Why he's parked there at this time in the evening I can't imagine.'

He lowered his binoculars, replaced them with his spectacles. The window gave an excellent view of the great hulk of the monastery with the open space in front of it. Horowitz bit his lip and went to the phone.

'We need reinforcements,' he decided.

He dialled the World Security number, asked to speak to Gareth Morgan. The operator wasn't sure whether he had left the building. A minute later Morgan's voice, irritable, came on the line.

'Who is it?'

'You can guess who is talking.' Horowitz paused. 'I have now surveyed the territory and need extra manpower. It must be your top men. Professionals. I emphasize that. And they must come up here on motor-cycles equipped with radios. And tooled up. I expect them to arrive within one hour . . .'

'That's impossible . . .'

'Then make it possible. I'm not prepared to argue the point. Call them at their homes. I know you have men who are skilled motor-cyclists. The leader reports to me, Anton Thaler, at the St Johann as soon as the team arrives.'

'Tooled up, you said.' Morgan made his final protest. 'This is Switzerland.'

'My knowledge of geography is pretty good, too. One hour from now . . .'

Horowitz broke the connection. Stieber, his round head damp with sweat from the high temperature of the heating, stared at Horowitz.

'You usually work alone. Why the motor-cyclists?'

'Because I am not sure we know Tweed's final destination. We need outriders to scour the whole area. Of course, when the final confrontation comes, I shall be alone.'

39

Latitude 32. 10. N. Longitude 21. 30. W. The *SS Helvetia* – formerly *SS Lampedusa* – was steaming through heavy seas well south-east of the Azores in the Atlantic. It was late afternoon, the cloud overcast was threatening, and Greg Singer, late of the SAS, was in the hold. Beside him stood Captain Hartmann.

'It's a huge brute,' Singer observed as he gazed up at the giant computer *Shockwave*. 'I suppose it won't shift in this swell?'

'They protected it against all weathers,' Hartmann replied.

Shockwave, its immense face exposed at the front, was packed on the other three sides, at its base and the top, inside a wall of six-inch timber. The base was reinforced with steel.

Singer, leaning against the outer hull to hold his balance, watched as the vessel swayed. *Shockwave* appeared to be totally stable. Singer's great fear was that it would break loose, smashing its incredible weight against the hull.

'How long now before we pass through the Straits of Gibraltar into the Med?' Singer asked.

'If this weather continues, it may be several days. If it improves, we may move through the Straits earlier. I cannot predict . . .'

Singer swore to himself as he followed Hartmann up the ladder out of the hold. All these bloody skippers were like that: they wouldn't commit themselves. In its approach to Gibraltar, the *Helvetia* was still following a devious course to keep clear of the commercial sea lanes.

'I'll go see Hoch,' Singer said as they stepped into the passageway, 'then join you on the bridge.'

It never occurred to Singer that Hoch, the radio op. was the sole survivor of the massacre of the *Lampedusa*'s original crew. That was a detail which belonged to the past. Singer reckoned he had Hoch under his control – psychologically as well as physically. He had warned the American that his wife and family on Cape Cod in the eastern United States were under constant surveillance.

'One code-word from me and on a dark night that nice frame house of yours will go up in flames – with no exit for those inside. They'll roast to death, Hoch. When they reach the bodies they'll find cinders . . .'

Hoch, a lean-faced man with a strong jaw, had regarded Singer with pure hatred. Now Singer nodded to the armed guard outside the radio room, opened the door and walked inside. A second guard, a pistol in his hand, sat facing Hoch who was perched at the edge of his bunk.

'Just to remind you once again, Hoch,' Singer told him, 'we have the code-books. When London contacts you again you'll behave yourself, won't you?'

Hoch merely nodded. They might have the code-books but he carried inside his head the two trick questions and answers. The odd thing was Monitor had only contacted him once so far, and it was Monitor who had posed the trick queries in his signal. Hoch, nerving himself, had not replied with the correct answers.

Hoch didn't really grasp what was going on in London. The other contact, Prefect, contacted him daily – but never once had he introduced the trick words. It was almost as though Monitor was the only man who knew them. He wished to God Monitor could contact him again.

Tweed, seated in the back of the Mercedes, gazed out as the car moved along the highway above the southern shore of Lake Zürich. It was a clear cold night. On the opposite shore lights of towns glittered like stars fallen to earth. By his side sat Paula, still seething over Beck's apparent lack of total trust. Beyond her Newman, the Magnum nestled inside the hip holster Beck had also supplied, was asleep. Georg, their driver, opened the glass screen dividing him from the rear compartment.

'This is where we turn off up into the mountains to Einsiedeln.'

Despite the heavy snow-covering Georg swung the car skilfully off the main highway and they began to climb a steep and twisting road into lonely country.

'I thought Beck had more faith in us,' Paula burst out after Georg had closed the screen.

'He's in a difficult position,' Tweed squeezed her arm. 'I think if I were in his position I'd be equally cautious. He can't be one hundred per cent convinced of my innocence yet.'

'You should have showed him the photo of Sylvia Harman . . .'

'And admitted we had made two break-ins? Bob in Basle and the two of you in Harman's apartment in Zürich? The Swiss regard burglary of private property with the same severity as murder. I'd have put him in an impossible position.'

'I suppose you're right.' She sounded edgy. 'Don't forget to remind Georg to stop at that supermarket in Einsiedeln. We must have provisions. There'll be nothing at that chalet.'

'Don't worry. I told him before we left. Relax . . .'

As they continued climbing the tortuous road a team of motor-cyclists overtook them, moving over the icy surface at high speed. Tweed automatically counted six of them. Sinister figures clad in black leather with helmets and snow-goggles. He also noted each driver had an aerial for radio transmission spearing up from behind his saddle.

'Lunatics,' Paula commented. 'Riding at that speed on roads like this.'

'Youth will have its mad fling,' Tweed commented.

'They didn't look all that young to me,' remarked Newman, who had been woken by the zoom-zoom of the powerful machines.

As they entered Einsiedeln they passed the *Bahnhof* on their left, the end of the single-track railway from Zürich. Georg pulled up in the near-deserted main street in front of the supermarket. Tweed turned to Paula.

'It will take you a little while to do your shopping. Do you mind if we drop you here, then drive on to where the mobile transmitter van should be parked? And, Georg, could you go with her as bodyguard? Good. How long do we have, Paula?'

'Thirty minutes at least. It's not the shopping – finding where everything is in a strange supermarket takes the time. It's all right – I've got enough money. See you . . .'

Newman took over the wheel, they drove on and the snow was deeper; drifts were piled up on either side of the road. The car turned a corner and the monastery came into view.

'Park here,' said Tweed. 'That looks like the van.'

'I'm coming with you,' Newman said, struggling into his coat as Tweed slipped on his own topcoat. 'This could be hostile territory.'

Standing by his hotel window Horowitz stiffened, snatched up his binoculars, focused them on the Ingold van. Two men were facing him, talking to the driver. One familiar face came up so clearly he could see light reflecting from a lamp in the street off the lenses of the horn-rim spectacles. A face familiar from his study of photos, of the film of a man who had crossed the Rhine at Laufenburg. *Tweed*.

'What is it?' asked Stieber.

Behind him stood a figure clad in black leather, holding a motor-cyclist's helmet. Bruno Zeller, leader of the team.

'Shut up!' said Horowitz.

His blank expression concealed his excitement, the exhilaration of the chase when he was hunting a target. This was his first live sighting of Tweed. The brilliant Deputy Director of the British Secret Service. The wily man who had eluded the ambush on the Freiburg auto-bahn, the man who later had escaped the bomb he'd personally placed beneath the Audi. The man who seemed to have gone out of his way to advertise the trail of his flight to Switzerland. He looked so mild.

Horowitz swivelled the binoculars a fraction to the other man. Robert Newman. You're a long way from Basle, my friend, he thought. So now the clan gathers. Excellent. He lowered the binoculars, handed them to the motor-cyclist.

'Zeller, study the smaller man by that builder's van. Then the second man. You'll have to follow them – without them knowing.'

'Who is it?' asked Stieber impatiently.

'Tweed himself at long last. The taller man is Robert Newman, the foreign correspondent. A dangerous man who, according to the file I read, has worked closely with Tweed in the past.'

Stieber, unable to conceal his exultation, unlike Horowitz who had spoken in an offhand manner, slapped his ample thigh.

'We've got him! Why don't you take him now?'

Horowitz gave him a scornful glance. 'First the range is too great. Second we'd never escape in time. Or have you forgotten? We're up in the mountains. Only two ways out. Back to Zürich or along a precipice road to Brunnen.'

'What are we going to do then? Morgan will be furious—'

'Morgan can put his head in a bucket of cold water. We wait. This is not the end of their journey.'

Tweed, hands thrust into his coat pockets, was wandering slowly back and forth across the open space in front of the monastery. Newman caught him up, glancing all round. First he checked the few parked cars. Then he scanned the hotels and restaurants.

'What the devil are you doing?' he demanded. 'Strolling about in the open. A perfect target for a sniperscope rifle.'

'I don't think so.' Tweed was watching his footing on the treacherous slope. 'That photo Marler took in Freiburg near World Security's HQ. Armand Horowitz. Europe's top assassin. Reputed to have killed fifteen men. And not a jot of evidence against him. He's very careful. My guess is he's here now.'

'Then . . .'

'Wait, Bob. You heard Turpil reporting my presence to Morgan in Shopville before his macabre death. The fact that he also mentioned Einsieden. This information will be

406

known by now to Horowitz. But if he attempted to kill me here how far would he get? One phone call from you and Beck would have road-blocks surrounding the whole area. And Horowitz could not escape across the mountains. In the snow? Impossible. He'll know all this. And if possible I want him to see me.'

'In God's name why?'

'So he'll walk into the trap I'm setting for him. That is why I wanted an isolated hideout in the mountains. A cul-de-sac. No way out.'

Tweed and Newman had disappeared from view as Horowitz paced his room. Zeller had left, to instruct his team. Horowitz was frowning, had an abstracted look. Stieber shifted restlessly in a chair.

'Something wrong?'

'Yes. Again with Tweed's behaviour. He puzzles me, and if I don't understand something it worries me. He spent five minutes wandering about in the open, almost as though he was deliberately showing himself. The same pattern as in Laufenburg – on the bridge, at the station. Even in Zürich he puts up at the obvious hotel. What game is he playing?'

'I just hope we don't lose him.'

'Zeller and his team won't lose him. And they can contact us by radio in the Mercedes. We'll go to the car now and wait for news. I don't think it will be long coming.'

'We haven't eaten for hours,' Stieber complained and rubbed a hand over his ample stomach.

'You have a genius for stating the obvious,' Horowitz told him.

Newman drove Tweed the short distance back to the supermarket. Paula, avoiding the sub-zero temperature, was waiting just inside the entrance with Georg and a collection of carrier bags. Tweed and Newman got out, helped Georg to carry the provisions to the car. Paula dived into the rear of the Mercedes and glowed in the warmth. While Georg slipped behind the wheel, Tweed pointed out to Newman a signpost to the left. *Apthal*.

'The road to Brunni . . .'

They soon left Einsiedeln behind and the narrow road ran straight through a wilderness of snow and forest. Paula was reminded of the Black Forest after they had passed through the hamlet of Apthal – in the headlights the black firs closed in on both sides. To the left below the unfenced road ran a small river. The headlight beams shone on it as they turned round a sharp curve. The river was frozen solid, a tumble of wavelets formed of ice and frozen waterfalls.

'This is a pretty lonely area,' Paula commented and pulled her coat collar closer.

'Where we're going,' said Tweed, 'under the Mythen, it's the end of the road. I was here once years ago for a few days.'

'The Mythen?'

'A mountain few foreigners ever see. A magic mountain.'

'Now you're being fanciful . . .'

'But I'm not being fanciful when I say we're being followed.'

It was Newman who had spoken as once again he glanced through the rear window. He still had his coat unbelted and open so he could reach the Magnum quickly. He glanced back once more.

'Do we want the actual chalet where we're staying located?' he asked Tweed.

'Preferably not. Who is following?'

'A motor-cyclist. Like one of those who passed us on the way up to Einsiedeln.'

'I don't think we can ask Georg to drive any faster.'

The Mercedes was speeding over the dangerous surface which shone like glass in the headlights. Newman tapped on the window and Georg opened the screen.

'Mind if I take over the driving now?'

'As you wish. Mr Beck said I was under your orders,' he replied in German.

'Then pull up for a moment and I'll take the wheel. You sit alongside me . . .'

The raw intense cold hit him like a hammer as he climbed out of the car and looked back. The pinpoint of light which was the motor-cyclist's front lamp was stationary. A giveaway. Now he was certain. He got behind the wheel, waited until Georg had fastened his seat belt, then left the engine running and lit a cigarette.

'What are you doing?' Tweed called out.

'A battle of wills. Will he wait there all night in these freezing temperatures – or will he decide to follow from in front . . .'

He had hardly finished the words when the motor-cyclist came speeding up behind them, overtook slowly, and then rode ahead. Newman began driving at speed. The motor-cycle swung round a steep curve, skidded, recovered its balance. Newman pressed his foot down. Paula tensed. Tweed leaned forward, intrigued by Newman's tactics. He drew, alongside the motor-cyclist, swung the wheel, tipped the motor-cycle. The machine spun wildly off the road, the rider somersaulted as his machine hit the ice of the frozen river. The motor-cycle skidded for a few yards, met an obstacle, a small waterfall of ice, its momentum vaulted it into the air and then it fell back with a crumping crash. The rider, sprawled on his back, slithered a short distance over the ice, turned painfully on his side.

'You've got a bad memory,' Newman told Georg as he drove on.

'Why? Did something happen?' Georg asked.

40

The Mythen.

The mountain looked enormous by the light of a rising moon. Its slopes, shrouded in deep snow, towered over the scatter of chalets which was Brunni in the valley below. The Mercedes was moving slowly as Horowitz peered out, first at one side, then the other.

'I thought we'd spot where they'd made for by the wheels of their car in the snow,' he observed.

'But there are so many recent turn-offs,' Stieber replied as he drove the vehicle even more slowly.

'There can't have been so much traffic in this isolated spot at this time of the year, at this hour of the night,' said Horowitz.

There were wheel tracks leading off the road in all directions, leading to the chalets dotted about the lower slopes. Horowitz was perplexed. He had no way of knowing that Newman, approaching the end of the road, had deliberately driven off the road at many points, then carefully backed the car on to the road through the same ruts without altering the angle of the wheel.

'We spent too much time trying to get some sense out of the injured motor-cyclist who ended up in the river bed,' Horowitz decided.

'He did manage to tell us the Tweed car rammed him off into the river,' Stieber recalled.

'And bearing in mind where we found him – that it was beyond Apthal – Tweed and his friends must have driven as far as Brunni,' Horowitz insisted. 'They

410

have to be hiding in one of these chalets.'

'A few of them have lights on behind drawn curtains. Why don't we call at each place and see who is inside?'

'Because Tweed is not so foolish as to permit anyone to turn on the lights. He has to be concealed inside one of the chalets without lights . . .'

'Then what are we going to do?'

'We drive back to Apthal and talk to Zeller. By now he must have called up a car to take that injured motor-cyclist to hospital. This is a cul-de-sac. The road ends by that cable station which takes skiers up the mountain. Tweed is trapped.'

From behind the dormer window in the unlighted room on the first floor of the chalet, Newman watched the Mercedes turn in the road and head back towards Einsiedeln. He went downstairs to where all the lights were turned on behind closed curtains, put his night glasses on a table.

'That car had Horowitz inside it. And I'm pretty sure the driver was the same round-headed thug I saw watching at the frontier crossing in Basle. They've driven away.'

'So you were right,' Paula said to Tweed. 'With our decision to put on the lights. I thought you were crazy.'

'There are enough other chalets with lights on. I imagined it would be Horowitz who would come to spy out the land for himself. He'd assume we were inside one of the many chalets without lights. There, that's burning nicely.'

He stood up from the log fire they had found laid, which he had lit and was now crackling and flaming. He rubbed his hands together.

'But don't forget it was a clever idea of Bob's to drive up to all those other chalets and make wheel tracks in the snow. That must have confused them more than somewhat.'

Paula still wearing her coat, sleeves folded up, shivered.

'It's like an ice-box in here. I'll be glad when that fire warms us up. And, by the way, a meal will be ready shortly. Thank heaven they have electric power even out here – and an electric cooker in the kitchen.'

'That's the Swiss for you. All home comforts laid on for us.'

'But what's the next move?' Newman asked. 'We must expect an attack at any time now Horowitz has appeared.'

'Use the phone, report to Arthur Beck that elements of World Security have appeared in Brunni. Meantime I'm going to the van parked in the barn at the back to call the *Lampedusa* on the mobile transceiver.'

Georg, the driver, opened his leather coat and exposed the gun he wore inside a hip holster. 'I'll come with you, if that's all right, Mr Tweed.'

'Be my guest . . .'

'And what about the meal?' Paula protested. 'I suppose you want me to slow it down?'

'You always could read my mind,' said Tweed and smiled as she marched off to the kitchen, head in the air.

Latitude 35. 20 N. Longitude 10. 0. W. Twilight fell over a sea the colour of deep purple. The offshore winds carried a faint musky aroma from the invisible coast of Africa to the east. The *SS Helvetia* was sailing at full speed across an ocean as smooth as a summertime pond.

In the radio room Hoch was receiving – and responding to – the signal from Prefect. By his side sat a seaman who had a reasonable grasp of Morse code. Behind him stood Greg Singer, holding a Luger pistol.

Hoch, tense inwardly, was calm outwardly as he attended to his job and wondered why Prefect never inserted the two trick questions. He completed the transmission, signed off, sagged back in his chair. The seaman by his side nodded approval to Singer, stood up and left the cramped cabin.

'That's a good boy. Now you can have your dinner,' said Singer and walked to the door.

He was opening the door when a fresh transmission started to come through. The American, Hoch, scribbled a note on his pad. Singer ran back, read it. *Signal now from Monitor.* Singer rushed to the doorway, peered down the deserted passageway. The seaman who understood some Morse had disappeared. Singer swore, closed the door, went back to the transmitter, stood over Hoch with his Luger as the radio op communicated.

Hoch responded to the innocent questions. Then came through what he had been waiting for.

'Are you still proceeding on schedule? And how is Tray?'

'We are proceeding on schedule,' Hoch replied. 'End of reply.'

'Is the cargo in good condition? And my regards to White.'

The reply to which should have been a reference to Cowes in the Isle of Wight. Hoch responded.

'The cargo is in excellent condition. Last part of your signal unclear.'

'Signing off. I will call you again as arranged. My regards also to North . . .'

Hoch removed his headset. He turned in his swivel chair and looked up at Singer. The ex-SAS man was watching him with a suspicious expression.

'Why would Monitor suddenly contact us again? We haven't had a signal from him for a while – and then only one. But Prefect signals us daily. What's going on?'

Hoch shrugged. 'I could guess.'

Singer placed the muzzle of the Luger against Hoch's skull and grinned. 'Then guess. And you'd better guess good.'

413

'Two possibilities. One, Monitor has been sick. Second, it's part of the intense security. First a signal from Prefect – then a signal from Monitor from the same transmitter. Just the kind of double-check they made earlier when I was aboard the *Lampedusa*.'

'You guessed good,' said Singer.

He nodded towards the bunk and when Hoch had lain down on it he fastened the handcuff to Hoch's wrist. The other cuff was attached to an iron leg screwed to the deck. Singer left the cabin and met a guard on his way to the bridge.

'Go to the radio op's room and keep an eye on Hoch,' he ordered.

It was very nearly dark when he reached the bridge. The *Helvetia* appeared to be gliding across the surface of the ocean. Captain Hartmann turned to watch Singer as he walked up to the skipper.

'When do we pass through the Straits of Gibraltar?' Singer demanded.

'In the middle of the night. When the lookouts are trying to stop falling asleep. By morning we shall be well inside the Mediterranean.'

'On the last lap. Turkey here we come.'

In London Lance Buckmaster returned from the special room at the Admiralty where he had just communicated with the ship at sea using his code-name, Prefect.

Arriving after dark at the Ministry building he ran up the staircase to his office. It took him only a few minutes to tap out the brief memo to the PM on his typewriter. He read it quickly, initialled it with his flamboyant 'B', put it inside an envelope, sealed the envelope, addressed it: *Highly Confidential. Personal attention of the Prime Minister*, called a messenger and told him to place it direct into the hands of the PM.

414

As with his previous memos on the subject, it was terse and to the point:

1930 hours. Contacted North. Cargo proceeding according to schedule.

Tweed was frozen stiff as he closed the padlocks on the outside of the barn door. Inside the building was the van containing the mobile transceiver he had used to contact the *Lampedusa*. Georg, who had provided the keys for the padlocks, stood beside him, glancing round.

The incredible silence of the night in Brunni was like a sinister pall pressing down on them. Tweed stamped his feet in the snow and paused on their way back to the chalet close by. In the moonlight the immense cone of the Grosse Mythen – the Big Mythen – loomed above them like a threat.

To the right of the 6,000-foot-high mountain rose the Little Mythen, a twin-peaked giant. Little? Its snow-covered slopes soared into the night. There were far higher mountains in Switzerland, Tweed reflected, but isolated above the dead end of the valley, the mountains seemed immense.

'They're dangerous,' Georg remarked in German.

'Why? How?'

'The exceptional weight of snow which has fallen. And with only a slight rise in temperature the danger would increase. The danger of a major avalanche.'

'Let's get inside, it's cold . . .'

The four of them were settled at the table, eating ravenously, when Paula asked Tweed how he had managed with the transceiver.

'You look pretty grim,' she added.

'I contacted the *Lampedusa* more easily than I expected – considering how hemmed in we are by mountains. The

415

news is bad. The ship has definitely been hi-jacked. The radio op didn't respond to either of the trick questions.'

'You're worried, naturally.'

'I'm very worried about what may have happened to the original crew. This is a ruthless opposition we're fighting.'

'One thing I can't understand,' Paula continued. 'Something I've been going to ask you before. Why on earth did the PM agree to *Shockwave* being transported by sea? The Americans have giant cargo planes – one of them surely is big enough to have flown the computer across the Atlantic?'

'The answer is simple.' Tweed's tone became vague and his eyes were half-closed. 'Buckmaster insisted using a plane was unsafe. Planes crash. The PM accepted his argument. Simple as that.'

'Really?' interjected Newman. They were talking in English so Georg wouldn't understand what they were saying. 'Simple you said? Then, if the PM trusts Buckmaster so much, why did she arrange for you also to check the *Lampedusa*'s progress? And why did she agree that only you – not Buckmaster – would know the trick questions to put to the radio op?'

'Normal security precaution,' Tweed replied with the same vagueness. 'Now, let's finish our meal.'

'When we have,' Newman suggested, 'I'd like to phone Marler at his flat in London. If I can get hold of him I want to find out what he's up to back home.'

'Do it,' said Tweed, who spoke as though his mind were miles away.

'And I'd better check with the Schweizerhof in case Harry Butler and Pete Nield have arrived. We do need reinforcements.'

'Do it,' Tweed repeated. 'If they're there, tell them to contact Beck at police headquarters.'

'What on earth for?' asked Paula.

'Just do it,' Tweed repeated again.

416

'What's that noise?' Newman asked suddenly and jumped up from the table.

He dashed up the open staircase leading to the first floor in the dark. Without switching on any lights he fumbled his way to the bedroom at the front with the large dormer window. He opened the door, slipped inside. The chug-chug of an approaching helicopter was much louder, heading straight for Brunni.

Newman peered out of the uncurtained window and stared. A Sikorsky was hovering over Brunni no more than a hundred feet up. The moonlight shone off its fuselage. An unmarked machine. Like an evil great bird it maintained its hover, rotors whirling, motionless in mid-air.

Newman moved back to the side of the window. The occupants of the machine could be using night glasses. The machine began to move forward slowly, heading for the Mythen. With great skill the pilot turned away from the cliff-like walls which meant death to the machine, cruised slowly over the chalets, then flew off back down the valley towards Einsiedeln.

At a remote sector of Kloten Airport outside Zürich four Sikorsky helicopters were drawn up on the tarmac. Men in leather jackets and heavy trousers tucked inside knee-length boots, were boarding the machines.

Morgan sat inside a Mercedes with Horowitz alongside him. Behind the wheel sat Stieber, clad similarly to the men climbing inside the helicopters. The engine of the car was running and, at Morgan's insistence, the heaters were turned full up.

'What do you hope to achieve by this airborne attack force?' Horowitz enquired ironically.

'They are all trained skiers. Their equipment went aboard earlier. In case of casualties, they're all wearing German clothes and carry no identification. I have thought this out to the last detail.' Morgan was unable to conceal the satisfaction in his voice. He tapped the phone by his side. 'I am now waiting for word from Zeller that he has located the chalet where Tweed and his colleagues are hiding out. We'll wait for days, if necessary.' He gave Horowitz a sideways glance. 'I'm just wondering what you are doing for the big fat fee we're paying you . . .'

Horowitz's left hand gripped Morgan's right wrist. It felt like a steel manacle, screwed tight. Morgan had trouble not wincing. Horowitz's voice was a soft whisper.

'I'm not accustomed to taking personal insults lying down.'

'Sorry. Maybe I didn't phrase that very diplomatically. I withdraw the remark.'

He flexed his fingers as Horowitz released the grip. The assassin continued in the whispering tone so Stieber couldn't hear him.

'I am waiting patiently for Tweed to make one slip. Sooner or later they always make a slip.'

'Tweed has walked into a trap,' Morgan asserted, trying to recover his position. 'Brunni is a cul-de-sac. No way out. Except one road back to Einsiedeln. No route over the top of the mountains at this time of the year . . .'

'I was there,' Horowitz reminded him. 'I was the one who described the geography to Zeller. And someone is walking into a trap.'

Newman came back from the kitchen where he had used the extension phone to avoid Georg overhearing him. He sat at the table and drank fresh coffee poured by Paula.

'Thanks. That's better.' He looked at Tweed. 'I managed to contact Harry Butler at the Schweizerhof. He'd just flown in with Pete Nield. They're going to see Beck first at police HQ. Then they're coming up here right away on motor-cycles – courtesy of Beck. Harry called him while I waited. They're going to wait by the ski-lift at the end of the road until I fetch them. I didn't trust an open phone to

418

give them our exact location.'

'You've done well . . .'

'That's not all. I called Marler and caught him at his flat just before he left. Had a very intriguing conversation with him. Howard has given him a photocopy of the report by the pathologist who examined the dead girl in your flat. It showed traces of skin and blood under one of her fingernails. Same type which stained the sheet. She was group O Positive. You're blood group A, if I remember?' He continued as Tweed nodded, watching him intently. 'The blood group of the stain on the sheet – and under her fingernail – was a rare blood group, AB Negative. The murderer's blood group. All we're needing now is the girl's identity, Marler said.'

'You told him?' Tweed enquired. 'About Sylvia Harman. The call girl from Rennweg, Zürich?'

'No. Never said a word. I still have a funny feeling about Marler. He said you could come home now. Wanted to know where you are. I said somewhere in Europe.'

'Then in God's name why are we staying here any longer?' exclaimed Paula.

'Because we need Arthur Beck's full cooperation,' Tweed told her, 'and he's still not convinced of my innocence. But a full-scale attack on me here *will* convince him.'

'We could fly back,' she protested.

'I'd risk it myself. Alone. But we're dealing with ruthless professionals. Don't forget Armand Horowitz. If he did find out I was flying back he's quite capable of putting a bomb aboard the flight. I can't risk the lives of innocent passengers.'

'Then let's use trains,' she pressed.

'Bombs have been placed on trains. In Italy and other places.'

'Then how the devil do we get back when the time comes?'

'Only one way. And for that we need Beck.'

She turned to Newman. 'I think you're wrong about Marler.'

41

Marler left his London flat after the call from Newman. It was dark as he drove his Porsche to the Buckmaster flat in Belgravia. He was careful to park a good hundred yards from the entrance and in a side street. Leonora answered the speakphone and released the front door.

Half an hour later he smoked a cigarette in her bed as she disappeared into the bathroom wearing only a flimsy silk slip. She had attended to her blonde hair he had mussed up when she reappeared and slipped back under the sheets.

'Have you got a girl friend?' she asked after lighting her own cigarette.

He considered his reply. Unmarried, the love of his life was his Porsche and his independence. He did have girl friends in half a dozen countries in Europe. Variety was the spice of life.

'You're my girl friend,' he said eventually. 'Are you sure we won't be interrupted by an outraged husband?'

'Lance is down on Dartmoor. He flew there early this evening. He has his fun. Why shouldn't I have mine?'

'How did you know that?' he enquired as she slid her naked arm under his back.

'I employed detectives to follow him . . .'

'Dangerous. He's an expert on security.'

'We all spy on each other. People think spies are foreign agents after another country's secrets. But I spy on Lance, and he spies on me. I had the devil of a job to shake the man who was following me this evening, but I managed it. He thinks I'm still back in Threadneedle Street. I left on the lights in my office before I sneaked off to meet you. Have you not realized how many wives spy on their husbands? They check their suits for the wrong hairs, go through their pockets for theatre tickets. And husbands do the same thing with their wives. They notice when their woman spends a lot of extra time on her make-up before she goes out on her own. Suspicion rears its lovely head. And a woman gets to know her husband so well she can tell from his expression when he's been up to something. Because she watches him – *spies* on him.'

If a lot of marriages are like this thank God I'm single, Marler was thinking. She laid her head on his shoulder.

'Did you bring that compromising photograph you promised to give me? The one with Lance lying on a couch with the girl? You did promise.'

'Yes. It's in my jacket. I'll give it to you after I've been to the bathroom. And I suggest you get dressed.'

He closed the bathroom door and heaved a great sigh. Anything to get away from that coaxing, insinuating voice. He knew she might well now be going through his jacket. Let her. He'd checked carefully before he'd left his flat. In his wallet all she'd find would be the fake card showing he was a senior executive of the General & Cumbria Assurance Company, the cover for the SIS.

When he returned she had dressed. She was sitting in front of her dressing-table mirrors, brushing her golden hair. His jacket over the back of a chair was not in exactly the same position as he'd left it. He put on his clothes very quickly. Extracting the envelope from his jacket, he took out the photograph, using a handkerchief to avoid leaving fingertips. She was absorbed in repairing her make-up.

'The photo's on the bed. Are you going to use it?'

'What do you think? Time I scared the louse. I'll say

I've got several copies – and how would the tabloid press like to see it?'

'Up to you,' he warned. 'But if you do go ahead show him it in a public place, a restaurant full of people.'

'My!' She swung round on her stool with a radiant smile. 'You're feeling protective towards me. That really is most sweet of you, Marler.'

Stuff it, he thought, but she was going on again in the same syrupy tone.

'Surely you don't think Lance is capable of violence towards a woman?'

The remark hit him like a blow in the solar plexus. It was so obviously a serious question masked by a whimsical tone. His mind flashed back to what had happened in Tweed's flat. He kept his expression blank.

'I just think he has a hair-trigger temper and you'd be much wiser to have any confrontation in a public place – if you must have one.'

'Don't forget what I said about the managing directorship of World Security. It could become vacant soon. I'm getting really pissed off with that horrid Gareth Morgan. Kiss me again before you go. And think about my offer . . .'

Marler stood on the steps of the portico of the old building with a Georgian façade before he descended onto the pavement. It was because he paused that he saw the small man standing in the portico on the opposite side of the street, a man standing well back and holding something up to his eyes with both hands.

Marler glanced both ways as he hurried down the steps, saw no one as snow began to fall. At speed he continued straight over to the building on the far side. The swiftness of his movement caught the little man off guard. He backed, tried to enter the building, pushing open the door to the empty entrance hall.

Marler followed him, grabbed his right arm above and

422

below the elbow, pressing his fingers into the nerve centres. The little man, a camera dangling from a strap round his neck, yelped with pain as Marler manoeuvred him inside the hall.

'Make any more noise, try to get free, and I'll break your arm. For no extra charge I'll make it a compound fracture.'

It was the calm, chilling tone of Marler's voice as much as the pain which petrified the man. He stood very still while Marler whispered in his ear.

'Now tell me. Who are you? Who hired you to take my picture?'

Marler waited. He was confident he knew the answer to the second question. If the right answer didn't come up he'd have to exert more pressure; maybe break one arm to start with. The little man, illuminated by a dim wall sconce, had a pasty complexion, a shifty expression, and his suit was frayed at the lapels. He gasped out the words.

'Halbert. Of Halbert Investigations. A private detective.'

Holding him with one hand, Marler reached into his breast pocket. He hauled out a wallet, told the little man to extract the contents with his free arm. With trembling fingers the man found a grubby printed card, showed it to Marler.

Halbert Investigations. Willy Halbert. With an address in Clerkenwell. Not exactly the most high-class district in London. Marler tucked the card inside his own pocket.

'I asked who hired you? Do get it right first time, chum.'

'She didn't say there'd be any rough stuff,' Halbert bleated in an aggrieved tone. 'Mrs Buckmaster. She lives in the house you came out of. Told me to be here an hour ago, to photograph any man who left the building.'

'You did? There was no flash and it's dark.'

Halbert nodded his weak chin downwards to the

camera. 'It's an infra-red job. A security camera. Cost me a fortune. Worth more than my office and the sticks of furniture inside it.'

'I see.' Marler paused. 'Now I'll tell you what we're going to do. First, you'll extract the film from the camera and hand it to me. You can do that without spoiling the negative? Good. Next,' he lied, 'I'm an ex-SAS man. I could snap your neck like a celery stalk. So you tell Mrs Buckmaster the film didn't come out. Technical hitch. And you never mention our cosy little conversation. Is it a deal?'

'Anything you say.' Marler had released Halbert, who moved away from the sconce and extracted the film with difficulty. His right arm was hurting him. He handed the cartridge to Marler.

'That's going to cost me money,' he grumbled. 'She won't pay the rest of the fee.'

Carrot and stick. Marler took out his wallet. 'How much was the balance. Don't try and fleece me, my friend.'

'A hundred nicker,' Halbert said quickly.

He stared in surprise as Marler gave him two fifty-pound notes. He couldn't make out this pale-faced, well-spoken intruder whose manner spelt out killer to the petrified Halbert.

'I've had another idea,' Marler continued. 'You phone Mrs Buckmaster and tell her there's a technical hitch with the picture you took, that you've had to give it to a specialist in printing and developing. That it will take up to a week.'

'Then what do I do?' Halbert asked, massaging his arm. 'You have the film.'

'I'll call you. Only then can you tell her it didn't work. No picture.'

Now the stick. Marler's hands moved in a blur. They grasped the injured arm, squeezed it. Halbert yelped again.

'Don't have second thoughts,' Marler warned. 'Bad for your health – to start thinking. And I know where I can always find you down Clerkenwell way.' He released his grip and grinned. 'At least you're not out of pocket with this transaction. Put it down to experience.'

The following morning, as previously arranged, Marler flew from Battersea helipad by the Thames in the heart of London to Dartmoor. As he travelled in Buckmaster's private chopper he reflected on the events of the night before.

We all spy on each other. The seductive Leonora carried her idea to its ultimate conclusion: she even spied on her lover. Before travelling to Battersea, Marler had visited Grubby Grundy, the Soho photographer.

Grundy had developed the film in double quick time, providing Marler with two excellent prints. They showed him leaving the Belgravia building as he'd paused at the top of the steps. And there was no doubt where he was leaving – the number on the pillar had come out clearly.

It didn't take too much imagination to foresee how Leonora might use the picture if the devious need arose. She could tell Lance that Marler had arrived unannounced.

'He said you had sent him. He had a message for me. I never learnt what this bogus message was. He tried to rape me. I hit him with my hair brush and he collapsed. He's small and slim – so while he was unconscious I dragged him into the hall and left him there to recover. It was a frightening experience . . .'

Some such story. And the photograph, 'taken by a reporter who happened to be watching the building,' had been bought for a good sum by Leonora. Or, on some occasion, she might threaten Marler with the cooked-up story. Anything to give her a hold on him.

She also used stick and carrot. Stick was the photograph, backed up by her lying story. Carrot was her veiled offer of the managing directorship of World Security. Was she planning to ditch her husband while she had control of the huge conglomerate, World Security? And the photograph he had given her could be a counter in the elaborate game she was playing. A threat to have it published, to destroy his political career?

I'm walking a tightrope, Marler thought as the chopper lost altitude and the snow-covered ridges of Dartmoor appeared. Ten minutes later they landed on the helipad in the grounds of Tavey Grange. Lance Buckmaster was waiting in his study.

'On time as always. I like that, Marler.'

Buckmaster clad in an immaculate sports jacket and slacks, sat behind his desk, his right leg perched on the desk top. The hand-made brogue shoe gleamed like glass. Buckmaster raised both hands and ran them through the unruly locks of his thick brown hair.

'Help yourself to coffee,' he said in the exaggerated public school voice he used to such good effect in the House of Commons. 'You've located Tweed by now I hope? The problem of his disappearance – to avoid a scandal – has become urgent.'

Marler thought quickly, concentrating on holding the coffee pot. Newman, the bastard, had refused to reveal where Tweed was hiding. But when he had met them both last in Freiburg Tweed had been heading for Switzerland. He added milk. All this took only a few seconds.

'I now know which country he's taken refuge in. And it's not a very big one.' He looked up at Buckmaster who was watching him closely. Time to guess. 'Switzerland. And I know his haunts there.'

Buckmaster clasped his two powerful hands behind his

426

neck and nodded. It had been a test. Morgan had already informed him that Tweed was in some nowhere place up in the mountains called Brunni, south-east of Zürich.

He twisted his foot on the desk while he thought. Morgan was confident he could solve the problem. And for back-up he had Armand Horowitz. But they'd muffed the job twice. Once on the Frieburg autobahn, then with a bomb in the Black Forest. Marler, on the other hand, was the best marksman in Europe.

'Howard is really not up to the mark,' he said suddenly. 'I do think the time is coming when I'll have to appoint his successor.'

He studied his manicured fingernails and Marler was careful not to say anything. Another big carrot was being dangled under his nose.

'You're sure you can smoke out Tweed?' he asked eventually.

'He trusts me. That's the key. The answer to your question is yes.'

'I gather Tweed also has with him that foreign correspondent chap, Newman.'

'I know that,' Marler told him.

'He's SAS trained. I've met that bunch in my capacity as Minister. Suppose Newman gets in the way?'

'We're all expendable.'

Buckmaster adjusted the crease in his slacks. 'And Tweed also has Paula Grey with him.'

'We're all expendable,' Marler repeated in his cold voice.

Buckmaster whipped his leg off the desk, stood up, straightened his jacket. 'Then you'd better get after them. Finish the job, for God's sake. Sorry to drag you down here, but it's the only safe place for a chat.' He gave his wolfish grin. 'And don't forget what I said about Howard's job needing a replacement.'

'I'll fly to Switzerland today.' He paused before he left

the study. 'I read a bit in the paper about a Dr Rose being killed in a road accident. Wasn't he the pathologist who carried out the post-mortem on that dead girl found in Tweed's flat?'

Buckmaster froze for a second, then shrugged his wide shoulders; a powerfully built man, the Minister for External Security.

'How did you know about Dr Rose?'

'Howard mentioned he was still waiting for the pathologist's report. Named him as a Dr Rose from St Thomas's.

'I see. Yes, I read the same bit myself. Dreadful how many of these hit-and-run drivers there are these days.'

Marler stared out of the window as the chopper flew him back to London. But he saw nothing of the snow-streaked countryside. In a mental trance, he recalled recent events.

He was being offered the top job by Buckmaster. And within the past twenty-four hours Leonora had suggested he could be the next managing director of a vast conglomerate. The income for each post would be enormous.

He pictured himself buying the latest Maserati, even a Lamborghini. Racing along the autobahns in Germany, overtaking everything in sight. A red job. It would drive his girl friends into a frenzy, sitting by his side. A leap into the stratosphere of the Service. Or the world of business where you lived like a king. Dreams . . .

The nightmare would be finding Tweed inside Switzerland.

PART THREE

The Killing – Shockwave

42

Langley, Virginia, USA. Cord Dillon, Tweed's opposite number, Deputy Director of the CIA, picked up the phone with his own special number. Prepared for most things, the crag-faced officer received a shock.

'Is that Cord Dillon? Good. This is Monitor calling. I've grim news. The *Lampedusa* has been hi-jacked in mid-Atlantic.'

'Jesus! Where are you calling from, Tweed? There have been some funny rumours about you . . .'

Dillon was a tall, well-built man with a thatch of thick brown hair, clean-shaven, and above a strong nose his eyes were a startling blue and ice-cold. Sunken cheeks emphasized the cheekbones and the mouth was wide, thin-lipped, and expressed determination.

'Just for once, Dillon, listen. Don't worry about the rumours. I have enemies. You know that. I've contacted the *Lampedusa* three times now. On none of these transmissions did the radio op answer the trick questions.'

'Sounds like you're right . . .'

'I am right. You've distributed those silhouettes of the *Lampedusa* as we planned two months ago?'

'Sure I have. To every naval ship in the world. In sealed envelopes as you suggested. Only to be opened and the signal acted on when I send the word . . .'

'Send the word. I want you especially to alert the US Sixth Fleet in the Med based on Naples. They're to look for a freighter with that silhouette – bearing in mind the hi-jackers may have altered its appearance, and its name, but they can't change the basic silhouette. Once located, the vessel must be stopped, boarded.'

'Listen here, Tweed. What makes you so Goddamn certain it's heading for the Mediterranean?'

'Because from its original course it only had two alternative routes to reach Russia. One was to head north for the Barents Sea and the ice-free port of Murmansk. It wouldn't go that way – because of the NATO naval exercise, *Sea-Trap*, now in progress. The other route is via Gibraltar – sailing through the straits in darkness and linking up with a Soviet warship in the Eastern Mediterranean. That's the route I'd have chosen.'

'You sound Goddamn sure of yourself, Tweed . . .'

'I am. So, for Pete's sake, alert the Sixth Fleet. Now!'

The connection was broken and Tweed was gone. Dillon sat at his desk for a couple of minutes and thought. He wore his plain grey suit, which was neatly pressed, but clothes were something you simply had to throw on in the morning. Then he decided, reached for the red phone.

'Get me Admiral Tremayne at the Pentagon. Urgently. If he's in one of those endless conferences, drag him out. Tell him we have to send a *Leopard* signal. That will move him.'

One hour later a flotilla of vessels from the US Sixth Fleet got under way from Naples, each ship heading on a different course to sweep the Mediterranean. The commander of each vessel had opened his sealed *Leopard* order. He studied the terse signal, looked at the stack of photocopies of the silhouette of the *Lampedusa*, and distributed them to selected officers and other rank lookouts.

Among the flotilla despatched from Naples was the missile-armed Kidd-class destroyer DGG 997 *Spruance*. Its commander, Hank Tower, was a short, thick-set man, clean-shaven and with an easy smile. His course was due south for the Straits of Messina. Passing through them he would turn east, heading towards Crete and the Eastern Mediterranean. Speed: 30-plus knots.

The Soviet heavy missile cruiser *Sverdlov* had left its base at Novorossiisk and sailed across the Black Sea. It was now approaching the Turkish Bosphorus strait. It would pass down the strait in the night, proceeding across the Sea of Marmara and down the Dardanelles into the Eastern Mediterranean. A rendezvous east of Crete had already been established.

Prior to its departure, there had been a special meeting of the Politburo in Moscow. President Gorbachev had expressed doubts about the operation. But his military adviser had urged him to seize this unique opportunity to acquire for the defence of the Motherland the new Strategic Defence Initiative, *Shockwave*, perfected by the British and the Americans.

'There must be no major confrontation,' Gorbachev had warned.

'The *Sverdlov* will rendezvous with the *Helvetia* and escort it by night back into the Black Sea. After that, the *Helvetia* and its vital cargo will simply disappear. No one will ever know what happened to the original *Lampedusa*.'

'Just so long as there is no crisis,' Gorbachev had insisted.

He knew he had no choice but to agree. There were more than enough hostile elements massing against his *glasnost* policy. To alienate the military establishment could well end in his being removed from power.

Latitude 36. 54. N. Longitude 16. 30. E. The *Helvetia* was sailing south of the Straits of Messina on an easterly course. Its speed was fifteen knots and there was a heavy

433

swell under an overcast sky. It pitched and tossed gently under the swell.

It was four o'clock in the afternoon and not the kind of day you expected in the Mediterranean, Singer thought as he clung to a rail on the bridge. Behind the wheel, Captain Hartmann reflected that the ex-SAS man was tireless. He seemed to get by on three hours' sleep a night. The rest of the time he was prowling the ship, checking, checking, checking . . .

'Will we make the rendezvous on time?' Singer called out.

'It all depends on if the weather eases. I guarantee nothing. The met forecast is not good.'

'Make this old tub move faster.'

'This old tub is a freighter. She is moving at top speed, Mr Singer.'

Hartmann was always polite. In his position many would have pointed out he was the skipper. And Hartmann was also a careful man. Singer carried a loaded Luger shoved down inside his belt and had already displayed his ruthlessness. Hartmann was secretly appalled by the massacre of the crew of the *Lampedusa*. No one had told him about that in advance.

Singer nodded and left the bridge for the aft deck. He had a problem. He was worried about what would happen when they made contact with the Russian vessel. Would the Soviets let him – or any of the crew aboard the vessel – go free?

He was beginning to doubt it. Clinging on to a rail as he descended a companionway, he thought of the fifty thousand pounds – half the agreed fee – he had deposited for this job in a Luxembourg bank. Was it worth risking disappearing for ever inside Russia for the other fifty thousand?

He stood at the bottom of the steps and stared at the surf-topped grey waves rolling towards the vessel. No sign of land anywhere. The second problem was how to escape from the ship.

In its circuit two hundred miles above the earth the American satellite *Ultra* passed over the Black Sea. Its sophisticated cameras recorded everything happening below. A continuous flow of information was passed down to Langley, Virginia.

A specialist hurried into Cord Dillon's office. He laid two prints on the Deputy Director's desk.

'What the hell do these show?' Dillon demanded.

'That tiny black mark has been identified by our analysts. It is the Russian missile cruiser *Sverdlov* approaching the Bosphorus. On its way to the Mediterranean would be my guess.'

'Jesus!' Dillon grabbed his red phone. 'Get me the Pentagon. Admiral Tremayne. Tell him it's a *Leopard* emergency. To call me back. Fastest.' He slammed down the receiver, muttering to himself. 'God help us. Tweed was right . . .'

It was dark outside the chalet at Brunni. The moon had gone down, the temperature had dropped again. Newman piled logs on the fire as Tweed sat with Paula and drank more coffee.

It was the middle of the night. No one had felt like going to bed. Georg was upstairs, on watch by the dormer window. Newman had suggested a duty roster for a watch to be kept on the road back up the valley. Georg had dismissed the idea, saying he'd slept during the day. The night seemed endless as they waited cooped up inside the chalet.

'I managed to get through to America on the phone,' Tweed remarked. 'Last night. I reached Cord Dillon.'

'That rough diamond,' snapped Paula.

'That rough diamond is a very able man. In an emergency he can react with the speed of light. You might as well know he was going to contact the US Sixth Fleet to search for the *Lampedusa*.'

'Assuming it is headed for the Mediterranean?'

'Knowing the distances involved, the speed of the *Lampedusa*, I'm gambling that ship is now well inside the Med.'

'Even if you're right, it's like searching for a needle in a haystack,' Paula objected.

'Not quite. The Sixth Fleet has a lot of ships. I have done all I can. It's the original crew of the *Lampedusa* I'm worried about, that I have on my conscience.'

'Time to change the subject,' Newman said briskly, brushing his hands together as he stood up from the fire. 'In the general excitement of coming up here I forgot to tell you a couple of things.' He opened his briefcase and brought out a sheaf of photocopies. 'These are other documents I asked Turpil to photograph when we broke into World Security at Basle.'

'Don't mention Turpil,' Paula protested. 'I can't get out of my mind that horrible moment when he disappeared beneath that tram.'

'He was betraying Tweed,' Newman reminded her. 'He asked for what he got.'

'What are these?' Tweed asked quickly, picking up the photocopies.

'Evidence of how World Security operates. Their so-called Research & Development Division is the spearhead they use when they bid for another company. To build up their huge conglomerate Buckmaster and Morgan have used sabotage, blackmail and intimidation on a huge scale.'

'I see what you mean,' Tweed commented, skimming through the copies. 'And you're right.'

'That's really awful,' said Paula. 'Think of the misery

they must have caused to countless people. That's awful,' she repeated.

'That's big business,' Newman told her. 'A lot of conglomerates operate that way these days. Human beings don't exist. Only winners and losers.'

'And what was the other thing you were going to tell me?' Tweed enquired.

Newman glanced at Paula. 'When I was talking to Marler he also told me the pathologist who examined Sylvia Harman's body from your flat in Radnor Walk was killed in a so-called hit-and-run accident.

'So-called?' Tweed asked sharply.

'Marler said it was cold-blooded murder.'

'That does it.' Tweed jumped up from his chair and looked at Paula. 'I've been unhappy ever since you insisted on coming with me. We have to find a way of getting you away from this chalet and back to Zürich. Beck will find a safe way of transporting you back home.'

'We've had this argument before,' Paula reminded him. 'I would like to know what's changed.'

'Nothing. But the murder of this pathologist . . .' He looked at Newman. 'Who was he? Do you know?'

'A Dr Rose from St Thomas's.'

'The murder of Dr Rose,' Tweed continued, 'highlights the fact that World Security will stop at nothing to eliminate me – and any witnesses. You're going back to Zürich.'

'Really?' Paula extracted the Browning automatic from her shoulder-bag, checked the safety catch, turned the weapon in her hand. 'Why do you think I'm carrying this? And why are we still waiting here?'

'I've already told you,' Tweed said in an exasperated tone. 'An attack will be launched on us here soon. I need that to happen to convince Beck. Damnit, I've already explained it to you.'

'And I've explained I'm sticking with you until this is all over.' She paused. 'One way or the other. The only way you'll get me out of here is to carry me. You're going to need all the support you can get. There are few of us with weapons anyway.' She checked her watch. 'My turn to relieve Georg on the night watch. And the two of you had better get some sleep. See you . . .'

Newman waited until she had disappeared up the stairs. 'She has a point, Tweed. She takes her job very seriously. You send her away now and she'll never forgive you.'

'But at least she'll be alive . . .'

'You think so? What do you think she might run into going back down the valley – even if we did give her the car?'

The attack Tweed had predicted came just before dawn broke.

43

Paula, stiff from sitting on a chair in front of the dormer window, a pair of night-glasses slung round her neck, was pacing round the bedroom when she heard the machines coming.

She ran to the window, stood to one side, and waited. The sound of the approaching engines was growing louder in the stillness of the night. She heard the creak of the door opening behind her, swung round, the Browning held in both hands and pointed at the shadowy figure.

'Don't shoot the cook, he's doing his best.' Newman said.

'In case you've forgotten, *I'm* the cook. And you shouldn't creep up on me like that. You're supposed to be sleeping.'

'I heard those motor-bikes coming. Maybe it's starting.'

'Of course! I couldn't identify the sound.'

With Newman alongside her, she turned back to the window, the gun still in her hand, the safety catch slipped on. The engine sounds were now a roar. A headlight shone on the snow below the chalet. Slowing down, the large motor-cycle came into view. The rider wore a black leather suit, helmet and goggles.

'Oh, God!' she exclaimed, 'it's one of those thugs who passed our Mercedes on the way up from Zürich.'

'But what's he doing? Give me the glasses.'

The motor-cyclist had stopped, the powerful engine purring, then it swung across the opposite side of the road and carefully followed one of the false trails Newman had made when they first arrived. The ruts had frozen solid. The cyclist stopped, raised both hands, took off his helmet and scanned the area.

'That's Harry Butler,' said Newman. 'And if I'm not mistaken here come Pete Nield.'

The second motor-cyclist appeared and performed a copycat manoeuvre of the tactic carried out by Butler. He nudged the spiked wheels of his machine inside another set of frozen ruts created by Newman. Paula grasped what they were doing immediately.

'Nobody following them will be able to detect where they've disappeared to . . .'

She was talking into air: Newman had dashed out of the room and downstairs. He grabbed up his coat, threw it on and ran out of the front door and down the icy steps. Both Butler and Nield had wheeled their machines out of sight behind the chalet on the far side of the road.

'We're in the chalet opposite,' he told Butler as he almost collided with him round a corner.

'I know. Beck told us, drew a map. And he gave us the key to this chalet which is another safe house.'

Nield appeared from the back of the chalet in time to overhear the remark. 'What's safe about this place?' he asked. 'It's a dead end – and I emphasize the word *dead*.'

'Come across and meet Tweed. He woke up when he heard you coming . . .'

The two men were a contrast in personality. Butler was well-built, in his thirties, clean-shaven, deliberate in his movements and speech and poker-faced. Nield was a few years younger, slimmer and he sported a neat black moustache. He was agile, quick-thinking and sometimes impulsive. They complemented each other and made a good team with Butler normally taking the decisions.

As they plodded over the iron-hard snow each man carried a canvas satchel looped over his shoulder, a heavy satchel which bulged. Tweed, fully dressed, met them at the head of the steps and ushered them inside. He came straight to the point.

'Welcome. I'm relieved to see you. We're expecting a full-scale onslaught from the opposition any time now. How did you get on with Beck?'

Newman was piling more logs on the fire; a freezing wave of air had penetrated the chalet during the short time the door had been left open. Butler and Nield stripped off their jackets, warmed their hands in front of the fire. Newman checked his watch.

'Time for Georg to take over watch duty from Paula. I'll go wake him up.'

Georg appeared at that moment, coming down the stairs from the second bedroom at the rear. He stared at Butler and Nield, nodded to Tweed and went into the kitchen to wash his face with cold water. No better way of getting the corpuscles racing after a short deep sleep. He went back upstairs and Paula joined them.

Nield greeted her with a grin and a kiss on the cheek as Butler dropped his satchel on the table and began to unpack.

'Beck,' Butler informed Tweed, 'was surprisingly helpful. I got the impression he's begun to worry about you. We tried to persuade him to provide us with hand-guns, but he refused. Instead he supplied these. They could be more effective – he told us he'd given you weapons.'

'That's right,' said Paula. 'But what on earth are those?'

Butler had produced a short-barrelled, wide-mouthed and ugly-looking object like a large squat pistol. He extracted a second object, a similar instrument but with an even wider mouth, followed by large shells.

'This one is a tear-gas pistol. And this one is a smoke gun. Acrid, choking smoke – and lots of it from one shell.'

'Me, too.' Nield grinned again at Paula and took the same objects from his own satchel. 'And back home Butler has given me lessons in how to ride a Honda on skid-pans. Most stimulating.'

'Sounds dangerous to me,' Paula commented.

'You should see Butler skidding at speed with a sharp turn. His machine is tilted at an angle of forty-five degrees and he keeps control. A real tearaway. That's what he's been teaching me . . .'

'I doubt if you could use those machines here,' Tweed said.

'The surface is ideal,' Butler commented. 'We tested it on the way here from Apthal. Went off the road up the slopes. The snow is frozen hard. Now, what's the pro-gramme?'

No word about what had happened in London, Paula noted. No reference to the dead girl in Tweed's flat. No doubt about whether Tweed was innocent or guilty. They'd just come to help out their chief, to do their job. She blessed them.

'We face an attack on us by a determined and profes-sional opposition,' Tweed told them. 'They want to kill me. So far they have tried twice. This third assault, I predict, will be quite something.'

'So we'll sort out the sods when they come,' Nield responded cheerfully.

'How about weapons?' Butler asked. 'Beck said you had some.'

Newman produced his Magnum .45. Paula fetched her Browning from her shoulder bag. Butler nodded at Newman.

'That's quite a cannon. But it's still only two handguns. Right?' He looked at Nield. 'We're going to have to spring a surprise on our expected visitors. Tactics rather than firepower.' He switched his gaze to Tweed and Newman. 'If you agree, Pete and I will take up quarters with our motor-bikes in that chalet across the way. If they come down the valley we have them in a crossfire. If they come down the slope behind here out of the forest Pete and I will go up after them. Surprise is worth a lot of firepower.'

For Butler it was a major speech. Tweed glanced at Newman who nodded. 'I like it. Harry has the right idea.'

'Then we do that,' Tweed decided.

'See you then.'

Butler and Nield repacked their satchels, looped them over their shoulders. Nield winked at Paula who gave him her warmest smile. Then they were gone, the front door slammed shut. The only sound for a short time was the crackle and spitting of the logs in the heavy silence.

'I'm so glad they've arrived,' Paula said. 'It gives us a fighting chance.'

A slim one, Newman thought, but he didn't say anything.

No one slept any more. Paula made more coffee. Georg came down briefly to report smoke rising from the chimney on the chalet opposite. Tweed told him not to worry and he went back to his post.

The chalet had the same musty odour of the lodge they

had occupied in the Black Forest, an odour which mingled with the scent of burning logs. Tweed paced around a lot, his brow furrowed.

'I wish now I had asked Beck for a gun,' he said at one stage.

'You'd only have shot yourself in the foot,' Newman joked.

'That's rubbish,' Paula snapped. 'He's a first-rate shot.'

'Lost your sense of humour?' Newman enquired and grinned.

She put her tongue out at him.

The monk appeared about one hour before dawn. He drove in from the direction of Apthal in an Audi and continued slowly past the chalets to the ski station at the end of the road. Paula ran up the stairs and then called down for Newman to come up.

Newman entered the front room where Georg and Paula stared out of the dormer. It took him a minute to adjust his vision to the night. The chalet opposite was in darkness.

'Look what he's doing,' Paula said. 'It doesn't make any sense.'

A door opened in the stationary Audi and a short figure clad in the robe and cowl of one of the Benedictine monks walked to the ski station building and stared up at the Mythen. Both hands were clasped in an attitude of prayer. It was one of the most bizarre sights Paula had ever witnessed.

'What on earth is going on?' she asked in German.

'Some of the monks have a mystic feeling about the mountain,' Georg told her. 'Personally I can never work out where one begins and the other ends – religion and mysticism.'

'In the freezing cold? At this hour?'

Newman's tone expressed sheer incredulity. Georg nodded and smiled.

'Suffering is their pleasure, their way of life . . .'

*   *   *

By the cable station Stieber stood motionless. He had grabbed a Benedictine monk on his way back to the monastery in a side street earlier the previous evening. In what was really a deserted alleyway, he had hauled the monk inside a doorway, one arm round his neck in a hammerlock. He had increased the pressure, intending to truss up the unconscious man and to hide him. He had felt his grip loosen and the neck had flopped sideways. Checking his pulse, he had found none. He had broken the monk's neck.

Couldn't be helped. Stripping off the monk's robe, footwear and cowl, he had thrust the body into a trough of frozen water. The weight of the corpse had broken the ice and Stieber had thrust it down deep. The ice had almost immediately formed afresh, sealing in the monk. The man's face stared up at him as he waited to make sure the ice was thickening. Then he had hurried away, stuffing the clothing into the boot of the Audi.

Now he bowed his head, concealed beneath the cowl. Turning slowly, he surveyed the chalets. As he began to swing round Newman jumped to one side of the window. Without asking why Paula moved quickly out of view of the other side.

'Get away from the window, Georg!' Newman hissed in German.

Georg moved, but his reaction was a little slow. Down at the ski station Stieber saw movement behind the uncurtained dormer window. He was careful not to stare at the chalet as, head bowed, he walked slowly back to his car. At this hour why should anyone be watching from a window in an unlit room? He counted chalets, marked mentally the position of the one where he had seen movement, climbed back behind the wheel of the Audi and drove back slowly the way he had come.

'Well, now I've seen everything,' exclaimed Paula. 'What do you think, Bob?' Tweed's voice.

Newman turned round. He'd forgotten how silently Tweed could move. Tweed stood to one side of the room where he had a view down through the dormer window towards the ski station.

'I think it's damned peculiar,' Newman said savagely. 'A monk driving here in the middle of a sub-zero night – just to stare up at the mountain. Convincing?'

'I think not,' Tweed agreed. 'A monk. It's a perfect disguise for a man to reconnoitre the area. I sense the hand of Horowitz.'

'So they could be arriving any time now,' Paula said grimly.

'Any time now,' Tweed repeated.

Stieber drove back less than a mile from Brunni and pulled in to the side of the road where a Mercedes stood parked, its engine ticking over. A short distance behind it stood a second Mercedes.

Sitting by Morgan, the driver in the first machine, Horowitz blinked through his spectacles as Stieber approached, opened the rear door and slipped inside, slamming the door shut.

'Well?' asked Morgan.

'I've located the chalet where they're holed up. Very near the ski station – the last but one chalet on the left from this direction.'

'You're sure?' demanded Horowitz sceptically.

'No more of that, please,' Morgan burst out. 'Stieber is reliable. I'm calling Kloten now. Let's get it over with.'

He reached for the microphone, gave the call sign, received an immediate response and gave the order.

'Operation Mountain Drop . . . Objective is . . . Repeat, commence Operation Mountain Drop. Confirm. Over . . .'

The confirmation came through from Zeller, brief, terse,

then Morgan hooked the mike back over the cradle. He checked his watch.

'They'll launch their attack just before dawn. Perfect. A man's morale is at its lowest ebb. So is his alertness. We may catch them all asleep.'

'And what about Zeller's motor-cycle corps?' Horowitz asked in his ironic tone.

'I sent them back to Kloten to join the assault team. What kind of reaction do you think we'd get from the locals with a fleet of motor-cyclists vrooming about at this hour? One of the chalet owners might even call the police.'

'And choppers don't make any noise? Is that what you're saying?'

'Of course they do. But in this weather you get the Rescue Service sending out choppers at any hour if they hear someone is in trouble on the mountains.'

'Theoretically you seem to have thought of everything.'

'*Theoretically?*' Morgan queried irritably.

'If Zeller withdrew his motor-cycle team who were those two motor-cyclists who drove past us towards Brunni like bats out of hell?'

'How do I know? Maybe Zeller decided to send a couple back to reinforce the assault. I give Zeller a pretty free hand.'

'I need this car solely for my own use,' Horowitz announced. 'You can use the one behind us.'

'Thank you very much. May I ask why?'

Stieber called out from the rear of the car. 'God, it's hot in here.' He had pulled back the cowl off his head but it was impossible to remove the robe. 'And about this use of transport. I need a car to take me back to the agreed look-out point beyond Apthal. So I need transport just as much as Horowitz seems to.'

'Use the Audi again,' snapped Morgan. He turned to Horowitz. 'I asked you why you want this car for your own use.'

'Because I always work alone. No passengers. That's final.'

'If you say so.'

Morgan was feeling jittery. He was convinced Horowitz had not given him the real reason for his insistence on using the Mercedes by himself. He sighed as he reached for the door handle and glared at his companion.

'It's all yours then. I suppose you're getting ready to run if the going gets tough.'

Horowitz ignored the sneer as he looked over his shoulder at Stieber who was clambering out of the car.

'What did you do with the original owner of those clothes? I told you to tie him up and leave him inside any empty shop so they'll find him in the morning.'

'Didn't work out like that.' Stieber sniggered. 'By chance his neck was broken. Had to hide the body somewhere. Shoved it in one of those water troughs. Had to use the body weight to break the ice. You should have seen him as the ice froze over him and his face stared up through it.'

Horowitz hid his disgust. Stieber was a man who enjoyed his work. A dangerous attitude. For Horowitz, killing a target was a clinical operation to be carried out efficiently without emotion. He was even more glad to have the car to himself. The discovery of a murdered monk would set the police on fire.

Nor was he too confident of Morgan's assault plan. From Horowitz's point of view it would at least serve one purpose – it would smoke Tweed out of his refuge. And I'll be waiting, he thought as Morgan stepped out of the car and shivered with the cold. Horowitz called out to him before he slammed the door.

'What is it now?' snapped Morgan.

'Just remember you're dealing with Tweed.'

'The guy's not superhuman.'

'He is the most dangerous and wily antagonist I've ever been up against.'

Silence. Like the grave. It was getting on Paula's nerves. The bloody silence of the mountains. The fire glowed but had stopped crackling, as though waiting. Tweed sat at the table, going through the photocopies of the documents in the safe at World Security in Basle, the documents recording sabotage, blackmail, intimidation. A damning indictment.

The front door opened and Newman came inside, locked and bolted it. He had been double-checking the heavy closed shutters protecting the windows on the ground floor. He started up the stairs.

'Where are you going?' asked Paula to break the silence.

'To check the rear bedroom now no one is sleeping there . . .'

On the landing he opened the door, switched on a pencil flash. The curtains were closed over this dormer. Walking across the room, he switched off the flash, drew back the curtains. He opened the first window, then the second one beyond which served as double glazing. The view was up a shallow slope of virgin snow. At the top great fir trees were staggered at intervals, row upon row, one behind the other. That was when he heard the faint chug-chug sound.

He listened as the noise came steadily closer. Nothing to see – the trees obscured the view. He shut both windows, went back to the door and ran downstairs. The swift clatter of his feet made both Paula and Tweed stare at him.

'I think they're coming at last,' Newman reported. 'More than one chopper from the sound of it. Approaching us from the back and behind the trees . . .'

'I'll go up and warn Georg in the front room,' said Paula, jumping up. 'Hadn't you better go across to Butler and Pete Nield?'

Georg appeared half-way down the stairs. Paula noticed he had unbuttoned his holster flap, exposing the butt of his Walther. Tweed had stood up from the table, was cleaning his glasses, his head cocked to one side.

'I heard them from the front,' said Georg. 'I'd better get back up. Agreed?'

'Agreed,' said Newman. He looked at Tweed. 'I'll watch the back. No need to warn Butler. He'll have heard them coming.'

'What about me?' Paula asked, the Browning in her hand.

'You stay down here . . .'

'For safety?' she flared.

'No.' Newman's voice was rough. 'To take care of the windows down here. They may try to smash in one of the shutters – so don't think you're not in the line of fire. You are . . .'

He ran back upstairs and into the rear bedroom. Opening both windows again, he listened. The steady chug-chug of several machines was close but still he couldn't see a sign of them. He leaned out of the window, peered round the edge of the dormer at the roof. A few places he could get a hand-hold. He sat on the edge of the window and thanked God he was wearing a long heavy windcheater. The cold was already penetrating through to his backside. He put one foot on the ice-filled gutter, tested its strength. Holding on to both sides of the window he put both feet on the gutter, eased his weight on it. The gutter held. He hauled himself back inside, closed the outer window. Now he could hear the chopper engines clearly through the closed window. They were landing. Out of sight.

In the living-room Tweed put on his glasses. He went to the fire and picked up the iron poker. It was a weapon of a sort. He glanced at Paula.

'At least the waiting is over,' he remarked.

'I'm glad. Now we'll know the worst.' She corrected that. 'Soon they'll know the worst, whoever they are.'

Upstairs in the front room Georg had left the door open – as had Newman in the rear room – so they were able to shout to each other. Newman held his Magnum .45 with spare mags laid out on the inner ledge. The sound of the helicopters flying in had stopped. They were on the ground. The loaded pause – while they prepared something nasty.

It went on, the pause. Nothing happening. No sound, no sight of any intruders. Newman's night vision was pretty good now. To the east streaks of pallid light appeared, the first of the dawn. Perfect timing on the part of the attackers. They'd be coming soon.

He saw them suddenly. Through half-closed eyes a twitch of movement appeared high up amid the trees. Dark figures moving at astonishing speed. Zigzagging in and out among the tree trunks. Of course! He shouted back to Georg and they heard him downstairs.

'It's a ski attack! Coming at us through the forest . . .'

Tweed appeared at the door as though by magic. Holding his poker, he joined Newman who was crouched over the window, holding the Magnum in two hands. The tiny figures were growing larger. They skied with great skill. Tweed lifted his glasses, saw each man carried an automatic weapon looped over his shoulders. A formidable force.

He heard a roaring sound from the other side of the chalet. Dashing across the room and the landing, he ran to the window where Georg stood, Walther in his hand. The front door of the chalet on the far side of the road was open. Butler was manoeuvring his powerful motor-cycle through the doorway, down the steps, swung on to the saddle and raced over the road and up the slope past Tweed's chalet. Nield followed on his own machine, but headed for the other side of the chalet.

Tweed reached Newman's window in time to see Butler riding his Honda up the slope to the left as Nield appeared to the right. They were executing a pincer movement on the flock of skiers who had emerged from the trees and were converging on the chalet. And Butler had been right: the surface of the snow slopes was perfect for the spiked wheels of the motor-cycles. Butler was roaring up the slope, out-flanking the advancing skiers. Way over to their right Nield was executing a similar manoeuvre.

'I'd better get downstairs with Paula,' Tweed said as Georg joined Newman.

He hurried agilely down the treads. Paula was crouched behind the table, holding her Browning. She glanced over her shoulder.

'What's happening at the front?'

Tweed told her. She smiled grimly and took a firmer grip on her weapon. It was again a question of waiting to see what happened.

Upstairs in the rear bedroom Georg threw open both of the other windows and crouched beside Newman. Zeller, clad in black leather like his men, leading the onslaught, saw the open window. He slowed down, stopped, whipped his rifle off his shoulder and aimed at the window. He was still out of range of a handgun. Nield rode his bike with one hand for a few seconds, raised the other, holding one of the pistols, fired. In the greyish light Newman clearly saw the shell arc through the air, land close to the leader. Black smoke poured into the air, became a cloud, enveloping Zeller. Newman heard the *crack!* of a shot which went wild.

Several skiers behind Zeller changed direction as the black cloud spread. Butler was now guiding his machine inside the trees, zigzagging as the skiers had done, taking the high ground. Over to the right Nield also disappeared inside the firs. The skiers appeared confused, leaderless.

Then Zeller skied out of the cloud, shaking his head,

451

coughing as he cleared his lungs of the acrid smoke. The whole group halted briefly. Newman glanced at Georg.

'They're going to change tactics . . .'

The words were hardly out of his mouth when the skiers were on the move again. Earlier they had moved down in a phalanx. Now they separated over a wide area. A more difficult, widespread target. Ski-ing down towards the chalet individually.

Several skied a long way to the left, heading down for the road. And the sound of the motor-cycles had vanished. It was briefly so quiet Newman could hear the swish of the on-coming skiers. He waited for them to come within range.

'Some of them will come at the side of the chalet,' Georg warned.

'I know. They'll cope downstairs . . .'

One of the skiers who had circled round the chalet carried a crowbar. His companion was armed with a grenade. The skier with the crowbar skied up to a side window, inserted the bar where the shutters met and heaved.

The first warning of lethal danger downstairs was when both Paula and Tweed heard the wrench of the crowbar. Tweed, grasping the poker tightly, ran to the side of the window. There was a terrifying splintering noise and both shutters flew outwards. A gloved hand grasped the window ledge to haul the owner inside. Tweed brought the poker down on the hand with all his strength. The unseen man screamed. The hand disappeared.

His companion, much taller, grenade in his hand, appeared at the window. He wore a ski-mask and goggles. Paula stared at the horrific apparition, saw the right hand move back to a throwing position. She fired twice in rapid succession. The skier, who had taken out the pin, fell out of sight. There was an explosive detonation. Miraculously the glass of the windows remained intact but its surface was

452

smeared with a red stain. Tweed glanced out, saw below a goulash of dark red flesh and bone staining the snow. He reached out, hauled the shutters closed.

'What happened?' gasped Paula.

'Hand grenade. Finished them both off.'

No point in going into the gory details. He smiled his admiration for her. She nodded, shoved a fresh mag into the weapon so it was fully loaded. It went very quiet again for a short time.

At the rear window upstairs Newman calculated the first skiers would be within range any second. Then he heard the roar of the motor-cycles coming again, speeding out of the forest as they raced for the skiers at top speed. A clutch of skiers had formed opposite the rear of the chalet for a mass onslaught. Butler raised his pistol, fired a projectile. It landed in front of the enemy group. White vapour billowed in a cloud, creating a wall between attackers and chalet. The lead skiers reached it and suddenly there was chaos as the tear-gas hit them. Choking, blinded, they fell, skis projecting criss-cross upwards.

The second line of skiers curved to left and right to avoid their fallen comrades. One halted, raised his rifle. There was a *thuck!* close to Newman's head. A bullet had lodged in the woodwork. He swung his Magnum, took swift aim with both hands gripping the butt, pulled the trigger twice. The skier flung up his arms, dropped the rifle, collapsed backwards. Georg aimed at another skier standing, rifle thrust into his shoulder, fired three times. The skier sagged, fell face forward.

Butler and Nield were now racing their motor-cycles amid the mêlée. Nield rode past one skier and used the large muzzle of his pistol to hit the man. Barrel connected with skull. Nield almost lost his grip on the weapon but left the man behind sprawled in the snow. The heavy silence was no more. The roar of the cycles mingled with the rapid fire of shots. From the skiers, from the chalet. This was the

453

decisive moment. It was also the moment when downstairs Tweed and Paula heard vehicles approaching at speed along the road from the direction of Apthal, vehicles with sirens blaring like banshee wails. And above the siren sounds they heard the heavy thump-thump of helicopters approaching.

Stieber, who had no difficulty in breaking the neck of a defenceless monk, had halted his Audi well back from Brunni. Too many bullets would be flying around for his liking. He had driven the car off the road behind a barn. He sat behind the wheel in his heavy suit: the monk's robe was buried under the snow a mile back.

He saw the four cars, marked *Polizei*, tearing past him towards Brunni. The lead car, driven by Beck, skidded round the bends, recovered control, raced on out of sight while the other three cars followed. Stieber reached for the ignition key, then withdrew his hand. He'd heard the sound of choppers coming. Opening the door, he grabbed his binoculars and waited. One helicopter flew almost at rooftop level, following the road. On the side of the fuselage the word *Polizei* stood out in the weird light of dawn which was like grey smoke. Stieber focused the binoculars. Despite the cold the door of the chopper was open. Projecting from it was the barrel of a swivel-mounted machine-gun.

Stieber waited until two more helicopters had flown past at a greater height, then tried to start the engine. It fired after three attempts and he drove round the barn and on to the road, turning away from Brunni, heading back towards Einsiedeln.

Beck stared up the slope as he skidded the car to a halt in Brunni. Skiers, lying in grotesque attitudes, dotted the slope behind the chalet. Two men on motor-cycles circled the scene warily. The side wall of the chalet was stained with a dark crimson splash and below it was a huddle of two bodies.

'A massacre,' he muttered to himself.

He snatched the microphone from its cradle. The waveband was already tuned in to his three helicopters hovering overhead. A handful of skiers were making their way back up the slope into the forest.

'Beck here. Ground all choppers behind that forest. If they attempt to take off, use the machine-guns . . .'

He rammed the mike back on to its cradle and ran out of the car up to the entrance to the chalet. The rear door of his car had opened earlier and uniformed police with automatic weapons were heading up the slope, joined by more men from the other three cars. He ran up the steps, stood to one side of the door and hammered on it.

'Open up. Police here. This is Beck talking . . .'

Tweed opened the door after unlocking it and drawing back the bolts. Poker in hand, he stood to one side. In the middle of the room crouched Paula, her Browning aimed at the doorway. She straightened up, lowered the weapon. Beck stamped snow off his boots and walked inside. Tweed shut the door.

'Better late than never,' he observed.

44

At Einsiedeln, inside his room at the St Johann, Horowitz stood by the window. It was from here he had watched the four police cars arrive. From here he had watched through his night-glasses as Beck got out of the lead car and stared all round the deserted open space, then climbed back inside and drove off, leading his motorcade.

It was from here that Horowitz had seen the three choppers with *Polizei* on their fuselages overfly the town and head towards Brunni. None of this had surprised Horowitz – this was Switzerland. He had warned Morgan when the Welshman had called in briefly to see him on his way back to Zürich. Morgan had shrugged his wide shoulders, had said he had urgent business to attend to and had left.

Outside his room Horowitz heard the floorboards on the landing creak. The room was in darkness to let him see clearly what was happening outside. He picked up the Luger pistol with a silencer off the table, walked to the door, stood to one side.

'Yes? Who is it?'

'Stieber. Just back from you-know-where.'

'So what is happening?' Horowitz asked after unlocking the door and letting Stieber inside.

'All hell's let loose out at Brunni.' Stieber was sweating despite the cold outside. 'I saw four police cars and three of their bloody choppers racing towards the Mythen.'

'I know. I saw them. Now you've arrived you can make yourself useful. I paid for this room in advance for three days. You stay here and report by phone what happens.'

'And where are you going?'

'That doesn't concern you . . .'

'I don't like it. Suppose they find that monk I dumped in a trough? They might come looking for me.'

'And why should they suspect you? Were there any witnesses to the incident?'

Horowitz was closing his case. He had packed earlier ready for a swift departure.

'No, the alley was deserted. No one saw me.'

'And you've got rid of the monk's clothes?'

'I buried them in the snow outside Apthal.'

'Then you have absolutely nothing to worry about. Should a member of the police call to ask why you're here, tell them World Security is thinking of opening a bank account. You know the name of the bank in the High Street?'

'Yes . . .'

'Then I'm off. Just keep your eyes open. Don't go to sleep. Report by phone to Morgan any development.'

'You're clearing out, leaving the whole business behind?'

Horowitz stared at Stieber. 'You seem to have forgotten – I have a job I undertook to do. What has happened out at Brunni will help me to complete that job.'

Beck had made Tweed's chalet his temporary HQ. 'While we clear up this mess.' He sat at the table in the living-room with Tweed, Newman and Paula. Police came in, reported to Beck and went again. Ambulances had arrived to transport the injured and the dead from the blood-spattered slopes behind the chalet. Tweed faced Beck across the table.

'Do you believe me now?' he asked brusquely. 'Believe that there exists an opposition out to kill me?'

'Yes. I apologize for not believing you completely earlier. And we have identified the opposition.' He picked up a green identity folder a policeman had brought him. 'Most of those skiers had no means of identification on them. A deliberate ploy. But one man slipped up, had this folder inside his pocket.' He read from it. 'World Security, Zürich. Heinrich Locher. Then a number. That gives me what I've been waiting for ever since Otto Kuhlmann in Wiesbaden told me about the World Security truck they caught trying to smuggle classified high-tech equipment over the border into East Germany.'

'What have you been waiting for?' Paula asked.

457

'A legal excuse for turning over World Security HQs in Zürich, Basle and Geneva. Of course what happened out here was not all that legal.'

'We protected ourselves against armed attack – with weapons supplied and authorized by yourself,' Newman pointed out.

Beck smiled. 'Yes, you're right, of course.'

'And how did you happen to turn up here in the nick of time? We would have been overwhelmed by sheer numbers,' Tweed commented.

'Simple. I do know what's going on inside Switzerland. That is my job. It was reported to me from Kloten that World Security helicopters were assembling, that they were taking on board large numbers of men with ski equipment. The official reason was they were being sent on leave. I didn't swallow that one. I organized a strike force to stand by – choppers and cars. When that chopper fleet took off from Kloten it was tracked by radar – in this direction. I left Zürich to come up here at once. Now, Tweed, what are you going to do next? Have you any idea?'

'I'm returning to London. But I need your help, then Kuhlmann's. I can't fly back on a scheduled flight – they might put a bomb aboard the plane. I can't risk the lives of the other passengers.'

'Then why not use a chopper?'

'World Security will stop at nothing to make sure I never reach London. They could use Stinger missiles to destroy the machine. Lord knows what they have secreted away. I have decided the least risk to myself – to other people – is to cross Europe by car along the German autobahns, then to cross the Channel secretly by boat. For the first part of the journey I'll need your cooperation, Beck. Once I drive over the frontier at Basle I'm on my own.'

Beck looked dubious. Georg came in through the front door to report three more skiers had been transported into

458

the waiting ambulances. Beck nodded and asked him to leave them alone, to take charge of the operation on the slopes. Only when they were alone again did he comment.

'Who do you think is behind all this?'

'Buckmaster or Morgan. Maybe both. I think one of them murdered that girl they found in my London flat. Not a job to hand over to a lackey – it would have provided a potential danger to the instigator of the crime if the murderer were caught. It's one of those two men – and I think I know who.'

'And the motive?'

'Colonel Romer of the Zurcher Kredit Bank could guess at that.'

'All right, you're evading the question. Now, your route to London. You do realize you will be the target of the entire World Security apparatus. They'll pull out all the stops to make sure you never reach London alive.'

'I'm counting on that.'

The reply was so curious they all stared at Tweed. Paula leaned forward, searching her chief's face. It was devoid of expression.

'What are you up to now?' she asked.

'Just trying to get home in one piece,' Tweed said amiably. He paused and looked at Beck. 'Isn't the Zurcher Kredit one of the banks which has provided Buckmaster with a huge loan?'

'I believe that may be the case,' Beck replied cautiously.

'The phone is in the kitchen. He's a friend of yours. Why don't you call him now – get him out of bed, if necessary. If my judgement of Romer is correct it will be a loan subject to swift recall. Maybe even at forty-eight hours' notice. Give Romer a message from me. I strongly advise him to call in that loan immediately. If Buckmaster tries to delay repayment Romer should hint he won't be able to keep the news from the press for long.'

'If you say so . . .'

459

'The phone is in the kitchen,' Tweed told him as the Swiss stood up. He waited until Beck had closed the door, then stared at Newman. There was something implacable in his manner which made Paula watch him with fascination.

'Bob,' Tweed began, 'when you were a foreign correspondent all the time, I gather you built up a network of contacts all over the world?'

'That's true.'

'You still keep in touch with these people?'

'Yes. In case some big story I like the sound of breaks. As you know, I still write the occasional piece.'

'Reporter friends in Tokyo, Sydney, San Francisco, New York and London?' Tweed persisted.

'In a lot of places – including all those you mentioned.'

'Then you could phone them at intervals and ask them as a favour to spread the question, *is World Security solvent?*'

A heavy silence descended on the room. Newman straightened in his chair and his eyes narrowed. Paula parted her lips and looked excited: like Newman she had grasped what Tweed was doing. It was Newman who broke the silence.

'Of course the major stock-markets of the world are in those cities you've mentioned. And World Security shares are quoted in those centres. Yes, I could phone friends who would regard that as an international scoop – and they'd begin to dig deep for follow-up stories. When Beck's come off the phone I could call Tokyo.' He checked his watch. 'The market is still open there.'

Tweed held up a hand. 'Not yet. I want to give Romer the chance to get his money back before the avalanche descends.'

'And just exactly what are you up to now?' Paula

460

asked. 'I detect a ruthless purpose behind what you're saying. That's not like you.'

Tweed had the same implacable manner but he spoke in an almost offhand way.

'It was Colonel Romer who gave me the missing link I was seeking behind this conspiracy. He told me the Russian Narodny Bank is holding five hundred million pounds in gold bullion ready for an urgent transaction. The potential recipient of that huge sum is a closely guarded secret. While I was in London I was working on a secret project known only to three people in Britain. The PM, Buckmaster and myself. It concerned the movement by sea of the key to the defence of the West. Further, only two people had the codes to contact the ship transporting the high-tech project, which I call *Shockwave* . . .'

'Something the Soviet military would give five hundred million pounds to lay their hands on?' interjected Paula.

'Exactly. I repeat, only Buckmaster and myself could contact the ship transporting *Shockwave*. Which is why I had to be got out of the way, sent running like a common fugitive. So, a murder is carefully planned – with Sylvia Harman's corpse found in my flat. I do start running – which leaves Buckmaster as the sole contact with the ship carrying *Shockwave*. At least, that is what he believes. That man, a minister, is handing over our defence against a rocket onslaught to the Russians to save his company. It's me against him – and I'm going to bring him down.'

'World Security is a huge international conglomerate,' Newman warned. 'And Buckmaster always wins in a business battle. If he's after a company to take over he always wins – by intimidation, by the power of his reputation, by using every trick in the book. You think you can defeat him?'

'I'm going to bring World Security crashing down across the face of the earth. The tricky part is to avoid involving a Minister of the Crown in a murder case because that could destroy the government. That one I haven't worked out yet.'

'There are other people I could phone,' Newman mused. 'I've been thinking – people who spread rumours high up in the financial world behind closed doors.'

'When the time comes, do it,' said Tweed.

Beck opened the kitchen door and walked in to join them at the table.

'I phoned Romer. He was already up. He's an early riser.'

Tweed produced a sheaf of photocopies from his briefcase, a selection of the copies Newman had obtained from Basle. He handed them to Beck.

'It occurred to me after you'd gone that Romer might like to know something about the methods they've been using in the so-called Research & Development Division of World Security.'

Beck scanned the sheets. He frowned, still standing, checked back through several sheets, then looked at Tweed.

'This is damning evidence . . .'

'I suggest you might like to make a fresh call to Romer.'

'I think I will at that . . .'

Paula waited until the kitchen door had closed. Again she leaned towards Tweed.

'What game are you playing now? I don't think for a moment that occurred to you after Beck went to make his call.'

'A small question of psychology. Romer is up. He gets the first call from Beck with my message. He's a cautious Swiss banker. So at this moment he's weighing up whether to act or not. He gets a second call from Beck with evidence of the most appalling malpractice on the part of World Security. As I said, he's a Swiss banker. That second call reporting the evidence will decide him. He'll pull out.'

462

'You really are being devious,' Paula remarked. 'Is there any other titbit I've missed?'

'On my instructions, Marler is attacking Buckmaster inside his citadel. We're getting at him through his wife.'

'My! This really is a no-holds-barred battle.'

'Buckmaster is a cobra . . .'

Tweed stopped talking as Beck reappeared. 'Romer is calling in that loan. Now we have to take a few days trying to plan how you'll get back to London alive. If that's possible.'

45

At 8 a.m. London time, Lance Buckmaster received the call in his Belgravia flat from Zürich. Colonel Romer himself was on the line. Buckmaster greeted him affably and then stiffened in his chair as he detected the coldness in Romer's voice.

'Could you say that again slowly?' he asked curtly.

'At a meeting of the board this morning it was unanimously decided we must request you to repay the loan we made to World Security.'

'You're getting good interest on the money, Lord knows. I paid over the odds for that loan. You've received all the interest payments on time. And you shouldn't be talking to me. I'm a Minister now, in case you've forgotten.'

'Since the loan was agreed before you became a Minister – was negotiated with you personally – I thought it courteous to call you. You would prefer I get in touch with the chairman, Mrs Buckmaster?'

'Hold your horses, Romer. This comes out of the blue. I've had no hint of this before now, no warning.'

'The agreement does not mandate for any warning notice. We have taken our decision.' Romer's voice hardened. 'It is irrevocable.'

'How many months before you need the money back?' Buckmaster snapped.

'Not months. Not weeks. The time here is just after 9 a.m. We require payment of the entire loan by 11 a.m. your time, within forty-eight hours.'

'That's ridiculous with a company like World Security . . .'

'Read the agreement you signed. I'm sure you have a copy at hand. Or should I go through the strictly regular channels and call Mrs Buckmaster?'

'No. As you said, I negotiated the loan with you. May I ask why this sudden decision was taken?'

'Oh come, Mr Buckmaster. You know well it is the policy of my bank never to reveal reasons for decisions.'

'I'm asking you for thirty days to repay,' Buckmaster said.

'My regrets, Mr Buckmaster. I said the board's decision was irrevocable. The loan must be repaid in forty-eight hours. By 11 a.m. London time, two days hence. A courier will be flying to you with written confirmation.'

'Not necessary. No courier. Save your money.'

Buckmaster slammed down the phone in the living-room, swore slowly, with calculated venom. Running his hands through his hair, he stood up and walked round the room. Why? Why? *Why?*

His brain began to function. Zürich. Switzerland. Tweed was in Switzerland! That had to be it. *Tweed.* Assuming he was still alive. The phone rang again. He snatched it up.

'Who is it?' he demanded brutally.

'Morgan. Speaking from Basle. Is is OK to go ahead?'

464

'It is.'

In his Basle office overlooking the Rhine, the snow-encrusted rooftops on the opposite shore, Morgan pressed his prominent belly against the edge of his desk. It didn't sound too good a moment to report what had happened, but Buckmaster had to be told.

'We still have a problem . . .' Morgan talked fast – get it over with, exude confidence. 'The first major onslaught on the target was made and, as so often occurs, it did not succeed.' Morgan began to embroider the story. 'The target would have been removed but he had official help up in the mountains.'

'The police took him into custody?' Buckmaster said quickly.

'Something like that. You can guess the rest. But this is just the start of the take-over campaign.' Morgan phrased it carefully. He never entirely trusted a phone: he had bugged too many in his time. The police might be tapping the wire from outside. 'I am moving to Freiburg as soon as I have completed this call,' he went on. 'The campaign will continue from there. I have people here who will keep me in touch with developments . . .'

'Is Tweed still alive?' Buckmaster shouted down the phone.

'Yes,' Morgan admitted reluctantly. 'It was very odd. After the first phase of our campaign he appeared in the middle of Einsiedeln, got out of a car, walked around. Our accountant, Armand, found that odd.'

'And how does Armand view the situation?'

Morgan took a stronger grip on the phone. He was on firmer ground now. 'Armand is cool as a cucumber. Says the situation is developing as he expected. We have someone on the inside who reported the target is travelling back to England by road. God knows why, but Armand says that suits him fine.'

'Travelling back to England?' Buckmaster's voice rose

several decibels. 'When for God's sake?'

'Within a few days. We even know the route the consignment will take. Which is why I'm leaving for Freiburg to take overall command of the situation.'

'As you have up to now,' Buckmaster commented sarcastically. 'You say Armand has a plan?'

'Yes. I won't bore you with the details . . .' Morgan thought he'd got out of that trap skilfully. Buckmaster would assume he was being cautious over the phone. The fact was that Morgan had no idea what Horowitz's plan was. Buckmaster's tone was like ice when he spoke again.

'Hand over complete control to Armand. Offer him a large bonus to deal with the problem. Permanently. You're out of a job if you let me down this time. I already have your successor lined up . . .'

Morgan opened his mouth to protest and heard the click. The connection had been broken. Buckmaster had gone off the line. He replaced the receiver and mopped his damp forehead. The conversation had been an ordeal. Was Buckmaster serious in his threat to sack him? You never could tell. He always kept you off balance.

To take his mind off the phone call Morgan went over in his mind the events of the past few hours. The assault at Brunni had been a débâcle. Worse still, his paid contact inside Police HQ at Zürich had warned him to expect a raid on all three World Security HQs in Switzerland. Staff were busy burning incriminating documents. A detail he had felt it wise to omit mentioning to Buckmaster at this stage.

His police contact had also told him Tweed was leaving for London by road during the next few days – that he would be travelling on the autobahns in Germany from Basle. This seemed madness on the part of Tweed to Morgan. He had said as much to Horowitz on the phone when he had called from Zürich from a public call box.

'It is the first slip Tweed has made,' Horowitz agreed. 'I have been waiting for that slip . . .'

For a time Morgan had refused to believe Tweed was still alive. Then Stieber had reported the news from Einsiedeln – that he had seen Tweed step out of several cars in broad daylight and walk around in front of the monastery.

Strangely enough to Morgan, who had taken the call from Horowitz in a public box after a brief message from Zürich, giving him the location and number of the box, this episode had impressed Horowitz more than the massacre at Brunni.

'He's playing the same devious game,' he had commented to Morgan. 'He got out of that car in Einsiedeln and showed himself in a very public way. He's using the same strategy as when he crossed the bridge over the Rhine at Laufenburg, when he then made a fuss over the tickets at the station, when he booked rooms at the hotel nearest the *Hauptbahnhof* in Zürich.

'And what strategy is that?'

'Cat and mouse,' Horowitz had replied.

'And who is the cat?' Morgan had rasped.

'I shall be. In the end . . .'

That had been several hours ago. Morgan checked his watch. The car would be waiting to take him over the border into Germany. He had to clear out before the police raid hit the Basle HQ. He picked up his case and went down in the elevator.

The Mercedes was waiting for him at the kerb. Morgan had another bad shock. Wearing a chauffeur's uniform and a peaked cap, Armand Horowitz opened the front passenger door for him. In case someone was watching he said nothing and climbed inside. Horowitz, who had taken his case, deposited it in the boot, slammed it shut and got in behind the wheel.

'How the hell did you get here so fast?' asked Morgan.

'Encouraging to receive such a warm welcome.' Horowitz drove the Mercedes away from the kerb, headed for the bridge over the Rhine and the frontier control post beyond. 'It's quite simple. I flew in one of your remaining choppers from Kloten to Basle airport. Fortunate that your chauffeur is my height and build. I noticed that earlier. I borrowed his uniform.'

'He gave it to you? Just like that!'

'A little gentle persuasion was needed. He's lying unconscious in your communications room in the basement.'

'Why the disguise?'

'We are crossing the border into Germany . . .'

There was silence for the next few minutes. Morgan was uneasy about the checkpoint. Had Beck alerted the guards? Sent them his description? He couldn't get out of Switzerland quick enough. He'd heard what it was like inside Swiss prisons.

'Just relax,' Horowitz ordered as he slowed the car, joining the short queue waiting to pass the control point.

Morgan had his passport ready inside his coat pocket as a Swiss official approached the car. Would they get through?

The Swiss leaned down, stared hard at Morgan, who gazed back. The stare was transferred to Horowitz who sat erect, looking ahead. The Swiss, a short stocky man, waved them on. They were through. Horowitz drove on to German soil.

The short stocky man hurried inside the building to an empty office. Standing up, he pressed the numbers typed on a slip.

'Freiburg Police HQ? This is Swiss control at Basle. You have a Chief Inspector Kuhlmann who is expecting this call urgently.'

He had to wait a few minutes. Then a gravelly voice came on the line.

'Kuhlmann here. That's Swiss control at Basle?'

'Yes. I'm carrying out the instructions I received from Berne. A World Security Mercedes has just left Switzerland for Germany. Inside were Morgan and a uniformed chauffeur.'

'How do you know it was World Security? How can you be sure it was Morgan?' Kuhlmann demanded.

'Berne supplied a complete list of registration numbers of all cars belonging to World Security. They also gave me a detailed description of Gareth Morgan. He's fat as a pig, grossly overweight, medium height, mid forties, clean-shaven, very black hair. Looked like a giant turnip . . .'

'Describe the chauffeur.'

'Just a chauffeur. Tall, thin, lean-faced, wore steel-rimmed glasses . . .'

'O.K. And thank you.'

Kuhlmann put down the phone and turned to his assistant. 'Get me Arthur Beck of the Swiss Federal Police. You'll contact him at Zürich police HQ . . .'

46

In the living-room of his Belgravia flat Buckmaster sat in a state of shock. An hour earlier he'd had the phone call from Colonel Romer. The withdrawal of the loan was a disaster. The withdrawal of any of his many bank loans at this point would be a disaster.

It was so nerve-racking. It was also going to be a race against time, maybe a matter of hours making all the difference. As soon as the Soviet military took possession of *Shockwave* half the enormous sum of five hundred million would be paid to him in gold bullion in Switzerland. From a portion of that sum he could pay off Colonel Romer and his bloody gnomes. The balance of the other two hundred and fifty million would be paid after their technical analysts had examined *Shockwave*.

Tweed. It had to be Tweed's hand behind this cata-strophic news from Zürich. Tweed was in Zürich. The coincidence was too great. It all depended on Armand Horowitz doing yet another smooth and perfect job. Tweed must never get back to England. The thought of the man filled Buckmaster with venom.

He took a deep breath and remembered a long article which had featured him in *Forbes Magazine* in the States. The writer had traced Buckmaster's phenomenal rise to power and riches. He had used a phrase which leapt back into Buckmaster's mind. *This man is at his best with his back to the wall*. He stood up. He would beat down the opposition once again – emerge from this temporary difficulty stronger than ever. It was at that moment that Leonora, who had slept in after a late night at the office, appeared from her bedroom.

'I'm glad you're still here. I'd like a word with you, Lance.'

Something in her tone made him stiffen. She was holding a cardboard-backed envelope. From it she extrac-ted a large photograph, holding the blank side towards him.

'I've decided I can't stand your playing around with so many girl friends any longer.'

'What the devil are you talking about?'

His voice was dangerously quiet, his expression frozen. She had chosen the wrong moment to make a scene. Half his mind was wrestling with the problem of the loans. The last thing he wanted was more trouble – and so close to him. He felt the fury bubbling up inside him and with a supreme effort he preserved an impassive manner.

'I'm talking about this. Photographic evidence of your fooling around with your hired tarts.'

She extended the photo towards him and he took it from her. He was careful not to snatch it out of her hand. Taller than Leonora, he towered over her as he examined

470

the print. His eyes were cold as he raised them and looked at her.

'Where did you get this garbage?'

'Yes, that would be a good description of her,' she continued. 'Garbage. How much does she charge for a quick lay? Or do you buy her presents? A diamond choker? I wouldn't mind choking her myself.'

'This is a fake,' he told her in the same quiet tone.

'Of course!' she laughed in his face. 'A fake. That's a good one. Really, Lance, you're a Minister of the Crown. At the moment. I'd have thought you could do better than that.'

'I asked you where you got this from.' He advanced towards her. 'I want an answer.'

'Haven't you heard of private investigators? Lots of women employ them when they've learned to mistrust their sneaky husbands. And sometimes they get lucky – they get photographic evidence. Like I got.'

'You . . . stupid . . . cow.' He spaced out the words. 'I recognize this picture . . .'

'Really?' She put up a hand and touched a curl into place. 'You mean you get someone to photograph you while you're doing it? Kinky as well as randy as a goat. May I look at your photograph album sometime?'

'This photograph,' he repeated in the same over-controlled tone, 'is a fake. This picture of me on the sofa was taken by a press photographer. God! I've lost count of the number of pictures taken of me. But I do remember this one. You've been cheated. I've never seen this girl in my life—'

'You would say that—'

'Shut up!' he roared at her. He resumed his controlled tone. 'Someone has produced clever artwork – they have superimposed the girl – a picture of her – on top of me. Then they'd photograph the whole thing again to hide the joins.'

'You really expect me to believe that? I do believe you are losing your grip when it comes to telling convincing lies. Maybe you're losing control of everything.'

It was just something savage to say out of the blue. But it had a different meaning to Buckmaster. His mind raced. Could she have something to do with the withdrawal of the Swiss loan by Romer? Treachery behind his back? His fury boiled over.

He transferred the photograph to his left hand. He raised his right hand and slapped her across the side of the face with a backhander. Her head jerked back. She lost her balance and fell sprawling on to a nearby couch. For one moment the ex-captain of the Airborne Division thought he'd hit her too hard. He took a step forward and then she was lifting herself upright, leaning back on the couch, her eyes blazing.

'You bastard! That's the first and last time you'll hit me . . .'

'You're going to feel silly when I go through the publicity files and find the original photograph of myself this girl has been linked up with. Now, I need to know who gave you this piece of rubbish.'

'And the police need to know who had access to the Threadneedle Street executive elevator – everyone – on the night Ted Doyle was murdered . . .'

'Murdered? What fanciful nonsense are you talking about now? The press has reported Doyle fell out of the window.'

'Oh, yes,' she jeered, 'and you also were fooled by the report Chief Inspector Buchanan spread. He's not satisfied, I can tell you. Buchanan is investigating it as a case of cold-blooded murder. Only three people had keys to the executive elevator which comes straight up from the underground garage. Me, Morgan – and you.'

'You told this Buchanan I still have a key?' he asked quietly.

'Not yet.'

'You have some sense. Now, listen to me, Leonora. I can remove you as chairman and put Morgan in your place tomorrow.'

'I don't think so . . .'

'Then you'd better read the articles of association governing the conduct of the company. I can throw you out just like that.'

He snapped his fingers at her contemptuously. Leonora stood up and touched the side of her face with her fingertips. A blue weal marked her where Buckmaster had struck the blow. She could see it in the wall mirror behind him. She spoke through her clenched teeth, spoke with great emphasis.

'At the first sign that you're trying to remove me I'll go to Buchanan and tell him who still has the third key to that elevator.'

'You can't drag me into the Doyle business.'

'You want to bet?' she mocked him. 'Bet your whole career? How long do you think you'd last as Minister for External Security if the press splashed you across its pages as one of the murder suspects?'

'You . . .'

'And,' she continued with deadly calm, 'if you call me a cow a second time that's it. Come to think of it, I don't have to go and see Buchanan. He's made another appointment to visit me at my office. That third missing key intrigues him.'

'Let's leave things as they are,' he decided. 'We're having too many domestic tiffs . . .'

'Tiffs!' she snorted. 'When you say leave things as they are, you mean I'm staying on as chairman. Is that it?' she pressed.

'You caught me on the raw.' He was under icy control now. 'Yes, that's it. Of course. I need someone I can trust in that position. Morgan is insatiably ambitious. Keep your eye on him.' He checked his watch. 'Hanson will be waiting to take me to the Ministry. Give me that envelope. I will hang on to this photo until I've found the original.'

'I do have other copies,' she warned him as she handed it to him.

'Fair enough. I really must go now . . .'

Outside the entrance he was his normal affable self with his chauffeur, Hanson, who opened the rear door of the Daimler. Once the car was on the move he sat tensely, thinking over recent events. His whole world was coming apart.

There was Romer and the withdrawal of the Swiss loan. He'd have to visit the room inside the Admiralty, check on the progress of the *Lampedusa*. The ship must be close to its rendezvous point. And now he had a fresh anxiety. He had read the papers and there had been no further mention of Doyle's death. Just a small report that the inquest had been adjourned at the request of Chief Inspector Buchanan. 'While we continue our enquiries . . .' What enquiries?

As Buckmaster was driven to Whitehall, Marler was not far away, driving his Porsche to Scotland Yard. He had delayed his departure for Switzerland after reading the papers. His attention had been caught by the item on the postponement of the inquest on Doyle, the chief accountant who had fallen out of a window at World Security.

Leonora had told him about the strange death of Doyle during pillow talk at her Belgravia apartment. By asking a few offhand questions Marler had built up a picture of what had happened during the fatal night. She had chattered on, relieved to have someone she could talk to about the weird episode.

Marler had made a brief phone call to the Yard. He had spoken to Buchanan briefly and they had arranged this appointment. He parked his car and walked inside the famous building. He was shown up to Buchanan's office immediately and had a shock when he entered to room.

There were two men inside the office. One of them Marler recognized. Chief Inspector Harvey of Special Branch, the weasel-like officer Tweed had always disliked. Marler concealed his sense of shock. What a contrast the two men were.

Buchanan, tall, elegant, cordial, got up from behind his desk, walked round it, extended his hand. His grip was firm. He wore a smart grey suit, a white shirt, a pale grey tie which matched the colour of his alert eyes.

'Thank you for coming to see me, Mr Marler. Do please sit down. I gather you know Chief Inspector Harvey of Special Branch?'

'We've met.'

Marler nodded to the other man. Black-haired, shorter and bulkier than Buchanan, he wore a blue business suit which didn't seem to fit him properly. A sneer lingered at the corners of his tight little mouth. His eyes darted all over the place.

'I don't quite understand,' Marler began when Buchanan had sat down again behind his desk. 'You're the Met – Metropolitan Police. Harvey is Special Branch. It's unusual to find the two separate forces working together.'

'What's that to do with you?' Harvey snapped.

'I do think we owe our visitor an explanation,' Buchanan intervened politely. 'You are, of course, quite right, Mr Marler. The two forces normally operate independently – and most of their activity is connected with your organization. Of which, I confess, I know very little . . .'

'Do you really think this is necessary?' Harvey snapped.

'I do. Mr Marler, I'm investigating the circumstances surrounding the death of Edward Doyle, chief accountant with World Security. Apparently he fell to his death from a window late one evening. There are aspects of the case which puzzle me. The investigation is continuing. Now, this is where Harvey comes in. There was – only a short time before Doyle's demise – the murder of an unknown woman in the Radnor Walk flat of a man called Tweed. I understand he is your immediate superior?'

'Correct.'

'Harvey is getting nowhere with his enquiry into this brutal murder . . .' He paused and Marler glanced at Harvey who was glowering. Not a welcome disclosure. '. . . and so far,' Buchanan continued, 'he hasn't had any luck identifying the victim. He found himself facing a dead end.' A grim smile appeared on Buchanan's face. 'Excuse me, that unfortunate pun was unintended. Am I explaining this clearly so far?'

'So far. I'm still waiting for the connection.'

'Which is what I'm coming to. Harvey has managed to keep the Radnor Walk murder out of the press – for obvious security reasons. Then he heard about the death of Doyle at the offices of World Security. That has appeared in the press. On the night of the murder in Radnor Walk three people turned up at that address. And this was in the early hours of the morning. One was Robert Newman, the foreign correspondent. Another was your ultimate chief, Mr Howard, alerted by an anonymous phone-call. Tweed subsequently disappeared. All clear so far?'

'I get the picture.'

Buchanan paused. Marler was beginning to grasp his mannerisms, his technique. He paused before saying something significant. 'A third man also turned up very promptly at the flat. Lance Buckmaster, Minister for External Security.'

'Really?'

'When are you going to talk, Marler?' Harvey burst out.

'I am talking.'

'Oh, yes.' The sneer was pronounced. 'In single sentences?'

476

'That's right.'

Marler answered Harvey's questions without looking at him. Buchanan was watching him closely with a hint of amusement. He turned to Harvey and smiled.

'Why don't you pop down and get yourself a cup of coffee at the canteen? I'll join you there in a few minutes.'

'I think I'd prefer to stay where I am.'

'Harvey, I started out by making it a request.'

'We're not getting anywhere with this iceberg.' Harvey pursed his lips and stood up. 'Maybe you'll find me in the canteen, maybe you won't.'

He closed the door quietly after leaving the room. Marler asked Buchanan if he could light a cigarette. The Chief Inspector told him that was quite all right. Marler lit his cigarette, blew a smoke ring, watched it circle above him, then spoke.

'What's the connection? I'd like you to spell it out.'

'The only possible – I repeat possible – connection is that Buckmaster arrived at Radnor Walk soon after the body was found. Then, shortly afterwards, we have another corpse at the headquarters of World Security – Buckmaster's company – in Threadneedle Street. I am beginning to wonder whether the two incidents are linked. I have no evidence, I stress. Why did you come to see me, Mr Marler?'

'I can't reveal my source. I work under the Official Secrets Act. But someone told me there is a private executive elevator from the underground garage at Threadneedle Street to the suites on the eighteenth floor. Is that so?'

'Yes, it is.'

Buchanan was no longer looking at Marler. The soul of relaxation, he played with a glass paperweight on his desk. He looked up as Marler asked his question.

'I take it this interview is between the two of us? That

you won't repeat this conversation to Harvey? I'm still talking about the Official Secrets Act.'

'You have my word. You may talk freely. In complete confidence.'

'Staying with that elevator. I understand there are only three keys which operate it. Mrs Buckmaster has one. Gareth Morgan has another. The third key is supposed to have gone missing.'

'That is the way I understand the situation.'

'Lance Buckmaster has the third key. It isn't lost. He kept the key when he became a Minister. So he has discreet access to the executive suites at Threadneedle Street.'

Buchanan stopped playing with the paperweight. He gazed into the distance, his manner still relaxed. This man could coax the truth out of most people, Marler thought.

'I'm greatly obliged to you, Mr Marler, for that interesting piece of information. I won't conceal from you it opens up a fresh line of enquiry. After all, Doyle was Chief Accountant. As the Americans say, he would know where the bodies are buried.'

'And we're talking about two bodies.'

'Indeed we are.' Buchanan paused. 'Would it be too much to ask why you didn't want to talk about this in front of Harvey? He is, after all, also covered by the Official Secrets Act – as you are.'

Marler checked his watch. He'd soon have to leave to catch his flight for Zürich. He gazed straight at Buchanan.

'I never flannel people. But I've been assessing you ever since I entered this office. I know Harvey. He'll make a balls-up of the whole business. I think you'll do rather better in bringing the investigation to a conclusion.'

'Thank you,' said Buchanan. 'I take that as a compliment.'

* * *

Driving to London Airport, Marler checked over in his mind what he had achieved. He remembered a friend whose security company had been taken over by Buckmaster with a hostile bid.

Every form of intimidation and pressure had been employed to demoralize him. Rumours had been spread that his family would be kidnapped and held to ransom. There had been a burglary at his home which seemed pointless – until too late he discovered his phone had been bugged.

A number of his security trucks had been sabotaged – involving very late delivery of consignments to old customers who had consequently withdrawn their business. His wife had suffered a nervous breakdown. To stop the pressure – none of which could be proved to the police – his friend had accepted a bid from World Security which hugely undervalued his firm.

Well, thought Marler, Buckmaster is going to enjoy a taste of psychological warfare himself. He felt confident that Leonora would show him the compromising photograph sooner or later. Probably sooner.

Now Buckmaster was going to face discreet but persistent cross-examination by Chief Inspector Buchanan into Doyle's death. The combined pressure was bound to have some effect on the Minister's morale. Most of all he'd worry about the press getting hold of one of the two stories. Well, chum, he said to himself – you're not the only one who can set about destabilizing the morale of an individual. With a sense of grim satisfaction he boarded the Zürich flight.

47

Marler made the call to Buchanan from a phone at Kloten Airport soon after landing. He had to wait awhile
before the Chief Inspector's voice came on the line.
Buchanan had just arranged an appointment to see
Lance Buckmaster that evening at his apartment in Belgravia.

'Who is this?' Buchanan enquired.

'Marler speaking. Didn't they tell you? I gave them
my name.'

'Just to check your identity, what were you wearing
when I saw you last?'

'Check sports jacket, grey slacks, blue shirt, yellow
tie.'

'And give me the name – just the surname – of the
man who was with me when you arrived.'

'Harvey. You are a suspicious character . . .'

'Merely careful. Where are you calling from?'

'A long way from London. Don't ask me the location.
I am careful, too.'

'I'm satisfied. What is it, Mr Marler?'

'Another possible lead I overlooked to mention when
I saw you.' Marler paused: Buchanan should grasp the
significance of that conversational ploy. 'The lead is a
hit-and-run – so-called – death which took place in
London recently. A man called Dr Rose of St Thomas's.
Buckmaster might be able to help you on that one.'

'Who is this Dr Rose? As you kept saying, what is the
connection?'

'Dr Rose was the pathologist who examined the body of the unknown girl murdered at a flat in Radnor Walk. Bye . . .'

Marler picked up the phone again and dialled police HQ in Zürich. He asked to speak to Arthur Beck, gave his name, and said he'd also like to speak to Paula. He waited and was put on to two different people. The second was a woman. He had to repeat what he'd said at the beginning. Another wait. He kicked snow off his shoes: they had brought a mobile staircase for disembarkation from the flight and the snow was thick on the ground.

'Arthur Beck speaking. Who exactly is this?'

'I thought they'd have told you by now. I'm speaking from Kloten. I just flew in from London. I'm trying to contact a man called Tweed. My name is Marler.'

'Who?'

'Tweed. Come on, Beck, you know him. You've worked together in the past. His assistant, Paula Grey, is probably with him. And Bob Newman, the foreign correspondent.'

'I think you'd better report to police headquarters. A taxi driver will bring you here.'

'You haven't answered my question about Tweed . . .'

'A taxi driver will bring you here. Goodbye, Marler.'

Now what is happening, Marler wondered? He picked up his case and headed for the taxi rank. Was Beck hostile towards Tweed? He'd have to box clever when he arrived at police HQ.

'That was a man called Marler,' Beck said to Tweed, Paula and Newman after he'd put down the phone. 'Just flew in from London, so he said. What do I do with him when he arrives here? You know him?'

'A key member of my team,' Tweed replied.

481

He looked up as a policewoman showed Butler and Nield into the large office overlooking the River Limmat. It was night and across the water lights glittered along the waterfront. Reflections from street lamps vibrated in the dark water. Butler and Nield had just returned from taking baths at the Hotel Schweizerhof. They sat down and watched Tweed.

It was two days since the massacre at Brunni. Since then Beck had installed Tweed in a guarded house in the Altstadt. He was brought to police HQ only after night had fallen. Beck flexed his hands.

'You haven't told me what I do with this Marler. Could he be someone else impersonating Marler? We can put him in the interrogation room and you can take a look at him unseen through a one-way window. World Security is like an octopus with its tentacles everywhere. I've only grasped that recently.'

'It might be a wise precaution,' Tweed agreed. 'Then if it is Marler he can join us . . .'

'I don't think so,' Newman intervened vehemently. 'How do we know we can trust him? He could be in Buckmaster's pocket by now.'

'I agree with Bob,' Paula chimed in. 'We can't risk it.'

Tweed looked at Butler and Nield. 'Your opinion of Marler?'

'He's always been a lone wolf,' Butler replied. 'But where Tweed is concerned I'd trust Marler with his life.'

'Which is exactly what you would be doing,' Paula exclaimed.

'Pete?' Tweed enquired, facing Nield.

'I go along with Butler. And on this cross-country run we are going to need all the help we can get.'

Beck stood up from behind his desk. 'One piece of information I omitted to pass on to you, Tweed. Chief Inspector Kuhlmann phoned me from Germany a couple of days ago. He reported that Morgan crossed the border into Germany at the Basle frontier post in the direction of Freiburg. Driven by a chauffeur – wearing steel-rimmed spectacles.'

'And that sounds like Armand Horowitz,' Newman said grimly.

'So,' Beck continued, 'do you still think, Tweed, it's a good idea to travel back to England by road? And along the German autobahns? I've had my doubts about that ever since the idea came up.'

'That's the route I'm taking,' Tweed told him. 'And we have made all the preparations for me to go by road.'

'You're stubborn.' Beck shrugged. 'Now you must excuse me while I go downstairs and make arrangements to receive this Marler.'

Tweed waited until they were alone. He then walked across the office and turned on a transistor radio. It was tuned to a police waveband. He noted its position, turned the station knob until he found music playing. Standing, he addressed his team.

'That's probably unnecessary – but it guards against the room being bugged. World Security have penetrated this building in another way. They have an informant inside the organization.'

'How on earth do you know that?' Paula asked.

'Because Morgan and – more important – Horowitz have crossed into Germany. And Beck said that they were pointed towards Freiburg – which is on the route I will be taking. Beck phoned here several times before we left for Brunni – and made advance preparations for my journey. The coincidence is too great.'

'Then we must change the route urgently,' Paula stated.

Tweed shook his head. 'No, we keep to the original arrangement. The same route.'

Paula glanced at Newman. He was sitting with the ghost of a cynical smile. She looked at Butler and Nield.

Butler showed no reaction. Nield winked at her. She turned back to Tweed.

'This is madness.' Her eyes narrowed. 'You look too innocent. What are you up to now?'

'I have already told you. I am going to smash World Security, I am going to destroy Buckmaster. The second part will be the more difficult – to accomplish it without a great national scandal. We'll have to play it off the cuff. Now I am going down to the transceiver inside the van Beck had driven down from Brunni and parked outside. I want to see if I can contact the *Lampedusa* again. It may be close to its rendezvous with the Soviet military establishment.'

'Then we're close to a major disaster,' said Paula.

Tweed turned the radio knob back to the police band, switched off the radio. Newman joined him as he left the room.

'I'm coming with you. It's dark outside . . .'

While they waited Paula poured everyone more coffee from a percolator on a hot-plate. They sat in silence. From outside the only sounds were the occasional wail of police sirens. Fifteen minutes later Tweed returned with Newman.

'I made contact.No reply to the two trick questions – as I expected. My main idea was to keep up the morale of Hoch, the radio op. I recognize his "fist" – we practised before the *Lampedusa* sailed. The position aboard must be very tense by now.'

Latitude 34.10.N Longitude 25.50.E. The *Helvetia* was sailing south of Crete on an easterly course. Although no land was in sight the freighter was about midway along the huge Greek island. Its scheduled progress had been considerably slowed down by worsening weather. Under a lowering sky twenty-foot-high grey waves like small

484

mountains rolled towards it. The foredeck was awash as the massive waves broke over it. The glass was dropping, a storm was brewing.

Greg Singer fought his way up the companionway to the bridge as the vessel pitched and tossed violently. He had checked once more the vast bulk of the monster computer in the hold. By some miracle it had still not shifted its position. He staggered across the bridge to where Captain Hartmann stood alongside the helmsman behind the wheel.

'How much time have you to make up?' Singer shouted.

'Make up?' Hartmann stared at the rugged-faced Singer as though he were mad. 'We are six hours behind schedule – and the latest met forecast promises a Force Seven gale. We shall be lucky to stay only six hours late. There is just a chance the gale will pass to the south. But look at it now.'

He waved a hand beyond the foredeck. The view was hardly encouraging. Giant rollers swept towards them from all directions. In the distance clouds like a black hand had smothered the horizon. Singer tightened his lips: there seemed little point in bullying the skipper any more.

And the problem he'd had on his mind earlier now seemed to be more menacing. When they made the rendezvous would the Russians simply let him go? He was beginning to doubt it more and more. On shore it had seemed a straightforward deal. Now at sea with nothing in sight but the accursed surf-topped rollers Singer felt trapped. Somehow he had to escape.

The missile cruiser *Sverdlov*, one of the Soviet Navy's most modern and heavyweight ships, had emerged from the Dardanelles Straits and was sailing south at high speed through the Aegean Sea for the rendezvous close to Eastern Crete.

The weather was good, the sea was calm, the huge

warship was proceeding at top speed. The commander had no doubts: he would reach the rendezvous with the freighter on time. His only worry was the latest met report. A fierce gale was raging south of him. But he didn't expect it to slow his ship's speed by more than a few knots.

The unseen eyes of the spy satellite *Ultra* looked down on the earth. Its circuit took it over the Black Sea, the Aegean Sea and then across the Mediterranean to Libya, its main target. At Langley, Virginia, Cord Dillon studied the latest photographs *Ultra* had transmitted. He compared them with the report prepared by the analysts. Copies had been sent earlier to Washington. The red phone rang. He grabbed it, announced his identity.

'Tremayne here,' the Admiral replied. 'You've seen the latest *Ultra* pics?'

'I was about to call you. They show the *Sverdlov* is already west of Rhodes. That's getting pretty close, Admiral.'

'Which is why I've sent Naples an urgent *Leopard* signal. In short, to move their butts . . .'

Approaching Crete, Hank Tower, commander of the Kidd class destroyer DGG 997 *Spruance*, was feeling frustrated. He was on the bridge when the decoded signal from Washington was handed to him. He scanned it quickly, then called for more speed.

In the engine room the crew looked at each other. *Spruance* was swaying like a ballet dancer in the heavy seas. Normally they would have reduced speed. But orders were orders.

Tower, feet straddled to counter the vessel's motion, stood on the bridge gazing ahead. His frustration sprang from his inability to launch his helicopter in this weather.

486

At the first sign of a slackening of its force, he would send the machine aloft. That was the way to locate any vessel in the area which had a silhouette even remotely resembling the *Lampedusa*.

48

An Oriental maid showed Buchanan and his assistant into the living-room of Lance Buckmaster's Belgravia apartment. As they entered the room Buckmaster stood up from a Georgian desk and came round it to meet them, his manner affable. He shook hands with Buchanan who introduced his assistant.

'This is Sergeant Warden. He'll take notes of our interview if that's all right with you, sir.'

'Make yourselves at home. Do sit down. Can I offer you a cigarette?'

'Thank you, but neither of us smoke.'

'Jolly good. Neither do I. Goes back to the days when I was with my airborne division. Thank you for agreeing to come here rather than at the Ministry. A hotbed of gossip, any Government department.'

'That's what I thought,' Buchanan agreed as he sat down in a carver chair and crossed his long legs.

'Wouldn't you prefer a more comfortable chair?' Buckmaster suggested.

'This will do me nicely, sir. I know you're a very busy man, so I'll come straight to the point.'

'Not enough people do that. Please carry on.'

Warden, seated in an armchair, his notepad in his lap, was careful to show no expression. This was typical

Buchanan tactics. A gentle opening to relax the target.

'We find ourselves in a bit of a quandary,' Buchanan began. 'We're hoping you'll be able to help us see a little daylight.' He paused. 'The fact is I'm concerned with two murders.'

'Two?' Buckmaster looked puzzled, intrigued. 'How can I possibly help?'

'You haven't asked me which two murders I'm talking about.'

Warden smiled inwardly. It was beginning. Buchanan's tactic of interrogation by psychological attack – disturbing the morale of his opponent. Buckmaster, wearing a hacking jacket and corduroy trousers, was sitting on a chintz-covered couch, legs apart, hands clasped lightly between them. He smiled wolfishly – as much as to say all right, I'll play your little game.

'Tell me, Chief Inspector, which two murders are you talking about?'

'The murder of Edward Doyle, your chief accountant, at the Threadneedle Street headquarters of your company . . .'

'Just hold it there a moment, would you? I understand Ted fell from a window in his office. Poor devil. I heard it could have had something to do with his gambling habits.'

'Gambling habits, sir? What kind of gambling would that be?'

'The gee-gees. Horses. I never knew it while he was in my employ, but apparently he gambled in a big way. And, sadly, usually lost. Most people foolish enough to make that their hobby do lose.'

'Does gambling really fit in with the character of a man who rose to be chief accountant in an international conglomerate as big as World Security?'

Buckmaster waved his hands in a vague gesture. 'I suppose that being concerned with figures he deluded himself that he'd worked out a winning system. I'm just guessing.'

'I'm always interested in guesses. Sometimes they hit the mark. The trouble is we've found no evidence at all that Doyle ever visited a racecourse in his life.'

'That's odd.' Buckmaster frowned as though in recollection. 'I'm sure someone told me something about betting slips being found in his office . . .'

'At his home, sir. Not at his office.'

'Oh, I see. Can't recall who brought the matter up. Maybe my wife. I gather you've interviewed her at Thread-needle Street.'

'What did you think was the significance of Doyle being in possession of betting slips, sir?'

'Well . . .' Buckmaster looked at Warden, then back at Buchanan. 'I assumed the poor chap had got himself in too deep and took the only way out?'

'Suicide? Is that what you thought?'

Warden kept his head down as he scribbled in short-hand. In a brief conversation Buchanan had led the Minister of External Security into the labyrinth of discussing the circumstances leading up to Doyle's death. And this man is a polished political performer he was thinking.

'Well,' Buckmaster said slowly, 'it does seem to follow.'

'You discount then the possibility that Doyle accidentally fell out of his office window. You're saying that in no way could it have been an accident?'

'I can't say I've discounted any possibility. I'm not sure how we reached this point in the conversation.'

'So you haven't discounted the option that Doyle might have been murdered?' A pause. 'Sir?'

'You seem to have forgotten the betting slips you say that you found at his home.'

'No, sir, I haven't forgotten them. There's a difficulty in that direction. A number of betting slips were found in his house tucked under a household article. They were tested

489

for fingerprints. Doyle's fingerprints. There were no fingerprints on those slips. Why would a man carefully wipe old betting slips clean of his fingerprints. Any guesses on that point, sir?'

'I don't quite like the tone of your question.' An edge to his voice now. He sat back and clasped his long jaw in one hand. The blue eyes were like chips of ice.

'To have reached your present position you have to be a man of wide experience and intelligence.' Buchanan paused. 'I simply thought you might be able to help me.'

'I really have no comment.'

Buckmaster relaxed. Warden again kept his expression blank. His chief was on top form. What was coming next?

'Then there's the second murder,' Buchanan went on genially. 'Where you, by your presence at the scene of the crime, seem to be the only link with the Doyle investigation.'

'Which murder is that?'

'The brutal murder of an unknown girl in Tweed's flat at Radnor Walk.'

Buckmaster's jaw muscles tightened. His body stiffened and he stared at the Chief Inspector, who patiently waited for his reaction.

'I understood Chief Inspector Harvey of Special Branch was in charge of that case.'

'Indeed, he is. Quite correct, sir. But informally he has suggested I include that case in my enquiries.' Buchanan reached inside his pocket, produced an envelope and held it out. 'This letter to you from him authorizes me to bring up the Tweed case.'

Buckmaster took the envelope, tossed it on the couch beside him, unread. He sat erect, buttoned up his hacking jacket. Now very much the Minister for External Security, Warden was thinking. Buckmaster's voice was terse, brusque.

'I refuse to discuss any aspect of what happened at

490

Radnor Walk. A matter of national security. The only officer I'm prepared to talk to is Chief Inspector Harvey – and he already has the meagre information I was able to supply.' He glanced at the red boxes piled on his desk. 'And now, if there's nothing else, I would like to terminate this interview. I expect to be up till midnight going through my despatch boxes.'

Buchanan stood up, followed by Warden. 'I would like to say I appreciate the amount of your valuable time you have given me, sir.'

Buckmaster, also standing, looked at Buchanan with bleak suspicion. Had he detected a note of sarcasm in this too polite police officer? He nodded.

'I'll show you to the door.'

Buchanan waited until his host was reaching for the handle before he spoke again. 'Incidentally, sir, I imagine, as you are going to be working here it will be no inconvenience that we have asked your chauffeur, Hanson, to visit us at the Yard this evening?'

'What on earth for?'

'It concerns Doyle's residence where the betting slips were found. A neighbour opposite, a lady, saw a stranger call at Doyle's house a little while ago. He apparently had a key since he went up to the door, paused, and then went inside.'

'I fail to see how this concerns Hanson.'

'I hadn't quite finished, sir. This stranger, a man, called after Doyle had died. The neighbour proved to be an observant witness, gave us a clear description of the stranger. We showed her half a dozen photographs of various men, one of them Hanson. She immediately picked him out as the man who had called.'

'Where on earth did you find a photo of Hanson?'

'Very straightforward, sir. You're one of the most well-known men in the country. We contacted a photographic library and they came up with several pictures of you

491

arriving at some function – with Hanson standing by the door of your Daimler as you alighted. We blocked out your picture, of course.'

'Obviously a case of mistaken identity.'

'That, sir, is what I wish to check this evening. I won't keep you any longer from your boxes. The work of the Government must go on.'

Warden waited until they were seated inside the unmarked police car parked further down the street. He asked the question as they fastened their seat belts. Buchanan was behind the wheel.

'He road-blocked us on the Tweed business.'

'Which is exactly what I anticipated,' Buchanan remarked as he started the engine and drove away from the kerb, his headlights playing over the snow-streaked street.

'So what was the point?'

'To rattle him. I'm sure he was concealing something from us. His eyes flickered briefly when I mentioned Hanson.'

Alone, Buckmaster walked into his study, closed the sound-proof door and poured himself a stiff Scotch. He felt like a man with a noose tightening round his neck. He swallowed the drink.

First there was Tweed. The agile bastard had so far eluded every effort to eliminate him. He'd check progress on that front in a minute.

Second there was the withdrawal of the Romer loan. He had just managed to cover that by getting Morgan to sell one small subsidiary company at a ridiculously low price. He had never sold before: he had always acquired. It was like losing an arm.

And now there was this smart-alec Buchanan, linking the two cases. He didn't like the sound of Hanson being interviewed. Would the fellow have the sense to say nothing?

The drink helped. He stared at himself in a wall mirror. He looked quite normal, poised, sure of himself. Some of his arrogant self-confidence returned that he would win again. He always won. I've won every battle I've fought, he reminded himself. Nothing's changed: I can do anything.

He sat down at his desk and used his private line to call Morgan in Freiburg. He drummed his fingers on the desk top while he waited. Morgan came on the phone.

'Buckmaster here. Any progress with locating the target?'

'We not only know his whereabouts – he's in Zürich – but we know the exact route he's following when he tries to return by road.'

'If you have to take risks, take them. That consignment must not reach its destination. *Understood?*'

'Fully. Everything has been laid on for his reception . . .'

'Your head's on the block with this one.'

'That doesn't worry me . . .'

'But maybe this will. I've had a visit from a Chief Inspector Buchanan. CID. He asked questions linking the murder at Radnor Walk with Doyle's demise in Threadneedle Street.'

'My God! How could he do that?'

'He's done it, take my word. Oh, there's something else. Apparently he has a witness who alleges she saw Hanson enter Doyle's house – after Doyle's death.'

'I don't like the sound of that. What bloody bad luck . . .'

'So, you see, Morgan, your head really is on the block.'

Morgan began to reply and realized the line had gone dead. He swore as he replaced his own receiver. Buckmaster had gone off the line after delivering the appalling news. Morgan reached for his hip flask, unscrewed the cap, upended the flask and took a heavy slug. The news had unnerved him. He was sweating like a pig. They were closing in on him – would Buckmaster throw him to the wolves if it came to that?

Tweed. He has to be liquidated this time, he told himself. Even if I have to pull the trigger.

Carrying his case, Marler walked into police headquarters in Zürich, announced his identity, said he had an appointment with Arthur Beck. The uniformed police receptionist asked for proof of his identity and Marler produced his passport. His profession was given as Insurance Executive.

He was escorted to a large room with a table in the centre and hard-backed wooden chairs pushed under it. The receptionist said someone would bring him coffee while he waited for Mr Beck.

Marler dumped his case on the spotless floor, lit a king-size cigarette and walked slowly round the room. The walls were painted white. The only furniture was the table and the chairs. The only object on the table top was a heavy glass ash-tray.

Three of the walls were blank. No pictures. On the fourth wall was a large rectangular mirror. Marler stood in front of it and studied the glass. Then he raised his right hand and flapped it in a little wave at the mirror.

On the other side in another room Beck stood alongside Tweed. They had a clear view of Marler. Beck stiffened in surprise when Marler gave his little wave. He looked at Tweed.

'Is that Marler?'

'Definitely.'

'What the devil is he waving at himself for?'

'He's waving at you. He's spotted this is a one-way window. As I said, that's Marler. I'd like to talk to him alone.'

'Be my guest. I'll lock this room and wait upstairs for you with the others . . .'

494

Tweed walked into the other room and Marler gave him a little salute as a policewoman brought in a tray with coffee and left them alone.

'You really are wicked,' Tweed observed as they sat at the table. 'Beck was startled when you gave your little wave.'

'The whole place screams interrogation room. So why a mirror? It had to be a one-way window for unseen observation. You're not showing signs of wear and tear considering you've been hunted across half Europe.'

'I'm all right. What's happening back at home?'

'I've been putting the wind up Buckmaster. You probably won't approve, but I had a faked picture concocted – showing Buckmaster on a couch with a luscious girl friend. Then I gave it to his wife, Leonora. Should set the cat among the pigeons.'

'I don't disapprove. The man is evil. I know that now.'

'I also had a chat with Chief Inspector Buchanan, the officer investigating the death of Doyle, the World Security Chief Accountant in Threadneedle Street. Told him Buckmaster still has a key to the private elevator up to where Doyle took his dive.'

'How did you find that out?'

'Again, you'll maybe not approve. It came out while I was in bed with the delightful Leonora. Pillow talk.'

'You have been busy . . .'

'Then I called Buchanan again, just after flying out here – and suggested he check the so-called hit-and-run death of Dr Rose. Very convenient. He conducted the post-mortem on the girl found in your bed.'

'You can't put too much pressure on Lance Buckmaster as far as I'm concerned. Anything else?'

'Yes. I may have cleared you of any connection with the girl murdered at Radnor Walk. What's your blood group?'

'A positive.'

'Which is the same as for forty per cent of the

population. I have a photocopy of Dr Rose's post-mortem report, courtesy of Howard. There were blood stains on the sheet – and more traces of blood and skin under one of the girl's fingernails. Her blood group is O positive. Same again as for forty per cent of the population. The punchline is the blood group of the traces under the girl's fingernail. I should have used the singular before. Her index finger. Same as the stain on the sheet. Blood group AB negative. A very *rare* group, the murderer's. My guess is we need to identify the blood groups of Buckmaster and Morgan.'

'Buckmaster's will be recorded at the Ministry of Defence. He's still a reserve officer in the Airborne forces. I have a friend at the MOD. When I get back home . . .'

'*If* you get back. What about Morgan?'

'That may be more difficult, but nothing's impossible . . .'

'Except your reaching London alive. How are you travelling?'

'By road. Now, don't start arguing – I've had enough of that from Paula, Newman *and* Beck.'

'Who's arguing?' Marler tipped ash into the glass bowl. 'I think that may be the safest mode of transport. Depends on the route.'

'That's decided.' Tweed pulled a map out of his pocket and spread it out on the table. 'From here to Basle. Cross into Germany at Basle, then straight up the autobahns at high speed. Later, veer off west through Belgium and arrange for a vessel to cross the Channel.'

Marler studied the route which was marked with a black felt-tip pen. He looked up at Tweed.

'This route has just been worked out?'

'No. I planned it a couple of days ago . . .'

'And told who?' Marler enquired.

'Paula, Newman, Beck and the police escort which will take us through to Basle . . .'

'Then change the route. There could have been a leak.'

'There probably has been. Morgan and Armand Horowitz crossed the frontier at Basle heading towards Freiburg two days ago.'

'I see.' Marler went quiet, blew a smoke ring, studied Tweed. 'You're setting yourself up as a target so they'll come after you. And you're relying on speed to get you through.'

'That and the cooperation of Otto Kuhlmann. I've spoken to him. He's alerting their élite group of counter-terrorist police.'

'You're not going to change your mind, so I won't waste my time. What I'll need is a chopper – preferably a Sikorsky – with a first-rate pilot. I'll also want a sniper-scope rifle.'

'You won't get either from Beck.'

'But I will from Kuhlmann. Then we'll run the gauntlet. It should prove interesting.'

49

8 a.m. The call from Tokyo came through to Buckmaster's Belgravia flat as he was preparing to leave for the Ministry. While he waited for the girl at the other end to put him through to his Far East Managing Director, John Lloyd-Davies, Buckmaster calculated the time difference. It would be 5 p.m., local Tokyo time.

'That you, Buckmaster?' Lloyd-Davies asked in a strained voice.

'Yes. Some problem?'

'You could say that. World Security shares dropped

twenty per cent today on the Tokyo stock-exchange. A tidal wave of selling. No buying.'

'For God's sake, why?'

'Due to strong rumours that World Security is going bust. That its liabilities vastly outweigh its assets. Some problem, as you said.'

'Where are these absurd rumours coming from?'

'I've been trying to track them. Which is why I waited to call you. Top financial consultants are advising clients to get out fast. I haven't traced the source yet. At midday I issued a reassuring statement. It did nothing to stem the panic.'

'Now, listen to me.' Buckmaster gripped the phone tighter. 'I want you to use every contact you have to find out who is behind this. Money, threats – whatever it takes. And report back to me as soon as you find the enemy. Then we can deal with him. That's it.'

Buckmaster put the phone down and stared into space. What would happen when the London market opened? Let alone Wall Street? They were all a lot of sheep. He didn't like the sound of what Lloyd-Davies had said. *A tidal wave of selling . . . It did nothing to stem the panic.*

Picking up the phone again he pressed buttons for the number of his main London broker. Jeff Berners might just be at his office early. He was. Berners answered the call himself, sounded impatient.

'Yes, who is it?'

'Buckmaster. I've just had a call from Tokyo . . .'

'I was about to phone you myself,' Berners broke in. 'You have heard about the big fall? So have we. Here they're already talking about marking down World Security shares by twenty-five per cent . . .'

'That's crazy . . .'

'Purely a precautionary move.' Berners now was soothing. 'Buyers should arrive in droves at that price. At least I hope so . . .'

498

'You hope so?' shouted Buckmaster. 'We're talking about one of the biggest conglomerates in the world. Quoted on the Tokyo, Sydney, New York, London and Frankfurt exchanges . . .'

'Which could fuel the flames,' Berners warned. 'There have been ugly rumours. One that a major bank in Tokyo is considering withdrawing its loan. Another that Zurcher Kredit in Zürich *have* withdrawn their loan. We called Zurcher Kredit but they wouldn't react, refused to give any comment.'

'Well, there you are.'

'Are we? No Swiss bank ever releases information concerning its transactions. Is it true by any chance?'

'Of course not. I'm surprised you ask me. Where are these rumours coming from?' Buckmaster demanded.

'No one can pinpoint them. There's even a rumour it's a massive bear-raid to force down the price prior to a huge consortium bidding for World Security. That could shove up the price today.'

'Will it do that?'

'You want my frank opinion?'

'For what it's worth.'

Berner's tone hardened. He didn't appreciate the sarcasm. 'People are doing their sums. They calculate you're needing at least five hundred million pounds just to stay afloat.'

Buckmaster felt ice-cold. Where was this precise information coming from? For a moment he was thrown off balance, then he recovered. No hint of his reaction must appear in his response.

'Then they'd damned well better do their sums again.'

'The trouble is,' Berners went on, ignoring the thrust, 'in the market everything is finally based on confidence and on trust. I'll keep you informed of developments . . .'

'Do that thing,' Buckmaster said and ended the conversation.

He sat behind his desk, his mind racing. A couple of minutes later the phone rang again. He snatched up the receiver.

'Yes?'

'Is that Mr Buckmaster? Chief Inspector Buchanan speaking.'

'Yes. What do you want now?'

'Simply to ask you did you ever meet a man called Dr Charles Rose?'

To Buckmaster it felt like a bombardment. His mind raced in a different direction. This was the last question he had expected. Should he deny all knowledge? Just in time he stopped himself falling into the trap.

'The name is familiar. Give me a moment to think. I meet so many people. Yes, it's coming back to me now. This subject does concern national security . . .'

'It also concerns possible murder. A third murder, sir.'

'Would you mind explaining that cryptic remark a little more?'

At the other end of the line Buchanan smiled to himself. He was up against an opponent worthy of his steel. No wonder Buckmaster was feared during debate in the House of Commons, noted for his ability to think on his feet, to slash an antagonist to verbal ribbons.

'Not at all, sir. Dr Rose was the pathologist who examined the body of the young woman found murdered in Tweed's flat. Not long after conducting his post-mortem he walked out of St Thomas's Hospital one dark evening. At his usual time. A great man for precise routine, Dr Rose. He was knocked down and killed in the street by an alleged hit-and-run driver.'

'Alleged?'

'That was what I said, sir. I have reopened the case since I have reason to believe it was cold-blooded murder. And in his appointments book is noted a meeting with you at the Ministry. Does that help your memory?'

'Yes, it does. I remember now. I can't say much about this for obvious reasons – of national security. But Dr Rose came to show me his post-mortem report on the girl found at Radnor Walk. Simple as that.'

'Thank you, sir. And did Dr Rose leave the report with you?'

'Of course not. He took it away with him. The interview couldn't have lasted longer than ten minutes. That's all I can tell you – because that's all there is to tell.'

'You see my problem, sir? I have three deaths to investigate. And the only link between the three is yourself. You were at Radnor Walk. Ted Doyle was your Chief Accountant. And you met Dr Rose.'

'I don't see your problem at all, Buchanan. I repeat what I said to you the last time we met. I am only prepared to discuss these matters with Harvey of the Special Branch. I suggest that from now on you go through the proper channels. Otherwise I may have to complain to the Assistant Commissioner. Do I make my meaning clear?'

'Perfectly, sir. And, of course, it is your privilege and your right to communicate with the AC at any time . . .'

'Don't lecture me,' Buckmaster rasped. 'I probably know the form better than you ever will. And now, if you don't mind, I'd like this line free for an urgent call I'm expecting from Frankfurt.'

'Thank you for your co-operation, sir . . .'

In his office Buchanan put down the phone. He had been talking into the air. Warden looked up from his desk and raised his eyebrows.

'Sounds as though it didn't go too well, sir.'

'On the contrary, Buckmaster is beginning to crack. He could easily have invoked national security to refuse to say a word about Dr Rose. The interesting thing is he went out of his way to explain why Rose came to see him. Which makes me wonder more about our esteemed Minister for External Security.'

'You think you'll break him down in the end?'

'I don't know. But as I've just said, Buckmaster is beginning to crack under the pressure.'

In his study Buckmaster sat with his hands clenched together. The whites of the knuckles showed. It *was* like a bombardment – coming at him from all directions.

He stood up, took the swagger cane he'd used as an officer from a drawer, and walked very erect round the room, slapping his thigh with the cane. During training with the Airborne Division he'd been under live fire. He hadn't flinched from that: he wasn't going to flinch from present difficulties.

The door opened and Leonora walked in. He glared at her. As she'd come in he'd been walking, slapping the cane he still held in his hand. She stared at him with a peculiar expression and then spoke cautiously.

'What are you doing, Lance?'

'Planning on how to conquer the world.'

She sucked in her breath as he continued marching round the room, holding himself ramrod erect. He held his head tilted back as he had when inspecting the troops.

'You're not in the Army now,' she remarked.

He turned on her. His eyes blazed. 'Why don't you knock before you enter my study. I don't want you in here. You're disturbing my planning – my strategic planning. Kindly get to hell out of here!'

She lost colour. She backed away from him. She fiddled for the door handle behind her back, found it, opened the door, backed out and closed it. Outside she leaned against the door and closed her eyes. She was convinced her husband was going mad.

50

Before leaving Zürich, Tweed had a final conference with Beck at police HQ. In the office sat Paula, Newman, Butler, Nield and Marler. Beck had marked the escape route on a large-scale map of Western Europe pinned to a wall. Seated behind the table Tweed looked worried.

'You're not sure this is a good idea now, are you?' Beck remarked.

'On the contrary, I'm more determined than ever to follow the planned route. What's on my mind is the fate of the original crew of the *Lampedusa*. I feel responsible.'

'If I were you, I'd get that out of your mind,' Beck advised. 'You have plenty to concentrate on getting back to London. Everything is organized.' He checked his watch. 'Midnight. You leave in one hour. And Chief Inspector Kuhlmann of the Federal Police has promised full co-operation once you cross into Germany.'

'I'd like a word with Kuhlmann once we're over the frontier,' Marler intervened. 'After all, I am the deception specialist.'

'That can be arranged.' Beck perched his backside on the far end of the table. 'Tweed, you're sure you have enough solid evidence to clear yourself of the accusation of murder and rape in your London apartment?'

'More than enough. Partly thanks to Marler,' he added without elaborating.

'And you think you know who the murderer is?' Beck persisted. 'Buckmaster or Morgan?'

'One of them,' Tweed replied cryptically. 'And I predict

my arrival in London will be the final straw which topples Buckmaster.' He looked at Newman. 'Not that he's in too good a shape now after those phone calls you made all over the world. World Security shares are dropping like the proverbial stone.'

'And I've more calls to make as we head north,' Newman told him. 'It will be a débâcle.'

'You're all assuming Tweed will get there alive,' protested Paula. 'After what happened at Brunni I've no idea what may face us once we arrive in Germany.'

'Not us,' Tweed corrected her. 'Arrangements have been made for you to fly home from Basle under an assumed name . . .'

'Then you can cancel your bloody arrangements. I'm seeing this thing through to the bitter end. You'd have to carry me aboard that plane.'

'Don't push it any more,' Newman warned as Tweed opened his mouth and then closed it without speaking.

'Unless,' Marler drawled, 'you're insinuating Paula would be a handicap on the trip.'

'Blast you both,' Tweed reacted with unaccustomed vehemence.

'Then that's settled,' concluded Paula, and gave him her best smile.

'I feel happier having Paula with us,' Butler remarked. 'A woman often observes something a man misses – she has a good eye for small details.'

'One more thing,' Beck informed them, looking at Paula, Newman, Butler and Nield. 'You're all carrying weapons I supplied. You can keep them while you're still in Switzerland, but before you cross the frontier at Basle you hand all of them back to me.'

Tweed picked up his briefcase and clutched it on his lap. It contained the previous year's appointments book of the call-girl, Sylvia Harman. Beck knew of her existence and had sealed her apartment while his men searched it inch by

504

inch. But Tweed had omitted to tell him about the book. Beck then sprang his surprise.

'If that is all I suggest we leave now. One hour ahead of the planned departure time.'

Tweed was intrigued. Did Beck suspect there was an informant inside his HQ? It had seemed strange he had not suspected the likelihood of a leak. He stood up and Beck led the way downstairs to the cars waiting outside. The others followed, carrying their cases. Tweed's return to England had begun.

Outside the HQ Tweed paused on Lindenhofstrasse before getting into the first of the cars. Paula fumed as he stood there, head cocked to one side. Zürich was very quiet at that hour. What was the unusual sound he had heard? Glancing up, he saw the icicles suspended from the roof gutter. By the light of a street lamp he saw globules of water forming, sliding down the icicles, dropping into the snow below with a soft *plop!* Behind him Beck spoke.

'Yes, the temperature has suddenly risen above zero. The big melt is coming. At last.'

'Which', Marler commented next to him, 'will make driving conditions on the autobahns diabolical if the same thing's happening in Germany.'

'We'll find out when we get there,' Tweed replied and sat in the front passenger seat.

Beck, who was driving him, slipped behind the wheel while Newman took a rear seat alongside an armed detective. As the car started off Newman checked his fully-loaded Magnum inside his hip holster. He could extract it swiftly even inside the car.

Marler took the front passenger seat in the second car and beside him another detective took the wheel. Paula and a third detective sat in the rear. Butler and Nield were inside the last car, one a front seat passenger, the other in the rear, and two detectives accompanied them.

The snow-streaked streets of Zürich were traffic-free as Beck drove out of the city of green spires and ancient buildings. He moved at high speed and followed a devious route towards Basle. Once clear of Zürich, he accelerated, way over the speed limit.

Inside his office at the World Security building in Freiburg, Morgan put down the phone. He shifted his bulk in the chair and gazed at Horowitz with a bland smile.

'My Zürich informant. Tweed & Co left just after midnight. Tweed, his mistress, Newman, three other men, and five detectives. They're coming towards us along the planned route. My informant slipped into Beck's office after they'd gone. And on the wall was a big map with the route marked. Straight up the autobahns from Basle towards Belgium. We're in business.'

'An odd lapse of security, that wall map.'

'Nobody's perfect. And Beck himself is driving the car which has Tweed inside it.'

'And the position at the Basle crossing?' Horowitz enquired.

'Everything's set up. Stieber is waiting there – on the German side, of course. In his Münich film studios van. The police checked him earlier.'

'And left him there?' Horowitz's tone was incredulous.

'Organization.' Morgan waved a stubby-fingered hand, his nails trimmed short. 'Stieber and his driver both have identity cards showing them as members of the Münich film unit. Stieber told the police wallah his van had broken down, that they were waiting for a repair truck. No one's worried.'

'Again, most curious.'

'If you don't like it, I'll handle the job myself,' Morgan snarled.

Horowitz nodded. The pressure was getting to Morgan despite his air of self-confidence. He checked his watch. They would know soon enough now.

It was the middle of the night when Beck stopped the car in an old village near the outskirts of Basle. For the third time during a journey at breakneck speed he took hold of the microphone, used the code signal, *Matterhorn*, and reported his position to Basle HQ.

'I'm going to stretch my legs,' said Tweed. 'You can spare a few minutes?'

'Just a few . . .'

Tweed stepped out into the darkness of a deserted street. Behind him Newman also left the car, the Magnum held by his side. He was followed by the detective, holding a Walther.

It was still cold as Tweed walked up and down in the snow. He looked up at the rooftops of the ancient houses with their dormer windows. Patches of tiles showed where the snow had retreated. He paused. There was a constant drip-drip as the icicles, shorter than in Zürich, sent a constant flow of water droplets into the snow. Underfoot it was soggy – the iron-hard crust had gone. The thaw was speeding up.

'We can provide a hot meal for you at headquarters before we drive to the frontier,' Beck called out.

'Thank you, but I'd sooner keep moving now we've started.'

He got back inside the car with Newman and the detective and Beck sped forward again. He stopped again a little later. Behind them the other two cars pulled up. Beck asked Paula and Newman for their weapons. He made a hand signal out of the window and in the rear car Butler and Nield surrendered their gas- and smoke-pistols.

Beck drove on, crossed a bridge over the Rhine. Within

minutes they had reached the control point between the two countries. Beck stopped his car at the cabin on the Swiss side and a short, stocky, broad-shouldered figure smoking a cigar appeared. Otto Kuhlmann. He shook hands with Tweed as the Englishman climbed out of the car. A detective fetched the cases from the boot.

'Good of you to meet us, Otto,' Tweed said. 'I certainly didn't expect to find you here at this hour. Now! What do we do next?'

'All arranged. We walk across to our frontier post where you see the silver Mercedes waiting.'

'We may be driving into an ambush,' Tweed warned. 'By now I reckon the opposition is desperate.'

'That's been foreseen, anticipated. And I have an account to settle with this World Security gang. One of their trucks once tried to smuggle forbidden high-tech equipment over the border into East Germany. We stopped them, but I could never make the case stick.'

'And you have a long memory,' Newman interjected.

Kuhlmann, an impressive and formidable figure in his dark business suit, grinned at Newman, held out his hand.

'Welcome to the party, Bob. A little while since we last met in Frankfurt. A lot of water has flowed under the bridge since then . . .'

Tweed had thanked Beck and said goodbye while the two men were greeting each other. Then he picked up his case as Paula joined him and they walked towards the Mercedes. Their feet slopped through snow which had become slush. Beyond the Mercedes a large black van was parked well to the side of the road with its rear facing them, a rear with two doors and a porthole window in each door. Tweed noticed by the street lamps it bore in German the legend, *Münich Film Studios Unit*. At intervals on the German sides of the road tall, tough-looking men in camouflage gear carried automatic weapons and watched them coming.

'Who are they?' Paula whispered.

'German anti-terrorist police. We are being received in style.'

Paula shivered. 'Let's get inside the car. It's one of the big jobs.'

She was right. The gleaming vehicle had the capacity to take Tweed, Paula, Newman, Marler, Butler, Nield and one other. Behind them Marler was making his request to Kuhlmann with all the reassurance that it would be granted.

'I'm a marksman. Tweed will confirm my statement. There will be an ambush, maybe more than one. I need a sniperscope rifle and a chopper. Preferably a Sikorsky with an expert pilot. I need to guard this car from the air.'

'You talk big,' Kuhlmann remarked in his gravelly voice. He studied Marler who stared back with his ice-blue eyes. 'OK. I'll oblige you. And with a Sikorsky. But you'll have to wait until we reach Freiburg.'

'Then what are we waiting for?'

Without a glance at the broken-down film-unit van, Kuhlmann ushered his flock inside the Mercedes. Butler and Nield sat on flap seats in the rear, facing Newman and Marler. Tweed ushered Paula into the front passenger seat and waited until Kuhlmann, cigar between his teeth, walked up to him.

'Otto, do you mind if I drive? I've been doing damn-all the past few hours.'

Paula winked at Kuhlmann. 'He just wants to let rip now we're on a German autobahn.'

'Well, I gather he was driving when that articulated truck tried to mow you down when you were last approaching Freiburg. If you'll risk it, I will.'

He went back, opened the rear door and squeezed himself in by Newman's side. Throwing his cigar into the snow, he slammed the door and called out to Tweed.

'I'll guide you. We hit the autobahn soon. Just try and get us there in one piece, there's a good chap . . .'

Morgan put down the phone in his Freiburg office and looked again at Horowitz.

'That was Stieber from his film-unit van. A silver Mercedes, 500 SEL, registration number . . . Headed towards here out from Basle. Tweed's inside it with other passengers. We've got them.'

'Maybe. The petrol tanker is ready?'

'Stationed in a side road just off the autobahn south of Karlsruhe. That where you're going to take them?'

'It's just starting. I'll see how things develop. I never finalize a plan until I have all the data.'

'You'll have a film show soon as Stieber arrives here with his van,' Morgan said jauntily.

Autobahn E 35 stretched ahead in the night endlessly like a huge unrolled carpet, a carpet streaked white and grey in their headlights as Tweed drove at high speed. There was hardly any other traffic. The grey streaks were dangerous – snow had melted, exposing ice below it.

The Mercedes glided through the night and Paula was lulled almost to sleep. She jerked wide awake suddenly as the car swung into a violent skid. Her hands clenched. She glanced at Tweed. His expression was calm as he drove into the skid and the steel barrier loomed up in the glow of the headlamps. Paula closed her eyes, waited for the impact. Tweed slowed, turned the wheel a fraction, skimmed past the barrier and drove on. In the rear Kuhlmann grunted.

'You handled that well. Some of this surface is shot ice.'

'I could have handled it better,' Tweed commented. 'I missed the gleam on the ice. I'll know better next time.'

510

A large sign appeared in the distance. Kuhlmann leaned forward to see it more clearly.

'You turn off right ahead. Direction Mulheim.'

'We're still south of Freiburg.'

'I said I'd guide you,' Kuhlmann said gently. 'I'm doing just that.'

'I want to be in Belgium before daylight. This is a detour.'

'And you'll see why when you take it.'

Tweed followed directions, took the turn-off for Mulheim. They drove along a deserted road which seemed familiar to Tweed. He waited awhile before he spoke to Kuhlmann.

'Surely we're heading up for Badenweiler Spa, for the Black Forest?'

'Only a short distance. Trust me. I have a little surprise waiting for you, for the opposition.'

Paula, wide awake now, stared ahead. The road was climbing, the snow was thicker on the surface. At least it covered that diabolical ice. Kuhlmann told Tweed to take a side turning to the right and he found himself driving along a road just wide enough for the Mercedes. And still climbing.

'Slow down,' Kuhlmann warned. 'You're coming to a gap in the trees to the left. Take it. And maybe you wouldn't mind slowing down.' He glanced at Newman. 'I didn't know your chief was an ex-racing driver.'

'Got the bit between his teeth,' commented Paula, then she gazed in astonishment as Tweed turned and they entered a vast amphitheatre which was a worked-out limestone quarry. The headlights shone on the walls rising, cliff-like, at the far end. But what held her was the sight of five cars parked in a semi-circular laager-like fashion. Tweed also stared.

Five silver Mercedes, all of them 500 SELs. And they all had the same registration number as the car he was

511

driving. He braked and spoke over his shoulder.

'What on earth is this circus, Otto?'

Kuhlmann chuckled grimly. 'I only had two days to set this up. Getting the cars was easy. Making up the number plates so they all matched the registration of this car was the very devil. But we managed it.'

'I don't quite see the idea,' Paula observed, 'or am I being dim?'

'You saw that Münich film-unit van parked near the border in Basle? That was World Security – filming Tweed's arrival – and this car we got into. I ordered the control police to question the driver superficially and leave it alone.'

'Why?'

'World Security runs its own espionage network. A dismissed employee came to me and spilled the beans. I've been letting them run on a loose rein, waiting my opportunity.' His tone became grim. 'This is it. You get it, Tweed?'

'I think so, but you explain.'

'That film unit will confirm you're travelling in a silver Mercedes with this registration number. They're stopping at nothing to prevent you reaching England alive. How do I know that? They bribed one of my assistants, Kurt Meyer, to give them information. I became suspicious of Meyer. Again I let him run loose for awhile. He used to report from a local public call-box. I had it bugged. Two days ago, when Beck told me you were coming through, I arrested him, put him in solitary.' He glanced at Paula. 'I grilled him myself.'

Paula gave a mock shudder, which was only partly mock. The thought of being cross-examined by Kuhlmann was not a pleasant thought.

'He cracked,' Kuhlmann went on, as though the outcome was the most natural thing in the world. 'Told me about the film van and that a major assault would be made on your way through Germany. So I prepared this.' He waved his cigar at the laager of Mercedes. 'Six cars will travel up the autobahn, all the same make and colour – and all with the same registration number. You, Tweed, will travel in one of them. But which one? They'll have trouble working that out.'

'And who will be inside the other cars?'

'The élite anti-terrorist unit armed to the teeth, all wearing business suits.'

'That reminds me,' said Newman, 'I'd appreciate it if you could loan me a Magnum .45 with spare mags . . .'

'And', Marler chipped in, 'you promised me a Sikorsky and a sniperscope rifle.'

'Waiting for you at the airfield at Freiburg. One of the cars will peel off and take you to the chopper. The pilot knows the plan, will easily catch up with us . . .'

'We'd also like weapons,' Butler suggested in his flat voice. 'Nield and myself. Walthers would suit us fine.'

'That's OK. One of those cars contains an armoury of guns.' He reached a sheaf of papers out of his pocket. 'Just sign these – they're temporary permits to carry weapons. Makes it all legal and above board. I prepared yours, Newman, in advance – and yours, Marler. Beck passed on your request while you were waiting to leave Zürich.' He looked at Butler and Nield. 'You two fill in your names, then sign on the dotted line.' He switched on the overhead light.

'Why are you doing all this for us?' Paula asked. 'And I'd like a Browning automatic . . .'

'Which is waiting for you, again courtesy of Arthur Beck's calling me. Here's your bit of paper. Why am I doing all this? To settle my score with World Security. They're going to attack our convoy, using some of their own personnel. They have some pretty dubious characters on their payroll – but always with no prison records. I want to catch them in the act . . .'

'With Tweed as the target, the tethered goat,' Paula said indignantly.

513

Kuhlmann threw up his hands. 'I thought it was your chief's idea that we do it this way . . .'

'It was,' Tweed said quietly. 'I'm quite satisfied. Which car will I travel in?'

'Second one in the convoy. You can decide who travels with you – on condition you don't drive. Too exposed.'

'I'd like Paula to come with me,' Tweed suggested. 'Then you can organize the rest of the seating arrangements.'

'OK. You sit in the rear with Paula. A couple of my men will occupy the front seats. I'll be in the third car – behind you. Newman can ride with me.'

'That's settled then,' Tweed said impatiently. 'Hadn't we better get the show on the road?'

'Why not?' responded Kuhlmann and opened the car door. 'We should hit the Belgian border before dawn.'

They stepped out into the raw night cold, their feet crunching on stones under the melting snow. In the silence of the darkness they could hear at the end of the quarry the sound of running water sliding down from the top of the cliff. Paula shivered as she glanced round while they approached the cars. The towering walls of the quarry reminded her of an ancient Roman amphitheatre where people died.

51

A short time after Tweed had turned off the autobahn towards Mulheim, Stieber drove his van north to Freiburg. Under the bonnet was a souped-up engine.

Half an hour later Morgan and Horowitz sat together in

the small cinema in the basement at World Security. Stieber sat behind them as the projectionist ran the film taken from the porthole window in one of the rear doors of the van.

Horowitz sat erect, his eyes motionless behind the steel-rimmed spectacles. He studied Tweed closely as he emerged from the Swiss car, ignoring the others. He noted the shoulders hunched against the cold but the head held high, glancing in all directions as he walked slowly through the snow towards the German post. The pause while he stamped snow off his shoes – an opportunity he seized to look straight at the van filming him. Laufenburg all over again – when he had gazed at the house above the Rhine filming his crossing into Switzerland. A reflection from a lamp caught the lenses of his glasses. For a few seconds they were silver, like laser eyes staring at the van. Then the glance swung away in an arc, observing everything at the frontier post. And, by his side, the Grey woman, also glancing all round.

To Horowitz there seemed something implacable in the slow deliberate walk into Germany. This was the man he had hunted across half a continent. Any other target would have been dead long ago.

'That's him,' Stieber whispered excitedly in the dark from a seat behind them.

'Shut your mouth,' Horowitz said with deadly calm. 'I am concentrating . . .'

Still motionless, he watched them approaching a silver Mercedes. 500 SEL. More men followed Tweed and the girl. A flock of them stood round the car as Tweed climbed inside. The registration number was clear – because the car was parked under a street lamp. Why? It would have been so easy to park it in the shadows. Odd. Very odd. Horowitz felt a warning tingle. The rest of the passengers climbed inside the car. One was Robert Newman. Of course . . .

The Mercedes moved off. Past the van. Out of sight.

515

Horowitz was convinced Tweed had known he was under observation. The whole film clip had the atmosphere of a stage-managed scene enacted for his viewing. The screen flashed white. End of film clip.

Horowitz still sat motionless as the lights came up in the cinema. Morgan stirred beside him, stared at his companion. He dug him gently in the ribs.

'That's it. Now we know the vehicle he's travelling in.'

Horowitz still stared at the blank screen. His voice was detached, as though he gazed into the distance and saw something invisible to Morgan and Stieber. Then he spoke, tersely, in a voice devoid of emotion.

'I need a silver Mercedes. 500 SEL. Like that car.'

'That we can provide,' Morgan said complacently. 'It just so happens we have one in the garage here. It's kept for when Buckmaster visits us. I give it a run now and again to keep the engine tuned up.'

'I'd also have liked the same number plates, but I'd assume there's no time to fake a pair.'

'Not really. We have to leave here at once. Stieber reported he didn't see the car when he was driving the van with that film here. And he can move fast in that van – he suspects they saw him coming, speeded up and took a turn-off. But they'll be back on the autobahn. That map inside Beck's office proves that.'

Horowitz stood up abruptly. 'Take me to the car at once. And your men are already positioned on the autobahn at intervals? And the petrol tanker south of Karlsruhe?'

He was walking towards the exit leading to the garage as he spoke and Morgan, his overfed frame wobbling, had trouble keeping up with him.

'Everything is laid on . . .'

'And your men are carrying no identification, I presume?'

'In the rush I didn't bother. No one in that car will survive the holocaust we've planned.'

'It's your company . . .'

Inside the huge underground garage it was cold and Horowitz slipped into his fur-lined trench coat. As he hurried to the Mercedes he put on his gloves. Reaching it, he scooped up handfuls of frozen snow dropped from the wheels of other cars and carefully smeared it over the front number plate. He repeated the process with the rear plate.

'I'm coming with you?' Morgan suggested.

'No one is coming with me. The keys . . .'

Unlocking the car, he climbed in behind the wheel and Morgan waddled over to open the automatic doors, pressing a button on a wall panel. The huge doors opened slowly with a grinding sound as they broke the ice.

Inside the car Horowitz took from his shoulder holster his Luger, checked the weapon. It was a 9-mm calibre Parabellum, probably the most widely used cartridge of its type. The muzzle had been adapted to take a silencer. Horowitz took the silencer from his pocket, screwed it on, laid the weapon on the seat beside him with spare mags. It had a magazine capacity of eight rounds. One should be enough.

For his steel-rimmed glasses he substituted a pair of horn-rims which altered his appearance. From his pocket he extracted a crumpled black beret and rammed it on his head. The transformation was complete. Without glancing at Morgan, who was running towards a BMW, he drove out, headed for the E 35 autobahn.

As the convoy of six silver Mercedes approached Freiburg the rear car peeled off, driving away up a turn-off leading to the airfield. Inside the car Marler sat in the front next to the detective driver. The other five cars disappeared north towards Karlsruhe.

Reaching the airfield, the car pulled up close to a Sikorsky helicopter with a ladder leading to the main cabin. At the foot of the ladder stood a uniformed policeman carrying an automatic rifle. Marler dived out of the car, thanked the driver, ran towards the guard with his identity card in his hand.

'Marler,' he said, handing the man his card. 'And I'm in one hell of a hurry to take off before someone is killed.'

The guard checked the card with the aid of a pencil flash, handed it back and gestured. Marler ran up the ladder and at the top a burly German in pilot's gear hauled him inside. Marler was talking fast again.

'You have a sniperscope rifle for me?'

'Ready and waiting, sir . . .'

'I have to sight it. Ammo?'

'Incendiary bullets, as requested.'

Marler fed the cartridges into the weapon, asked the pilot, who had retracted the automatic ladder, to leave the door open a moment. He aimed the rifle through the opening, the stock firm against his shoulder. The pilot suddenly pointed.

'There's that wild rabid dog again. The brute's already bitten one of the airport staff. Had to be rushed to hospital. Touch and go whether . . .'

Marler was staring through the night 'scope. Standing in the snow, forelegs apart, was a large mastiff. The 'scope brought the dog's head up close, its mouth smeared with foam, its teeth showing. It began trotting towards the chopper. Marler adjusted the sight, the dog's ugly head and chest filled the 'scope. He pulled the trigger. The report echoed across the airfield. The mastiff disappeared in a bursting cloud of blood, flesh and bone.

'It's been running wild in the woods,' the pilot said. 'I can take off for the autobahn when you're ready.'

'How about now?'

*   *   *

Morgan drove the BMW on to the autobahn and headed north. Beside him sat Stieber with a detailed map of the autobahn and the surrounding areas open on his lap. At certain points a cross marked different areas alongside the E 35. These were the carefully chosen ambush areas – where World Security guards waited with various weapons to annihilate the silver Mercedes.

All the waiting ambushers were in radio communication with a control point at Freiburg to co-ordinate the information. Morgan drove at medium speed for two reasons as the occasional flash of distant headlights indicated a vehicle coming towards them on the southbound lanes.

'You did give Horowitz one of those marked maps?' Morgan asked Stieber.

'He has a map with the same markings I have.'

'Good. And keep that radio connection open so we know what is happening.'

One reason Morgan drove at a medium speed was the state of the autobahn. The thaw was continuing. At intervals the streaks of melting snow exposed gleaming patches reflecting in their headlights like glass. Solid ice . . .

The second – and more important reason – he held down speed was he didn't want to run into the holocaust when it happened. He wasn't paid to take risks like that. The head of the Research & Development Division which had planned the ambushes was Stieber. He was an ideal choice for the job. He *enjoyed* his work.

'Shouldn't you step on the gas?' Stieber suggested. 'We're going to miss all the excitement . . .'

'The only thing I may step on is you. Shut up while I drive. It will all happen soon now.'

Inside his silver Mercedes Horowitz drove at high speed along E 35. Under the Luger on the seat beside him was the map with the ambush locations. He drove with great skill, avoiding the deadly ice, hands holding the wheel lightly. Horowitz was quite relaxed: at last he was alone and could handle the situation in his own way.

As at Brunni, he foresaw another débâcle – after all it had been organized by Morgan, a man for whom he had the utmost professional contempt. A con-man, a lackey and lickspittle for his boss, Buckmaster.

Ahead the autobahn followed a great curve, which gave him an excellent view. He sat up straighter. Spread out at intervals round the curve was a convoy of no fewer than five silver Mercedes. For a moment Horowitz was puzzled before he understood the strategy.

Driving with one hand on the wheel, he quickly examined the cars through a small pair of night glasses. His eyes narrowed as he spotted they all had the same registration plate number. He put down the glasses. Clever, very clever. He sensed the hand of Kuhlmann.

In one of those five cars Tweed was riding. *Which* one was the intriguing problem. He watched as they continued driving round the long curve. Car Number Two moved closer to Car Number One. Like a ballet Car Number Three closed up to Car Number Two. The remaining two Mercedes kept their distance at the rear of the convoy. The last Mercedes was a long way back. The rearguard.

The ghost of a smile appeared on Horowitz's normally expressionless face. Tweed was in Car Number Two. First part of the problem solved. Target located. Second part of the problem – how to get alongside Car Number Two.

Horowitz glanced at the map. The first ambush point was about five miles ahead. Horowitz had already worked out his operational plan. The rear car was quite a distance behind the convoy. The first ambush would be launched where the autobahn again followed a long curve. At that point – providing conditions were favourable – he would carry out the first phase of his plan.

*   *   *

Inside the second Mercedes Tweed sat in the rear seat closest to the steel barrier. Beside him sat Paula, erect, her shoulder bag looped over her left side. In front a detective was driving. In the passenger seat next to him was another detective.

There was so little traffic that the fast-moving convoy was occupying the inside lane. Tweed sat relaxed, eyes half-shut. By contrast Paula was like a coiled spring, staring at the car ahead, turning to check the position of the car behind them.

In the third car Kuhlmann sat beside another detective who was driving. In the rear seats Newman sat next to Butler – who also kept glancing round, a Walther resting in his lap. Newman also appeared to be half-asleep. The steady drumming of the convoy's engines had a hypnotic effect. Butler stirred again.

'Stop shifting about,' Newman suggested.

'I prefer to keep my eyes open, to see what's happening.'

'We'll all know when it happens,' Newman told him.

'That's a fact,' agreed Kuhlmann and bit on his unlit cigar.

At Freiburg Airport Marler was inwardly fuming. Just before take-off they had detected a mechanical fault. Men in overalls were working on the engine, fighting to correct the fault quickly. Outwardly, Marler waited calmly in his seat, staring out of the window at the bleak night. Beside him the pilot rolled cigarettes, placed his latest one inside an ancient tobacco tin. Between his lips dangled an unlit cigarette, tobacco dripping out of the tip.

'It shouldn't be long now,' he remarked.

'When they're ready I'd appreciate it if you move fast.'

'Will do. I've radioed the delay to Kuhlmann. He replied.'

'What did he say?'

'Something unprintable.'

'I can guess.' Marler resisted the temptation to check his watch. When they were airborne, they were airborne. If they were in time.

Morgan kept up his medium speed which would keep him miles behind the silver Mercedes transporting Tweed. There had been only one brief message on the agreed radio band. From Horowitz.

'Preserve radio silence at all costs . . .'

What the hell did that mean? Morgan wondered. It sounded promising – as though Horowitz knew what he was doing. He glanced at Stieber as he began moving round a long curve.

'How far to the first attack point?'

'About twenty miles from here.'

'We should hear something then. I hope. Tweed must be almost there now.'

Horowitz turned the wheel as he began moving round the second long curve. He could see only the last two cars and then the first of these disappeared. He glanced again at the map. The first ambush point was coming up. They might get Tweed at a first attempt, but he doubted it.

He began to put his manoeuvre into operation. Inside the silver Mercedes he saw the blurred outline of a figure glancing back. They'd be puzzled at first by his appearance. The fact that his number plate was obscured wouldn't worry them over much: slush had been whipped up by the wheels for long stretches. He increased speed, closing the gap between himself and the other car.

He lowered the window alongside himself. For two reasons. He had to hear the sounds of the ambush the moment it was launched. The second reason was more deadly. Both cars were moving at speed, which suited Horowitz's purpose. As he froze from the icy air flooding in he listened for the ambush . . .

The first Mercedes in the convoy was a long way round the curve, still in the inner lane and close to the steel barrier. There was no other traffic in sight ahead. The first warning they had that they had run into an ambush came when a rattle of bullets from two Uzi machine-pistols hammered the rear of the car. The driver did the unexpected. Instead of speeding up he slowed down.

'OK, Arber,' he said to the man alongside him. 'Respond.'

Arber lowered the automatic window. The sound of the fusillade had become a cannonade. Beyond the barrier figures clad in Balaclava helmets and ski suits stood behind the barrier, their weapon muzzles aimed. Arber had extracted the pin from a grenade, hurled it. He grabbed the second grenade in his lap, extracted the pin, hurled it. All this in fractions of a second.

The detonation of the grenades murdered the night. The men behind the barrier flung up their arms, fell backwards. The window behind Arber had been lowered. A machine-pistol projected, a hail of answering fire swept along the barrier as more Balaclava-helmeted figures appeared. Like targets in a shooting gallery they collapsed as the bullets ploughed into them. More grenades were thrown from the car. Detonations succeeded each other so one almost merged with another. One attacker held a rocket launcher. His finger was on the trigger when a stream of bullets laced across his chest. He jerked backwards, the launcher pointed skywards, its projectile exploded in the night high above the autobahn. Then silence. The convoy moved on.

In the third car Kuhlmann grinned, spoke to his driver as they sped on.

'The damned fools assumed Tweed was in the first car.

523

Not a bullet hit Tweed's vehicle.' He reached for the phone. 'Thor speaking. Our location is . . . Send the meat wagons. No hurry. Let them bleed . . .'

In the distance Horowitz heard the cannonade, the detonating grenades. This was the moment. He accelerated. Driving with one hand, his other hand rested on the ledge of the open window, holding the Luger. He aimed for the rear tyres of the Mercedes, fired three times. The target car slewed out of control, smashed into the barrier. Metal screamed against metal. The car stopped.

Horowitz rammed his car to an emergency stop, jumped out a few feet ahead of the other vehicle, ran towards it. Behind the windscreen he saw movement. He held the Luger gripped in both hands, fired twice. The windscreen crazed, two bullet holes appeared. In the front seat two detectives sagged, dead.

Horowitz hauled open the rear door. One man was slumped forward, unconscious. The other man moved. Horowitz fired and the movement stopped. He felt the pulse of the slumped man, detected it. Placing the Luger muzzle against his skull he pulled the trigger. The detective jerked convulsively. Once. Seven shots gone. He rammed a fresh mag into the Luger, opened the front door. One man lay back in his seat, a red stain in his forehead. Slight movement from the other man. Horowitz aimed calmly, pulled the trigger twice. He closed both doors, ran back to his own car.

Five minutes later, moving at high speed, he saw the rear of the convoy moving ahead of him. He slowed down, kept the same distance between himself and the fourth car he had observed earlier, settled down to maintain that speed.

Inside the fourth car a detective glanced back through the rear window. He nodded to his companion.

'It's OK. Tail-end Charlie has caught up. Our rear is all right.'

524

The convoy sped on through the night with Horowitz bringing up the rear. He glanced again at the open map by his side. The main onslaught – the petrol tanker attack – was several miles away yet. That was when, in the confusion, he would complete his mission, would kill Tweed.

The massive petrol-tanker was parked at the side of the slip road leading down to the northbound lanes of the autobahn. The driver sat hunched behind the wheel, his engine ticking over. The tanker was laden to the gills with petrol. On the seat by his side was the radio-control device which was tuned to transmit the beam which would detonate the bomb inside the tanker, a bomb sealed inside a heavy box.

His companion, muffled in a fur coat and hood, stood where he could look down the autobahn. In his gloved hand he held a walkie-talkie ready to warn the driver the target Mercedes was approaching. Through the night-glasses looped round his neck he could see a long way down the straight stretch of the autobahn – far enough to check the registration number.

When the time came he would call the driver, who had his own walkie-talkie. Then he would run back to the juggernaut to take the radio transmitter from the driver. It would be up to the driver to do his job, jump from his cab and clear of the immense mobile bomb.

He saw the lights of a car approaching, pressed the glasses to his eyes. Wrong registration, wrong make of car. Audi. He relaxed, beat his gloved hands round his body to keep the circulation going. They should be here soon now. He hoped.

Inside the second Mercedes Paula was breathing heavily, releasing the tension which had built up during the attack. Beside her Tweed nudged her gently in the ribs.

'You see, they can't even shoot straight,' he commented, recalling General de Gaulle's famous reaction after the assassination attempt in August 1962.

'It was frightening at the time though.'

'Well, that's behind us.'

'What worries me is what may lie ahead of us. They haven't given up yet, I'm sure.'

'On that point, I agree.'

'You really think we'll make it to Belgium in one piece?' Paula asked.

'I believe we will,' Tweed lied. He had grave doubts on that score. 'The unexpected may come to our aid,' he added.

Inside the third Mercedes Kuhlmann sensed the major crisis was close. He picked up the microphone linking him with the other vehicles. 'Kuhlmann here. From now on red alert. Repeat, red alert. And our chopper is grounded. Message ends.'

In the cab of the petrol-tanker the driver would have given anything for a cigarette. Instead he chewed gum. He dare not risk smoking with the cargo of liquid dynamite behind him.

Outside, the lookout, perched at the top of the slip road, half-frozen despite his layers of clothing, pressed his glasses to his eyes once more. He frowned, stared harder, perplexed. In the far distance headlights were approaching. A whole convoy of lights. All silver Mercedes. An awful suspicion entered his mind. He picked up the walkie-talkie.

'Manfred,' he called the driver, 'get ready. They may be coming. Four or five Mercedes. I can't pick up the registration number of the lead car yet. Stand by . . .'

'Can't be the target,' Manfred responded. 'They said only one Mercedes.'

'I said hold on! And get ready to move.'

'If you say so, Karl.'

The lookout strained his eyes. The first car was still a good distance away. He held his glasses fixed on it, desperately trying to read the registration plate. Still too far away. The cars were travelling one behind the other, hugging the inner lane next to the barrier.

From his elevated position in the cab Manfred looked beyond the barrier. He couldn't see them, but he knew a group of heavily armed men was waiting. There was no way the men travelling in the Mercedes could survive the weight of the planned assault. He was about to put a fresh stick of chewing gum in his mouth when the voice of Karl came over the walkie-talkie as he ran towards the tanker.

'Get ready to move, Manfred . . .'

Out of breath, he hauled open the door of the cab on the opposite side to the driver. He reached in, grabbed hold of the radio transmitter. He was shutting the door when he yelled at Manfred.

'Move! Go! Go . . .!'

Karl was running back up the slip road to his observation point, slithering on ice, recovering his balance. Behind him he heard the tanker moving down to the autobahn, driving down to position itself at right angles to oncoming traffic. To block the autobahn.

Arriving at the top, again out of breath, he turned the safety catch lever on the radio transmitter. It was now activated. Only one button to press – then the holocaust. Karl raised his glasses again, then stiffened. The cars were still a distance away and the night was oppressive with the silence of the cold. But the silence had been broken. He could hear the chug-chug of a machine in the sky. A helicopter was approaching.

*   *   *

'There's the convoy,' Marler observed as he sat next to the pilot.

He looked down on the autobahn below and counted. Five cars. The correct number. The last car was closing up on the convoy.

Once more Marler raised his own night-glasses. Across his lap rested the sniperscope rifle, fully loaded. The chopper moved ahead of the convoy and suddenly Marler tensed. The pilot glanced at him. Marler had the glass glued to his eyes.

'Trouble?' the pilot enquired through his mike.

'You could say that. A bloody great monster of a petrol-tanker has been parked across the autobahn. And a man is watching from the top of the slip road. Maintain your present height. You see the tanker? Good. Keep us in a hover one hundred yards this side of that tanker. Not an inch closer. Hell is coming . . .'

Marler wrenched off his headset, released his seat belt, moved swiftly back into the main cabin, holding the rifle. Standing with his shoulder pressed against the interior of the fuselage, he opened the door. The Arctic rushed in. Marler peered out backwards. The convoy was approaching. The forward movement of the Sikorsky ceased, the pilot was holding it in a hover. Marler eased his way to the other side of the door, looked forward and down.

The tanker had just stopped moving. It was stationed like a wall across the autobahn. The cab door was open. The driver was climbing out. Marler steadied himself against the fuselage. The pilot was holding the machine almost motionless. Marler raised his rifle, rammed the stock into his shoulder, peered through the sight, his finger on the trigger. The full-bellied side of the tanker jumped into the crosshairs of his weapon. He pulled the trigger. Three times in rapid succession as he sent the incendiary bullets into their target. He sat down in a seat and gripped the arm.

A blinding flash. The world came apart. The bomb inside the monster detonated by itself. The tanker disintegrated. Sheets of burning petrol enveloped the fleeing driver. The flaming curtain swept over the barrier where figures stood with Balaclava helmets, weapons at the ready. The detonation had come too early. There was a tremendous roar. The pilot saw the figures behind the barrier running, clothes alight, like weird illuminated ghosts in the night. The blast hit the Sikorsky. The machine wobbled crazily. The pilot gripped his controls, stabilized the machine. A lake of burning petrol spread down one side of the autobahn. The tanker had disappeared.

Inside the third Mercedes Kuhlmann saw the flash, heard the roar, grabbed the phone, shouted the order to the other vehicles.

'Laager. Laager. Laager!'

The drivers performed the previously agreed manoeuvre. The three rear vehicles drove into the next lane, pulled up in a semi-circle. Kuhlmann could see the two cars in front of him. The one carrying Tweed, the car ahead of him, had stopped just in time, short of the inferno flaring in a curtain of flame. Black smoke began to drift up.

Horowitz, in the rear car, reacted instantly when he understood the manoeuvre. He pulled out into the fast lane and past the two vehicles in front of him, stopping alongside the second Mercedes. Confusion. Chaos. The rattle of gunfire. Men shouting. He opened the door of his car, stepped out, the Luger held close to his side. He wrenched open the door of the second Mercedes. In the front two detectives. In the rear on the far side, Tweed, staring back at him. Horowitz's Luger moved in a blur, shot the driver, shot the detective next to him. The driver slumped, injured with a bullet in the shoulder. His companion groaned. A bullet in the ribs. Horowitz noted the girl sitting next to Tweed, aimed the Luger at Tweed. Two more shots echoed inside the car.

A looked of astonishment crossed Horowitz's lean face. Still gripping the Luger, he staggered back. Paula, holding her Browning in both hands, fired a third time. Horowitz was still upright, still moving. He stumbled round the front of the car, silhouetted against the sheet of flame. Newman, standing a few feet in front of his car, fired the Magnum, muzzle aimed at Horowitz. The heavy slug hit him in the right-hand side of his chest, hurled him backwards. He pirouetted like a ballet dancer, fell forward over the barrier and was propelled out of sight.

Newman ran to the barrier – in time to see Horowitz diving head first on to an ice-surfaced lake twenty feet below. As Tweed, Kuhlmann and Paula joined him, he saw the cracking of the ice. Horowitz disappeared through a three-foot-wide hole.

Kuhlmann had been shouting orders, forming his men into an irregular line of attack as they advanced towards the flames, firing with machine pistols at the surviving members of the assault group. He walked rapidly to join Tweed, carrying a powerful flashlight. He shone it down on the icebound lake.

'I don't understand how he was still able to move after I'd fired twice at him,' said Paula.

'He's the most professional assassin in Europe,' Tweed reminded her. 'I once heard of a man with six bullets in him who walked a mile for help.'

'That ice is six inches thick,' Kuhlmann commented. 'He must have gone through a thinner patch. He's still alive.'

Horowitz had drifted up under the ice, seeking the opening. In the glare of the flashlight they clearly saw his hands hammering at the solid surface of his ice tomb, the blurred outline of his head. 'I can't watch this,' said

530

Paula and went back to the car. Horowitz continued bobbing up and down beneath the ice, many feet from where he had dived into the lake. His hands were still beating at the unyielding ceiling above him, more feebly now.

'I'm not getting my feet wet rescuing that,' Kuhlmann remarked. 'For what? The expense of a long trial, a prison sentence, then later he breaks out. No thank you. Tweed, you shouldn't be out here. Newman, escort him back to the car. That's an order.'

Kuhlmann waited by himself, moving the flashlight, until the hands of Horowitz became still. The water beneath the ice shimmered as the corpse slowly sank. Kuhlmann turned back to the cars.

'That's that,' he said to himself.

He walked over to Tweed's car after looking at the dying flames. The firing became desultory, stopped. He bent down to speak to the new driver.

'The fast lane is clear. I'll order another car to lead the way for you. Go slowly until you're past this mess.'

'Same route?' the driver asked.

'Same route. You'll be in Belgium by daybreak. You'd better be.'

He stood up, saw Newman staring skywards to where the chopper hovered over the scene. Newman was making a thumbs-up gesture. Inside the Sikorsky's cabin Marler, watching through his glasses, smiled drily.

'When they start moving follow them. We'll escort them out of Germany.'

52

WORLD SECURITY EMPIRE CRUMBLING. SHARES DROP 40% ON WALL STREET

BUCKMASTER CONGLOMERATE CRASHING. RESIGNATION OF MINISTER?

MAJOR US BANK CALLS IN WORLD SECURITY LOAN

At 7 a.m. Buckmaster stared at the headlines of the newspapers strewn on the floor of his living-room in Belgravia. He had sent out early for the papers. He ran his hands through his hair. Who the hell had organized this conspiracy? It had to be a conspiracy: he'd organized enough of them in his time.

'I'll still beat them into the ground,' he thought, and then the phone rang. It was Morgan. Calling from Freiburg.

'It went wrong,' Morgan reported. 'The opposition outnumbered us by ten-to-one,' he lied.

'Present location of the target?'

'Last seen heading north along the same route. Middle of the night.'

Buckmaster had always trusted his intuition. 'He went in via Belgium. He'll return that way. Have you someone you can send to conclude negotiations there?'

'Yes. Stieber . . .'

'Then send him. To Brussels. Use the Lear jet. Alert our Belgian organization – to observe and locate. The negotiation must be concluded by Stieber,' he repeated. 'Board the jet yourself, drop off Stieber in Brussels, then fly here . . .'

Buckmaster clasped his hands and stared again at the spread of newspapers. At least he could still take decisions. If Tweed reached London, he was finished. Tweed would only return if – by some unknown means – he had cleared himself. Climax very close.

Tweed abandoned the idea of returning secretly to England by boat. He announced his decision when Newman was driving him into Brussels. He looked at Paula by his side and smiled.

'Remember? This is where it all started?'

'Where I fought you over coming with you.'

'And thank God you did. You saved my life when Horowitz opened that car door. A pro killer to the last, that man.'

'All part of my job,' she said dismissively. 'And how are we going to cross the Channel?'

'By air. I hate the sea. It never stops moving. Bob, the airport is the next stop.'

Marler, sitting alongside Newman, looked over his shoulder. 'Is that wise? Throwing caution to the winds on the home stretch?'

'When I phoned from Aachen I was calling the PM. She has laid on an executive jet for us. Officially, it is to take an EEC Commissioner to London.'

Paula stared at him. 'What's been going on? How could you call the PM when officially you're still a fugitive?'

Tweed lifted the briefcase he was holding in his lap. 'It is all here – the evidence to clear me. The story of Sylvia Harman. Her desk diary you found at her Zürich apartment. The photocopies Bob brought from World Security in Basle.'

'There's something you're not telling us,' she said.

'All will become clear.'

*　　*　　*

Morgan had disobeyed Buckmaster, had changed his plans. He was waiting near the check-in counters at Brussels Airport. A dozen yards away Stieber sat reading a newspaper. He was waiting for the signal from Morgan warning him that Tweed had arrived.

For Morgan it was desperate measures – a long shot. He had no information from his lookouts in Belgium, all of whom had a photograph of Tweed. He was hoping against hope that Tweed would decide to fly direct to London.

The Lear jet was parked on the tarmac – waiting to take him on to England. The thought of facing Buckmaster and confessing total failure appalled him. He stood close to a bookstall. It was a strategic viewing point: he could see all the check-in counters. He looked at his watch again, then at passengers approaching the counters. No sign of Tweed.

Newman drove along the approach road to the airport. He was worried about one factor: they carried no weapons. At the German frontier Kuhlmann had insisted they surrendered them. Quite correct, but damned inconvenient. He looked in his rear-view mirror.

'Butler and Nield are keeping up with us,' he remarked.

The two men were travelling in another Renault. Kuhlmann had phoned ahead to his opposite number in Brussels, Chief Inspector Benoit, an old friend of Tweed's. The two cars had been waiting at the frontier.

'Benoit is meeting us at the airport,' Tweed informed the others for the first time. 'He wants to wish us *bon voyage*.'

'It will be *bon* when we are airborne,' Newman said grimly as he reached the airport building and pulled in to the kerb.

Tweed carried his own case as he walked inside with Paula close to him, her eyes scanning the concourse. She still thought this was a bad idea but kept her mouth shut. Behind them Newman made a gesture to Butler and Nield to fan out. Unbeknown to Tweed, he had talked to the two men and Marler privately.

Tweed was the only one who showed no signs of tension as he walked across the concourse. A familiar figure appeared by his other side. Benoit. A jovial, portly man in his forties, he had a great beaked nose, light brown hair and shrewd eyes.

'You had a tough time in Germany I hear from Kuhlmann. Welcome to peaceful Belgium.'

'Don't say things like that,' Paula interjected. 'It's tempting fate.'

'My felicitations, Paula,' Benoit replied and then he hugged and kissed her on the cheek.

Tweed had paused near the check-in counters. Benoit turned to explain. He waved towards the counters.

'You need not go near them. I will escort you to the executive jet which has arrived and is waiting to fly you back.'

Morgan nodded to Stieber and moved out of sight behind the bookstall. Stieber looked round, spotted Tweed. Standing still. A perfect target. Holding the newspaper in his left hand he grasped the butt of the Walther inside his raincoat pocket. A range of no more than ten feet. Point-blank . . .

More people were coming in, swirling in a crowd. Outside a jet took off, its engines roaring. Stieber began to pull the weapon out of his pocket. So many people. In the confusion escape should be easy. Everyone would dive for cover. The gun was half-way out of his pocket.

Newman was walking by himself, looking everywhere for danger. He saw a man sitting on a seat. Familiar. Why? Where? A rounded-headed man. It hit him. The night he had driven into Basle past the frontier post. The car waiting. Two men in the front seat. The driver a round-headed man. He moved.

Stieber had the gun almost out of his pocket when an

arm was wrapped round his neck in a hammerlock. Another hand grabbed his gun-hand. There was a struggle as Stieber tried to stand up, to free himself. The gun twisted, was rammed back inside his pocket. His finger pressed the trigger. Another jet roared into the sky, muffled the sound of the shot. He sagged back on the seat.

Newman glanced round. No one was taking any notice. He put his hand round Stieber's neck in a seemingly friendly gesture. His fingers felt for the neck pulse. Nothing. Stieber was dead. In the struggle he had shot himself. Newman eased his body upright, let it flop back against the seat.

Hurrying to a bar, he bought a bottle of Scotch, stripped off the covering, loosened the cap. When he walked back to the seat Stieber was still slumped like a man asleep. Still no one took any notice. Newman uncapped the bottle, placed it carefully upright alongside the corpse, walked away to join Tweed and the others who were following Benoit through an open doorway. Marler caught up with Newman.

'You managed that skilfully. Thought I'd have to lend a hand.'

'You'd have botched it up.'

'Nice to know you have confidence in me, old chum.'

They didn't tell Tweed what had happened at the airport. In mid-air over the Channel Newman and Marler agreed he'd been through enough. Tweed and Paula sat together three rows in front of the two men.

'One thing I ought to tell him now,' Marler said. 'Be back in a minute.'

He made his way along the narrow alley and sat down in the empty seat across from Paula. Tweed had been checking his dossier of evidence, arranging it in sequence. Marler leaned over the aisle.

'You'll have something to add to that once I've visited a certain safety deposit in London. A copy of the post-mortem on Sylvia Harman by Dr Rose. The vital data is, of course, the blood groups.'

'And I have a friend inside the Ministry of Defence who can check the records and give me Buckmaster's blood group in confidence,' Tweed told him.

'And if Buckmaster doesn't have the rare blood group?'

'Then Morgan killed and then raped her. It has to be one or the other of them. They'd never delegate such a grisly task.'

'Have you any idea which of them did it?' Paula asked.

'Yes,' said Tweed, 'I know for a certainty. It all fits in with the *Lampedusa*. That's the key. Now, no more questions.'

Latitude 34. 30. N. Longitude. 27. 20. E. The US missile destroyer *Spruance* was motionless in broad daylight east of Crete. As Hank Tower, commander, studied the silhouette of the *Lampedusa* with the officer who had brought the outline to him, the sea was calm.

A short distance to the north of the destroyer a freighter was continuing on a north-easterly course. When the weather had slackened Tower had launched his helicopter and it was this machine which had located the freighter, *Helvetia*.

'That ship is twin-funnelled,' Tower objected. 'The *Lampedusa* has only one funnel.'

'Agreed, sir. But when you put an arm over the rear funnel and compare the silhouette of that freighter with the silhouette in your hand they match perfectly. I think they've erected a dummy funnel.'

'You just could be right. We'll test them. Give them the order to heave to.'

He waited, staring at the silhouette, comparing it with

the freighter, while the signal was sent. There was no response. The freighter proceeded on its course, leaving behind a wake as it increased speed. Tower pursed his lips, gave the next order – to fire a shot across the bows of the *Helvetia*.

Aboard the freighter Singer stared at the destroyer, calculating the distance between the two vessels. He decided he could swim it easily in these calm waters. Below, in the radio cabin, Hoch, the radio op, was gazing out of the porthole. The shot fired across the freighter's bows filled him with hope. He had to leave the *Helvetia*. His only problem was the armed guard who slouched in a chair, pistol in his lap.

The shot across their bows alarmed the guard. He stood up, pushed Hoch aside from the porthole, and peered out himself. He felt he had to go up on deck, to check what was happening. He turned to Hoch, raised the barrel of his pistol, struck Hoch on the temple. At the last second Hoch moved slightly. The barrel grazed his forehead. He collapsed to the floor.

The guard ran out, slamming the door. Hoch waited, heard his running footsteps disappearing along the passageway. He stood up, shook his head, went to the door, opened it and peered in both directions. The passageway was deserted.

The guard ran on to the bridge. Most of the crew were crowded on the foredeck. Captain Hartmann had taken over the wheel from the helmsman. In the distance he could see the heavy bulk of another vessel approaching. The *Sverdlov*. He was going to make a run for it.

The aft deck was empty as Singer climbed the rail, dived into the sea, began swimming with powerful strokes towards the *Spruance*. Behind him on the deck appeared Hoch. The radio op glanced round, saw no one, climbed the rail and dived after Singer.

Hoch also was a good swimmer. For long stretches he

swam underwater before breaking to the surface to take in air. He could see that Singer would arrive first but that did not deter him.

Aboard the *Spruance* a lookout ran up to the bridge, reported to Tower.

'Two men jumped overboard from the freighter. They're swimming towards us, sir.'

'Lower a ladder. Prepare to take them aboard . . .'

On the foredeck of the *Helvetia* Captain Hartmann had lost control of his motley crew. He was concentrating on reaching the *Sverdlov*. All eyes were on the Soviet cruiser. No one noticed the two men swimming in the sea. Singer had reached the ladder, had dragged himself out of the water, was mounting the ladder. Close behind him Hoch surfaced, saw the ladder, took a deep breath for one final effort.

Aboard the *Helvetia* was a seaman called Levitt. Once the skipper of an American freighter, he had lost his ticket for being drunk on duty. He hated the Americans. The shot across their bows had infuriated him. Goddamn Yanks! He'd show them. He whipped off the canvas cover, exposing the machine-gun. Aiming for the *Spruance*, he opened fire, sweeping a hail of bullets along the hull of the destroyer. Hartmann was appalled. He screamed at him but the machine-gun continued its chatter.

Aboard the *Spruance* American seamen ducked. One man fell, laced with bullets. He lay still on the bridge. Singer had reached the deck. He crouched low, saw to his amazement the figure of Hoch scrambling over the side on to the deck. Hoch, who could expose him.

Singer reached inside his shirt, grasped the Luger pistol inside his waterproof holster. He hauled out the gun, aimed it at Hoch, who stared at him in horror. An American officer reacted. Lowering his bullet-shaped head, he ran forward as Singer stood up, hit him in the middle of the back. Singer was thrown forward to the side, slipped on the deck, fell overboard. The officer used his walkie-talkie to call the lookout at the stern.

The engines of the *Spruance* were moving the vessel out of range of the machine-gun. Singer surfaced, saw the hull sliding past him, desperately tried to swim away from the warship. At the stern the lookout peered over, caught a brief glimpse of Singer as he was caught in the undertow and dragged towards the huge slicing propellers. The churning white wake turned crimson for a few fleeting seconds. The lookout saw something like a decapitated head bobbing up and down. It disappeared as he retched over the side.

On the bridge Tower was issuing more orders as his ship put distance between himself and the freighter. His instructions from Naples were specific. If all else failed, in an emergency the *Lampedusa* must be sunk. He gave a fresh order to ready a missile for firing.

Standing with his feet spreadeagled, he watched the *Helvetia* speeding towards the still distant *Sverdlov*. He gave the final order.

A missile *whooshed* into the clear sky, described an arc, fell, and landed square on the freighter amidships. A perfect shot. There was a thunderous boom as the missile exploded. Seconds later the freighter's boilers blew up. Its rear funnel toppled. Tower glanced down at the silhouette he still held. Yes, the so-called *Helvetia* was the *Lampedusa*. He looked up again. The freighter had come apart amidships. The bow upended, slid below the sea out of sight. The stern shattered into a million fragments. A giant column of water soared into the air. Reminded Tower of the geyser, Old Faithful, in Yellowstone National Park. The water seethed and boiled as the relics of the freighter plunged to the bottom of the Mediterranean, taking with it the cargo in the hold. Then the sea began to settle. The crew stood gazing at the place where the *Lampedusa* had floated less than a minute before.

In the distance the *Sverdlov* began to change direction, heading back on a northerly course. Tower gazed at Hoch, brought to him by an officer.

'I'm the only surviver of the original crew of the *Lampedusa*. That man who tried to shoot me and went overboard was Singer. He masterminded the hi-jacking of the ship.'

'Better come below to my cabin, tell me your story . . .'

53

The executive jet was descending towards London Airport. Tweed looked out of the window. It was good to see England again. Most of the snow had gone. Only a north-facing rooftop here and there showed relics of the white blanket which had covered the country.

'You look worried,' Paula commented.

'I am. The big problem is Buckmaster – the national scandal which could break out if he goes down. Imagine the headlines: MINISTER FOR EXTERNAL SECURITY INVOLVED IN WORLD-WIDE FRAUD. Makes me shudder.'

'There has to be a simple solution,' chipped in Marler, who still sat opposite them across the aisle.

'Tell me one,' said Tweed.

'Oh, I didn't say I'd thought of one. I just said there has to be one.'

'Very helpful,' snapped Paula, then stared at Marler. 'And two unsolved murder cases – Sylvia Harman and Ted Doyle, the accountant, from what Benoit told us just before we boarded this jet.'

'So where do we go when we touch down? Marler enquired.

'Straight to Park Crescent. To report to Howard. And to the PM.'

'There we go again,' complained Paula. 'I still don't understand your present relationship with the Prime Minister.'

'Cordial,' said Tweed.

'More mystery,' Paula sighed and braced herself for the landing.

Morgan's Lear jet landed half an hour later. His pilot had been given a longer flight path than Tweed's. He walked through Passport Control and Customs without much delay – although the official checking his passport examined every page.

As soon as Morgan had left the official closed his window, picked up a phone and spoke to Jim Corcoran, Chief of Security.

'Gareth Morgan has arrived. He went through Passport Control a couple of minutes ago.'

'Thanks. Excuse the brevity – I have a call to make myself.'

Hanson, the chauffeur, was waiting with the Daimler. Morgan settled himself in the rear seat. He waited until they had left the airport before asking his question.

'Any problems while I was away? With Leonora?'

'Not with Mrs Buckmaster. With myself, sir. I have some bad news. The police have been questioning me. It seems some nosey-parker bitch saw me when I entered Doyle's house to plant those betting slips.'

Morgan leaned forward. 'How the devil could she identify you?'

'I'm still trying to work that out. The police had me in a line-up and the old bag picked me out immediately.'

542

'We'll get you the best lawyers in the land. You haven't admitted anything, I trust?'

'Simply to deny that I was anywhere near the place. Then I clammed up. It's her word against mine.' He paused. 'I should warn you of something – they have a Chief Inspector Buchanan on the case. He's like a dog with a bone, insists that Ted Doyle was murdered.'

'I've met the flatfoot.' Morgan waved a contemptuous hand to reassure Hanson. 'I can handle him any day of the week. Let's get to Threadneedle Street immediately.'

Tweed opened the door of his office and paused. The room was full of people. Howard sat in the armchair, one elegantly-pressed trouser leg over the arm. Monica sat behind her desk. Two other men sat in hard-backed chairs, swivelled in their seats as he entered, followed by Paula. The significant factor was his own seat behind his desk was unoccupied.

'Welcome home,' Howard began. 'I got your signal from the jet. The PM got her signal, also. She'd like to hear from you when convenient. But first these two gentlemen are anxious to have a word with you. Chief Inspector Buchanan and his assistant, Sergeant Warden. Jim Corcoran informed them you were on your way from the airport – with my permission.'

Tweed nodded at the visitors, took off his coat, which Monica took, and sat behind his desk, slapping his briefcase down on the top. There was an urgent knock on the door and Chief Inspector Harvey of Special Branch appeared.

'I hope I'm not late . . .'

'You are,' Howard told him. He pointed to a chair. 'Sit.'

Tweed took command of the meeting, gazing at Buchanan, who looked as though he had all his marbles.

'Have you identified the dead girl found in my flat?'

'Not yet, sir. In spite of extensive enquiries.'

'Well, I have now . . .'

Tweed emptied his briefcase, arranged Sylvia Harman's diary alongside the pile of photocopies and started talking. He spoke tersely for ten minutes and during that time Buchanan's grey eyes never left his. As he concluded, Tweed pushed the diary, protected inside a cellophane bag, across the desk together with the photocopies.

'When my assistant . . .' He nodded towards Paula seated behind her own desk. '. . . acquired that diary in Zürich she placed it in that bag which was originally wrapped round a new pair of tights. So Harman's fingerprints should be on it.'

'Very helpful, miss.' Buchanan smiled approval at Paula. 'I do have on record the deceased's prints, so comparison should be straightforward.' He paused, looking at Tweed. 'From what you have told me it appears Morgan procured high-class call-girls for Lance Buckmaster. It also seems Sylvia Harman could have been transported quietly to London by this Lear jet. The fact that she was resident in Zürich solves the problem of why we were not able to trace her here.'

'You are the detective,' Tweed replied.

Buchanan stood up. 'I've also been informed Mr Morgan is back in London. With this evidence I think my next visit should be to interview him.'

'You're the detective,' Tweed said again with a smile.

'But what is the motive for all this?' demanded Harvey.

'That comes under the heading of national security,' Tweed replied.

'That simply isn't good enough . . .'

'It's good enough till hell freezes over,' Howard snapped. 'Now I think Tweed has earned a rest. I'll show you gentlemen out.'

'You've made my life very easy,' Buchanan told Tweed and he left the office.

544

'He said a rest,' Paula reminded Tweed who shook his head.

'It's not all over by a long chalk. Get me Cord Dillon at Langley. Now, please.'

Paula pursed her lips, reached for the phone. A few minutes later she said Dillon was on the line. As soon as the American had identified Tweed he began talking urgently.

'Big news from the Mediterranean. The *Lampedusa* was located just in time. It opened fire on one of our destroyers. The crazy bastards. A Soviet cruiser was heading within a mile of the incident. The destroyer responded, as instructed. A missile sank the *Lampedusa*. The radio op, Hoch, survived. The rest of the original crew were massacred during the hi-jack . . .'

'Oh, no! That's awful, really awful.'

'Fortunes of war.' Dillon sounded laconic. 'What do we do now?'

'Activate Tiger One.' Tweed's voice was decisive. 'Immediately.'

'Will do. I'll send a fuller report from the survivor, Hoch. Stop worrying.'

Tweed put down the phone. Monica and Paula waited. When he didn't say anything, Paula probed.

'Are we allowed to know what Tiger One is?'

'I'm afraid not. At least, not yet.'

IS WORLD SECURITY SOLVENT? SHARES NOSE-DIVE ALL MARKETS

The newspaper headline shrieked at Buckmaster. He paced his living-room. The door opened and Leonora entered, her face grim. She closed the door and gestured at the newspaper on the floor.

'What is going on? I have a right to know. I am the chairman . . .'

Buckmaster lost control. 'You're nothing. You've no right to know anything. Haven't you realized it yet? You're just a figurehead. Someone I put in because a Minister must be seen to be impartial. It's the law that I have to divest direct control of the company when I accepted my Cabinet post. That's all.'

'It's not all.' She clenched her fist. He was in a dangerous mood but she didn't care. 'It was my money which started you in business . . .'

'A feeble pittance!' he shouted at her. 'Since then I've multiplied it millions of times. Built it up into a mammoth.'

'The company is now worth nothing, you idiot. Read the headline again. The shares will soon be worthless. And so will you. And all that will be left will be this apartment and Tavey Grange on Dartmoor.'

'Don't kid yourself,' he sneered. 'This place – and the Grange – are mortgaged to the hilt.'

He regretted the outburst as soon as the words had been uttered. Leonora stared at him in sheer disbelief. She had to get her breath back before she reacted.

'You never told me, you bastard. Well, I can get my own back on you. I may have another chat with that nice detective, Buchanan. About Morgan. He *was* with Doyle later on the night Ted died so mysteriously. I'd forgotten my car keys. I came back up to my office and saw Morgan disappearing inside Ted's office. Very late in the evening.'

'You'll keep your mouth shut,' he said savagely.

'Will I? Don't count on it.' Then she regretted voicing her threat. Buckmaster was advancing on her with a peculiar expression. She backed away, ran to the door, opened it and turned before she slammed it shut.

'Just don't count on my silence any more,' she shrieked.

He heard her running down the staircase, the slam of the front door. Followed by a car engine starting, moving away. He stared once more at the newspaper headline, picked up the phone, dialled.

'Hanson, bring the car round. I want you to drive me to the helipad at Battersea. Call the pilot, tell him to have the chopper ready. He's flying me to Dartmoor.'

Behind his desk in his Threadneedle Street office Morgan sat facing three men. Buchanan, Warden and Harvey. Buchanan had been talking for about fifteen minutes while Morgan listened, his obese figure slumped in his chair.

On the far side of the desk was Sylvia Harman's diary still wrapped in cellophane, the pile of photocopies Buchanan had handed him one by one as he explained what he knew.

What he knew? Buchanan knew everything. Morgan was stunned when Buchanan had gone methodically over the dates marked with an 'M' in the diary – when he had then compared them with the dates of the payments of six thousand francs a time which coincided. Buchanan again sat well back from the desk so he could cross his long legs.

'I have already warned you,' he continued, 'you are not obliged to say anything but anything you do say will be—'

'All right! I've got that. No need to go on about it.'

'I also repeat that if you decide to cooperate by making a statement there is the possibility that may be a point in your favour later. No guarantee, Mr Morgan. I am in no position to guarantee anything.' He paused. 'It is entirely your decision.'

Buchanan said nothing more. He had purposely omitted at this stage the fact that a further examination of Doyle's office had detected Morgan's hand-print on the edge of the window the accountant was supposed to have fallen from by accident. A hand-print which matched several found on Morgan's desk. That could come later. When he was charged with the murder of Edward Doyle.

The silence in the office was heavy, like the oppressiveness before the breaking of a storm. Morgan played with an unlit cigar. He'd been set up, pushed into the front line by Buckmaster. How else could that diary be lying on his desk – together with those photocopies? And instead of the initial 'M' which had been used for camouflage, the initial should read 'B'. It was for Buckmaster he had procured the high-class call-girls. Including Sylvia Harman and her last flight to London aboard the Lear jet.

Morgan lit the cigar, began to talk.

Washington, DC. It was dark, when the massive C-5A transport plane began its take-off from Andrews Air Force Base. The pilot had received the Tiger One signal direct from Cord Dillon. The crew had boarded the plane, surrounded by armed guards.'

The huge machine lumbered down the runway, had almost reached the end when it lifted off. It gained height rapidly, headed out across the Atlantic on a north-easterly course. At fifteen minute intervals the radio operator reported their position by coded signals.

In accord with the very precise time schedule, the C-5A landed at the British airfield, Lyneham, in Wiltshire, just after nightfall. Heavy lifting-gear moved towards the plane and the large rear doors were opened, the ramp dropped. An immense mobile transporter drove close to the ramp and the disembarkation operation began.

The enormous cargo was carefully transferred from the plane to the transporter. Even though Lyneham was an isolated airfield in the middle of the countryside, great canvas screens had been erected round the rear of the aircraft.

During that night many roads in England were closed by police. The explanation given – where inevitable – was that a giant electrical transformer was on the move. But aboard the transporter were heavily armed SAS troops. Other soldiers rode on motor-cycles ahead of and behind the transporter.

It was not possible to move the transporter to its ultimate destination in Yorkshire overnight. So, during daylight hours from the following morning until the next night, the great vehicle was housed in an aircraft hangar on an old wartime airfield.

When night came the transporter resumed its slow journey on the last half of its route. Again roads were sealed off and the vehicle trundled north. Before daylight it arrived at its final destination in Yorkshire.

Top secret signals were immediately despatched to London and Langley confirming its safe arrival. Two men – Tweed and Cord Dillon – breathed sighs of relief.

54

In the underground garage below World Security HQ in Threadneedle Street, Marler had indulged in a little arm-twisting. Literally.

He had pounced on Hanson from behind when the chauffeur got out of the Daimler he had just parked. With one hand over the man's mouth, he used the other hand to bend the arm backwards until it was almost wrenched from its socket. Hanson had moaned with the pain, then heard the whispered question.

'You've got one chance to give the right answer. Make just one small mistake and I'll break every bone in your body. The question is very simple. Where is Lance Buckmaster?'

'Took him to the chopper waiting at Battersea. Ease up a bit, mate, for God's sake . . .'

'Go on.'

'The chopper was flying him down to Tavey Grange, Dartmoor.'

Marler released his grip a little. He waited while Hanson gasped and wheezed before he spoke again.

'Now this conversation is going to remain our little secret, isn't it? If I find you've even hinted to a soul that we had our little talk I'll not only come after you – I'll find you.'

'Don't want any more to do with you,' Hanson had replied.

Marler had left the garage, walked round the corner, climbed behind the wheel of his Porsche, and driven off. Within an hour he was well away from London, driving just within the speed limit to the West Country.

It was when he was bypassing Exeter that he realized most of the country was free of snow but Dartmoor was still in the grip of the freeze. In the distance its high ridges rose like great white waves and not an inch on the moor was freed from the dense blanket. He began climbing, the snow became deeper, the ice-ruts like iron.

Passing through Moretonhampstead, he slowed as the road curved and he skidded. Five minutes later he was moving along the winding drive leading to the Elizabethan turrets and chimneys of Tavey Grange. He pulled up in the courtyard, jumped out and hauled at the bell-pull of the front entrance. José, the butler, opened the door.

'I'm looking for Mr Buckmaster,' Marler said casually. 'I was in this part of the world and thought he might want to have a word with me.'

'You've missed him by five minutes, sir,' José responded. 'He has gone for a drive to Princetown. Said he needed a breath of fresh air. Drove out of here like a madman. Sorry, sir, I shouldn't have said that.'

'Don't worry,' Marler said breezily. 'I didn't hear what you said. And there's no need to leave a message. I must hurry back to London . . .'

Marler retraced his route along the drive, but when he reached the lodge gates he turned left. Towards Princetown, not London. A quarter of a mile away he pulled up briefly. From under his seat he unclipped the Magnum .45, checked that it was fully loaded. It was ironic: he was always joking with Newman about why use that old cannon? He laid the gun on the seat beside him and drove on.

As he climbed high up to the moor he found the snow deeper still, the patches of concealed ice more treacherous. There was no other traffic about and it was bitterly cold. Everywhere it was a white world, a wilderness with the occasional tor rearing up, a white monument.

He slowed down again when he came to the steep curving stretch of road above Shark's Tor. Here the ice was very dangerous. He drove on and still he hadn't passed another car in either direction. The sky was like lead. Was even more snow on the way? Half an hour later he reached the sombre prison-like Princetown.

Driving behind the wheel of his own Porsche, Buckmaster's mind was in a whirl as he drove back into Princetown from Yelverton. He was on his way home. Home? Had he got one anymore? Had he got anything left? The magnitude of his fall from the heights stunned him.

The PM had sent a message saying she wanted to see him. Stuff her! He had had the phones taken off the cradles at Tavey Grange. No way she could communicate with him. He had to work out a fresh plan to beat the bloody lot of them. He had been in tight corners before and fought his way out. What he had done before could be done again.

Driving down the main street of Princetown, past the bleak granite buildings, he peered through his goggles. For a moment he couldn't believe his eyes. A red Porsche coming towards him. It was the registration number which caught his attention. Buckmaster had not built up a world-wide security organization without an exceptional memory for detail. Marler's Porsche!

A whole new stream of thoughts flooded through his mind. Marler. Of course! That was the solution to his problems. As the other vehicle came close he opened the window and waved a defiant hand. Catch me if you can! He'd race Marler back to the Grange!

Marler understood the gesture, gave a little mock salute as the two cars passed each other. Then he swung his car in an illegal U-turn and followed the other Porsche. In his wing mirror Buckmaster saw the manoeuvre and grinned. There had always been something of the schoolboy beneath his ruthless exterior. That was it. Race Marler back. Loser coughed up a bottle of Krug!

Buckmaster was leaving Princetown behind, accelerating, driving up on to the moor as Marler sped forward a hundred yards behind. Buckmaster worked out the plan as he increased speed. Sack Morgan. Throw him into the street. Put Marler in his place. Marler was an expert on security, was just the man for the job. With Marler by his side he'd build a new and bigger empire.

Exhilarated with the idea, he rammed his foot down, racing up on to the heights of the moor. The car skidded on an ice patch. He grinned with excitement, drove with the skid, regained control on the edge of a deep drop. This was the life – took him back to his days with the Airborne Division. He was climbing steeply now and round him spread the empty wilderness. No sign of life. Just the day for a race. Flat out! He sucked in cold air through the open window, drunk with excitement.

Behind him Marler maintained the gap of a hundred yards. Too dangerous for an emergency stop on this surface. He heard the boom-boom of Buckmaster's exhausts. He was increasing speed even more. Marler's lips tightened. He pressed his own foot down. It dawned on him that at any hint that he was closing the gap Buckmaster accelerated even more.

Marler glanced up ahead beyond the two speeding Porsches. A mist like steam was drifting over the moor towards the road. If it reached the road visibility would suddenly drop to nil. Now they were at the top of the moor, coming close to the point where the road dropped suddenly and turned sharply at the same time. He reached for the Magnum, driving with one hand. His own window was open: he had lowered it back in Princetown immediately after the U-turn.

Resting his arm on the ledge of the window, he took aim. At all costs he mustn't hit Buckmaster. And no bullet must dent the car. He timed it carefully as the bend and the drop approached, fired once, then again.

Buckmaster heard the heavy reports of the Magnum, looked in his mirror, saw the hand holding the gun, realized Marler had closed the gap. What the hell was happening? Had Marler gone mad? He'd offered him Howard's head on a plate. A third shot hummed past his window. God! Marler was trying to kill him . . .

He rammed his foot down. He'd out-run him. He could drive faster than any amateur driver in the country. He was on the crest of a hill. A fourth shot winged past his window. He glanced again in the mirror, took his eyes off the road ahead for only a matter of seconds.

Marler had gone stark raving mad. Buckmaster remembered he had a gun in his study. He'd get back to the Grange first, rush upstairs, grab the gun. He remembered he was driving at high speed. He looked ahead. There wasn't anything ahead . . .!

Marler saw the Porsche drive straight off the road and over the edge. He slowed down carefully. Buckmaster's car was leaping into space. The car described an arc, then began its fall. It swung sideways in mid-air, plunged down.

553

The nose hammered into the summit of Shark's Tor. The impact toppled the car head over heels, cast it out into the abyss. The Porsche dropped like a torpedo heading for its target, reached the rocky gorge below, slammed into the granite and exploded. Fire blazed from the crumpled wreck, was then blotted out by the swirling mist. Marler drove on, past Tavey Grange, through Moretonhampstead – heading for London.

Epilogue

'So *Shockwave* is now in place at Fylingdales in York-shire,' Tweed concluded.

Seated in his Park Crescent office were Monica, Paula, Newman and Marler. Tweed had explained how the giant twin computer, the key to SDI, had been flown secretly aboard the US transport plane to Lyneham and then moved north by road.

'I don't understand any of this,' said Paula. 'What was all that business about *Shockwave* being aboard the *Lampedusa*?'

Tweed sighed. 'The key to a highly complex operation approved by the Prime Minister. The original intention was to fly *Shockwave* to Britain. Then Buckmaster intervened, insisted that with so many planes crashing these days sea transport was the safe way to move the computer. Made a very big fuss about the whole affair. Too big a fuss. So we decided to test him.'

'We?' queried Newman.

'The PM and myself. I sensed something was very wrong and I'd been uneasy about Buckmaster since his appointment. He was too good to be true. To my surprise the PM agreed with my plan. She was beginning to have her own doubts about Buckmaster.'

'What plan?' Paula persisted.

'Only five people would know about my plan. The PM, myself and Cord Dillon at Langley. Plus the head of the US Joint Chiefs of Staff, and the President. The Americans were very happy with the idea – they'd been worried stiff about *Shockwave* travelling by sea.'

'But it did,' Paula protested.

'What was loaded aboard the *Lampedusa* was a brilliant mock-up of the real thing. A dummy *Shockwave* constructed in the US by the two British scientists who helped design the real thing. This was the test – the trap, if you like – we prepared for Buckmaster. Only he and I knew the codes for communicating with the ship. On this side of the Atlantic, that is. Had the *Lampedusa* reached Plymouth safely, without interference, then Buckmaster would have been cleared and I would have resigned. Instead it all went horribly wrong. I underestimated Buckmaster badly.'

'I think I see the light,' Newman remarked. 'Do go on.'

'First, Buckmaster, knowing I had the codes, that I would be communicating with the ship, had to get me out of the way – a task he accomplished brilliantly. He framed me with the suspected murder and rape of Sylvia Harman. And he was the man who did the dirty job on the girl. We know that now – and this is highly confidential like the rest. Morgan has talked his head off. Buchanan kindly came here to tell me. It was Morgan who procured call-girls for Buckmaster, who arranged for Sylvia Harman to fly to London by the Lear jet and drove her to my apartment. He told Harman Buckmaster wanted another session with her.'

'And what about the call from Richter, your Freiburg informant?' Paula queried.

'That was Morgan's doing – at Buckmaster's suggestion. To get me away from my flat long enough on the fatal night. They paid poor Richter ten thousand pounds to entice me to the Cheshire Cheese with the excuse of meeting him. Morgan has admitted this. So, I had to run for it – to stay free and try to communicate with Hoch aboard the *Lampedusa*. And while aboard Buckmaster was confident I could have a fatal accident. As I said before, it all went horribly wrong – in every way, I deeply regret.'

'What does that mean?' Newman asked quietly.

'I wrongly assumed that even if the *Lampedusa* was hi-jacked the crew would be put ashore somewhere. Instead they were massacred. I'll have that on my conscience for the rest of my life. I underestimated Buckmaster's ruthlessness.'

'You couldn't have foreseen it,' Paula told him quietly.

'And you did counter-attack,' Newman pointed out. 'Turned the tables on him brilliantly.'

'It's little compensation. Oh, by the way, Kuhlmann is cooperating wonderfully. He's told the press a group of terrorists penetrated World Security in Germany and were out to kill him. My name won't be mentioned. Otto is a good friend.'

'How can you be sure Buckmaster strangled and raped Sylvia Harman?' asked Newman.

'I checked with my friend at the Ministry of Defence. The records show Buckmaster had the rare blood group – AB Negative. The blood group found under Harman's fingernail and the blood stain on the sheet. Morgan's blood group has also been checked. It's O Positive.'

'But won't a lot of this come out at Morgan's trial?' suggested Newman.

'No. Morgan will plead guilty to the murder of Ted Doyle – and get a lesser sentence. It will still be ten years inside, and he has a wife and children. The Crown will accept the plea and no evidence will be offered.'

'And was Dr Rose, the pathologist, murdered?'

'Yes, by Stieber, who flew over here and drove him down in a stolen car. Morgan admitted that, too. Said he was acting on Buckmaster's orders and he, Morgan, only heard about it later. Which I doubt. That won't come out either, now Stieber is dead.'

'Can I ask where that leaves me?' Newman enquired.

'In the clear. No one saw the incident at Brussels Airport. Incredibly, Stieber's body was found only two hours later. It's assumed he committed suicide. His fingerprints were on the gun.'

'And World Security?' Paula asked. 'What's happened to it?'

Tweed picked up a newspaper on his desk. 'It's in the Stop Press. World Security shares have been suspended on the London Stock-Exchange. No more dealings. End of story. And I'd like to thank you all for your support. Without you, I'd never have made it. May be you should all go home now, take a well-earned rest.'

He waited while Newman and Paula left the office together. Marler was still sitting in his chair. Tweed stared at him.

'You've had very little – in fact, nothing – to say. Was it very cold on Dartmoor yesterday?'

Marler lit a king-size cigarette, looked at Tweed in surprise. 'I've no idea. It's a week or two since I was down there. I expect all the snow has gone by now.' He stood up, the cigarette tucked in the corner of his mouth at a jaunty angle. 'I think I should push off now, get a bit of shut-eye. Cheers!'

'What was all that about?' asked Monica when they were alone.

'A poor joke on my part.'

Tweed opened the newspaper to the main headline set in large type. It gave him a certain satisfaction.

CABINET MINISTER DIES IN TRAGIC MOTOR ACCIDENT ON DARTMOOR

LANCE BUCKMASTER NOTED FOR HIS RECKLESS DRIVING

Tweed looked up at Monica. 'Now I want you to take down my letter of resignation to the Prime Minister. I'll sign it immediately and I want it sent to Downing Street by special courier.'

'She'll persuade you to withdraw it.'

'Not this time, Monica.'